A
SWARMING
OF
BEES

Published by Acorn Digital Press Ltd, 2012.

Cover artwork by Louise Millidge © 2012

ISBN 978-1-909122-22-2

www.acorndigitalpress.com

*For Whitby Writers Group – in thanks for their
support and encouragement*

A
SWARMING
OF
BEES

THERESA TOMLINSON

CONTENTS

HISTORICAL NOTE

In the year 664, Oswy's Kingdom of Northumbria covered a vast stretch of land from the Humber to beyond the present-day Scottish borders. These lands were divided into two sub-kingdoms: Bernicia in the north roughly corresponded to present-day Northumberland and Deira in the south, roughly corresponded to present-day Yorkshire and Cleveland.

'Be still, wise-ones
Do not fly wildly to the woods
Be mindful of your keeper's welfare
As each man is of eating and of home'

This is an Anglo-Saxon charm, which would have been chanted over a hive to prevent honeybees from swarming – author's own version.

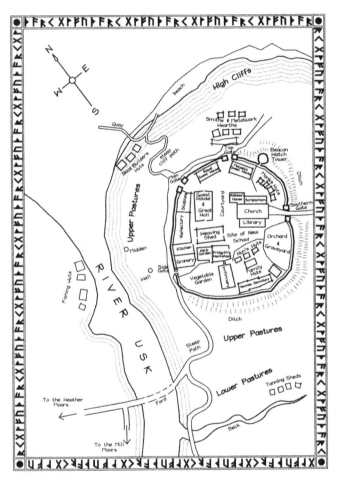

Streonshalh

King Oswy's Northumbria

CHAPTER 1

THE GREAT MEETING

Streonshalh, in the Kingdom of Deira – the year 664

The herb-wife struggled to her feet, the tools that swung from her girdle clinking as she moved. Black dots swam in front of her eyes, and her bones creaked as, once again, she got up too fast.

"Take it slower, Fridgyth," she chided herself.

It was getting harder to straighten these days, especially after rising from a crouched position. As she leant forward to brush herself down, she fought back a growing sense of vulnerability.

The greater part of a sunny morning had been spent dropping tiny leeks into holes that she'd made in the well-manured soil of the monastery gardens. A cutting north wind would often lash across the high clifftops of Streonshalh, but this favoured spot faced due south and was protected both by a high fence and the sturdy timber-framed monastery buildings, which made it the pleasantest place to work. Summer was fading fast. Just as the herb-wife surveyed her finished task, thunder rumbled in the distance. The job of planting leeks should have been done much earlier in the year, but with everyone so busy preparing for the Synod, it had been neglected. If the threatening storm brought rain, at least Fridgyth wouldn't have to water in the little green shoots.

With the exception of the herb-wife, the gardens were quiet and all but deserted. Over the last few days a deluge of important visitors had descended upon Streonshalh. Fridgyth's usually willing gang of helpers had been requisitioned to serve the guests, leaving her to fend for herself.

This extraordinary gathering, called for by King Oswy, had brought all of the most powerful Christians in the land together, and they were now sitting in the great hall of the guest house, discussing pressing questions of the day.

Fridgyth had little personal interest in the fierce arguments that raged between the different factions. The Romans looked to the pope as their leader and insisted that their way of worship was the only true way, bcgecause it originated with Saint Peter, whereas the Irish monks who had come to Northumbria from Iona made a similar claim, though John was the apostle they followed. Bitter resentment had developed about the differing methods of calculating the date of Easter and even the varying styles of tonsure adopted by the monks.

Fridgyth could only shrug with contempt when she heard them furiously disputing the way in which a monk should shave his head. She'd been raised to honour the old gods – Freya, Woden and Thor – but she understood well enough that these questions were of great importance to Abbess Hild, who not only ruled over both the monks and the nuns, but was also a princess in her own right.

She folded her arms and smiled with satisfaction at the result of her morning's work: leeks were a precious winter crop and needed more than ever as the monastery grew with every year that passed.

A heavy wooden gate slammed at the edge of the garden and Fridgyth looked up to see one of the nuns hurrying along the path beside the cabbage patch. She stared in amazement, for though the undyed monastic habit and linen veil could signify any one of the religious women who inhabited the monastery, the quick step and small stature told her that it was the abbess herself. Surely, as royal hostess, Hild couldn't have left the meeting before it finished? The discussion had been expected to last all day and tomorrow too.

As the diminutive shape disappeared through the side gate in the high wooden stockade, Fridgyth brushed the soil from her palms and set off in the abbess's wake, curious as to what had made her behave so erratically.

Once, she'd feared this forceful little woman, who was kin to both the King and the Queen, but Hild had cleverly managed to make a friend of one who might otherwise have become an enemy; the two women were the same age, they'd lived through the same hard times and they understood each other well.

Soon after she'd arrived in Streonshalh, the abbess had shocked many of the older monks and nuns by asking the Usk Valley cunning-woman to become the monastery's herb-wife. Fridgyth had accepted the invitation with equal pragmatism, seeing, at once, that standing out against these wealthy and powerful Christians would only bring more death and destruction to Deira. The kingdom had suffered far too many years of strife, and as the newly appointed monastery herb-wife, she would have status and acceptance amongst both the older inhabitants and the newcomers

Fridgyth had stoically dug up the roots of her most valued medicinal plants, taken cuttings from others and moved into the newly built herb-wife's hut without fuss. She quickly discovered that the role of herb-wife suited her well, for it meant she could move with ease almost anywhere, within the monastery and throughout the seaboard town

Now, keeping the small figure of Hild in sight, Fridgyth followed her through the side gate. As she gained on the abbess, she saw rare signs of agitation – Hild yanked sharply at her linen veil, as though she thought it might slip awry. Her usual expression of lively curiosity had been replaced by one of rage. As the herb-wife approached her, she turned, blue eyes blazing, her thin cheeks flushed.

"In God's name…" she cried. "They cannot do this to us!"

"What can't they do?" Fridgyth demanded.

Hild stared at her for a moment and then fled again, breaking into an undignified run. Fridgyth followed with dogged determination until the abbess stopped at last and sat down with a little more decorum in a grassy patch hidden by thick gorse bushes, halfway down the hillside. The herb-wife eventually caught up with her, struggling somewhat to catch her breath.

There were few who'd dare to approach the abbess in such a mood, but the herb-wife sat quietly down beside her in the grass. They both stared into the distance in silence for a while the abbess distractedly fingering the gleaming black jet cross that hung at her neck. When at last Hild glanced at Fridgyth, her eyes were still blazing.

"How could he? How could the King do this to us?" The herb-wife kept her silence and waited for the abbess to go on. "It's all Wilfrid's fault," Hild's lips gave a bitter twist as she spoke the name. "Bishop Agilbert was meant to lead the Roman delegation but, as he cannot speak our language, he gave Wilfrid free rein to represent him."

"Ah," Fridgyth sighed, understanding better now.

Wilfrid, the young abbot of Ripon, was famed for his handsome face and clever words, but Hild was not one of his many admirers.

"Sweet words drip from Wilfrid's mouth like honey," the abbess said. "He slips smoothly from one language to another, and of course he won the women over as soon as he opened his mouth, nay, as soon as he stood up and smiled, but I never thought King Oswy would be swayed by him."

Fridgyth looked up sharply.

"So the King has decided…? Already?"

"Yes. He's gone over to Rome."

Fridgyth stared, open-mouthed. Like everyone else in Streonshalh, she'd thought the decision of the Synod a forgone conclusion: King Oswy would come down on the side of the simple form of religion that he and his brother had learned as youngsters in exile on Iona – the ancient, Irish form of Christianity, brought to these lands by Bishop Aidan.

"So… does this mean that your Easter feast is to be calculated by the Roman method now?"

"Yes," Hild said.

"Is it still to be named for Eostre then?"

Hild gave a wry smile and shrugged.

"Nobody seems to care that the feast bears the name of a pagan goddess."

"And the tonsure?"

She nodded grimly.

"The tonsure too… all monks are to shave the crown of their heads, in the Roman style. I'm glad that I'm a woman, for I would never do it."

"Hmm," Fridgyth raised an eyebrow, hoping to recover the abbess's usual dry sense of humour. "No indeed... I cannot see you with a shaved crown."

The ghost of a smile touched the corner of Hild's mouth – but quickly fled.

"I feel we betray Aidan and all the monks who came with him from Iona," she said.

"I know nought of these things," Fridgyth admitted. "But I'm surprised the King deserts the faith of those who reared him."

Hild glanced up, her expression scathing.

"Oh... but you should have heard Wilfrid speak... he has convinced the King that Saint Peter will refuse him entrance to heaven if he displeases the Church of Rome! Bishop Colman spoke for the Irish side, and did his best, but he had to use an interpreter. In any case, what could he say to contradict an argument like that?"

The herb-wife sighed... it was all beyond her understanding. They sat in silence again until the raucous honking of geese, flying arrow-straight out to sea, caught their attention.

"We used to say wild geese flying like that spelled disaster," Fridgyth said. "A warning perhaps the King will come to regret his decision."

"Oh I'm sure he *will*, but he may realise it far too late and if I quarrel with him over it, we could set Deira at war again."

Fridgyth saw Hild's chin tremble and reached out to press her arm, but the abbess shook her off.

"Don't – you'll make me weep!"

"Then weep! Why should you be shamed to weep, when a trusted hearth-friend has done you down? That's a true reason to weep, I'd say."

Hild laughed, but the laughter turned quickly to harsh gulping sobs.

"You weep!" Fridgyth said more quietly now.

Hild nodded frantically and unable to say more, she buried her head in her hands. Thunder still rumbled in the distance, and a bank of smoky grey cloud moved steadily towards them from the south, threatening rain. Seagulls fled the clifftops, following the path of the wild geese.

"You'll feel better for letting it out," Fridgyth said.

Suddenly the abbess was sobbing and howling like a she-wolf, whilst Fridgyth sat there stolidly keeping watch over her friend.

Hild had ruled the monastery at Streonshalh with the confidence and capability of a warrior chieftain. Now, at the age of fifty, she'd gained a reputation for wisdom, decisive judgement and not suffering fools with gladness, but she had no power over the High King of Northumbria and his decision would become law, both in Deira and Bernicia, and the many smaller kingdoms that paid tribute to him.

A few light raindrops fell as the abbess wept and the herb-wife stared resolutely out to sea. Lightning flashed high above the far side of the valley, and thunder rumbled again, but the storm did not break overhead and gradually, as a warmer wind rose in the south, the pattering of rain ceased. Shards of sunlight came slowly and pierced through the heaviest clouds as they headed out to sea, while a rainbow glimmered faintly across the valley.

Hild's sobbing subsided, and her breathing grew calm, though she still hid her face in her hands.

"I think you should look up now," Fridgyth said at last.

Hild lifted her head and gasped in wonder at the rainbow.

"A sign of hope?" she whispered.

"A better sign," Fridgyth agreed.

Familiar girlish voices rang out from somewhere down below them on the quayside. The rainbow's colours intensified as the warmth of the sun grew and the cheerful cries below them gained in strength. The clacking of wood on wood followed them.

Hild knuckled all traces of tears away.

"I must look a fright… thank goodness it's only you that can see me, Fridgyth. Is that Elfled I hear down there?"

"It sounds like her."

They both struggled to their feet to see better down the bankside. Hild's ward, the Princess Elfled, was racing along the quayside, screeching like a fisher girl. Oswy had placed his daughter into Hild's care when she was less than a year old, demonstrating to everyone his friendship and complete trust in the abbess.

"What on earth is Elfled up to, and where is Wulfrun?" Hild said.

The quay below was bathed in sunlight now.

"Ah, there she is. Such a clattering sound – I see now what they're about."

Elfled howled in pleasure as she whacked a wooden quarterstaff forward. She was blocked and tackled carefully by Wulfrun, her protector and companion. Mathild of Eforwic, an older, orphaned princess who'd recently come to live at Streonshalh, shrank back from them, nervous of their wild behaviour.

Hild and Fridgyth glanced at each other, their mouths twitching and their spirits lifting at the sight of the girls' cheerful combat.

"I don't recall telling Wulfrun to teach the princess how to use a quarterstaff," Hild said. "But what a good idea it is! See them go at it. Elfled can defend herself using nothing but a strong stick, but poor Mathild... she is fearful I think."

"Mathild is the one who needs to learn to fight," Fridgyth said. "There's few who'd tackle Elfled, with or without a stick."

Hild smiled.

"And I still have the care of her, despite her father's decision." She glanced hesitantly at her companion with a conspiratorial, almost coquettish, look as her usual reserve weakened. "Did you know that Oswy once asked me to marry him?"

The herb-wife's mouth dropped open, and the abbess chuckled at her reaction.

"I thought that would shock you. It was a long time ago, but he and I are almost of an age you know and when his first wife died he sought me out. 'You are a true princess of the ancient Deiran line,' he said. 'Marriage to you would bring me a strong claim to rule Deira.'"

"What sweet talk!" Fridgyth said.

Hild shrugged.

"He's never hidden his ambition from me, and at least he spoke honestly, as though I was a hearth-companion."

"Whatever did you say to him?"

She smiled.

"I told him firmly that I was determined to dedicate my life to the

Christian God, and I pointed out to him that Eanfleda would make a younger, much prettier bride and that as King Edwin's daughter she'd provide him with an even stronger claim on Deiran lands."

Fridgyth stared amazed.

"But you could have been Queen of All Northumbria by now. Don't you regret turning him down?"

"No I do not," Hild answered with relish. "As abbess of Streonshalh I have much more independence and I'm happy to share my own small kingdom with the gulls. He has given me his daughter to rear, and she's a great comfort to me."

"She could have been your child."

"And I love her as though she were my own; now for her sake, if for no other reason, I *must* remain on good terms with her father."

"Even as abbess you are answerable to him."

Hild pulled a wry face as she rose and brushed soil and grass from her habit.

"Yes, I am," she straightened her veil. "And I'd better go back and force myself to smile at our guests. Cuthbert hates this outcome too, but he bows to it for the sake of peace. I will try to do the same."

Fridgyth nodded, relieved that the moment of anguish seemed to have passed. Hild gave her a swift kiss on the cheek.

"Thank you," she said. "A straight-talking friend is a blessing, especially one who passes no judgement!"

The abbess set off back towards the side gate, gathering speed as she went.

Fridgyth stayed out on the hillside, looking down at the river; the sun was past its zenith and the sky was blue and cloudless now. She was relieved that Hild's immediate sorrow had eased, but at the same time she couldn't help wondering what Oswy's decision might mean to those like herself, who lived at Streonshalh. Would there be other changes made? Would a pagan herb-wife still be tolerated?

The herb-wife had not been the only Streonshalh inhabitant to benefit from the arrival of the royal abbess. Hild had also taken Ulfstan, the powerful village headman, as her reeve, inviting him and his family to take up residence in luxurious quarters in the new visitors' guest house. He'd accepted the position without much hesitation, so that under the auspices of the monastery, the King's law was now administered in Usk Valley much as it always had been. Hild had even put the chief boat-maker on her payroll, too. Thus, she'd swiftly bought up any possible local opposition, tactfully turning a blind eye when pagan rites were still quietly observed. Fridgyth wondered what would happen if orders were to come, not from the abbess or even the King, but from Rome? From this day forward, their lives would surely be different, for good or ill.

She sat down again, lost in these thoughts, and didn't notice when Caedmon, the cowherd, waved to her as he brought the white vellum calves up the steep hillside, and headed towards the lush foraging ground of the upper pasture. As the sun began to sink down towards the horizon, she stirred herself, sensing some subtle shifting down below, where the boats were moored. Struggling to her feet once more, her keen eyes focused on the quayside, crowded with visiting vessels. She puzzled as to why the strong hempen ropes seem so dark down there and seethed with movement.

"Ah," she breathed as understanding dawned. "Rats… ship's rats!"

Black rats were creeping along the mooring ropes and scurrying in a dark line across the quayside into the grassy bank close to the boat-makers' huts. As she watched, the sight seemed to add to her sense of foreboding. At last she forced herself to turn away; the rats were Freya's children and had a right to come ashore and dwell in Streonshalh, just as the rest of them did.

CHAPTER 2

LATE VISITORS

Fridgyth turned her face towards the ever-growing monastery, built high above the wild ocean, where sea eagles and gulls soared, set back a little way from the exposed clifftops. The fine carved pediment of the guest house and the wooden cross that crowned the church could both be seen above the strong, protective stockade that surrounded the monastery buildings. The ancient beacon of Brigs Headland towered higher than anything else, where long ago the Chieftain Streon had built his roundhouse. The site commanded such a fine view of land and sea, that it made the inhabitants feel that they need never fear sudden attack, either by an approaching army or a fleet of ships.

The herb-wife marched purposefully back towards the side gate, just as two riders made their way up the steep pathway from the river crossing. At first she took them for latecomers to the Synod, but as they came closer she saw that they were boys of no more than fifteen summers, travel-stained and weary, their undyed religious habits covered with dust from the road. One was tall and fair like the Angles, the other slender and dark, with a nut-brown complexion. Both were tonsured in the Irish style that would soon be banned in Deira: their hair left long at the back, but shaved across the front from ear to ear. As they approached, they slowed their horses and dismounted, bowing respectfully to Fridgyth. Their heads were covered in stubble as though they'd been too lazy, or in too much of a hurry, to keep their tonsures neat.

"Welcome to Streonshalh," she said. "But you're far too late for the Synod; it's all over and done with."

They looked baffled, and she saw that they both moved stiff-legged, as though saddle sore.

"Haven't you come for the great meeting?" she asked. "Even the King is here."

She thought that they glanced at each other with a touch of alarm, but then the fair-haired lad seemed to recover. He bowed formally.

"Sister… we seek Abbess Hild and did not know of this important meeting. We've had a long and difficult journey to get here."

He spoke the English language well, but with a lilt that was similar to that of Brother Brandon, the Irish guest master.

"All are welcome here," she said. "But most of the beds are taken at the moment. From your speech, I'd say you were a fellow countryman of our guest master; we'll go and find him and I daresay he'll do his best for you. Who shall I say you are?"

"I'm Flann," the fair-haired one said, "and my companion is Samson."

Fridgyth glanced at the dark-haired boy for a moment and thought he looked uneasy, but then he bowed and suddenly gave her a shy, delightful, smile. She examined him more closely and decided that, beneath the grime of the road, he was almost as handsome as Wilfrid and, if anything, his diffident manner made his looks more appealing.

Softening a bit, she introduced herself as the abbey herb-wife and gestured to them to follow her towards the main gate. The guards stood smartly to attention; their weapons were polished and honed while the King was in residence.

"We crossed the sea and came overland through the kingdoms of Gwynned and Mercia," Flann said. "I'm afraid we are ragged and travel-stained, for we came in great haste and lost our way many times, but I met Lady Hild once when I was a young child and she promised warmheartedly that if ever I needed help I should come to her."

"So you are in need of help?" Fridgyth said, slowing her steps to give herself a little more time to think.

Were these lads bringing more problems for the abbess? There were many who arrived like this seeking aid or advice and none were turned away, but this really was the worst possible timing.

She stopped and looked them up and down again.

"The abbess is very busy," she told them frankly. "Since King Oswy summoned this meeting we've had no peace here at all. Streonshalh has seen nothing like it. The most powerful folk in the land are here to discuss the future of the Christian church, and there's no sleeping places left in the monastic guest house or the visitors' hall. All benches and pallets are body-crammed, though our guest master will do his best for you."

The travellers had stopped too; this time there was no doubt about it – they looked troubled.

"You say King Oswy is here?" Flann asked.

"He is indeed."

"And his queen too?"

"Oh yes, Queen Eanfleda's one of Rome's staunchest supporters; she wouldn't have missed this meeting for the world. It seems she's had her way too, for the King *has* decided in favour of Rome."

"We should leave," Samson said quickly, with the burr of Ireland in his speech.

Flann frowned for a moment while he considered, but then he firmly shook his head.

"No, there is nowhere else for us to go – and those who turn and run must run for ever."

Fridgyth could not help but smile, amused that such a mature and sagacious pronouncement should come from one so young. She made a quick private decision, for this lad's open face, and gravity appealed to her just as much as Samson's dark troubled looks did.

"You sound thrice your age," she told him roundly. "As I say, all monastic accommodation is packed with visitors and their beasts, but I'm herb-wife here and, as we've fortunately no sickness at the moment, I could let you sleep in my infirmary. It's not what I *ought* to do, but Brother Brandon has his hands full and I think you'd be quite comfortable in there."

They exchanged uncertain glances again, and Samson gave a brief nod.

"Sister, you show us much trust," Flann said. "We'd be very grateful for the accommodation you offer; we're not vowed monks, needing monastic cells, simply scholars raised in Irish monasteries."

Fridgyth nodded.

"Well... I'm not a nun either, though I take pleasure in you calling me sister so respectfully. You may sleep on the infirmary pallets and shelter your horses in my lean-to, if you're not too fine for that."

"We're most grateful for your help," Samson said. "But tell me, does a religious woman known as Cloda still live here?"

She raised her eyebrows, surprised that he should know the woman.

"Oh everyone knows Frankish Cloda and even though her mind wanders into dreams sometimes, she's still a treasured member of our community."

"Ah... Cloda still dreams," the boy said softly, and it was clear that he was revisiting old memories.

Fridgyth was held for a moment by the distant look in his eyes, deep-set and dark with amber flecks. She had a strange, fleeting sensation that she too might be dreaming and have to wake at any moment. With an effort, she shook herself back to duty and practicalities.

"I *ought* to announce your arrival to the guest master and tell him what we plan, but..." she hesitated and the boys looked agitated again.

Then Flann spoke cautiously in a low voice. "Do you think it would it be possible to tell only the abbess of our arrival? I pray she will remember me."

Fridgyth narrowed her eyes at such an extraordinary request.

"If you'd tell Abbess Hild privately that Flann Fina is here," he went on, "I think she'd understand."

"Flann Fina...?" Fridgyth puzzled. "I've heard your name somewhere before, but cannot think...?"

The young man flinched a little, but he went on, his message becoming more intriguing with every word.

"We'd be grateful if you would tell the abbess – 'the *young bee*, is discovered by enemies and in need of protection'. We know these words must sound strange, but..."

They didn't need to say more. Fridgyth's interest was captivated by this small mystery. The dim, brooding sense of unease that she'd felt out on the hillside had vanished, for here was something much more immediate and interesting to worry about, instead.

"I'll tell the abbess as soon as I can. The *young bee* you say!" She glanced from one to the other, wondering what or who the mysterious words could possibly refer to and then she chuckled. "Well – I am a beekeeper, so of course I should take care of any *young bee.*"

Both boys grinned foolishly and suddenly seemed very young to be travelling without armed guards to protect them.

Samson bowed.

"Sister, we regret putting you to such trouble, but our safety depends on your discretion."

"Say no more," she told them. "It's a good job it was *me* you met first. I shall find a way to speak to the abbess privately, for I think there's no need to trouble Brother Brandon after all."

She led them back the way they'd come and took them inside the stockade by the small side gate, telling herself that if she broke one rule by putting them up in her infirmary, then she might as well break two and avoid awkward questions at the main gate.

They guided their horses carefully around the deserted gardens and tied them up in the lean-to shelter where Fridgyth kept her gardening tools. The small infirmary had been built of timber, as had her workshop, but also provided her with a hearth and living space. The separate chambers were divided by a wattle and daub filled frame, with an open arch leading from one space to another. Her small sleeping cell was set in another lean-to on the far side of the workshop and from every possible wooden beam hung bunches of drying herbs. The whole place reeked with the sharp, medicinal scents of the plants.

Wyrdkin, the fat brindled cat, came out to greet them, sniffing at their boots as they lifted heavy saddlebags down from their horses. Fridgyth then showed them into the infirmary and pointed out straw-stuffed mattresses set on low wooden truckles that were covered with woollen rugs.

"Not much, but clean and free of rats," she told them. "You'll find fresh water in the barrel outside for your horses to drink, and for you to wash in, a lad brings a cart up here every day to fill it from the well. There's a good sack of oats, so your beasts won't starve."

They both smiled.

"This will be much better than sleeping under the stars," Flann said.

When they had taken oats and water to their horses in the lean-to, Fridgyth led them into her workshop and invited them to sit on stools, while she built up the smouldering fire in her hearth.

"Now then, help yourself," she said, indicating a small loaf and a hunk of goats' cheese on the table top. "I eat in the monastery refectory as a rule, but as they are so busy today I thought I'd bring my lunch over here. Take a good beakerful of my elderberry wine… that should clear the road-dust from your throats, though I do say it myself."

They thanked her and sat down, staring about her hut with fascination. The workshop was lined with shelves that were crammed with pestles, mortars, pitchers, pots, cauldrons and crocks full of salves to treat different ailments. Baskets of lamb's wool and clean linen were stacked beneath her table, while knives, spoons, scoops and brushes hung in neat rows from every available nail. Though every nook and cranny was covered with her equipment, all was clean and orderly, and everything was in its proper place.

Fridgyth chuckled to see their amazed expressions.

"This may appear to be a magpie's hoard," she said. "But everything has a use, and I know exactly where to lay my hands on whatever I need. Ah well, I'll leave you both to settle in. You could come to the feast in the great hall tonight… nobody would notice two extra guests."

But they shook their heads.

"Until we greet the abbess, we must remain here," Flann said, with polite insistence.

"Then I shall bring you some food myself, but before I do anything else, I must go to the garden and water in my leeks."

As the light faded, the great hall of the visitors' guest house became flooded with lay brothers and sisters setting up trestles and benches around the long central hearth in preparation for the evening feast. To one side of the fire, stood the raised royal dais where the King would sit, surrounded by his family and most esteemed guests. It commanded both the best view of the gathering and the warmest spot. This hall was the largest communal space available within monastic bounds, and many of the guests had to sleep there too.

As dusk fell, candles and lamps were lit, and the eminent visitors began to wander back inside to take their places. Having supplied her secretive guests with good, plain food from the kitchens, Fridgyth stared about her as she entered the hall, finding herself almost deafened by the babble of different languages. Brother Brandon rushed about frantically, trying to organise the workers and, watching him, Fridgyth felt vindicated in her decision not to trouble him with her late arrivals.

The abbess appeared, smiling and giving orders with her usual calm, good humour, conducting herself as the perfect hostess. Fridgyth could see that this took a deal of covert patience on Hild's part, as the guests were determined that they should receive due deference and many were sensitive to any slight, real or imagined. With so many kings, queens, bishops, abbesses, sub-kings and princes crowded together under one roof, it was difficult to decide who should sit where. At last, the blare of horns rang out when King Oswy and Queen Eanfleda entered and some semblance of order fell over the gathering.

The pro-Roman guests were triumphant at the success of their mission, while those of the Irish persuasion were desolate at their failure. The victorious young Abbot of Ripon, Wilfrid, was invited to sit on the royal dais between the Queen and the King's eldest son, Alchfrid, Sub-King of Deira. The Queen and her stepson had recently made an unlikely alliance in favour of the Roman ruling. Bishop Agilbert, who should have led the Roman party, was relegated to the second bench – fortunately he made no complaint about it, seeming simply relieved that his side had won the day.

Hild carried the ceremonial drinking vessel, made from a huge aurochs' horn, to the King's table, struggling a little with the weight of it,

"Welcome and drink hail!" she cried.

Oswy rose to his feet to accept the precious cup from the abbess, towering over her. He was still a good looking man – with fading fair hair, ice-blue eyes and a warrior's frame. He drank deeply and everyone clapped; the feast had begun.

As the abbess moved on, carrying the drink-horn to her other guests, Fridgyth took a heavy pitcher from a nervous young lay-sister.

"I will act as pitcher bearer to the abbess," she said.

The girl willingly slipped away, and Fridgyth went to stand at the abbess's side. The two women exchanged glances.

"I want to speak to you when there's time," Fridgyth whispered.

"I don't know when that will be," Hild said.

The King complimented the abbess on both the strength and sweetness of the mead, and then offered the horn to the Queen, who presented it, at once, to Wilfrid. The young abbot shook his head modestly at this honour, but took the horn and drank nevertheless. Fridgyth filled it again, and it was passed on amongst the most honoured guests, Wilfrid's handsome face soon grew flushed with both mead and compliments.

CHAPTER 3

FRANKISH CLODA

Despite the formal cheerfulness, which was only to be expected at such a feast, Oswy ate little. He turned away from the Queen to converse with Colman, the bishop of Lindisfarne, who'd been placed on his left hand side. He spoke quietly to the old man in the Irish language that he'd learned as a young exile growing up on Iona. The Bishop's thin cheeks were drained of colour.

"Colman suffers, I think," Fridgyth commented.

Hild nodded and agreed, "Of course he does!"

Oswy looked rather concerned and disconcerted to find the elderly bishop so shaken by the decision that he'd made, ruling against the Irish tradition.

"I think Oswy is regretting it already," Hild said quietly. "He speaks of trade and powerful allies in Rome, but Colman cares nothing for that."

"Could he go back on his word?" Fridgyth asked.

Hild shook her head.

"Not when honour is at stake!"

Cedd, Prior of Lastingham, who'd patiently acted as interpreter throughout the great meeting, sat next to Colman, joined in the conversation, and tried to offer reassurance. He, too, had been raised on Lindisfarne in the Irish tradition and was privately disappointed with the result.

It had been agreed, with Hild's usual practicality, that the Synod should coincide with Streonshalh's Harvest Feast, so the kitchens had been preparing for many weeks ahead. Sister Mildred, the foodwife, fussed over her dishes, red-faced and fretful. It was a very important occasion and the season of plenty, so nothing was stinted. The diners appreciated the rare treat of soft white bread seasoned with poppy seeds. The loaves were broken to cries of delight and shared amongst the guests, followed by rich stews of venison and platters of roast boar and goose. Steaming vegetables cooked in butter and sprinkled with rosemary were also carried round.

Dogs bayed outside as the meat bones were cleared away. A troop of tumblers climbed up onto each other's shoulders and then leapt deftly down again, careful to avoid the glow of the fire. The feast was finished with a touch of sweetness as great platters piled with pancakes dripping with honey and berries, and garnished with thick, golden cream were served.

As the meal drew to a close, the mead-horn was passed around again. The King called Wilfrid forward and announced that the Queen had a gift for him. Wild cheers came from his supporters, as Eanfleda, pink-cheeked and quivering with pride, draped a wide cloak of costly purple silk about the young abbot's shoulders. More cheers broke out amongst the Queen's supporters, while the Irish contingent clapped coolly and politely, their faces glum.

When Wilfrid had returned to his seat, the abbess spoke up and entreated Eadwig, the bard, to sing for them. Everyone cheered as the man came forward to claim the harp-stool. He was dressed in a rich red tunic, his arms decorated with many gold rings, for Eadwig had earned great wealth and fame as the King's musician. He placed his hands on the harp ready to play and silence fell.

> *"Wise is the warrior king*
> *The wide-ruler who trusts in God*
> *Strong and shrewd is his judgement*
> *Brave in the face of his enemies*
> *His judgement is highly prized*
> *His praises will be sung through the years"*

Eadwig's voice was rich and pleasant, and the audience listened with hushed respect as he went on to sing of Oswy's battles for his kingdom and his holy and heroic defeat of Penda, the fearful pagan king of Mercia. The end of the performance was greeted with a loud stamping of feet and wild applause. The King took a gold band, which was skilfully decorated with red garnets, from his arm and proffered it as a reward. Eadwig received it gracefully, adding it to his already valuable collection. When the abbess called for another singer from amongst her own herdsmen and lay-folk, they begged that she, herself, should sing. Hild reluctantly took the harp and looked around at her audience; Fridgyth could see that she struggled to find the right psalm for the occasion. As leader of a religious community, it would be improper for her to sing of daring deeds in the language of the people, though she knew that this was what they craved. Most of the company lolled back in their seats, now mellow with the rich food and plentiful drink – some of the older guests were already struggling to keep awake. At last, the abbess chose the psalm best known to them and began to chant.

"*Dominus regit me, et nihil mihi deerit.*
In loco pascuae ibi me collocavit."

To many in the audience the Latin words meant nothing, but still they listened for Hild was a skilled musician and her voice was deep and soothing. When they politely begged her to sing again, she gracefully demurred and handed the harp to Coen, the leader of her own small warrior band, who also had something of a reputation as a musician. Coen recited the daring deeds of brave warriors and heroes who had battled against foul monsters – stories so popular and well known that the audience could join in with gusto. Those who had been nodding off to sleep struggled upright again and gave him their full attention.

Fridgyth saw Hild slip away to sit in one of the quieter corners, and she too made her way towards the shadowy space, secure in the knowledge that the bard held the attention of any potential eavesdroppers. She bent close and whispered her mysterious message about the *young bee*.

"I didn't take them in through the main gate, or introduce them to Brother Brandon, seeing as they begged for privacy," she added defensively.

The abbess glanced hastily up at the high table.

"Flan you say... the *young bee*? Dear God," she murmured. "Why now? Haven't we got enough to deal with? What have you done with them Fridgyth?"

"I've set them up on two of my sick-beds and served them with baked herrings, bread and mead."

Hild nodded.

"Are they content, do you think?"

Fridgyth shrugged.

"They seem to be."

"Yes... well... it's the best that we can manage for now. And Fridgyth – they must be kept away from our guests, and Elfled too; they mustn't speak to her, not yet."

Fridgyth was in truth more fascinated than ever.

Hild's mouth twitched just a little.

"Well... despite you're flouting of my rules, it may turn out for the best."

Fridgyth smiled broadly.

"They've asked for Frankish Cloda," she added.

"Yes, they would," Hild seemed quite unsurprised by that. "Speak to Cloda privately and take her to them; she will be very pleased, I think."

But the task of taking the old Frankish woman to see the visitors privately, posed something of a difficulty for she found Cloda with her old friend Begu, Elfled's old nurse, sitting at table with the young princesses and Wulfrun. Fridgyth arrived to find Cloda berating Elfled and her companion over the state of their clothes.

"Shame, I say, at a feast like this," Cloda wagged an admonishing finger. "Princess Elfled should have worn her finest gown. Look at Mathild! She knows how to dress like a true princess. Begu, you should have made them change their clothes – anyone would think they'd been fighting."

Begu rolled her eyes in frustration.

"What makes you think they'd take notice of me? And anyway nobody is looking at *them* tonight – all eyes are on Wilfrid."

Cloda, an aged religious woman from the Frankish lands who'd arrived at Streonshalh seven years earlier, was well known for speaking her mind. Fridgyth could see that shy Mathild squirmed at the unwelcome praise; she'd much rather *not* be held up as an example to the other girls.

"Beg pardon Sister Cloda," she interrupted at last. "But I had a dream last night."

"A dream you say!" Both Begu and Cloda turned to Fridgyth, their faces full of sudden interest, distracted immediately as she'd hoped they would be. Those two spent a great deal of time together discussing the deep significance of their dreams.

"I too had a dream last night," Cloda said. "I knew it warned of some great change that was to come, so I was not at all surprised by Oswy's decision."

Elfled caught Fridgyth's eye and flashed a mischievous glance in her direction, grateful for this timely interruption.

"Now Cloda," she said. "If poor Fridgyth has had a troubling dream, you must give her your advice, here and now. You know how important dreams can be; you always say so yourself."

"What kind of a dream was it?" Cloda asked in a practised and businesslike manner. "Was it a vision, a terror or a fretful dream?"

Fridgyth looked thoughtful for a moment, for she still struggled to see her way forward.

"It was… a mysterious and rather secret dream," she said at last. "I cannot tell it here… I really cannot."

Cloda's mouth dropped open in eager anticipation, surprised and flattered by this unusual request for help from the independent herb-wife. She got up from the table without another word and followed Fridgyth out of the Great Hall. The girls grinned at each other, relieved to have been freed from her lecturing.

Once outside, Fridgyth took Cloda by the arm and began to lead her down the path towards her hut. The nun went willingly enough, until at last Fridgyth stopped.

"Sister Cloda, please forgive me," she began. "I told a lie. I needed to get you out of the feast so that we could speak alone."

Cloda was shocked.

"You mean there is no dream? You lied about a dream? That is a serious offence, herb-wife. How can you take God's messages so lightly?"

"I'm very sorry, but I couldn't think how else to speak to you discreetly. Travellers have arrived from Ireland, and they wish to greet you privately. Their names are Flann and Samson."

"Samson!"

The effect of the name on the woman was extraordinary. Her eyes immediately filled with tears; when she clutched Frigyth's arm, the herb-wife could feel her trembling.

"Samson... my dear boy, he is here – here in Streonshalh? Now I understand my dream. I saw a huge skep, and I could hear bees buzzing fiercely inside it, but when I lifted the skep... well never mind... you say he is here?"

"You'd better come and see him for yourself," Fridgyth said, urging her gently on towards the hut, touched a little by her emotional response.

The two boys had washed and brushed their habits, so that they looked much more presentable now than when they had first arrived. They were just finishing their makeshift meal when the women came in. Both of them rose to their feet, and Samson held out his arms.

"Dear boy!" Cloda cried in a trembling voice. "I never thought..."

"Nor I," he responded, throwing his arms about her, lifting her bodily off her feet.

"I see you know each other well," Fridgyth observed.

Flann smiled, watching them with quiet satisfaction.

"Put me down!" Cloda ordered. Then she pushed him away a little, so that she could look at him properly. "So tall... so tall, but far too thin," was her verdict. "And your hair..." she reached up and rubbed her fingers through the rough stubble at the front of his head. "You remember what I told you?"

"Of course. How could I forget?" Samson laughed and hugged her again.

"I'll leave you alone to enjoy your reunion," Fridgyth said. "I daresay Mildred and the kitchen workers will be overwhelmed tonight and in need of my help. I'm sorry that your visitors have to suffer my humble hospitality."

Cloda smiled.

"Samson and I have sheltered in far worse places than your hut," she said with a mysterious smile.

Questions swirled through Fridgyth's mind as she wandered back towards the great hall. Cloda must be far too old to be the boy's mother… could she be his grandmother, perhaps? But the boy was Irish not Frankish. A great urge to share this interesting gossip grew with every step she took.

Later that night, when she returned to her hut, she found Cloda was still there, talking in an animated manner, having ignored the bell that called all religious persons to the prayers of the night. Fridgyth's arrival recalled Cloda to her duties, and she rose to go.

"The abbess doesn't want Elfled to know about your visitors?" she remembered to say, just as Cloda was leaving.

The old woman looked at her sharply.

"No… of course not," she said, clearly understanding it all much better than Fridgyth did. "Least said, soonest mended."

Flann got up too and nodded.

"The wise man enjoys silence," he added, which made both women smile indulgently.

Wyrdkin rubbed herself around his legs, purring loudly; it seemed the cat had taken to this quiet young man just as quickly as her mistress had.

Cloda walked away into the darkness, having promised to return early next morning. The two young visitors went to find their infirmary beds and Fridgyth settled to sleep on her narrow straw pallet, Wyrdkin curled round her feet as usual, but sleep did not come quickly even though she was so tired. Unanswered questions plagued her and refused to be pushed to the back of her mind: Cloda came from the Frankish lands, but Samson was clearly Irish… so what was the connection between them? How and why had they once sought shelter together? It must have been when Samson was very young. What a day... what a day! Finally, bone-weary, she sank into sleep.

She was woken by an urgent knocking at the door of her hut. The cat leapt to the floor while Fridgyth struggled out of bed and wondered if it was morning. She found Brother Brandon, the guest master, on her doorstep with a flickering lantern in his hand, for it was still dark.

"Bishop Colman is sick," he said at once, as she peered out at him.

His thin face was pinched in an anxious expression. He hopped from foot to foot; his head was hooded to keep out the morning chill.

Fridgyth turned to grab her own warm cloak.

"I've attended him through the night," the guest master explained. "But it's all to no avail; we need your skills."

They hurried through the damp dew and past the quiet buildings. Colman was in a cubicle on the upper floor of the monastic guest house, unable to rise from his bed, looking whiter than ever in the shadowy candlelight and hardly able to speak. The Lindisfarne monks were all up and fussing around him, repeatedly calling down heavenly retribution on the heads of the Roman supporters.

Fridgyth examined the old man carefully, and then took Brother Brandon outside so that she could speak frankly to him.

"The bishop suffers from shock and despair," she said. "I saw it in his face last night. I doubt there's any underlying disease, but I don't take this grief lightly, for I've known folk to wither and die from such a thing."

Brandon's face turned paler still at the thought of the grave responsibility he bore. It would be no light matter for him, were the bishop to die in his care.

"Keep him warm, well fed and rested," Fridgyth advised. "Allow only his closest attendants to remain with him; make the others leave him in peace. I shall bring him honey, crushed heather-tips and camomile to drink, and I think you should ask the abbess to visit him. Maybe *she* can lift his spirits a little."

"Damn this decision of the King's," Brandon muttered. "Though I'd say that to no other but you, Fridgyth. These Lindisfarne monks swear they'll never grow their forelocks and I, for one, don't blame them."

Fridgyth was surprised. The guest master was usually a model of courtesy and discretion.

"That attitude won't help Colman," she said sharply. "He needs to see a way forward, just as we all do."

Brandon looked embarrassed at his brief outburst and spoke in a conspiratorial whisper.

"They say the shaved forehead was the ancient mark of the priest long ago, before ever Anglian kings came to raid these shores. You know what I mean by that... herb-wife!"

She did indeed know what he meant.

"Yes," she admitted, "They say it was the mark of the Druid priest. But you Christian monks are not Druids, are you? If the bishop is to live, he must find a way to accept this decision."

Brandon nodded, shamefaced now.

"So must we all! You are right in that, herb-wife. I beg pardon that I spoke so carelessly!"

Fridgyth sighed as she walked away; it wasn't going to be easy to keep the peace between the differing groups. Deira had been torn apart for many years, with blood-feuds and bitter quarrels over land ownership and tributes. Were these Christians now going to set themselves at each other's throats and bring more bloodshed here?

When she got back to her workshop, she was a little taken aback to find the abbess seated at her board, breaking her fast with bread and cheese in the company of Flann and Samson. They all looked up as Fridgyth walked in, and their conversation paused.

"I must make a camomile brew for Bishop Colman," she announced. "He suffers sadly and blames himself for the Irish defeat; a visit from you, dear Abbess, might help, I think."

"I'll go to him now" Hild replied and got up at once.

"Those Lindisfarne monks spit fury at the king, but it won't help the bishop; he needs to recover his sense of purpose, just as you have somehow managed to do."

"Our herb-wife is known for her bold speech," Hild said dryly, she then sighed. "Well... I'll do my best for the bishop, but my own sense of purpose ebbs and flows like the tide at the moment."

Fridgyth turned to her visitors. "I'm glad you've all found food," she said, as she picked up a pot of dried heather tips.

"The abbess honoured us – she served us herself," Samson smiled.

"Did she?" Fridgyth raised her eyebrows.

Hild ignored her friend's meaningful glance and turned back to the young men.

"Now," she said, "are we agreed as to what we should do?"

"Yes indeed," Flann said.

To Fridgyth's surprise, Samson rose from the board as though to take his leave.

"Will you act as hostess to Flann a little longer?" Hild asked. "Samson will be found accommodation in the royal guest house, and I'll introduce him to the King and Queen."

Fridgyth's eyes widened, but she nodded.

"Yes, of course," she said. "Flann is welcome to stay here as long as he likes."

CHAPTER 4

WISE SAYINGS

The abbess left with Samson at her side, and Fridgyth turned to search out her dried camomile bundles. She set water to boil on the hearth and began rubbing the leaves and stalks into a small bowl, biting back the many questions that came into her mind. Meanwhile, Flann settled himself companionably in the corner of her workshop. He took a small leather-bound book from his saddlebags and began to read, absently stroking Wyrdkin who had curled up on his lap. He didn't appear offended that Samson had been invited to stay in the luxurious royal guest house, while he was left in the herb-wife's humble dwelling, and he clearly *was* the scholar he claimed to be.

Fridgyth made herself concentrate on the job in hand as she poured boiling water over dried camomile and added a spoonful of honey, followed by a few drops of her heather tips infusion. Then she strained it all into a small jug, murmuring:

> *"Freya wife, Freya wife,*
> *Let not life be lost!*
> *And save us all from bleak despair."*

Flann glanced up, a little startled to hear the pagan prayer. Fridgyth recalled that she was making this remedy for a Christian bishop, so turned hastily to the east and made a small bow.

"In the name of the heavenly Father... amen, amen, amen," she added.

Flann reverently added another amen and went back to his book.

Fridgyth covered the jug with a clean cloth and set off to deliver her potion. Rain spotted as she hurried towards the monastic guest house, where she found the abbess sitting at Colman's bedside, strumming her harp and softly chanting psalms.

"Now here is our good herb-wife," Hild said, as she set the instrument aside. "Her medicines are always laced with honey, and we put great trust in her."

Fridgyth left the bishop in a calmer mood, sitting up in bed to sip his soothing potion. Passing the kitchens on her way back to her hut, she noticed a young man and woman looking hesitantly in at the doorway.

"Are you lost?" she asked. "Can I help?"

They were a handsome pair, but neither face was familiar to her, and the girl's expression was glum.

"I am sent to the kitchens," she said, and Fridgyth recognised the accent as Frankish, similar to Cloda's.

"You've found the right place then," Fridgyth told her. "You're new here I think."

The girl nodded, but it was the young man who answered.

"My name is Guy, and this is my sister Gunda. We came in the train of Bishop Agilbert."

He bowed politely and gave Fridgyth a charming smile. The Synod had brought many ambitious young men to Streonshalh, and this one was tall and strongly built as well as good looking.

"Visitors are served their meal in the great hall," Fridgyth explained helpfully.

The young man nodded.

"We've been there and eaten well in the company of royalty, and now the abbess has generously given us her permission to stay here in Streonshalh."

"My brother is a talented scribe," the girl explained. "And now that he has seen the fine scriptorium here… "

"Ah," Fridgyth understood, she nodded at the lad. "You wish to stay."

Guy shrugged, almost bashful in his manner.

"Bishop Agilbert has agreed that I may leave his service," he said.

"And Brother Cenwulf has taken me as a religious oblate, to study in the scriptorium."

"But this – Cenwulf – says I must go to the kitchens," Gunda cut in, full of bitter resentment.

"Huh!" Fridgyth spoke with sympathy. "Brother Cenwulf would… he has a very low opinion of women. Cenwulf doesn't even approve of the two princesses receiving instruction in the skills of reading and writing. I will speak to the abbess on your behalf, but she's so very busy at the moment. Go into the kitchens for now, honey. In Streonshalh we deem all work to be of equal value."

The girl looked both offended and amazed at this suggestion.

"But surely not kitchen work!"

"My sister is surely worth more than kitchen work," Guy cut in, protesting.

"Oh, even kitchen work is valued here," Fridgyth insisted, for this was something that she and the abbess were in total agreement over. "Where would any of us be without good food? The rules at Streonshalh state that all honest work is of equal value – none shall be rich and none shall be poor. Other monasteries may be different, but here in Streonshalh this is how things are. Do you wish to be a nun?"

The girl glanced at her brother, and then shook her head.

"Go into the kitchens," Fridgyth advised and gave her a warm pat on the shoulder. "You won't be there for ever. There are many ways to live in Streonshalh – we don't all have to be nuns. Lay brothers and sisters are welcome here, and we have family huts full of growing children."

Gunda looked at her brother again and, when he gave a slight nod, she agreed at last.

"I will go there for now."

"And I'll go into the kitchens with her and make sure that she'll be well treated," Fridgyth assured the anxious brother.

"I thank you," he said and hesitated for a moment as though he might kiss his sister, but thought better of it and headed back in the direction of the scriptorium.

Fridgyth led Gunda into the noisy workplace, where she was a frequent visitor. The kitchens were thatched, with side walls open like a barn to emit smoke and steam from the many cooking fires. Two more sheltered areas were filled with tables and troughs, where women kneaded dough and roasted malted grain. The clatter of pots and pans combined with the loudly shouted instructions was deafening, though the smell of baked bread was good.

Fridgyth sought out Mildred the foodwife and bellowed in her ear.

"This young woman is to be given work – see you treat her kindly. I shall be keeping my eye on her."

"We treat them all decent, so long as they work hard," Mildred said, as she lifted flour-covered hands, offended at the very suggestion.

"Well, do you want more help or not?" Fridgyth demanded.

"Oh yes, we need all we can get," Mildred admitted. "They say the King is anxious to get back to Bamburgh, but the tides and winds keep him here. Meanwhile, he holds another feast tonight for his kin and special guests. I expect Alchfrid 'the Stranger' will be at table again!"

"Oh aye, lording it over us all!" Sister Redburgh added resentfully.

Mildred wiped her hands and took Gunda by the arm, steering her towards the scullery area where the loud-mouthed red-handed scouring women scrubbed trenchers and dishes clean with sand, before they were rinsed.

"You look like a decent, tidy lass," she said approvingly. "If you work well today, you may serve the King tonight."

Gunda's expression changed, so that she looked a little more interested.

"I might serve the King's guests?" she said,

"Of course – but you must help us get this scrubbing done first."

The girl glanced back at Fridgyth and she almost smiled, then she obediently lifted a dirty griddle from the pile and set about cleaning it in a capable manner.

"I shall have my meal in my hut," Fridgyth announced, taking up a wooden tray. "You've enough to feed without me as well."

She helped herself to a loaf of bread, fresh from the oven, a good slab of goats' cheese and a pitcher of ale.

"I see you're not starving yourself," Mildred observed.

"And I'll be back after noon for a bit of charcoal to smoke my bees with!" Fridgyth retorted.

"All right for some," Mildred said.

Fridgyth ignored her grumbling and carried the food back to her hut, where she shared her meal with Flann.

"What are you learning from all this reading?" she asked him curiously.

"A great deal," he said, with a thoughtful smile. "This is an ancient book of wise sayings that I copied at Slane Monastery – one day I mean to write such a book myself."

Fridgyth smiled and shook her head.

"It must have taken you a long time to copy all those marks onto the vellum – you have an old head for such young shoulders."

"Now that might make a wise saying, in itself," he said and, pulling a small wax tablet and scraper from his pack, he proceeded to make a note of it.

Fridgyth laughed loudly.

"Oh – I have many wise sayings," she said. "And another one is – never collect honey after dusk, or you'll be stung. I must see to my bees while it's still light."

When she got back to the kitchens, she found Gunda deftly whipping a bowlful of cream with a wooden spatula and looking as though she'd done it all her life.

"This girl I brought you seems to know what she's doing," she commented.

"She'll do well enough," Mildred agreed grudgingly. "But I never thought to see this day," she complained, as she pinched round the edges of a crust to decorate a pie. "Alchfrid 'the Stranger' sitting at my board day after day, night after night, and once again I must bow and scrape and serve him all the best food we've been saving for the bitter months. There'll be nowt left for us when they've all gone home. Why do they all have to sit there and eat up our precious stocks, now that their great meeting is over?"

Sister Redburgh looked up from a steaming cauldron of pottage.

"Mildred's going to spice Alchfrid's bread with rotten plums and drop hellebore into his salad," she cackled.

Fridgyth grinned with answering malice.

"That's the way! Rotten plums should make him run – fast back to his palace at Eforwic!"

Alchfrid 'the Stranger' was King Oswy's eldest son by his first wife, a princess from Rheged. Oswy had set him up to rule Deira as sub-king, but this was an unpopular move. Deirans wanted Queen Eanfleda's son, Prince Ecfrid as their lord, for he was the grandson of the great King Edwin.

Fridgyth didn't really care who ruled them, so long as there was peace in the land, but it was always useful to keep in with the kitchen workers. She glanced along the many wooden shelves that lined the side of the kitchens, and helped herself to a tall beaker and a roughly made earthenware bowl. She lifted down a pair of iron tongs from their nail and used them to fish about in the cooking fire to filch a small amount of charcoal, which she then dropped, hot and glowing, into the rugged container. Ignoring the chorus of cheerful insults that followed her, she carried it outside and headed for the upper pasture. Caedmon, oblivious to the importance of the Synod and the royal guests, strode about the meadow mending wattle fences. He was the oldest of the cowherds, and many sneered at him and called him simple, but Fridgyth knew that it was only an embarrassing awkwardness in his speech that gave that impression.

She waved at him as she arrived, and headed straight for the hives. On the way, she searched for a small piece of cow dung from a dried up pat, which she then placed on top of her glowing charcoal so that it smouldered there, making thick, smelly, smoke. From her girdle, she took the old drinking horn with the tip sawn off that she kept especially for this purpose and held it in readiness.

She moved stealthily, creeping towards the hive nearest to her, then, holding the horn over the smoking bowl, she blew a steady stream of smoke, which she aimed into the small entrance of the straw-made skep.

"Now my darlings," she murmured in a soft, sing-song voice. "I must tell you that we have important visitors here in Streonshalh, but things have not gone as the abbess wished."

The bees buzzed louder than ever while she continued in the same crooning tones. She blew a little more smoke inside, then eased open the top of the skep.

The bees buzzed gently round her now and, drowsy with smoke and sweetness, they allowed her to reach inside and pull out a frame of honeycomb. They were used to this quiet tax, levied in exchange for comfortable accommodation and whispered confidences. The more secrets she told the bees, the sweeter the honey they produced. In turn, they enjoyed the dreamy state that the smoke induced and were less likely to sting her.

Fridgyth half filled her collecting bowl with delicate pieces of comb that oozed glorious golden honey, then blew a little more smoke inside and set the skep in order once again.

She left the bees to recover from her small robbery and wandered off to sit down near the well in a patch of late sunlight, where she licked the last scraps of sweetness from her fingers. Caedmon went to sit by her in comfortable silence, while his calves cropped the grass and gulls swooped crying above their heads.

"We're all upside down," Fridgyth told him at last. "I don't know what's going to happen now. The abbess is distressed. She hides it well, but I know she feels wretched."

"Poor Lady," Caedmon sympathised.

"Everything's going to be different," she warned him. "The monks are to shave their heads in the Roman style, and we must expect new rules coming in. Will I still be tolerated, I wonder – a pagan herb-wife?"

"But the abbess is your f-friend," Caedmon said quietly. "And surely the sun will still rise and set?"

Fridgyth looked at him and smiled. She took a deep breath of fresh salt-laden air; Caedmon's rare view of the world was just what she needed. She looked across the river to where the sun was sinking behind the hills, painting both land and sea pink and golden. A double skein of lapwings fluttered above the water, forming speckled black patterns that swooped and looped against the brilliant sky.

The cowherd's deep love of the earth and beasts around him made him content with the simple things in life. Kings and bishops were of no interest to him.

She turned to Caedmon.

"Your calves look well," she observed.

He smiled and nodded. Caedmon's sole concern was that his white vellum calves should have the best life he could give them. The young beasts were chosen at birth for their spotless hides and lived only until Bloodmonth, when the slaughtering gangs would come for them. They'd be swiftly garrotted in order to spill no blood and, when the first winter frosts arrived, the tanners would set to work on their hides. Their snow-white skins would be scraped, dipped, stretched and dried, then made into the finest vellum for the most skilful scribes to write and draw upon. The cowherd would weep for them as the weather grew cold and Bloodmonth approached, but for now the young beasts could still enjoy the lush grass as he watched over them.

"*Sun goes to rest in golden glory,*" he sang the words gently under his breath.

"Golden glory," Fridgyth echoed his words. "I like that... sing more for me. I wanted you to sing last night, but knew you wouldn't."

The shy cowherd would rarely lift his voice in song, but sometimes when he did, words would fall from his mouth like the joyful warble of a rising lark, banishing all his awkwardness of speech.

> "*Sister Sun goes down to her slumber*
> *Golden-gowned, adorned with garnets,*
> *Clouds her hair, fine-fluffed as fleeces*
> *She touches the river with rosy rays,*
> *And paints the meadows, like mackerel's pelt.*"

Fridgyth felt content for the first time that day.

"All this fretting and worrying over Easter and tonsures is nothing when I hear you sing," she said.

Caedmon sang on, his face rapt and rosy with the reflection of the sunset.

> "*Sister Sun – purge us in your pure light.*
> *Bathe us in butter-gold warmth.*

Sleep soft in night-dark wool
Greet us with gladness in the morning."

When at last he fell silent, Fridgyth turned to him and wagged a bossy finger.

"Next time the reeve calls for a bard, you take the harp and sing. Were the King to hear, he'd give you jewels or an armband of gold."

Caedmon shrugged diffidently and shook his head.

"C-cannot," he said, his painful stammer returning at once. "And what would I do with a g-gold armband?"

Fridgyth leant across and gave him a smacking kiss on the cheek.

"You're too good for us all, that's the trouble," she said.

Reluctantly Fridgyth got to her feet, feeling creaky from sitting there so long.

Caedmon too got up, to gather his calves and herd them back to the sheds.

CHAPTER 5

FLANN FINA

With a last lingering look at the sunset, Fridgyth set off back to the kitchens, thinking that it must almost be time for the summoning bell for the evening meal. Still lost in thought, she loaded up another tray of food and drink, enough for two, and carried it through the gardens, back towards her hut. She suddenly stopped at the sight of a young lad who hovered outside her door with a large hunting dog that he held on a leash.

"Now what?" she murmured.

As she moved closer, she saw that the hound was Oswy's favourite dun-coloured beast.

"What are you doing here?" she asked.

The lad gave her a haughty look and ignored her question.

Fridgyth strode past him, slightly irritated at this new invasion of her domain. As her eyes adjusted to the dimmer light of her hut, she saw that Flann had a visitor – a broad-shouldered man who sat with his back to the doorway, his wolfskin cloak had been flung over a stool.

"I've managed to get us a good mutton pie this time," Fridgyth announced as she came in through the doorway. "And there's warm bread and some honey fresh from the hive."

Flann looked up at her blankly, seeming to have temporarily lost his good sense and courtesy. Fridgyth walked past the man with the wolfskin cloak and lowered the tray down onto the table, but when she turned to look at the newcomer, her jaw dropped. It was King

Oswy himself who sat at her table and drank her elderberry wine from an earthenware beaker, while Wyrdkin mewed at his feet.

Fridgyth stared for a moment and then managed a clumsy curtsey. "My lord!" she murmured.

Oswy smiled wearily and waved a dismissive hand.

"Herb-wife, I thank you for your hospitality. Hild tells me that we can trust in your discretion, and I'm grateful for the opportunity to speak to my... young friend, in private." He indicated Flann, who looked more uncomfortable than ever. "I'm very glad to hear from the abbess that Bishop Colman is recovering, thanks to your medicine and administrations."

Fridgyth looked from one to the other and dropped another curtsey. "I'll leave you to speak together in peace," she said. "This food will come to no harm if left for a while." And, with that, she went hastily outside again.

She walked fast away from her hut; her breathing grew rapid and her legs threatened to give way. "Flann Fina... Flann Fina?" she whispered. That name had always seemed somehow familiar, right from the start? Why was Flann Fina sitting there in her hut, playing host to the king? The abbess would know, but Fridgyth could not press her for answers.

"Curiosity will be the death of you," Fridgyth's mother had warned, but it had never stopped her wanting to know other people's business – not then, not now, however trustworthy she might be about it.

It was no more likely that Cloda would reveal Flann's secrets than she would Samson's. Fridgyth stood still for a moment... where should she go? Darkness had fallen all around her and torches flared around the entrance to the great hall. Everyone would gather there for the evening meal, and Fridgyth's feet took her in that direction, though she had no clear idea in her head of what she might do next. The hall was crowded, and there was an air of restlessness, for the meal could not be served until the King appeared. Her mouth lifted in a smile when she spotted Sister Begu at one of the lower boards; there was a small space left beside her and Fridgyth went to join the old royal nurse.

"Where is Cloda today?" she asked.

Begu shrugged and waved a gnarled hand.

"Haven't seen her since last night, though I heard she was summoned to the royal guest house this morning... translating I expect. I've never heard such a babble of foreign tongues... and all of them wanting to be fed!"

"It'll be better when they all go back to where they came from," Fridgyth agreed, trying to sympathise.

Begu refused to be comforted.

"But will it ever be the same again? I'm far too old to change to Roman ways."

More immediate questions concerned Fridgyth. She swallowed hard and took a risk.

"I heard the name Flann Fina mentioned," she said. "One of the guests I daresay."

Begu looked up at once, bright-eyed as a sparrow.

"Flann Fina?" she said, then shook her head vigorously. "Oh no, they couldn't have Flann Fina here, not with the Queen in residence."

Fridgyth struggled to remain calm. "And why is that?" she asked vaguely.

Begu's eyes were narrow with intrigue.

"I shouldn't really speak of it... it was very much hushed up, but it's all so long ago. Flann Fina is the son of the Irish Woman."

"The Irish Woman?" Fridgyth frowned, vaguely remembering some scandal. "What was that all about?" she asked.

"You must tell nobody," Begu said wagging a bony finger at her. "I only know because the Queen came to stay with Hild at the time. It happened just a few years after Oswy's marriage to Eanfleda, when he was struggling to fight off King Penda of Mercia. He went to visit Irish Dalriada seeking aid and warriors from the princes he'd grown up with, on Iona."

Fridgyth nodded; the time Begu referred to was before Oswy ruled the kingdom of Deira as well as Bernicia – before Abbess Hild had come to Streonshalh too. Little news from the wider world reached the small harbour in those days.

"Well," Begu went on, her face alight with mischief, "Oswy was given the warriors he asked for and more, for he met up again with his childhood sweetheart, the beautiful Princess Fina, granddaughter to the Irish king, Colman Rimid."

"He never!" Fridgyth leant forward to catch every word.

"Oh yes," Begu nodded. "A love affair sprang up between them, and when the princess's royal kin learned that she was pregnant, they demanded that Oswy set Eanfleda aside and take Fina to be Queen of Bernicia in her place."

Fridgyth gasped.

"Oh well, Eanfleda was furious…" Begu continued. "You can imagine! She threatened to return to Kent, taking her young children with her, spoiling any chance Oswy might have of claiming to rule Deira through her line."

"What happened then?"

Begu shrugged.

"Princess Fina died giving birth to her son."

Fridgyth was stunned; Flann Fina – blood of Fina – the son of Fina. Suddenly she knew who her quiet visitor was.

"What happened… to the child?" she asked.

"Oh they agreed that the princess's kin should raise him in Ireland and that he would never to lay claim to Oswy's throne. It was all hushed up… but *I* haven't forgotten it and they say his half-brothers know of his existence and *shouldn't* rest easy while he's alive."

"So… of course, he couldn't be here in Streonshalh, could he?" Fridgyth said firmly. "I must have misheard."

Begu shook her head.

"I doubt he'd risk it," she said. "How old must he be now? Quite a young man I'd think."

Fridgyth was relieved when horns suddenly blared to announce the arrival of the king, and the whole gathering rose to their feet.

"I must go to see how the bishop fares," she said, to Begu in a low voice.

She slipped away, knowing that Flann would be alone once more, and strode out from the great hall, not in the direction of the monastic guest house, but out into the herb garden, where she sat down on a rough wooden bench amongst dark shadows and rustling leaves.

"Fina's son… here in my hut," she whispered. "He was speaking with his father, the King, and he's the most courteous young man I've met in a long time."

It took a while for her to catch her breath and think through this astonishing discovery. She could see that it was safer that Alchfrid of Deira and Prince Ecfrid remain in ignorance of their half-brother's presence at Streonshalh. The abbess seemed content to offer Flann sanctuary even though she was so busy and preoccupied. Fridgyth had warmed to the young man at once, and knowledge of his true identity did nothing to diminish that warmth. She now understood why he must hide in her hut, while his friend lodged in the royal guest house. The more she puzzled over it, the more protective her feelings grew towards the solemn young man in her infirmary.

She sat on in the darkness, listening to the mewling cries of gulls and the scurrying of small creatures, and it was only when she began to grow cold that she at last got up and went slowly back to her hut. She found Flann there alone, reading by the light of a candle. The food she'd brought was untouched.

"Your visitor has gone?" she said.

Flann nodded.

"By rights you too should be lodged in the royal guest house," she said. "You should be feasting there in the great hall, not sleeping in a rough hut like this for I know now that you are Princess Fina's son."

Flann closed his book carefully.

"I've slept in many places," he said. "An honest welcome means more than flattering words."

Fridgyth smiled.

"More of your wisdom?" she said.

"I would not, for all the world, dishonour the Queen by my presence," Flann went on. "And I hope I haven't brought troubling gossip to her ears."

"Nobody could be dishonoured by *your* presence," Fridgyth told him warmly. "And apart from the abbess, I'm the only one in Streonshalh who knows who you are. When I saw you with the King, it set me thinking… and now I realise."

Flann shrugged.

"My half-brothers fear I would lay claim to Northumbria some day, but my father understands, I think. I've no desire for kingship; what I wish is to become a scholar. Learning makes a poor man king."

"My humble hut is honoured by your visit," Fridgyth said. "But now you must eat."

Flann pulled his stool up to the table.

"Your cat is named after the Wyrd sisters of fate," he said. "A name from the old gods, I think?"

"Aye," Fridgyth admitted. "And you heard me chanting Freya's spell over the bishop's herbs! Well... I'm not like the nuns, I try to be Christian in many ways, but I still have respect for the old gods I was raised with. People can't change what they believe over night, whatever your father might think. Oh – I've been too bold with my words!"

"No, no," he reassured her with a smile.

She sighed.

"Till now I've been tolerated by the Christians for my skills, though what this new ruling might bring I cannot say. You too must disapprove of me?"

"I'm a Christian," Flann admitted. "I was raised a Christian, but I pass no judgement on others. You see, in our own ways we are both outsiders."

"Yes," Fridgyth agreed, nodding thoughtfully.

"So as two outsiders, let us share this excellent pie," Flann said, and he pulled a stool forward for her.

"I will then," Fridgyth said and, as she sat down, she felt that she was more favoured than any of the Streonshalh folk who feasted with their important visitors in the hall.

They ate and chatted comfortably, while Wyrdkin begged for scraps and Flann fed her generously.

"When the abbess first offered me work in her monastery, I accepted gladly," Fridgyth mused. "But that very first night I sat alone in this hut and wondered what I was doing amongst strangers. Then I heard a faint cry outside and went out to discover a skinny kitten, soaking wet and trying to shelter between two panels of the lean-to."

They both smiled at the picture her words brought to mind, and Flann bent down and gave Wyrdkin another firm stroke and a titbit. He put his hands on either side of the cat's stomach and tested her girth.

"Not skinny now, I think."

Fridgyth laughed.

"Oh no... she's the fattest cat in Streonshalh now. The poor creature wailed like the Wyrd sisters themselves and trembled with fear. I had to climb up high to get hold of her, and she bit me and raked at my hands, but when I brought her to my hearth and fed her on goats' milk she began to purr and I felt that I wasn't alone anymore. I called her Wyrdkin, for I thought the three Wyrd Sisters of Fate had sent her to me and she's the only kin I have."

Flann nodded sadly, and Fridgyth wondered if he too was lonely now that his friend had gone.

"You've a half-sister here," she gently reminded him.

He looked up thoughtfully.

"I feared Princess Elfled's presence might make it impossible for me to stay."

"Leave that to the abbess," Fridgyth advised. "She'll know how to deal with Elfled; the princess answers to none but Hild and, believe me, the girl has a will of her own."

When at last they got up to go to their beds, the cat followed Flann to the infirmary, ignoring Fridgyth. She frowned at such inconstancy, but admired the creature's discernment.

The next morning, Fridgyth got up and went to fetch food from the kitchen, more determined than ever to see her guest well fed, but when she got there she found a great hustle and bustle going on.

"They're off... the King is leaving," Mildred told her, relief in her smile.

Word had flown around the monastery that both tide and winds were right for the royal barge to set sail for Bamburgh. The King's household thanes had gone down to the quayside to prepare the *Lady Acha*.

It seemed that almost everyone had set aside their work to make their way down to the harbour. The leave-taking of the King would be a rare sight, not to be missed.

Fridgyth hurried back to her hut with food.

"Do you wish to take leave of your father?" she asked Flann.

"Thank you, but I think not," he replied.

She left him contentedly examining her stock of herbs and set off again to follow a growing crowd that headed for the main gate. As she passed the kitchens, the girl Gunda emerged, and she called to her.

"Come and see the King and Queen set off for Bamburgh, I gather Bishop Agilbert is leaving too."

But Gunda shook her head, looking rather flushed and agitated.

"Good riddance to him," she said. "I must find my brother and then get back to work. Your foodwife says I am good at table... I serve well."

"Was the bishop a strict master, then?" Fridgyth asked sympathetically.

"He was," the girl said.

"It sounds as though you are doing very well working with Mildred, after all."

"I am content," Gunda said. "Now I must go to find my brother."

The girl set off towards the scriptorium, just as a wave of monks and nuns came flooding out of the tiny huts in their separate enclosures. Fridgyth accompanied them as they jostled their way down the steep hillside, soon to be joined by the metal-workers, glass-makers, potters and rope-makers; the whole of Streonshalh turned out.

When she reached the bottom of the hill, Fridgyth glimpsed the abbess and Princess Elfled standing at the quayside with Wulfrun and Mathild. They'd stationed themselves by the gangplank to oversee the loading of goods aboard the *Lady Acha*. The King's household warriors took their places at the oar thwarts, and there was an atmosphere of eager anticipation. Fishermen in their own small vessels skulled around the King's great barge, eager to escort the larger craft safely out into deeper water. Fridgyth boldly pushed her way through the crowd to reach the abbess, so that people turned to frown at such discourtesy but as soon as they saw who it was, they let her pass.

"Blessings herb-wife," they murmured dutifully, for they lived in constant fear of sickness and knew that they might need her help at any time.

Many who outwardly professed Christianity still kept tiny, carved wooden images of Freya tucked away under their doorframes, and many prayers to Thor drifted upwards with the smoke from Streonshalh hearths whenever a fierce storm rose at sea. Some still claimed descent from the ancient Chieftain Streon and kept tiny rotund carvings of Brig, the ancient tribal goddess, hidden in their thatches.

At last, Fridgyth stood just behind the abbess and the two princesses. Hild acknowledged her presence with a friendly nod. At the sound of horns up near the main gate of the stockade, the excitement of the crowd grew keen. A slow procession appeared and threaded its way down the steep cliff path from the monastery.

"Here they come! Here they come!"

"Ey now, look at them with their grand cloaks floating out behind 'em!"

The King strode at the front, and Wilfrid and Alchfrid walked just behind him. Oswy responded half-heartedly to the polite cheers that rose around him, but his impatience to be off was thinly disguised. Wilfrid of Ripon, in contrast, resplendent in the purple cloak that the Queen had given him, waved magnanimously to the crowds.

The royal women were carried down the hillside in open litters, Queen Eanfleda first, followed by Princess Audrey with her much younger husband Prince Ecfrid marching along side her.

Suddenly the air was warm with greeting. "Bless you," the fishwives chanted as they passed and some shouted boldly, "Ecfrid for Deira!"

"Oh but look," cried Elfled, when she glimpsed the head of the procession. "Wilfrid looks more like the King than my father does!"

CHAPTER 6

CUTHBERT

Nobody could disagree with Princess Elfled's frank comment, for the Prior of Ripon did look much more like a king than either Oswy or Alchfrid 'the Stranger'. When Oswy arrived at the quayside, he came forward to kiss the abbess on both cheeks and thank her cordially for her hospitality. He kissed his daughter perfunctorily and went aboard the *Lady Acha*. Wilfrid followed him and soon appeared on the deck flanked by Queen Eanfleda and her stepson. The young prior had been invited to stay at the royal fortress of Bamburgh while the reorganisation of the church was discussed in detail. All three leaders of the victorious party smiled and waved at the flood of adoring monks and nuns who now pushed forward to catch a glimpse of them.

"Wilfrid's to be made a bishop you know!" a young pink-faced novice whispered in Fridgyth's ear. "Hasn't he got the holiest and heavenliest of faces? And the Roman tonsure looks so good on him."

Fridgyth rolled her eyes at such silliness. Wilfrid possessed powerful charm, she couldn't deny it, but she thought it very much the earthly kind. With his dark hair, strong features, warrior's build and powerful voice, most women found him irresistible. Many of the young monks who crowded close to the waterside had already shaved their crowns in the shape of the new Roman tonsure, skin scraped pink and raw from the blade, in emulation of their hero.

"Where's the King now?" Elfled searched for a last glimpse of her father.

"He's there beneath the awning," Wulfrun pointed him out. "Look – Bishop Agilbert sits with him."

"Why will he not look this way?" Elfled's disappointment could be heard in her voice.

"They're studying charts and lists," Mathild told her kindly, "So much to do... such busy men."

Fridgyth saw that a dainty new jewel graced Elfled's small index finger. "Oh... what a beautiful ring you have," she said, trying to distract her.

The princess saw little of her parents and this important political visit had left her particularly short of any demonstration of parental affection. She smiled and held up the ring to be admired, it was crafted into the shape of a golden bee.

"It was given to me by my new cousin Samson," she said with a smile. "He's a distant cousin to both me and the Queen, though I'd never heard of him before he came to feast with us last night."

Hild, who'd overheard the last bit of the conversation, exchanged a meaningful look with the herb-wife. Fridgyth raised her eyebrows, but made no comment – Samson was acknowledged to be of royal blood so giving out fine gifts, jewellery in the shape of a bee, was normal. But could this dainty gem be somehow linked to the *young bee* the boys had referred to?

At last, the *Lady Acha* was ready. Forty of the King's household warriors hauled in unison, and the barge pulled slowly away from the quayside, and sunlight glinted on the shields slung over the oar thwarts. It was a magnificent sight: the swan-like lines of the twin prows dipped and lifted as the keel cut through the water, while a powerful backwash sent fishing boats bobbing wildly as they endeavoured to keep pace.

The crowd surged forward, so that the princesses had to be protected, and the abbess called out to warn those that pushed to the front to get back. At last, order was restored and as the vessel unfurled its sail and vanished northwards, the smaller boats headed for the fishing grounds. The watchers on the shore turned away reluctantly and set off to climb the hill once again and return to their regular tasks. The excitement was over.

As Fridgyth gathered herself for the steep ascent, a young girl whose face was flushed and wet with tears ran towards her from the direction of the boat-makers' huts.

"Please mistress – please?" she cried, grabbing Fridgyth's arm. "My sister said I must run and fetch the cunning-woman – her little bairn is terrible sick. Please come to our hut!"

Fridgyth felt a pang as she recognised the girl – the youngest of the family born to Ketel and Berta.

"I'll come at once Della," she said, pushing away a touch of reluctance. "But don't call me the cunning-woman, honey, you know I serve the monastery now."

She turned to follow the girl down to the largest of the old wooden boat-makers' huts that stood close to the quayside. Berta appeared in the doorway, chasing two fleeing rats with her broom. She neglected to greet Fridgyth with her usual formal nod and waved her inside.

"Thank goodness you are here," she muttered.

There seemed little doubt that a rat had bitten the baby or that the wound had festered. Both mother and grandmother were distraught, and the child was weak and feverish, while Ketel the boat-maker hovered quietly by the hearth. Fridgyth sighed – she'd seen many a baby lost to such a nasty bite.

"Keep her cool when she sweats and warm when she chills," she advised, as she endeavoured to make her voice steady and businesslike. "If you send Della up the hill with me. I'll give her sage and thyme sweetened with honey. It's a cooling, cleansing mixture that can be stirred with goat's milk for the babe."

"It was good of you to come," Ketel said as she left.

She gave him a meaningful look and answered quickly.

"I help all who are sick."

"But still it was good of you," he repeated, and his hand brushed her shoulder in a familiar way.

Fridgyth moved away from him.

"Too many rats down here," she said gruffly.

Della scrambled willingly up the hill at her side, unaware that the herb-wife was mindful of an ancient sore, long since healed – or so she'd thought.

While Fridgyth made up the medicine, the girl chatted excitedly, awed by the visit of the King and Queen and confident now that the herb-wife would heal their little babe. As she strode of back down the hill with a good-sized stoppered jar of the cooling mixture, Fridgyth thrust those long-buried memories away and decided to go to see how Bishop Colman fared.

When she passed the stables, she was greeted by the ripe smell of manure and the clatter of hooves as Elfled and Mathild trotted out on horseback with Wulfrun in attendance. Elfled's expression was thunderous; she ignored the herb-wife and urged her lively pony Seamist into a canter. Mathild followed more sedately on a quiet grey.

"I see she's still unhappy that her parents and brothers have gone," Fridgyth observed.

"Yes indeed," Wulfrun replied, steadying her mount for a moment with a practised hand. "She won't settle to lessons, so I thought a gallop over the clifftops might help to cheer her."

"A good idea," Fridgyth agreed, as she stood back to allow Wulfrun to catch up with her royal charges.

Fridgyth gazed after them for a moment.

"Elfled still has a brother here, if only she knew it," she murmured to herself.

She arrived at the monastic guest house, to find the abbess at Colman's bedside again, deep in conversation with the old man. There was much activity around the simple lime-washed cubicle as the monks bustled and packed the sparse belongings that they carried with them.

"I'm glad to see the bishop looking so much better," Fridgyth approved, for the old man had a little more colour in his cheeks.

Hild's expression was resigned.

"His grace will not be travelling back to Lindisfarne," she announced.

"No indeed." One of the young monks who'd been so angry yesterday turned to Fridgyth and smiled. "We go to Iona; there at least *we* can worship as we wish – there will be no Roman forelocks for us."

"A hard choice to make," Fridgyth said.

Hild nodded sadly.

"Yes – a hard choice, but it may save his life, I think. I'll send a message to Bamburgh – the King must find himself a new bishop for Lindisfarne. Young Brother Dunstan threatens to go with them and, I daresay, Cenwulf will want to follow when he hears what they intend."

Fridgyth gathered up the beaker and jars that she had brought her medicine in and wondered how the King would take this news. Having returned them to her hut, she went on to the herb garden and spent the remains of the morning cutting rosemary and thyme. When the bell rang for the noontide meal at last, she fastened her bundles and hung them up to dry in her workshop.

"Now that the King and Queen are on their way to Bamburgh, I think you should be free to wander where you please," she told Flann.

He looked up from his book and smiled.

"I'm quite content."

Fridgyth called in at the kitchens to make sure that a good tray of food and drink was taken to the infirmary. Gunda looked up from scrubbing pots and wiped her forehead.

"How are they treating you?" Fridgyth asked at once.

"They treat me well," she replied.

"She's a good girl," Mildred called. "I've no complaints about her."

Gunda got on with her work again, and Fridgyth went on to the refectory. The abbess was seated at the high table with the princesses and Samson. When she saw the herb-wife she beckoned her over.

"Come and join us, Fridgyth," she said. "We're back to plain, wholesome fare I'm glad to say. Does your patient in the infirmary still thrive?"

The glint in the abbess's eye told her that the inquiry referred to Flann. Samson, who was seated between the two princesses, looked up with concern.

"Those in my care thrive well," Fridgyth announced carefully.

"Fridgyth! Fridgyth!" Elfled called, waving a narrow roll of parchment from her seat at the far end of the table. "See what beautiful work Guy the new oblate can do; his painting is almost as good as Eadfrith's."

Eadfrith was the young tutor who had charge of the princesses' education. A quiet young man who struggled with Elfled's boisterousness, he was the best scribe in the abbey and produced exquisite pictures to illustrate his work.

"Almost as good as Eadfrith," Fridgyth raised her eyebrows in mock surprise. "Can that be possible?"

"Come here and see."

The princess unrolled the thin strip carefully amongst the dishes and Fridgyth went over to look at it. It was painted with images of young calves, lifelike in the softness of their hide and the playfulness of their movements. Everyone around them smiled in delight; it was exquisite.

"Brother Cenwulf has set Guy to work in the scriptorium," Elfled continued excitedly. "But the abbess says he may help us with our studies too. There are three new Frankish oblates that have left the bishop's service to stay here and Wulfrun makes sheep's eyes at them, but I like Guy best! He makes me laugh all the time."

"I do not make sheep's eyes," Wulfrun said quietly.

"Hush princess!" Mathild chided. "It's not dignified for you to say such things."

"I have met this Guy," Fridgyth admitted. "He's certainly a fine looking fellow, but his sister has been sent to work in the kitchens."

"We're going to show these pictures to Caedmon," Elfled insisted, as she rolled the parchment carefully up again, uninterested in the sister. "He'll love to see the calves so beautifully drawn."

Wulfrun whispered low to Fridgyth, "I do not make sheep's eyes, but I have to admit that the new Frankish goldsmith is very handsome."

The herb-wife chuckled.

"How does he compare to Wilfrid?"

"Nobody's better looking than Wilfrid," Elfled butted in. "Not even my new cousin Samson."

Samson looked up.

"Do I hear my name mentioned?" he asked.

Mathild looked down and blushed.

"Those who have big ears may wish they'd never listened," Elfled told him, cheekily and then she bent close to Fridgyth, cupping her hand mischievously over her mouth. "You must ask Wulfrun what we saw when we were out riding!"

"We said we wouldn't speak of it," Mathild whispered, shocked.

"Oh, it's fine to tell Fridgyth, nothing offends Fridgyth."

Samson obligingly turned away again to speak to the reeve.

"I think you'd *better* tell me." Fridgyth said.

"Well... Elfled saw him first," Mathild began.

"Saw who?" Fridgyth demanded.

"A naked man," Wulfrun whispered.

Elfled shook her head. "He was not quite naked for he wore a loin cloth, and it was not just a man – it was Cuthbert."

"Still as a wooden carving – like one of the ancient gods," Mathild said dreamily, as she demonstrated with grace, her palms outstretched.

Fridgyth could see that the quiet girl had been moved by what they'd witnessed.

"He was praying," she went on. "And there beside him in the water, we saw three black shining snouts... a miracle."

"Seals," Elfled breathed the word, her eyes were bright. "Wild creatures... if I try to go near they slip and slide away, diving deep beneath the waves, but seals don't flee from Cuthbert."

"It was his stillness that did it," Wulfrun added with practicality. "That's what made them come to him. He stood as still as the rocks, and I must admit that even Caedmon cannot rule the beasts like him."

"You'd think he'd catch his death of cold," Fridgyth commented.

"Yes," Elfled agreed and she shuddered at the thought. "And when he got out of the water, we thought they'd swim away. But instead they followed him, and while he dried and dressed himself, they heaved their fat bodies up the beach to loll beside him, waving their tails and flippers."

"You won't tell anyone we looked, will you?" Wulfrun begged.

Fridgyth assumed a serious expression and pretended to judge them, but the consternation in their faces made her relent. "Well... it seems there's been no real harm done, so I'll keep it to myself. But you're not to go watching naked men again"

"He wasn't quite naked! I told you that," Elfled insisted.

Then she was suddenly shocked into round-eyed silence, for Cuthbert himself appeared in the refectory. He bowed when the abbess invited him to their table, and they all saw that he had stubble at the front, and a freshly shaved round patch on his crown, his flaxen hair was clipped and short at the back. It would take a while for the Roman tonsure to form properly, but it seemed he'd made a start.

"You too, Cuthbert!" Hild said.

He shrugged and smiled.

"Mother Hild, how we look has little importance."

"Dear Cuthbert, you are quite right," she agreed. "Are you ready for your journey?"

"You are not going already!" Elfled's cheerfulness vanished. "Everyone is leaving us!"

"I will set out for Melrose tomorrow morning," Cuthbert said quietly.

Elfled recovered quickly, determined to make the most of the short time left in his company.

"Well… in that case I order you to walk along the cliffs with us this afternoon!" she said, taking hold of his sleeve and looking up at him pleadingly.

"You order nobody, Elfled," Hild cut in quickly.

"But the seals swim below the cliffs and Cuthbert must help us find them; he is the only one who can do it."

Cuthbert shook his head, while Wulfrun and Mathild exchanged an anxious look. Had Elfled given them away?

But Cuthbert smiled.

"This afternoon the tide will be in, so you must look in the water meadows for your seals. We might take one of the boats and row upriver – with Mother Hild's permission of course."

Elfled brightened.

"I offer my services too," Samson put in.

Hild nodded, seeing how this must cheer her ward.

"You'd better take one of the bigger boats," she said, "for of course Begu must accompany the girls."

This stricture dampened the youthful spirits somewhat, but only for a moment.

"How do you know where the seals will be found, dear Cuthbert?" Elfled asked.

"I think he asks them," Wulfrun said with a smile.

CHAPTER 7

CENWULF

The young people got up from the table and left to get ready for their seal hunt. Hild beckoned Fridgyth to her side, and her cheerful manner vanished.

"Brother Cenwulf hasn't been seen today," she said quietly. "I know he's distressed at the King's ruling, but I'm surprised he's not here to make his protest. Will you go to his hut to ask if he's ill? Tell him… he has my permission to speak."

Fridgyth's spirits sank at the thought of visiting the strict, ageing Brother Cenwulf, who openly belittled women both as nuns and scholars. She went off to her workshop, muttering under her breath that many in Streonshalh would be only too glad if Cenwulf decided to go off to Iona with the bishop; then she chided herself, for it was not a herb-wife's business to make such judgements.

She placed a few stoppered bottles in her basket and a small selection of her most effective salves – comfrey, marigold, goose grass and thyme – then picked up her burden with a sigh, thinking hopefully that if Cenwulf was ill he'd be more vulnerable, and that might mean kinder. She braced herself as though for battle and set out.

The stark cells of the dedicated monks were built inside their own enclosure, to the south east of the church; women were forbidden here and only the abbess and herb-wife were an exception. Each tiny hut was constructed of daub-plastered panels, set in a wooden frame, and each roof was thatched with heather. There was barely space to lie down in these cells and little protection from the bitter north wind that blew from the sea. Fridgyth found it hard to understand what it was that made these men and women want to live like this, deprived of all comfort in their lives.

She knew that she mustn't open the door of Brother Cenwulf's cell herself; she should stand outside and beg him to come out to her or wait until he threw open the hatch at the top, so that they could speak. Fridgyth doubted Cenwulf even approved of Abbess Hild, if the truth were told – a women set over men to rule a double monastery!

"Brother Cenwulf?" she called, when she arrived outside his hut. Her voice sounded shrill in the quietness of the rows of cells. "Brother Cenwulf! Mother Hild fears that you are sick. Do you need help? Mother Hild gives permission for you to speak."

There was no reply, though she waited some time. What was she supposed to do now? Though a metal latch-lifter swung from her girdle amongst her many small tools, it would be most discourteous of her to lift the latch herself and blunder in. She drew breath and shouted his name loudly once again. Immediately a shutter in one of the nearby scriptorium windows creaked open, and Eadfrith looked out. It seemed that Elfled's young tutor had remained in the monastery, while the others had gone to find seals, and Fridgyth was relieved to see him there.

"The abbess is worried that Brother Cenwulf's sick and I'm to see if he needs help," she explained.

Eadfrith came out from the scriptorium and down the outer steps, into the monk's enclosure. He went, at once, to tap on Brother Cenwulf's door.

"That won't do any good," Fridgyth told him.

He knocked hard then, but still there was no response.

"Should I call him again?" she asked.

Eadfrith shook his head and tapped his lips, to indicate that he kept silence, as many of the dedicated monks did at this time of day. He pushed at the door to see if it would open, but it didn't.

"I think he has set the latch inside," she said. "I don't *like* to force my way in, but…"

The young teacher nodded and pointed to the latch-lifter that swung from her girdle. Fridgyth unhooked the curved strip of metal and handed it to him. He put his face up to the small hole and pushed the small implement through, knowing well how the door would be fastened; but then he stopped, looking disconcerted and turned to Fridgyth tapping his nose.

"Yes, I smell it too," she said, understanding at once; he was quite right, an unpleasant smell hung over Cenwulf's hut. "The stench of sickness," she said. "We must open the door – he does need help."

Eadfrith eased the latch-lifter down until there came the clear, metallic sound of it catching and then the door swung open.

Fridgyth's stomach leapt with revulsion; Cenwulf was far beyond any help she could give. In her work she'd seen many a dead body, but never one like this. The monk had slumped backwards, but the narrowness of the cell meant the back wall supported him, so that it appeared he knelt almost upright. His fingers were locked together in an attitude of prayer, but dried vomit stained the front of his habit. His eyes were open and staring, and he had an empty goblet fallen at his feet.

"Dear God!" Eadfrith cried, driven to break his silence at the shock of what he witnessed.

Fridgyth clapped her hands over her nose and shut her eyes, for the stink of sickness and death that came from the opened cell was much worse than anything she'd had to deal with in the infirmary. She wanted very much to turn and run back to her clean hut, but she forced herself to look more closely and caught another familiar smell, the faint odour of garlic.

"He's dead," Eadfrith whispered.

It was a certainty, not a question, for it didn't take a practised eye to be sure of it.

"Yes," Fridgyth agreed. She braced herself to touch Cenwulf's bony cheek, and when she did so she found it cold. "And he's been dead for some while, I think. Can you detect garlic amongst the other foul smells?"

Eadfrith nodded.

"I can."

"Oh blessed Freya… how has this happened?" she whispered.

A great many dishes at the Synod feast had included garlic and more again for the King's smaller feast the following night, but it seemed most unlikely that the strict, aged monk would have been invited to the King's private celebration.

Eadfrith hastily made the cross-sign on his breast.

Fridgyth looked carefully at the gold-rimmed goblet on the floor; picking it up gingerly, she sniffed at it. There were traces of dark red wine left in the bottom and the strong smell told her that it was the expensive, potent drink that was brought across the sea to Streonshalh from the Frankish lands.

Eadfrith too sniffed and recognised the stale odour of the dregs. "But Brother Cenwulf disapproved of strong drink – and this quality of wine is served only at the royal table."

"Aye… he's always made his disapproval clear," Fridgyth answered dryly. "But sometimes those who complain loudest are the ones who feel temptation most."

"But surely red wine could not kill him?"

"No," Fridgyth agreed. "But sudden excess might cause death to one whose stomach isn't used to rich food and drink. I've known many a man die from choking on his own vomit."

"But not Brother Cenwulf," Eadfrith insisted, horrified at the idea.

Fridgyth shook her head and pressed her lips together; unlikely though it seemed, the evidence of the goblet was there for them both to see. "There's the smell of garlic too," she said. "Brother Cenwulf was at the Synod's feast as we all were. Maybe he gorged too much and got a taste for strong drink, then followed it with stolen wine."

"Stolen from the King's table?" Eadfrith could not countenance such a thought.

"How else could it have got here?" Fridgyth asked.

Eadfrith had no answer.

"See how emaciated he is," she observed. "He's been so strict with himself, his stomach might rebel at sudden excess and…"

"What a terrible way to go!" the young teacher cut in, and he shuddered.

They crouched there together in silence for a while, simply staring at the dreadful sight. It was a hard thing to believe, but the evidence was unassailable. Cenwulf seemed the least likely of all the monks to be tempted by the sin of gluttony, for he above all had proclaimed fasting as the greatest source of holiness and spoke constantly to the young oblates about denying the appetite.

"Why did he not cry out for help?" Eadfrith asked.

Fridgyth's early revulsion fast turned to sadness as she looked at the gaunt cheeks and hooked nose. She sighed.

"To him dishonour might seem worse than death. How could he allow himself to be discovered in this state?

"But to die, rather than call for help?"

"He couldn't know he was dying," Fridgyth's practical mind saw that. "He'd maybe hope to weather the sickness, and none of us would be any the wiser."

She struggled to her feet and straightened her apron as dark dots swam in front of her eyes once more.

"I must tell the abbess what's happened. I'm sorry I made you break your silence," she added with an apologetic smile. "Let's leave it all as we've found it, for the abbess may wish to see for herself and the reeve too."

"It was not your fault," he said, as he also rose to his feet. "I only keep silence by choice. I'm not a professed monk as yet, and it wasn't you who made me speak. I think I should come with you to see the abbess."

He quietly closed the door to the hut.

Fridgyth was glad of his company as they walked slowly back to the abbess's house. She was reluctant to trouble Hild with more bad news. The abbess was shocked when she heard what they'd found, and sent for the reeve to accompany her to Cenwulf's hut. She asked that Fridgyth and Eadfrith keep their knowledge of his death to themselves, until she and the reeve had a chance to make their own judgement.

Back at her hut, Fridgyth filled a jug with fresh water from the barrel, for she felt the need to wash. She added a few drops of the precious lavender essence that she brewed and scoured her hands until the dreadful smell of death was drowned out by the fresh, clean scent of the herb.

Flann looked up from his reading with concern.

"A bad case of sickness," she explained.

Longing to free her mind from the dreadful image, she wandered out into the upper pasture to find Caedmon. He sat amongst his calves, studying the vellum parchment Elfled had given him.

"The princess s-says I may keep it," he said. "I will treasure it. The maker has copied the calves perfectly."

Fridgyth examined the painting again, cheered a little at the sight of such skilful work.

"Yes, this young oblate, Guy, is talented, no doubt of that," she said. "We've made our visitors far too comfortable; so many seem to want to stay, but talented lads like this one will be welcomed by the abbess I think. He's made a fine impression on Princess Elfled too. She swears he makes her laugh all the time, and Elfled could do with someone to make her laugh. Eadfrith does not count that among his many talents."

Caedmon nodded, for he too had worries about the newcomers.

"A Frankish st-stockman has been here in the pasture to examine my calves," he told her. "I hope he doesn't w-want my job!"

"No," Fridgyth assured him. "The abbess knows nobody could care for the vellum calves as well as you do."

The cowherd went back to his silent perusal of the tiny strip of drawings. When at last he tried to speak again, he was overcome with emotion.

"I w-wish I could have shown this l-lovely thing to mother," he managed at last.

Fridgyth sighed in sympathy, for Caedmon's mother had spent her life as a slave. Descended from one of the old British families, she'd been taken captive as a child when the Angles came and forced into serfdom, her family were too poor to take flight to the western kingdoms as many of the old chieftains had done. When at last the abbess had learned of her plight, she'd bought the old woman her freedom, but it was to be enjoyed for only a short time - at the end of her first winter of liberty, her spirit fled.

"I w-wish I knew where mother had g-gone," Caedmon said.

Fridgyth nodded. She'd like to know where her dead husband and children had gone too.

"I was brought up to believe that Hretha, the death-goddess took those who died to the summer land, and brave warriors to Woden's feasting hall, but the abbess tells a different tale. The Christians speak of a perfect place called heaven."

"A p-perfect place," Caedmon said, sighing. "Like a bright meadow?"

Fridgyth smiled at the idea.

"What would you want for your mother?"

"I'd want a meadow f-filled with flowers."

"Sing of it," she begged.

Caedmon glanced around to make sure that nobody else was close enough to hear; then he began to sing softly and the stammer vanished, as Fridgyth knew it would.

> *"I see a far field*
> *Buttercup-bright*
> *Showers fall and feed the land*
> *Gentle, greening*
> *And a rainbow, brilliant-hued*
> *Bridges earth to sky.*
>
> *Cows forage, milk-heavy,*
> *They call to their calves*
> *Beasts with spotless hides*
> *Sleek and snowy-white*
> *Never to see a slaughtering knife*
> *Nor ever leave their dams."*

"Yes, I can see your mother there in that meadow." Fridgyth sat back and smiled at the picture that came to her mind. "And I see my little ones running through the grass. You are a word-weaver and a bard, just like Eadwig. You must take your turn in the mead hall," she urged.

"N-no," Caedmon shook his head. "I t-tried, last night in the herdsman's hall, but they laughed and threw their meat bones at me... I was tongue-tied, nothing but fool-speak came to me!"

"How dare they?" Fridgyth was furious. "Who did that? I'll set them bleating like lambs!"

Caedmon shook his head and wouldn't say.

Fridgyth suspected it would be the gatekeepers, who thought themselves fierce warriors though they'd never been put to the test. Coen, their leader, considered himself a famous bard since he'd sung for the King. She sighed, for she knew that if she berated Coen over their treatment of Caedmon, they'd whisper that the cowherd hid behind woman's skirts, and it would be even worse for him.

"It's n-no matter," Caedmon insisted.

They sat quietly in the meadow, side by side, while Fridgyth's anger cooled a little, but it wasn't long before they were interrupted by a clamour in the distance.

"The herb-wife! I want the herb-wife! Please let me inside the gates!"

Fridgyth got up quickly to see what was happening. Those same boorish lads that she suspected of cruelty to her friend stubbornly barred the way against a young girl who cried out in distress.

"I'm here," Fridgyth called, and she waved wildly. "The herb-wife is here."

Caedmon stood up too and swung his arms above his head to catch the girl's attention. Fridgyth set off towards the main gate then recognised Della. She picked up her skirts and ran.

"Help us... help us!" Della cried.

"What is it, honey?" Fridgyth panted when she reached her.

"Mam is taken sick now, and my sister too; her little bairn has died. Father doesn't know what to do! I said I'd find you."

Fridgyth's heart thundered at the news. She took the girl's hand.

"I'll come at once. Help me fetch my bundles and herbs."

CHAPTER 8

BY THE QUAYSIDE

It was dark when Fridgyth returned to her hut that night, and she was so tired that, for a moment, she was surprised to see the gleam of a candle there; then she remembered her secret royal visitor.

She found more than she'd expected, for the abbess was with Flann, sipping elderberry wine, while Wyrdkin enjoyed another feast at their feet.

"You're late," Hild said with concern, rather than accusation.

"Ketel the boat-maker's wife and oldest daughter are both sick and the grandchild has died... nowt but a bairn she was."

Hild frowned and murmured "Poor babe. Yet another death. What a sad day this has turned out to be."

Fridgyth nodded.

"I've done all I can think of, but I still fear for them."

"You've done well," Hild approved. "And you look worn out. Come sit with us and drink some of your own good wine; there's bread and cheese to eat. We've said all we need to say for the moment. I understand you've discovered the identity of your guest?"

"Nobody shall hear of it from me," she said quickly.

Hild smiled and turned to Flann.

"There's not much that gets past our herb-wife, but we can trust her."

"A trusted friend is of greater value than gold," he said quietly.

"Yes indeed." Hild nodded approvingly. "But Fridgyth... tomorrow your guest will move into new accommodation. I'm having a chamber prepared, so that he can join Samson in the royal guest house and I'll take Elfled to meet him. I'll tell the princess the truth, but to everyone else our visitor is to be known as Aldfrith, a scholar like Samson and an Irish prince. Cloda will move into the royal guest house to act as housekeeper and see to their comfort."

"That sounds like a good arrangement," Fridgyth agreed.

"Now eat," Hild said, as she pushed the trencher of bread towards her.

Flann got up, bade them both good night and went to the infirmary, leaving them alone.

"What of Cenwulf?" Fridgyth asked when he'd gone.

"The reeve agrees; it seems he's died of excess – there's no other explanation. But I would rather we didn't voice this abroad. It's a matter between him and his maker, I think."

Fridgyth nodded. Many would gloat if they knew the truth.

Hild gave a sad smile.

"The rumour flies around that he's died of a broken heart," she said. "He was so deeply distressed at the outcome of the Synod."

"Ah, well," said Fridgyth. "A broken heart shall save his reputation then."

"Yes," Hild replied, and added with a grim touch of humour. "He's likely to become a saint, I think. I've made arrangements for him to be buried with the usual ceremony due to a respected member of our community, in the monastic cemetery."

Fridgyth tried to eat a little and struggled to keep up a conversation; the abbess saw how exhausted she was and left her to settle for the night. It was only when she lay down and closed her eyes, that she dared to remember the terrible evening she'd spent down in Ketel's hut.

She'd found his wife, Berta, in a bad way – flushed and vomiting, with a nasty swelling in her armpit as though she too had been bitten by a rat. At the same time the poor woman was distraught at the loss of her grandchild. The baby's mother was sick as well, so Fridgyth had done her best to make both women comfortable and had fed them her fever brew, while Della worked hard to help, doing everything the herb-wife asked of her.

Ketel had sat and wept by his hearth, thanking her constantly for her help.

"I thought you might refuse us," Berta whispered, between rasping breaths. "Ketel's mother delivered my bairns, and she treated us with her herb simples and brews, but now she's gone."

Fridgyth had glanced up to where Ketel sat, then bent close to whisper in the sick woman's ear. "It's long forgotten now, Berta. I didn't even know you knew about it."

For as long as anyone could remember, boatmaking had been one of the most important skills on that rocky shoreline and Berta's father had been the chief craftsman of his time. He'd no son of his own, so he'd picked out Ketel from the Streonshalh lads as an ambitious, reliable, skilled young man who was worthy to be his son-in-law and follow him into the trade. But Ketel was Fridgyth's first love and they had had every intention to wed, but when the tempting offer was made to Ketel by the boat-maker, suddenly the cunning-woman's daughter seemed less of a catch. So Ketel had married Berta and Fridgyth had been broken-hearted, though she'd recovered enough to accept marriage with Ingild a year later. She'd gone to live with him on his smallholding on the hillside above Ruswarp Mill. The land they farmed was rich, and Fridgyth had been happy enough with Ingild, as three children were born to them in swift succession.

The year of King Edwin's defeat had been harsh for everyone – the year of terror, as it was still thought of. Fridgyth, like many others, had lost both her husband and her children. Ingild had died defending his land against Cadwalla's rampaging gangs and Fridgyth herself had been badly burnt, trying to stamp out the flames in their burning barley field. Having lost both her husband and the crop, she found herself injured and unable to care for her children adequately, and one by one her little ones had died of hunger and cold. She'd fallen into deep despair and might well have died too, were it not for small pots of food that began to appear on her doorstep from time to time. The gifts had given her strength to survive, knowing that someone had taken the trouble to tramp out from the village to the remote half-ruined dwelling and leave her sustenance.

Eventually she'd gathered together the strength to return to Streonshalh, only to find her mother sick. She had set about nursing her and learning from her the skills of cunning-woman.

All long ago she told herself as she tried to push the painful memories away. Cadwalla was the enemy, not Berta, and she'd a suspicion that it might have been Ketel who'd quietly seen her fed.

As she drifted off to sleep, she resolved to get up very early in the morning and go straight down the hill to help them again. What a day! The dreadful picture of Cenwulf came unbidden to her mind, the door of the cell swung open again and again.

Fridgyth rose at daybreak and set off as she'd planned. She found Berta even worse, and the swelling needed to burst. She fed her meadowsweet tea, which seemed to comfort her a little, but racked her brains in desperation as to what to try next.

"A seaweed poultice," she muttered, "dulce and sea salad!"

"I will fetch the weeds for you," Ketel offered.

"Do you know which ones to gather?"

He shook his head.

"I'll be back," she said.

She picked up a small willow-woven skep and touched his arm gently as she went out.

She set off across the rocky beach, beneath the cliffs and went skittering from rock to rock, as she searched for the spreading green sea-plants that she'd used in the past with some success for treating boils and tumours. These particular seaweeds weren't easy to find, but as the tide washed in, she managed to gather a useful sized bunch. She turned to hurry back, when she saw with a slight jolt that she was not alone. A hooded figure was hunkered down in the shadows between two rocks; whoever it was they kept very still, but they had a good view of the sea. As she stared, the figure rose and bowed courteously in her direction. She saw with surprise as the hood fell back that it was Samson.

"I'm sorry to startle you," he said. "I love the sea and sometimes find that I need my own company."

"The princesses will be missing you," she told him. "And I believe that your friend will be moving into the royal guest house today."

"Yes, I must go back to welcome him," he said and turned, at once, to clamber over the rocks towards the cliff pathway. Fridgyth tucked the damp bundle of seaweed into her basket and followed him, feeling just a little uneasy. It seemed a strange place to find him when he was about to be reunited with his friend. She wondered if his dark, good looks and disarming manner had made her trust him too quickly.

That night, Fridgyth trudged back up to the monastery from the quayside in darkness. She went in through the stockade by the side gate, to find that, once again, a candle burned in her hut. Hadn't Flann gone yet?

But it was Hild who sat there alone, save for Wyrdkin.

"It's as well you're here," Fridgyth said at once, forgetting in her urgency the courtesy due to the abbess.

"What's wrong?" Hild asked, ignoring Fridgyth rudeness, for she sensed trouble as Fridgyth came just inside the doorway.

"You'll have to know soon enough," she said. "I don't want to start panic and fuss, but I can't pretend anymore."

"You're never one to fuss. What is it that you can't pretend about?"

"This sickness…" Fridgyth's mouth trembled a little. "Down amongst the huts by the quayside… it's very bad. I hoped it was just the stomach rot, but this is something I've not seen before. I don't know that you should be here with me, for it's spreading from hut to hut. I will go straight back to Ketel's family to stay with them for good or ill."

Hild frowned, for she liked the sound of it less and less.

"Tell me more," she commanded.

"First it was Cynfrid's baby," Fridgyth began. "And I thought it was a rat bite, for the huts down there are rat-ridden. Then Cynfrid fell sick, followed by her mother, Berta. The girl Della has helped me care for them, but now she's taken sick herself. Rat bites do not spread like this. I fear it's some contagion."

Hild gasped, and Fridgyth hurried on.

"The sickness has spread to the next hut and the next. Sage and thyme does nowt but soothe their pains a little and a foxglove purge is useless. I gathered seaweed to make poultices today, but I was too late."

"Ah no… too late you say?" asked Hild leaning forward in alarm.

Fridgyth shook her head.

"Berta and Cynfrid were dead when I returned. I used the seaweed I'd gathered to treat Della's swelling, poor lass."

"What is this sickness like?" Hild asked.

"I've never seen it before, but I fear I've heard of it. It starts with vomiting and the sufferer pukes until they've emptied themselves, then a lump like a great boil grows – and those boils come fast. Cynfrid's baby had a nasty swelling below her ear and Berta a painful lump in her armpit. With Cynfrid it was the groin."

Hild's face turned pale in the candlelight; she too had heard of just such a sickness that had raged across the Frankish lands and Ireland too. There'd been reports of it in the southern kingdoms. She always faced up to trouble, though she feared to speak the word. "It is… the plague," she said at last. "Yellow plague! Isn't that what they call it?"

Silent dread hung in the air between them.

"Yes," Fridgyth said at last. "We thought we'd stay free of it, so far away from the Frankish lands, but I fear we are plague-free no longer!"

Hild put her hands to her head in a sudden gesture of distress.

"What can we do? I can't think straight," she admitted.

"Nor I," Fridgyth agreed.

"Is this God's wrath – God's judgement on our Synod? You don't think Cenwulf died of the plague?"

Fridgyth stared. Poor Cenwulf; in her frantic work down at the quayside she'd forgotten him.

"There were no lumps or boils on him," she said uncertainly. But perhaps she hadn't examined him thoroughly enough to be sure of such a thing. Perhaps they'd judged Cenwulf too quickly and too harshly after all.

"Dear God, what have you sent us now?" Hild cried.

Fridgyth was shocked to hear the abbess sounding so desperate. She struggled to regain her usual common sense and spoke more calmly, for she knew that if panic spread they'd all be lost.

"Maybe I'm seeing the worst," she said. "If we were right about Cenwulf's death, then this sickness remains quayside-bound, and we must try to keep it there. Flann is safe in the royal guest house now, isn't he? Has Elfled met him?"

Hild nodded and swallowed hard, as she tried to regain her composure.

"Elfled has accepted him as her brother, with some fascination I think; she'd heard servants gossip in the past and knew something of his existence. She understands that it's a tricky situation with her mother, and there's little that she learns about her father that surprises her. She will call him Aldfrith and treat him as the visiting scholar that he is."

Fridgyth nodded.

"I saw Samson down on the beach today, when as I scrambled over the rocks to gather seaweed."

Hild seemed unsurprised and nodded.

"I have decided that both of these young Irish scholars may claim protection here, but Samson must not go down the hillside again for fear of the plague and I shall tell him so. They're clever lads, both nobly born and that's all that must be said of them. Though if we *do* have pestilence here...?"

"Let's not be hasty," Fridgyth was determined to stay calm. "I'll return to the boat-makers' huts for now."

"But you put yourself at risk."

"That's a herb-wife's job," Fridgyth insisted. "I'll gather my medicines and go. You must manage without me for a while. Call on Begu and Cloda if needed, they both have healing skills, and keep the monastery closed as best you can. If any come down to the quayside, they'll be risking their lives."

Hild nodded, more hard-headed now.

"Tell poor Ketel to carry the dead around to the southern gate. I'll see the cemetery opened for them. It's a blessing Cuthbert set off this morning in Colman's train." Then the abbess glanced up sharply, as her own words brought with them a dreadful new realisation. "Yellow plague... it spreads like fire... that is well known. Has this disastrous Synod sent the seeds of sickness all across the land?"

"Don't let your thoughts fly that way!" Fridgyth advised. "Keep faith – you are good at that."

She stepped back from the door so that Hild could leave without touching her.

"I would embrace you," the abbess said.

Fridgyth smiled fiercely.

"But you must not."

"Then come up to the outer well at sunset tomorrow. I'll meet you there in the open air and keep my distance and then at least I'll know how you fare."

"At sunset," Fridgyth agreed.

"I must inform the reeve and Brother Brandon too," Hild muttered half to herself, as she hurried away into the darkness.

Fridgyth went back into her hut and allowed herself one long, heartfelt, heavy sigh. What lay ahead now?

She stroked her cat.

"And you… you must fend for yourself for a while," she said. "It'll do you good. You're fat enough to last a month, and there are plenty of rats about."

She set off back to the boat-makers' huts in the moonlight, loaded with bottles and more bundles of herbs.

Fridgyth worked so hard the following day that her mind became blurred. More of those who lived in the ramshackle row at the quayside had died; only a few stayed strong. Ketel sought to numb his misery with action now, and she was glad to find that as she went from hut to hut, to apply poultices and feed meadowsweet and horsetail tea to the sufferers, he was always at her side and willing to do any dirty job despite his losses. There was no time for them to discuss the past. Young Della's foul swelling seemed to be responding to the seaweed treatment, though her fever still raged. The poultices were growing stale, and all the fresh seaweed had been used up, so that afternoon Fridgyth set out across the slippery rocks to gather more.

CHAPTER 9

SEAWEED

A warm sun lit the sea, touching the waves and sand with silvery light. Cormorants perched on the rocks to perform their awkward wing-drying dance, while gulls wheeled overhead. It would have been pleasant to be there if her purpose had not been so desperate, but the tide came in fast and there was little time.

She couldn't help but glance across the rocks to where she'd seen Samson, but today there was no sign of him. She gathered the seaweed as quickly as she could, enough for several poultices. Then, as she turned to go back, something else caught her eye. A small boat came in on the tide and headed for the rocky beach beneath the high cliffs that the monastery crowned. She stopped, puzzled at the sight of it, because none of the local boats would ever choose to land up there, where the rocks are treacherous.

Streonshalh had a fine open harbour where the river flowed out into the sea. There was a wooden quay for the larger vessels to tie up and smooth, protected sandbanks, where the fishermen hauled their boats.

Despite her urgency to return, she shaded her eyes and watched as a tall man leapt from the boat into the shallow water. The craft pulled away, at once, and rowed back out to sea, with a great deal of effort against the incoming tide. The tall newcomer purposefully waded ashore. The fellow's broad shoulders and easy stride made Fridgyth think of a warrior, and she thought that she could see the dark silhouette of a sword at his waist. She glanced out towards the horizon again to see that the small boat had moved fast through the waves towards a much larger vessel that stood offshore in the distance.

When she looked back to the rocky shore, the man had vanished into the darkness beneath the cliffs. There was a steep winding path up to the monastery round there, but a newcomer would be most unlikely to find it without help or someone to meet him. Could Samson have been on the look out for that small boat? Fridgyth shook herself back to the present; it was all very strange, but she should be ashamed to be gawping at things that were not her business while her patients waited for help. She set off again and hurried back across the rocks to the boat-makers' huts.

When she got back, she found that Ketel had prepared the bodies of his wife, older daughter and grandchild for the rites of the dead. He'd laid them out respectfully in his workshop on woven wicker litters and dressed them in their best clothing with strings of glass beads about their necks. In Berta's hands he'd placed her wooden weaving shuttle, beautifully carved in the shape of an open boat. He'd wrapped the baby in clean, fine linen and set a string of tiny shells about her neck, then laid her at her mother's side.

Fridgyth caught her breath at the sight of them, and tears flooded her eyes.

"Poor little mite," she murmured.

Their bodies were still swollen and distorted with the plague-swellings but the flush of sickness had gone from their skin, and the pallor of death brought a touch of peace and beauty.

Ketel turned and saw her.

"I've done my best, but…"

"You've done very… well…" she managed, though her throat clamped tight on the words and she found she couldn't say more

He struggled to smooth Berta's hair with a fine-toothed bone comb.

Fridgyth remembered what Hild had said.

"The abbess has offered you her burial ground," she said, as she touched him gently on the elbow. "She'll make arrangements to open the southern gate to you."

Ketel shook his head and made no reply.

"What is it?" Fridgyth asked. "Are you not content with that?"

"It is good of the abbess," he said, "But *we* still fear the ancient gods. We don't want to offend Lady Hild. We know she means well by us, but… many of us see Thor's anger in this sickness. We must return to the old ways and take our dead onto Thorden Sands."

Fridgyth rubbed her aching back and considered his words; she could well understand his attitude. Respect for the abbess and gratitude for her fair treatment had suppressed most open adherence to the old religions, but desperate times brought back old fears.

"So… you'd build a pyre on the sands near Thorden, as we used to do?"

Ketel nodded.

"Yes," she said. She accepted that he must do what he thought to be right. "I'll explain to the abbess when I go to the well tonight."

"Will you come with us and sing a lament as you once used to do?"

Fridgyth hesitated and glanced into the hut where Della tossed restlessly on her bed.

"Better not," she told him gently. "I'll go to the abbess for food and milk, then come back here. You have a child that still lives, and while she lives, I shall do my utmost to save her. I go now to make a fresh poultice for her."

He nodded.

"Of course you are right."

She went inside and mashed the seaweed to bring out the juices, then formed them into a poultice, but as soon as she'd made the girl as comfortable as she could, she returned to Ketel.

"May I help," she offered. "I'm more used to this work than you."

He allowed her to take the comb from him, and she set to work carefully, arranging his wife and daughter's hair.

"I could mark out your Berta's weaving shuttle with Freya's runes," she offered uncertainly. "I have not forgotten how to do such things."

"I'd like that well," he said.

So Fridgyth fished inside the leather pouch that swung at her belt and brought out her short rune-stick with its sharpened point and a tiny, stoppered vial of elderberry ink.

"You made this for her, I think," she said, as she carefully lifted the carved shuttle from Berta's hands.

He smiled wistfully.

"I carved it for her while she laboured to bring Della to birth. It's made from ash, the sacred tree."

"She must have loved it so."

He gave a sudden, painful bark of derisory laughter.

"No! Berta complained that it never worked well, for it caught at the warps."

Fridgyth looked up at him and saw, for a moment, the man she'd once loved – his hair was thin and silver now, but he still had the strong shoulders and upright stature of his youth. She turned hastily back to her task, and marked out the runes.

"This rune means travel," she said, thinking carefully what would be appropriate.

And this one represents the sea.

This has the meaning of summer

and this one happiness."

Then she spoke formally.

> *"I pray you Freya of the midnight cats.*
> *Let this good woman Berta,*
> *Travel over the sea to the summer halls,*
> *Where she will know perfect happiness,*
> *Pray send her daughter*
> *And her daughter's babe too*
> *So they may all be together in the happy lands."*

Ketel sighed, and his eyes filled up with tears.

"I thank you for this," he said quietly. "It means a great deal to me."

Then almost as an afterthought, Fridgyth added the rune for generosity.

She was uncertain why… perhaps it represented her own sorry feelings toward poor Berta. She replaced the boat-shaped shuttle in the dead woman's hands and forced her mind to more practical matters.

"I think you should take all this bedding with you to be burnt," she told Ketel. "I don't like to say this, but I've heard that fire destroys the pestilence."

He grunted a brief acknowledgement.

"I've heard it too."

"When will you set out?"

"At sunset. Three of our lads have gone ahead already to build the pyre." Then he sighed. "I've no proper funeral urn so I thought to use her best cooking pot for the cremation bowl."

"That will represent them all well," Fridgyth agreed. "You'll bury it up at Thorden?"

"Yes, I will."

"You're a good man," she said softly.

The sudden, shocking, misery they were forced to share had wiped away the awkwardness that had grown between them over the years. They'd slipped back naturally into working together as trusted friends, and this brought a crumb of comfort at this desperate time.

Ketel left for Thorden, accompanied by those from the boat-makers who were still well. They carried the bodies and bedding in a solemn procession towards the distant sands. As soon as he'd gone, Fridgyth fed Della more of her sage brew and then left her briefly while she climbed the hill to the outer well. She found Hild waiting there for her, accompanied by Sister Redburgh and Gunda. They carried fresh bread, milk and cheese.

"How does it go?" Hild asked.

Fridgyth wearily passed on the news of the latest deaths.

"Come back with us," Hild urged. "There is little you can do down there."

But Fridgyth shook her head. She couldn't abandon Ketel and the only child left to him.

"Della still lives," she said. "The swelling has burst, and I think my seaweed poultices are doing some good. While she lives and there is hope, I cannot desert them... there are others too."

Hild nodded, respectful of her decision, but she'd more to say.

"We'll come to the well each evening to bring you food. I've made arrangements for the burial of the bodies." She spoke with unsentimental practicality.

Fridgyth shifted uncomfortably.

"I beg pardon lady. The boat-makers have gone to carry the bodies of their families along the sands to Thorden."

Hild flashed a look of anger, for she understood what this meant at once.

"My pardon! Do you think they can have my pardon for that?"

Fridgyth would not be cowed by fierce words.

"They fear their old gods visit sickness on them because they work for Christians, and I can understand why they should think that way. They believe with all their hearts that they must now appease their ancient gods."

Redburgh and Gunda looked shocked that the herb-wife should answer the abbess so frankly, but Hild simply frowned in thought. It was a harsh blow, but the abbess knew well that many of these recent conversions to Christianity were fuelled mainly by payment, shelter and the security the abbey offered. The Irish style of Christianity that Hild had learned from Bishop Aidan held to the belief that tolerance and patience would eventually win against pagan ways.

"It seems I must accept," she said at last. "I accept and shall try to understand."

Fridgyth added her own matter of fact advice.

"In this case I think it better that they *do* burn the bodies. Old clothes and bedding often seem to spread disease, but fire cleanses."

"I'll pray for their souls," Hild said. "Please tell them that, and Fridgyth, you needn't fret that we have no herb-wife; a Frankish monk, Brother Argila has arrived today. He's a leech, skilled in the healing arts, and though I did not look for visitors, I felt *his* arrival must be heaven sent."

Fridgyth suppressed the small protest that rose in her throat and nodded her head. She immediately hated the sound of this 'healer monk', who could so easily step into her shoes. Was this what she'd feared ever since the Synod; was it the beginning of the end for her? The services of a leech-skilled 'religious brother' might well be preferred by the monks, though perhaps not by the nuns.

She waited until Hild and her helpers had gone back inside the main gate and then went to look for Caedmon. She found him just as he had rounded up the calves, ready to take them back to the sheds for the night.

"Don't come close to me," she warned. "But I must speak with you. Have you seen this new Frankish monk that arrived today? What manner of man was he? Was he old, was he young?"

Caedmon frowned and shook his head. "I saw n-no new monk."

"But there is one," Fridgyth insisted. "A leech, so the abbess says."

"Nobody like that has passed this way," Caedmon maintained.

Fridgyth went back down the hill to Ketel's hut, bothered at what she'd heard. She could see flames rising in the distance on Thorden Sands, but still she was distracted by what she'd heard about the new visitor. How did this Brother Argila get here if he didn't pass the cowherd in the upper pasture? Then she stopped, for she had remembered the small boat that came in on the tide. If that was this religious leech's arrival, then it was a strange and secretive way for him to come.

She tried to push away the disquiet she felt, as she carried on down the hillside. She told herself that she should not take offence, for there was enough to worry about without her making mysteries out of simple things.

She knew Ketel wouldn't be back from Thorden until the morning, so she decided to make herself as comfortable as possible. Looking for clean straw, she went out to the nearby stables that housed the tough little mules that pulled carts up the hill to the monastery. She helped herself to armfuls of the mules' bedding, disturbing and scattering a family of rats as she gathered it. When she got back she saw that Della laid quietly, her breathing steady; perhaps there was still hope for the girl.

Having dosed her patient with more meadowsweet and horsetail brew, Fridgyth lay down to rest. She was exhausted, but as she closed her eyes, the sight of the man on the rocks came back to her. When the King came to Streonshalh for the Synod, the whole town had been on the look-out for his barge – there'd even been rivalry to be the first to spy it in the distance. As soon as the horn was sounded, they'd all hurried down to the harbour to greet him, but of course this Brother Argila was only a leech-monk, not the King. She shut her eyes, determined to put the mystery out of her mind.

Next morning she woke with the scent of wood smoke in her nostrils. Ketel had returned from the rites of the dead, smudged with soot and ashes, grim-faced, with the news that two more of the young boat-makers who'd gone with him had collapsed with the sickness overnight.

Fridgyth struggled to her feet, ready to go to them.

"So, it's not over yet."

The day passed in another muddle of miserable work, but Fridgyth made more seaweed poultices for Della and the girl continued to improve. There were now only two of the quayside families still free of the plague, and they packed their few belongings and headed inland, children and bedding piled into mule carts. Fridgyth couldn't blame them; she felt she'd have done the same. That night, as the sun went down, she toiled up the hill to find the abbess by the well again.

"Della's propped up in bed and supping broth," Fridgyth told her, for she hoped this might bring some cheer.

"That's something," Hild acknowledged, her face still a picture of utter misery. "But I am the bearer of bad news tonight."

Fridgyth glanced up at the well-built wooden stockade. Had their struggle to keep the sickness from the monastery been in vain? Had Cenwulf really died of the plague after all and spread it among the monks and nuns?

"No," Hild saw the way her thoughts strayed. "It's not bad news of Streonshalh, but of Lastingham. A messenger came to tell me that Prior Cedd took sick and died almost as soon as he arrived back from the Synod. Now others are sick at Lastingham."

"So it *has* spread inland," Fridgyth said, "Despite our efforts."

Hild nodded.

"You look exhausted," she said. "I fear greatly for you. Come back with us."

Fridgyth shook her head; she longed to go back to her comfortable hut, but she'd promised Ketel that she'd see him through this trouble, and she was determined to keep her word. She took the food and bundles of herbs that Mildred and Gunda had brought for her and set off back down the hill, walking fast before she could change her mind. Flames leapt again in the distance on Thorden Sands, and the wind carried a plume of thick black smoke far out across the sea.

"Freya carry them to the happy halls!" she whispered.

Ketel would be relieved to see that the smoke rose high into the sky, for it was seen as a symbol of acceptance from the gods. The smoke carried with it the spirits of those who'd died.

"And Christ take up their souls," she added for good measure.

CHAPTER 10

THE HERB-WIFE'S APPRENTICE

Once again Fridgyth fell to an exhausted sleep and, at the first sign of morning light, she tried to get up. Her stomach heaved, and when she tried to rise to her feet, she vomited a mess of bile and blood painfully onto the earthen floor. She'd eaten little the day before, and as she bent to vomit again, she recognised with dread an uncomfortable stiffness in her neck. Her fingers snaked upwards to find that a throbbing lump had appeared there.

"Ah Freya… not me too!" she muttered.

Della got up from her pallet and came towards her on wobbly legs. She pushed Fridgyth back onto the straw.

"I'll fetch you water," she said. "And your sage potion… that did me good, for I am better."

Obediently Fridgyth lay back, aware that her whole body was burning up.

"Why me? Why not me?" she muttered.

She lay on her straw bed throughout the day and drifted in and out of fear-filled dreams that brought back memories of the Year of Terror. Once again she raced through fields of burning barley, searching hopelessly for food to keep her children alive. Sometimes softer fancies came to her, and she thought herself in Caedmon's meadow, where she lay amidst buttercups and daisies, nuzzled softly by calves as they tugged at the grass. Once she opened her eyes to see a rat scurrying past, looking for crumbs.

At last she lost consciousness, aware of little more than a great deal of pain and Ketel, who stared down at her with wide anxious eyes. The pain in her neck and head had become so severe that she sometimes wondered if she'd died and gone to the Christians' hell. Time swirled around her so that it seemed that years had passed while she lay in a helpless state.

Snatches of conversation reached her.

"I fear she's going."

"No! We won't let her!" Della's determined voice came through to her. "She saved me! We will save her! We must."

The terrible pain in her neck grew worse; it throbbed and throbbed until it became unbearable. She heard shouts, curses and screams that sounded strangely familiar. Could that be her own voice shouting? She thought, at one time, that Ketel had stabbed her in the neck. Was that punishment for allowing his wife to die? The agony peaked and, when it eased a little, it seemed that something warm and damp was pressed against the painful spot, while the cool water that trickled down her burning throat carried the bitter taste of sage.

Then, one morning, she opened her eyes to find that she was lying on a clean feather-stuffed mattress, covered by a soft woven rug. Her forehead was cool and her mind clear. Sun shone in through the half-open shutter, and she could hear the cries of gulls and the wash of the sea as it lapped at the quayside.

Her hand went up to her neck to touch a huge, tender scab still freshly forming.

"I'm alive," she murmured.

Della came at once to kneel beside her.

"Lie back and rest," the girl ordered.

Fridgyth heard the sound of sobbing and looked past Della to see Ketel sitting by the hearth, his head in his hands.

Fridgyth struggled to make her numb, cracked lips form the words. "Is your father sick?"

Ketel hastily wiped his tears away and looked up at her.

"No, no. He weeps with joy that you live," Della said. "I made him lance that swelling with his knife, and he feared he'd killed you when it bled so. I went to find the seaweed that you used on me, and we made a poultice."

"You did very well," Fridgyth murmured. She struggled weakly to rise, her mind still fuddled. "But… I must go to see the abbess."

"No, lie back," Ketel ordered, his voice strong now. "I went up the hill to see the abbess and told her you were sick. She sent new bedding and linen sheets and rugs to make you comfortable."

"Has the sun gone down yet?" Fridgyth asked, still puzzled.

They both smiled.

"The sun has gone down and risen again four times," Della said. "You are slowly getting better, just as I did."

Fridgyth lay back obediently.

"Who made you herb-wife?" she asked.

"I made the appointment myself," the girl responded with a touch of humour. "There was nobody else to do it."

All that day Fridgyth lay as weak and helpless as a newborn babe. That evening she managed to sip a few spoonfuls of the fish broth that Della had made.

"Are you going to Thorden tonight?" she asked Ketel.

"We've no more dead to burn," he said. "Only us three left."

Fridgyth looked at Della for confirmation.

The girl nodded, solemn now.

"They've either gone to the happy halls, or fled," she said.

There came the sound of a knock on the side of the hut and a familiar voice called Fridgyth's name. Della looked alarmed for it seemed the abbess herself was stood outside.

"Don't you dare come into this hut," Fridgyth ordered, though her voice croaked like a young lad's.

"Praise God!" Hild made a happy response. "Fridgyth… you must come back to us now!"

Ketel helped the herb-wife to her feet and supported her as she stumbled to the threshold. He opened the door, and the chill air took Fridgyth's breath away, but she was cheered to set eyes on the abbess again.

"I want all three of you to come up to the monastery," Hild said. "I'm convinced that you've saved my monastery, by keeping your suffering to yourselves. The danger must have passed by now. It is time to let *us* look after *you*."

Fridgyth nodded acceptance.

"We'll stay here for two more days to be quite sure, but then we'll come," she said. "I fear these huts must be burned to the ground, along with our clothing – for safety," she said, turning to Ketel with uncertainty.

He nodded sadly, and Fridgyth knew he was thinking of the pyres on Thorden Sands.

"Fire cleanses," he agreed. "These huts hold nothing for us now, and they're rat-ridden."

"New workshops shall be built," Hild promised. "And I will supply all the materials that you need, but I think we must wait until the spring for that. For now, you'll be our honoured guests in the abbey."

Ketel looked uncomfortably down at the ground.

"You saw our fires Lady?"

"I saw your fires," Hild shrugged. "You honoured your dead as you thought true. Nobody can judge you for that. Our reeve has made space ready for you and your daughter in the visitors' guest house, and in two days' time I'll see you there."

The abbess left, and Fridgyth accepted Ketel's help to struggle back to her bed. He set her gently down and covered her with the rug. She was touched by a moment of sheer elation; she was alive, the abbess was welcoming her back, and Ketel was treating her so very kindly. Tears welled in her eyes, then exhaustion came and she slept again.

The two days passed, and Fridgyth continued to recover and strengthen. There were no signs of sickness on Ketel, which seemed a miracle to both his daughter and the herb-wife.

On the third evening, Ranulf, one of Fridgyth's gardeners, came down to the quayside with his two oldest sons. In their arms they carried dry straw, tinder and flint. Fridgyth staggered out of Ketel's hut, still wobbly-legged but glad that the time had come for her to return to her home.

The boat-maker and his daughter took one long last look at their hut.

"Nobbut a row of tumbledowns," Ketel said.

He carried only a hempen bag full of the precious tools that couldn't be left behind and set off with determination to climb the hill to the abbey. Looking miserable, Della hovered at Fridgyth's side.

"This is the only home I've ever known," she said.

Ignoring the weakness that she still felt, Fridgyth took the girl's arm and began to lead her away towards the hill. "The abbess will build a new home for you," she said. "And the abbess builds well – no flimsy work satisfies her."

"But… I do not think I could bear to come back here again," Della said, as they began to climb the hill.

"Then we'll find you something else."

An idea that might quell Della's fears had come to Fridgyth over the last two days. She'd grown close to the girl as they struggled for life together. She wasn't sure what Ketel would think of her idea, for he might well consider that *he* had the right to decide his daughter's future, but Fridgyth would only feel happy if the girl herself made the choice. She stopped for a while to catch her breath.

"I've no daughter left to me," she said. "And I've been thinking that I need an assistant, a young woman I'd teach healing skills to, so that she might be herb-wife after me."

She resolutely pushed to the back of her mind the presence of a leech-skilled monk.

Della had stopped too, her face suddenly alive with surprise and interest.

Fridgyth went on, encouraged by the girl's eager expression, "So… I have been thinking – why shouldn't it be you? I'm getting too old to manage alone, and we worked well together. How you found the right seaweed for the poultice, I cannot think."

Della smiled at the new image of the future that these words had brought to her.

"I looked carefully at the old poultice you used for me," she said, "and I took a small sample with me; then I searched across the rocks to find a plant that looked just the same."

"You see?" Fridgyth smiled broadly. "You are a resourceful young woman, that's just what any good herb-wife *would* do. Well? What do you say?"

"Oh yes, please," Della answered at once.

Fridgyth nodded and held out her hand again.

"Then, with your father's permission, you shall become my apprentice. Now come, we must somehow get ourselves up to the top of this hill."

Ranulf had cleared the area around the huts to make sure the wooden quay would not catch fire, and soon they heard the crackle of dry, burning, timber behind them. Soot and sparks flew into the air, and the light scent of wood smoke followed them.

Della stopped again.

"Don't look!" Fridgyth advised, as she urged the girl onwards.

Throat-catching billows of smoke trailed up the hill after them, but they struggled on and at last found Ketel and the abbess by the well, with Gunda in attendance. Hild moved as though she'd embrace the herb-wife, but Fridgyth still would not allow it.

"Our clothes must be burnt," she said, "but Ketel and Della have nothing else to wear."

Hild turned at once to give orders.

"Gunda, go to the royal guest house and tell Cloda to search out some good spare clothing. Please take it to the herb-wife's hut at once. Fridgyth, you look as gaunt as a half starved cat, but praise God you are alive!"

"Aye, my legs are stiff as posts, but as you say… I am alive and glad of it."

The abbess accompanied them to the main gates and then turned to speak again.

"Gunda has kindled a fire in your hearth and set water to heat. Mildred says she may stay to help you settle into your hut again, and there's something of a surprise waiting for you, I think." She smiled as she spoke these mysterious words, then grew practical again. "I'll leave you to your cleansing. Come over to my house as soon as you are all ready."

The abbess walked away, still smiling knowingly and, as Fridgyth led them towards her hut, Wyrdkin came out to greet them, purring wildly. The cat looked considerably thinner, but as soon as Fridgyth put out her hand to stroke her, the creature leapt back skittishly and vanished inside.

"Forgotten me so fast?"

Fridgyth was offended. But when they stepped inside the hut, they saw why Wyrdkin was so jumpy. She guarded a mewling litter of six kittens that she'd stowed in one of Fridgyth's herb baskets for safety.

They gaped at the basket full of tiny tumbling bodies.

"So – life goes on," Fridgyth murmured.

Della went, at once, to pick up a wobbly-legged handful of fur. She lifted it to her cheek and the tiny creature immediately started to purr, bringing some small comfort.

They left Ketel standing awkwardly outside the hut, while they stripped naked and washed themselves in a tub of warm water they'd filled from the pot on the hearth. Gunda was sent to burn their clothes in the space that Fridgyth used for garden fires outside. The herb-wife couldn't bear to destroy her precious leather girdle, so she removed all the tools that were attached to it, scrubbed it with soapwort and hung it in the smoke above the fire to dry.

"Mother would be outraged at the waste of a decent gown," Della said guiltily, though she glanced eagerly at the pile of new clothing Gunda had brought.

Fridgyth understood.

"But it must be done," she said. "Go and see what Cloda has sent us."

Della helped herself to a fine linen under-shift and one of Mathild's old woollen overdresses that was dyed dark yellow and trimmed with narrow tablet braiding at the sleeves.

She put it on with small cries of delight, "So soft and warm. I've never had such a gown."

Fridgyth had her own old gowns stowed away in a chest, but she'd never been one to miss an opportunity, so she took a good plain woollen gown, dyed green that she thought she'd seen on Prince Ecfrid's wife.

Gunda appeared again and stood beside them awkwardly. Fridgyth saw her wistful face as she watched Della try on the braid-trimmed overdress.

"I do not see why you shouldn't benefit just as we do," she told the girl, and she pulled out a woollen madder dyed gown, trimmed with braiding.

She held it up in front of Gunda.

"But the abbess never said…" the girl began, though her words faded away and Fridgyth could see the keen desire in her eyes.

"Try it on," she ordered.

She helped the girl get into the dress and laced her up at the back. The colour brought out the delicate roses in her cheeks and the lightness of her fair hair.

"As fine as any princess," Della told her warmly.

"But I cannot," the girl protested as tears sparkled in her eyes.

"I told you that kitchen work is valued here," Fridgyth reminded her, hands on hips. "This is your reward for all your hard work. Our royal visitors have discarded this finery, and we don't want the moths to feed on it. Hild has never approved of waste; I shall make it right with the abbess."

Gunda snatched Fridgyth's hand and kissed it, her mouth trembled with emotion.

"No need for that," Fridgyth laughed and pushed her away. "Now, go and fetch the boat-maker in and Della, let me comb your hair!"

When Ketel came into the hut, he stared at them both, awestruck. Fridgyth had caught Della's long brown hair back in a smooth plait.

"You look," he murmured. "You look like the reeve's daughter and you Fridgyth, you look—"

"And you will soon look like the reeve," Fridgyth cut in cheerfully. "Make the most of this opportunity – we all deserve it. Try this fine, blue woollen tunic and here's a cloak of the same hue; you'll look grand in that."

They went outside to give him privacy, and when he reappeared Fridgyth caught her breath. Ketel stood upright, if a little awkward in his new clothes; but he'd trimmed his beard and combed his hair neatly. Once again she glimpsed the strong, attractive young man he'd been.

"You *do* look like the reeve," Della cried. "No – better than the reeve! Don't you think, Fridgyth?"

"Aye… I do," she said quietly, and she smiled at him.

CHAPTER 11

WINTER MOON

They were all ushered into the abbess's house; both Della and Ketel looked nervous despite Fridgyth's reassurance that they would not find Hild at all high and mighty when they got to know her better.

The little hall was cosy with wall hangings that depicted the snakestones that could be found so plentifully in the cliffs all around Streonshalh. The abbess had taken delight in the curled stone creatures and adopted them as her symbol, for she thought them something of a miracle. She'd even had them carved into a pattern on the lintel of her house.

Fridgyth and her friends were treated to a drink of warm mead, which raised their spirits and made them feel more comfortable. Begu and Wulfrun brought trays of food over from the kitchens, and the two princesses came to join them at their board. They were served roast duck and boar, made sweet and tasty with herbs and honey.

Hild proffered the gold-trimmed cup of mead for them to drink again.

"Drink-hail to you, herb-wife," she said. "And drink-hail to my two new guests. I hope you will be comfortable in our guest house, at least until the spring."

All three accepted the cup again; they blushed at the honour. As she returned the vessel Della spoke up, emboldened by the drink. "I beg your pardon Mother Hild," she said. "I'm truly honoured to be here as your guest, but… the herb-wife has asked me to be her apprentice, and I'd like nothing better than that."

"That's if my services are still needed," Fridgyth put in smartly.

Ketel looked up at them both with surprise, and Hild stared open-mouthed at Fridgyth. A brief silence followed.

"Whatever do you mean by that, herb-wife?" Hild asked at last.

The room crackled with tension, and everyone looked at Fridgyth. She shrugged uncomfortably. Why had she sounded so touchy or chosen this moment to make her fears known?

"Perhaps…" she began. "Perhaps a monk who has studied the healing arts might now be preferred to an aged cunning-woman."

She cringed inwardly at the whining defensiveness that she could hear in her own voice.

Again there was stunned silence for a moment; then Elfled spoke out in her usual forthright manner.

"How can you say such a thing Fridgyth? Mother Hild has done nothing but fret while you were away, and when she heard you'd caught the plague… well, we all knew how distressed she was."

Hild rose silently from her seat and came to hug Fridgyth warmly.

"I have missed you more than I can say," she said. "Brother Argila has done his best, but he has other purposes in life. I cannot tell you how glad I am to have you back. You've been missed most bitterly."

"I thank you," Fridgyth gulped, feeling very foolish, suddenly weak and watery-eyed.

"And I don't see why you shouldn't take Della as your apprentice, so long as her father approves," Hild said, turning back to Ketel.

The boat-maker still looked a little stunned, but he managed to reply with dignity.

"My daughter is old enough to make up her own mind, and I thank the herb-wife for her generous offer."

Fridgyth nodded and wiped away a shameful tear that trickled down her cheek. Elfled clapped her hands.

"Good," she announced. "So that's settled now, and everyone is happy. Could Della join us in our lessons, do you think?"

The abbess raised her eyebrows at this second unexpected request, but Elfled would not be put off.

"Mother Hild, you know I work so much better with friends

around me, and now we have Samson and Aldfrith as tutors we need more students. Poor Eadfrith will soon have nothing to do but scribe all day."

The princess hadn't always shown such interest in her education and Hild had to smile.

"Well… I've been thinking of building a school for girls," she admitted. "The boy oblates have their school, and I'm thinking that more young women should be educated too. So… yes Della, you may join the princesses in their lessons, whenever Fridgyth can spare you."

Ketel flushed, cleared his throat and bowed.

"I thank you lady."

"I'm so glad," Elfled said, and she reached out to press Della's arm. "Guy is such a tease. He makes us laugh all the time and Aldfrith is serious, but wait till you see Samson's lovely eyes. Of course we will have to put up with my old nurse, who fusses around us when the young tutors are with us."

Begu put down the pitcher of mead that she carried, reached out a bony hand and gave her royal nursling a smart slap.

"I'll give you fussing!" she said.

Della watched wide-eyed and shocked.

Elfled simply shrugged and rubbed her arm.

"You see what I have to put up with," she said, and then suddenly everyone laughed.

"I know another who might join your school," Fridgyth turned to Hild. "Guy's sister, Gunda – she's a clever girl."

The rest of the meal passed smoothly, but Hild saw that her new guests struggled to come to terms with their new circumstances – and nobody could forget that they were so recently bereaved. As the light began to fade, she suggested that they retire to their new accommodation.

"You should stay with your father tonight in the royal guest house," Fridgyth told Della. "But tomorrow I will fix up a small cubicle for you at the end of the infirmary and make you comfortable there."

"I could help with that," Ketel offered.

She smiled, nodded and then set off back to her hut, weary but contented.

Next morning Fridgyth woke up to sharp sunlight, startled to find herself back in her hut again. A flood of sadness overwhelmed her as she thought of the boat-makers' huts, but she pushed grim thoughts aside and got up to start sorting through her pots and jars; there was work to do – Della to be accommodated, herbs to be gathered and dried, medicines and salves to be prepared before the coldest weather came.

Later that day, Hild brought Brother Argila to visit her. He was older than Fridgyth had expected from the distant glimpse she thought she'd had of the man who leapt from the boat. He behaved in a courteous manner towards her and appeared to be respectful of her skills. He examined her small workshop with interest.

"You've no written labels on your pots," he said. "How do you remember which is which?"

Fridgyth's hackles rose. "By their odour and taste," she said sharply. She wasn't going to betray her lack of education.

Argila frowned for a moment, but then nodded.

"Simplicity," he murmured. "That's true skill."

Fridgyth was mollified a little, but unsure of his sincerity; she couldn't dredge up warmth towards the man. When they left, she stood in the doorway of her hut to watch them go. The monk towered above the small figure of Hild as he strode along at her side. They both walked fast, and Argila didn't walk like a monk at all – he marched like a strong and active warrior, despite the fact that he must be at least Fridgyth's own age. She remembered once again the boat she'd seen, or thought she'd seen.

"But I was sickening for the plague," she told herself. "Who knows what I saw! And the abbess rushes everywhere. She doesn't walk much like a nun."

Fridgyth settled back into her old routine, cheered by the company of her new apprentice. Time and good food served to restore their full strength, though many remarked on the slight touch of yellow in their complexions.

They were well fed, for Samson and Aldfrith spent their afternoons out hunting whenever the weather was fine, so the monastery kitchens were supplied with good stocks of wild boar and venison. The young noblemen made themselves at home in Streonshalh, and the princesses and Wulfrun often rode out with them after their lessons, returning pink-cheeked and healthy, while Della came back willingly from the scriptorium schoolroom to help Fridgyth powder herbs and pound ointments.

Sometimes Guy escorted Della back to the herb-wife's hut and stayed there to drink elderberry wine; he made both her and the herb-wife laugh. Fridgyth wondered if he admired her young assistant and worried a little about it. The lad was sweet-tongued and good looking enough to turn any girl's head, though officially he was oblated to the monastery. The role of herb-wife would not require chastity, as Abbess Hild was tolerant of those who preferred the family huts to the stark existence of the dedicated monks and nuns.

As time passed, the ugly scab on Fridgyth's neck hardened and began to shed, bit by bit, leaving behind a raw purple scar. On occasions, she looked at herself in the bronze hand-mirror that had been a gift from Princess Elfled and frowned a little. Why should she care about such things, at her age? She applied marigold balm regularly, but knew from experience that little could be done to smooth it.

The weather turned chill as the month of offerings finished and Bloodmonth began. On most days Ketel wandered over to Fridgyth's hut, and she saw that time lay heavy on his hands, so asked him to do some jobs for her. First he built a small sleeping cubicle for his daughter and then he replaced some of the rotting timber that supported the wattle and daub walls of the infirmary. His skills as a carpenter were excellent, and Fridgyth soon found her dwelling warmer and more watertight than ever before. In the evenings he sat by her hearth, alongside his daughter and the cowherd, while Wyrdkin struggled to contain her brood and kittens tumbled everywhere.

Caedmon refused to join them at first, sensing that a warm friendship had been rekindled down in the boat-makers' huts, but Fridgyth wouldn't allow him to hide in the cowbyre mourning his slaughtered calves.

She confided in Ketel.

"Words come to Caedmon like magic when he sings, but Coen's gang tease him roughly if he tries to play the bard and then his courage fails. Just the sight of the harp coming round in the servants' meadhall makes him want to puke."

"I could beat them into silence," Ketel offered, rising immediately to the cowherd's defence. "I don't fear that wean-faced gang."

"No, no," Fridgyth laughed and slapped his arm. "I don't fear them either. I'd box their ears if I thought it'd help, but this is a battle that Caedmon must fight alone."

Ketel frowned and looked thoughtful.

"Does the cowherd play the harp well?" he asked.

Fridgyth sighed.

"As well as most I think, but he gets little chance."

Ketel said no more, but the next evening he turned up at her hut with two short lengths of planed, seasoned oak and his bag full of tools.

"Am I to have another shelf?" Fridgyth asked.

"No, this is a new craft I'd learn," he told her, stroking the smooth wood with reverence. "I want to try my skill as harp-maker. A man can get good payment for a fine instrument, I'm told, and while I've the time..."

Caedmon looked up with interest.

Ketel set himself up on Fridgyth's work trestle and took a small adze from his bag. He began working steadily, gouging out the wood until the shallow, hollowed-out shape of the lower section of a harp began to emerge. Fridgyth and Della sat together in the firelight, companionably rubbing dried herbs and measuring them into the keeping bowls.

Caedmon said little, but he watched Ketel's work intently. At last, he could keep quiet no longer.

"I th-think it needs to be deeper here," he said pointing to the depth of the sounding board. "Making it deeper there, will give r-richer tone, I think."

"I thank you," Ketel nodded, acting on his suggestion.

When they left to go to their beds that night, Fridgyth kissed

Ketel's cheek and pulled his beard.

"You're a kind man," she whispered.

The weather grew worse, and Fridgyth treated all the usual ailments that winter brought: breathing troubles, streaming noses, chilblains and boils. One of the older monks fell and cracked his leg in two places and of course needed a bed in the infirmary. When death came to him after just one week, it seemed a relief, as it did for two of the oldest, frailest nuns, who died as the first frosts came. Three babies were born in the family huts, which Fridgyth thought balanced things nicely, though the babies could have chosen a more auspicious time of year to arrive.

One afternoon late in Bloodmonth, Fridgyth was surprised to look through her shutters to see Samson hurrying towards her hut.

"What is it?" she asked, going out to meet him.

"Please come!" he begged, his voice low but urgent. "There's been an accident. We were out hunting; Flann is hurt – that is Aldfrith," he quickly corrected himself. "They've taken him to the royal guest house."

Fridgyth snatched up her basket, her heart beating fast, and threw bundles of herbs into it. Then she looked at the lad more carefully and saw that his fine-boned face was swollen and battered all down one side.

"You too are hurt!"

"I was thrown," he admitted. "But Aldfrith's more in need than me… a wild boar… please come! Cloda is doing her best, but she needs your help."

"I daresay Brother Argila's more highly skilled," she felt obliged to say. "Have you sent for the abbess? Are the princesses safe?"

Samson shook his head.

"Thank God they didn't come with us today. My friend wants only you. He trusts you, Fridgyth. We don't want to bother the abbess – she's had enough to upset her of late."

That was true enough… Fridgyth snatched up her basket and hurried out with him.

She found Aldfrith pale and shocked, for he had lost a lot of blood from a deep wound on his shoulder. Fridgyth examined the hurt carefully and began to see, at once, why they might not want to worry the abbess.

"An accident?" she queried.

She'd seen such injuries before and was convinced that no wild boar had been the cause of it, but rather a spearhead. She quelled her curiosity and set about cleaning the wound quickly, while Cloda fed drops of poppy juice to the lad. The herb-wife took a fine curved bone needle from her pouch and, ignoring the groans that came involuntarily from Aldfrith's lips, she put three stitches in place to nip the wound together.

"That wound needs to be sealed with honey now," she said. "And then marigold ointment needs to be smeared around the edges for bruising."

She finished by strapping it tightly with a wad of lambs' wool and a strong linen bandage.

"Well!" she said with some satisfaction. "That should stop it festering, but you are going to have to rest in order to heal it clean and fast."

"I'll see that he rests," Samson said.

It was only when Aldfrith was at last propped up in bed – with Cloda fetching cushions to make him comfortable – that Fridgyth took another look at Samson, whose bruised face grew darker as every moment passed.

"Now you sit down," she ordered, "and I'll see to you. Marigold ointment will soothe that bruise, but first it needs to be cleansed."

He did as he was told and allowed her to patch him up.

"An accident you say?" she spoke low now. "Aldfrith took a spear-thrust I think?"

Samson flinched as she touched the raw skin and hesitated over his answer.

"I'm left wondering how such a spear thrust could hit the hunter," Fridgyth said, determined not to let the matter drop.

Samson nodded.

"We were chasing a boar that turned on us. My horse threw me and – well, my spear flew wild and caught Aldfrith's shoulder. I'm ashamed to say it is my fault."

"Hmm," Fridgyth was still not sure she'd heard the truth. "I'm surprised to hear of such a thing, for Princess Elfled tells me that you are both fine horsemen, but I can see why you don't wish to trouble the abbess. You should take better care of the monastery's steeds."

Cloda looked up annoyed having heard that last remark, angry that the herb-wife should treat royal guests to such frank criticism.

"Silence is discretion," Aldfrith murmured weakly from his bed.

With an amused twitch of her lips, Fridgyth nodded agreement.

"Aye, maybe so. I'll look in tomorrow to see how you both fare."

CHAPTER 12

THE SONG OF THE HARP

She left them in Cloda's care and set off back to her hut. As she passed the stables, she glanced inside, curious as to which of the horses had thrown Samson. Apart from the princess's Seamist and her twin, the gelding Seacoal, most of the monastery steeds were reliable plodders.

Four stable lads were hard at work rubbing the horses down as she strode in and confronted them.

"Which was Lord Samson's mount?" she asked, "Which beast threw him?"

Cenric, whom she'd known from a babe, looked up from stroking the withers of a strong dappled gelding.

"Teasel's never thrown a rider before," he said, defensively. "It's not my place to say so, but I'd never treat a horse like *he* did – royal guest or not!"

"What do you mean?" Fridgyth asked, stepping closer. "I thought Samson was a good horseman."

"So did I," Cenric admitted, "but not after today."

The lad moved carefully round the front of the gelding, stroking and soothing all the time, and pointed at his knees. Fridgyth saw a raw, bleeding wheal that cut across both of Teasel's joints and must have been very painful. She bent down and sniffed at the cut, recognising the clean, sharp scent of an ointment Cenric had applied.

"Mashed comfrey and pig fat?" she said.

Cenric nodded and grinned.

"Just like you showed me!" he said.

"You've treated him well," she approved, but frowned at the raw, painful mark. "What's caused it, I wonder?"

"A whip," Cenric said, "either that or the beast's charged into a rope!"

Fridgyth suppressed a gasp of surprise. Had they encountered more of an ambush than accident? If so, why had neither young man complained of it?

Her attention wandered to the other horses that were being rubbed down. She recognised Periwinkle, a steady mare that the abbess rode whenever a journey was necessary, she, herself had sometimes exercised the mare for the abbess. Periwinkle stamped her foot and lifted her nose in recognition.

"Who's been riding the abbess's mare?" she asked.

"The Frankish healer-monk – the visitor."

"Argila? He rode Periwinkle?"

"Always does," the other groom replied shortly, as he threw a woollen rug over the beast.

"But Periwinkle is the abbess's horse."

"The foreign monk exercises the mare for the abbess most days."

"Does he indeed?" she muttered, feeling more resentful than ever. "And when did Argila return?"

Cenric shrugged impatiently.

Fridgyth's suspicions grew. If Argila had been out and anywhere near the two lads, surely he would have been expected to help with Aldfrith's wound there and then. Why had he not?

"Did the leech-monk come back with the others?" she asked.

Cenric merely frowned, tired of her questioning.

"Do you know where he went?" Fridgyth persisted.

"It's not my job to question such as him," Cenric said peevishly, "or the young lords either."

"No, indeed," she said and turned to go.

Guy arrived in the courtyard as she came out, leading his sister on a bay gelding. He lifted her down and kissed her before she set off for the kitchens. Fridgyth nodded vaguely at them with approval. The girl needed a brief escape from her kitchen duties, and the horse was strong enough for two.

She continued back to her hut, trying to suppress the bubble of resentment that rose in her at every mention of Argila's name. The monk appeared to move about the monastery as freely as she did, even though he was a visitor and had only recently arrived. She sighed and pushed the unworthy thoughts away. Whatever the truth of it, her main concern must be for Aldfrith. If, as she feared, there was something sinister in this incident, it might mean that his identity had been discovered. Prince Ecfrid's supporters hated Alchfrid 'the Stranger' most of all, for he ruled Deira in their favoured prince's place, but they'd be just as likely to see Flann Fina as another threat to their darling prince. There were many such supporters in the monastery, Mildred the foodwife for one. But although Mildred championed her prince boldly and complained openly of Ecfrid's plight to anyone who'd listen, she'd never plan secret harm to anyone. Sister Redburgh had said something about putting hellebore in 'the Stranger's' salad, but that had certainly been in jest – Mildred was no more capable of poisoning than she was of planning an ambush.

Fridgyth shook her head to rid herself of such thoughts. There was not much she could do, other than heal the lad as best she could and keep a sharp eye out for signs of unusual activity as she went about her work.

She arrived at the infirmary determined to give her patients her full attention: there was a monk with an ulcerated leg and a woman who'd just given birth. But once she'd seen them both well fed and possetted to make them sleep, she allowed her thoughts to stray again to the strange accident. Then another thought had come to her. There'd been four horses all being rubbed down: Teasel, Periwinkle, a young bay gelding, and Aldfrith's mount. Who'd been riding the fourth horse? She would have to find out about that, whether Cenric liked it or not.

The following morning, Fridgyth set off early for the royal guest house and found Aldfrith sitting up in bed; he'd recovered well. She examined the gash for signs of putrefaction while Samson watched with interest. The honey and marigold ointment seemed to have done its work and the wound remained clean.

"Fate's Wyrd sisters smile on you," she said. "But you must be careful for a while and rest."

"Let me dress the wound," Samson begged. "I wish to learn more of the healing arts."

Fridgyth sat back and instructed him, impressed at the deft way he handled the dressings.

"He's got other skills," Aldfrith confided. "Last night the wound pained and made me restless. I begged them to fetch me more poppy juice, but instead, Samson talked me into a deep sleep, and I woke refreshed this morning."

"Talked you into a deep sleep? I've heard of such things. That's a skill I'd gladly learn," Fridgyth admitted with a touch of envy.

Samson nodded.

"I must find the time to show you, a much respected healer-monk in Slane Monastery taught me the skill."

But Fridgyth was not to be distracted, there was more that she wanted to know about their 'accident'.

"Who else rode with you yesterday?" she asked.

They exchanged the briefest of glances before they answered.

"Argila rode out with us," Samson admitted. "But we left him far behind, with Fredemund the Frankish goldsmith."

Fredemund was the goldsmith that Wulfrun admired.

"Doesn't Guy ride with you?" she asked.

Samson nodded.

"Yes, usually he does, but he wanted to take his sister out yesterday, for she was released from her kitchen work and that is rare – brother and sister see little of each other."

Fridgyth pressed her lips together in frustration; they'd answered her courteously, but told her nothing.

"Shame he wasn't there with you," she said. "I shan't report your accident to the abbess, as you wish me to be… discreet, but you must promise me that you won't ride unattended again."

"Of course," Samson nodded.

"Take a few of Coen's lads with you," she suggested. "They need something useful to do, something better than sitting round the main gate jesting and gaming all day!"

Fridgyth left the royal guest house satisfied that Aldfrith was on the way to recovery. It was, in many ways, natural that Argila and the goldsmith should ride together, for they'd both come recently from the Frankish lands and must understand each other well. Perhaps she saw trouble where there was none. Hild seemed to trust Argila with her horse, and the abbess was an excellent judge of character, none better.

The next day she was called upon to treat a burn that had begun to fester. Brother Gorm, one of the metal workers, came to her in great pain, supported by his friends.

"We told him he should've come yesterday, herb-wife, but he'd have none of it."

"Maybe the new healer-monk might look at him," one of them suggested.

Fridgyth huffed and ordered them out of her infirmary fast. She treated the burn with ragwort juice and honey, and then applied a poultice of mashed lavender and soft, fresh moss, but she'd seen that the wound was suppurating and agonising for the poor man. Could a leech-skilled monk maybe do better?

"Stay here and feed Brother Gorm sips of poppy juice," she told Della, "while I fetch Argila to look at this wound. We shall have two opinions instead of one, I think… and sometimes two birds can be killed with one stone," she muttered as she left her hut.

She marched over to the monastic guest house and asked Brother Brandon if she might speak to the healer-monk. Brother Argila emerged from the building, somewhat surprised that the herb-wife should summon him.

"It's Brother Gorm," she said. "He works in the metal hearths and has suffered a painful burn. He's left it for a day, and now it's festering. I'd be glad if you'd come and look at it and give me your opinion. Maybe you'll know of a Frankish cure that will work for him."

"It will be my pleasure," he agreed.

But as he came down the steps to join her, Fridgyth saw, at once, that he moved awkwardly.

"But you yourself are hurt I think," she said.

"No, no," he insisted. "Just a touch of ague. This damp weather sometimes brings it on."

"Have you tried a ragwort poultice?" she asked.

"No – I haven't heard of that," he answered humbly.

"Oh I use ragwort for many ills."

Fridgyth walked alongside him, more puzzled than ever. Why had his easy, warrior-like stride vanished suddenly? He hobbled beside her, unable to disguise his pain. Ague did not usually come on so fast, nor affect only one leg like that.

When they reached the infirmary, Argila examined Gorm's burn competently and compassionately; he approved her use of honey and the poppy juice, which had relieved the pain a little.

"Can you offer a leech-skilled treatment?" she asked.

He shook his head.

"To apply leeches would only make him weaker. It's not always the answer – your herbs will work better I think. Perhaps a little nettle stew sweetened with honey might give him strength and cleanse the blood. Honey inside and out, I always say."

Fridgyth nodded, acknowledging the compliment he'd paid her and wishing she'd thought of the nettle stew herself.

"I'm always at your service," Argila said and bowed politely, "any time."

As he limped away, Fridgyth vowed to control her childish resentment. What's more, his advice proved effective, for after a few more days of nettle stew and herb and honey poultices, the redness that had surrounded Brother Gorm's wound subsided and the patch of badly burned raw skin appeared to be healing cleanly.

Aldfrith too recovered from his wound and, as the weather grew much colder, the two royal scholars avoided further hunting expeditions. The larder was now well stocked and preparations for Christmas underway. The abbess seemed none the wiser as to the accident and very much occupied by the special arrangements that must be made for the winter festival. The usual feasts and entertainments were rather muted, for travelling bards and tumblers were feared to carry the pestilence in their wake.

The celebrations came and went mixed with much anxiety, for

news arrived, via one of the trading ships, that the plague had spread along the coast to many of the seaboard towns. The King and Queen were safe and well in their stronghold at Bamburgh, but they forbade Elfled from visiting them as she sometimes did for the Christmas celebrations. They heard that Wilfrid had been appointed Bishop of Eforwic, but rather than take up his position and set about the organisation of the churches, he'd set out to travel to Compiegne before the snows arrived, for he complained that there were no true bishops in the Anglian or Saxon kingdoms qualified to set him on his bishop's throne. Queen Eanfleda had provided Wilfrid with ships and servants for the journey, but Hild confided to Fridgyth that Oswy saw little need for the journey and was displeased. It seemed the great meeting of the Synod had not entirely resolved dissension between the royal pair.

After Christmas life grew hard at Streonshalh, as it always did at that time of year. A fierce north wind blew straight from the sea and snowstorms swirled around the high cliffs. The sea was tossed, wild and empty of trading vessels; even local fishermen feared to take their chances on the whale-roads at that time of year.

Fridgyth took Wyrdkin's growing brood one by one and gave them away to lay-families who needed rat-catchers. The kittens settled by new hearths, happy to entertain the children through the long dark evenings, greedy for titbits that came their way.

During these harsh months a comfortable friendship grew between Ketel and Caedmon, as they sat by Fridgyth's warm hearth. The harp took shape as Ketel fitted the top to the base with mortise and tenon joints. He fashioned six willow tuning-pegs to tighten the horsehair strings, and smoothed the whole body of the instrument with a hand-sized block of wood that he'd dipped in fishbone glue and sand, until the wood felt like silk. Caedmon collected horsehair from the stables for the strings and spun the strands together for strength. On the day the harp was finally finished, Ketel tried clumsily to tune the strings, and Caedmon took it from him eagerly.

Ketel and Fridgyth smiled at each other; Caedmon, sensitive to mockery, caught their glance and gave the harp back to its maker.

"No, it's yours," Ketel waved it away. "It's only the making of the instrument that interests me. I shall be more than satisfied if you can fetch a tune on it, then I'll set to work on another, and it will be better than the first."

Caedmon took the instrument with trembling hands, and set it upright to rest on his thigh. He stroked the surface of the smooth sound-box with reverence. Then, supporting the upper part of the instrument against his shoulder, he reached up to the tuning pegs and tightened each of the six strings as he listened to the sounds they made until at last he was satisfied.

"You look just like the King's bard," Della approved, her face bright with expectation.

Biting his lip with the effort to get it right, Caedmon placed his hand in position on the strings and began to strum.

"Oh! A lovely sound," Della cried at once. "So deep and sweet – now sing for us!"

He frowned in thought, then made to start, but hesitated again.

Fridgyth nodded encouragement to him.

"You can do it," she whispered.

And at last he gathered courage, cleared his throat and began to sing softly.

"*A seed allowed me birth… an acorn…*" he paused uncertainly, fearful that they'd sneer.

Neither Fridgyth nor Ketel made a sound, afraid to shake his fragile confidence, but Della had no such qualms.

"An acorn? Oh I understand – you sing of the oak tree that the harp is made from! Sing more! Please sing more?"

Caedmon cleared his throat, searching for words; then tried again:

> "*Mother Earth fed me,*
> *Sister Sun warmed me,*
> *Cousin rain, quenched my thirst*
> *I looked to Lady Moon at night*
> *And let my limbs,*
> *Reach up towards her placid light.*"

"Don't stop," Della whispered, when he paused once more.

"*An axe-man felled me*," he continued, the words seeming now to fall readily from his lips.

> "*And I wept, shedding sap.*
> *But a woodman bore me to his hearth,*
> *His sharp adze shaped me.*
> *His hands, hewed sweet music from my heart*
> *Now I shall sing unceasingly.*"

There was awed silence, when he finished.

"That is the s-song of the harp," Caedmon said, his words stumbling once more. "But it has little merit, and I should have added that the horse hair was given by the beasts!"

Ketel's eyes were bright with tears. He blinked hard, looking down at his hands.

"Your song moved me, Caedmon," he said quietly. "The woodman's hands, they 'hewed sweet music from my heart'. I couldn't want anything better to be said of me... not ever!"

"Word-weaver, you are a true word-weaver and a singer," Della cried, and she leapt up to bestow a kiss on the Caedmon's cheek.

Fridgyth smiled with satisfaction.

"Now you must take your turn in the mead hall," Della said.

But his frantic head-shaking told her that he could never do that and, as the days went by, they settled to enjoy his singing in the privacy of Fridgyth's hut. He sang of his lost calves, of the wonders of nature, of winter's bitterness and the anticipated joy of spring. Ketel cut more wood and set to work on a new harp.

CHAPTER 13

SPRING

The snows vanished with the thaw, as Mudmonth arrived. The religious ritual of Lent began, and the most dedicated monks and nuns set about their fasts. Hunting was still difficult, so the little meat that came the monastery's way was reserved to keep up the strength of the lay-brothers who repaired the wattle and daub, and the thatchers who dealt with roof leaks. Salt, dried fish, eggs, and cheese were eked out in small quantities to children and pregnant women.

Hild's rule required that all ranks should be provided with good, strong turnshoes and, though the shoemakers and tanners cut and stitched all year, feet grew ingrained with filth throughout Mudmonth, however well shod they were. The cold and damp weather brought chilblains and sores, and Fridgyth was always busy with her salves.

The year wore on and at last, spring approached. The heifers grew big with calf and needed a lot of Caedmon's care, so that the cowherd's visits to the herb-wife's hut grew rare. Fridgyth found herself sitting alone with Ketel one night, after Della had settled to sleep. She nervously fingered her scarred neck.

"I made that mark," Ketel said, watching her gloomily. "I made it with this knife."

Fridgyth shook her head and smiled at him.

"You saved my life," she said.

"There's so much that I regret," he admitted at last, low voiced.

"And my greatest regret is that I left you to follow the path of ambition."

She had known the time would come for this conversation, and it was something of a relief to speak of it at last. She had rehearsed what she would say many times.

"But you became a respected craftsman," she said, and her voice dropped to a whisper. "Without Berta there'd have been no Della and that girl is a joy to both of us."

She indicated the sleeping form on the straw pallet in the corner

"Yes and Berta was a good wife to me, but I never forgot you."

"Somebody left food by my door after my children died," she looked at him questioningly. "I thought it might have been you."

He shook his head.

"It was Berta. She was distraught when she heard you'd lost both your man and your little ones."

Fridgyth stared, deeply touched.

"She was the last person I'd have thought of," she said. "Your Berta *was* a good woman."

She remembered the criss-cross rune, the mark of generosity, which she'd added to Berta's shuttle, and suddenly she felt very glad that she'd put it there.

There was silence for a moment, but then Fridgyth spoke again, determined to chase his gloom away and make him look to the future.

"When the weather turns warm there'll be new boat-makers' huts and the workshops the abbess promised. Be ready to tell her what you want. We could ask the Frankish oblate, Guy, to draw us up a plan."

Ketel chuckled.

"When did a boat-makers' workshop need a plan?"

But Fridgyth was not to be put off, and she'd been pleased to hear him laugh.

"The abbess has plans drawn up on vellum for her buildings. Why shouldn't you? She is determined to see that you are compensated in some small way the losses you bore last autumn. She will be the winner in the end, for the finer the workshop, the better the boats you'll build for the monastery."

"A plan?" Ketel was still amused at the idea.

"Shall I speak to Guy? He is most attentive to your daughter," she warned gently. "He may well wish to please you."

Ketel looked surprised.

"But Della is too young for that!" he said.

"Fathers always think that," she told him, with a smile. "She's no younger than you or I when..." and her voice trailed away.

"No," he admitted, as he wistfully acknowledged the truth of her words.

Fridgyth sat alone after Ketel had gone and wondered what it would be like to sleep beside a man again. She sighed regretfully as she thought of her worn body and many scars; then told herself that, at her age, she should not entertain such ridiculous thoughts. But she did speak to Hild about the prospect of building the new boat-makers' workshops.

On a bright spring morning, the abbess, Ketel, Fridgyth and Guy walked down the hill to the old quayside. It was the first time Ketel had been there since the day the huts were burnt down, and Fridgyth had been anxious that he would be distressed on his return, but it helped a great deal that Hild had made sure that the quayside had been cleared and swept clean. After a brief moment of hesitation, Ketel started to pace up and down the site to measure it with his stride. Guy followed behind him, recording the correct numbers on a waxed slate. Both men grew excited as they discussed the different methods of boat building and the workspace that would be required for the process, both inside and outdoors. Hild and Fridgyth left them to their discussions and began the long walk back up the steep hill.

"What a good thing," Hild said her voice full of warmth. "I should have seen to it sooner... your Ketel needs this to keep him busy and make him look forward, I think."

"Not *my* Ketel," Fridgyth bridled.

"Is he not?" Hild smiled, knowingly.

Fridgyth looked up with a sharp reply on her lips, but her words died as Argila marched out of the main gate and set off fast towards the cliff edge.

"No sign of the ague today," she muttered.

Hild looked puzzled, and Fridgyth remembered that she'd promised to keep all knowledge of the accident and her suspicions to herself. "Argila strides about the place like a man half his age," she added, trying to sound vaguely admiring of the man.

"Yes indeed," Hild agreed.

When Fridgyth glanced up again, she saw that Samson and Aldfrith, apparently deep in conversation, stood close to the cliff edge. Argila hurried purposefully towards them, but then suddenly slowed his steps to seek shelter in the shady lee of a thatched metal worker's hut. He stood there, so very still, for a while that the blackness of his clothing hid his shape amongst the shadows.

"What is it?" Hild asked, for Fridgyth could not help but stare in his direction. "You look as though you've seen a vision and I've come to expect that distant look from Begu and Cloda, but not from you."

Fridgyth shrugged.

"Just foolishness, I daresay, but it looked to me as though the leech-monk was spying on Fina's son. What is he doing skulking there in the shadow of that hut?"

Hild turned to look where Fridgyth pointed.

"I cannot see him at all."

"That's just it – you can't see him because he stands so still in the darkness, watching them. Should they be allowed to wander towards the edge of so high a cliff do you think? It would take only a moment for someone to…"

"Ah… now I see Argila," Hild said, and she smiled serenely. "Fridgyth – it is nothing for you to worry about."

The abbess continued calmly with the upward climb.

"But… but…" Fridyth began.

"There… you see."

The two young men had turned round to wander back to the main gate, and Argila went openly to join them.

Fridgyth clamped her mouth shut, she felt foolish. By the time they reached the top of the hill, Aldfrith, Samson and Argila had walked slowly back together, chatting amicably.

"Our visitors enjoy the rare treat of a bright spring morning," Hild said. "They stroll in the fresh air just as we do and I don't think Fina's son very likely to run into trouble with the sharp eyes of our herb-wife looking out for him. Argila is a good man; I trust him and wish you could too."

Fridgyth flushed and nodded, but later that night it occurred to her that Argila strolled and chatted on the clifftops at a time when most monks were keeping silence. But then so had the abbess. Hild had set aside her own strict Lenten rules in order to see Ketel's project underway. These Christians make the rules up to suit themselves, she thought, still annoyed that she'd made herself appear ridiculous. Fina's son *had* run into trouble at least once that she knew of and, whatever the abbess said, she would continue to keep a sharp look out for him.

As Easter approached, the young men began to hunt again, and Fridgyth was relieved to observe that they now took an escort of Coen's warriors along. They brought back fresh venison and wild boar, while the abbess and her dedicated followers fasted more strictly than ever. Fridgyth's leeks and kale were harvested and made into pottage, as were the fresh alexander shoots that grew all around the edges of the upper pasture. Early vegetables were important, for they lifted the spirits of those who strictly refused meat.

When Easter came at last, the new way of calculating the day made it no less joyful after all the fasting that had gone before, though a few of the older monks and nuns muttered that they felt disorientated. Fridgyth and Ketel went to listen to Brother Bosa's Easter sermon, joining the gathering at the preaching cross in front of the church. Hild nodded with pleasure that both of them were there. A chorus of Latin chanting, led by Deacon James, followed the sermon. Fridgyth found it pleasant to listen to, even though she couldn't understand a word of it.

The news was whispered all around that Bishop Wilfrid still remained in Compiegne, and the King was angry at his slow return. As Eastermonth drew to a close, new calves were born, and Caedmon was busy in the cowsheds day and night.

Ketel was cheered when two boat-makers' families who'd fled the plague returned, all of them healthy and looking to rebuild their lives. The abbess approved the plans that Guy had drawn up for the new buildings and ordered trees felled in preparation for the work. The young Frankish scholar showed great interest in the project. In addition to drawing up the plans, he often went down to the site to discuss the skills of the boat-makers' trade with Ketel. As the weather improved, the two of them took Ketel's small fishing boat out to sea and returned with baskets full of fish.

"That lad soaks up all I can teach him," Ketel told Fridgyth with pride. "He knows all the sea-roads round here and he learns fast. Perhaps, he would make a good son-in-law, if were he released from his oblation to the Christian God."

Fridgyth smiled, glad that Ketel sounded so purposeful again.

"Well, as you say, Della is young as yet, but if she wants the lad and he's as keen as he appears to be, I'm sure the abbess would approve. She'll want to keep such a talented lad here in Streonshalh, but I've heard that oblation can be set aside before the final vows are taken. I must speak to Hild about his sister, for that lass still slaves away in the kitchens."

One morning early in Three-Milking Month, Fridgyth was out in the vegetable garden supervising a gang of lay brothers. She'd insisted that they get the root vegetables planted while the moon was still on the wane. It was now the last day before the new moon and, as everyone knew, parsnips planted as the moon waxed would never thrive.

The herb-wife preferred to give out vociferous instruction now, rather than lead by example as she'd once done. As the morning went on, she sat down to rest and Ranulf stopped his work to smile at her.

"What has six legs and two arms, but just one mouth and squawks a lot?"

Fridgyth shook her head and rolled her eyes.

"I'm sure you'll tell me, Ranulf."

"A gossip sitting on a bench," he said. "Do you see it? Four legs for the bench and her own two… that's six?"

His older son smiled at Fridgyth, shook his head, and got on with his work.

"What if it's a two-legged bench?" Fridgyth asked.

Ranulf scratched his head.

"Never mind," Fridgyth told him. "Don't even try to answer. You shall have the honour of taking the hand cart round to the chicken huts; we need more fowl droppings to manure the ground. What has four legs, a wheel and stinks a lot?"

Ranulf's son laughed at his father's expression of dismay.

"The wise man keeps his counsel, Father," he said. "Fridgyth's got the better of you, I think."

Ranulf stuck his spade into the rich crumbly earth and set off cheerfully in the direction of the chicken huts.

"You sit there in the sun, herb-wife," he said, as he passed her. "Last Winter Moon we thought you lost for ever and I for one am glad to see you still sitting here, giving out orders."

Fridgyth smiled and sat on in the bright sun, until it began to cloud over and the morning turned chill. The gardeners had built up a sweat as they worked. For a while they were more comfortable in the cooler air, but at last it grew so cold that they began to snatch up their cloaks.

"Rain's coming," Ranulf's boy warned.

Fridgyth held out her hand, but could feel no raindrops.

"This chill comes on fast!" she muttered. "You must all dig harder. If we can get all these seeds into the ground, a bit of rain will suit us fine."

They carried on digging, but the sense of unease only increased, and each began to stop work to stare up at the sky. The herb-wife sat on, irritated that they were making such a fuss when she needed to get her seeds into the ground.

At last Ranulf's younger son threw down his spade and pointed upwards.

"Stop! Stop! This is unnatural – the sun fails us and it is not yet noon."

When at last, Fridgyth shaded her own eyes to look up and judge for herself, she too was shocked, for a strange, dark bite had appeared up there, gnawing into the golden disc of the sun.

"Look – look at that!" Ranulf's lad cried. "A dragon's maw is swallowing the sun!"

"Some sky-beast for sure is eating our sun!"

"But what will happen, if the sun is gone?"

"Eternal darkness comes!"

"But we cannot live without the sun!"

"Is this the end of the world?"

They threw down their spades, shaded their eyes and stared in horror. While they watched, it seemed the great dark bite in the sun grew and grew.

Fridgyth struggled to her feet, and felt as frightened as her workers. Yet somewhere at the back of her mind she felt that this had happened once before. Then memory flooded back, bringing a wave of sadness with it. This strange mid-morning darkness had come the year her mother died.

The light was failing fast and frightened cries broke out in the distance.

"Heaven help us!" one of the workers cried. "I'm off to find my mother!" He ran towards the family huts, and others followed him.

"Wait!" Fridgyth begged, but they took no notice of her and they ran, only Ranulf's boy remained at her side.

His father reappeared without the handcart and looked distraught. At the same time screaming rose from the courtyard.

"Day turns to night," he cried. "This cannot be."

"By Freya," his boy cried. "Father – this is what comes of you insulting the herb-wife! She is still protected by the goddess, I think."

"No," Fridgyth was quick to refute that idea. "Your father and I are old friends; we tease each other all the time. This darkness has happened before."

"I think the King's decision is the cause of it!" Ranulf said. "We should never have turned to Rome – no never!"

He was so fearful that he couldn't hear Fridgyth's efforts to calm him.

"He said to turn to Rome would bring disaster!" he went on. "It broke his heart! We must go to pray!"

"But we have parsnips to plant," Fridgyth objected weakly.

"Parsnips be damned! Nothing planted this day will grow!"

CHAPTER 14

BOTHER DUNSTON

The light waned further and darkness gathered round them. The cries of terror in the courtyard had not abated. And, as though in reply to the chaos, the church bell began to ring insistently.

"We go to pray," Ranulf said decisively, and he set off towards the church.

Fridgyth sensed Hild's hand in the urgent ringing of the bell and followed him.

"The abbess summons us, I think. Yes, hurry!"

It would be like Hild to recognise the need to gather everyone together, to try to bring calm into this calamity. They hurried past the kitchens, just as Mildred led her workers out into the gloom, and with them came a warm mist of steam and the reassuring smell of baking. The courtyard was filled with cries and shadows as people ran wildly in every direction. Dedicated monks and nuns left their cells and poured out of their separate enclosures.

"Judgement, judgement!" they cried.

"We must turn away from Rome! It was all wrong!"

"It's Wilfrid's fault! And where is he now that we need him?"

"Aye, we must go back to Aidan's ways! Why have we shaved our crowns like this?"

Lay-folk called fearfully for little ones they couldn't find. The madness was bewildering, but the church bell continued to ring as darkness fell across the land, and the shadowy frenzy took on some direction.

"To the church! To the church!" everyone shouted.

Nuns, monks, layworkers and labourers all stumbled towards the tall thatched building with its high, carved cross set in a circle, which loomed black against the greying sky. But the church doors seemed to be closed, and it was clear that there wouldn't be room for everyone to crowd inside even if they managed to open the door. Hild's voice rose above the tumult.

"Gather round the preaching cross!" she ordered, and people struggled to obey.

The carved cross stood on three stone slabs in front of the church, and the abbess climbed up to stand beneath it. Her small figure could be seen dimly now, and her voice rang to reassure them that it was indeed their leader. Everyone gathered round.

"Be still and listen!" Hild commanded. In the moment of hush the abbess grasped her opportunity: "We must behave with dignity and charity to one another. Brother Bosa will explain what is happening. Wise men do understand these things."

Her sharp words seemed to bring something of a sense of calm; Hild was in charge and all would be well, but as they waited restlessly for Brother Bosa to come, they muttered fearfully of omens.

"Mother," Elfled's voice piped up. "Aldfrith, the scholar understands this darkness."

She'd been allowed to stand at the front – despite such fear and panic, Elfled was still the King's daughter.

Hild responded to Elfled's interruption with interest.

"Does he? I too remember something like this that happened in the year Eanfleda our queen arrived from Kent to marry the King. So we'll have no more talk of omens. It was a joyful portent then. Where is Aldfrith? Come forward at once. Is this right? Can you explain this sudden darkness?"

"Lady," he replied breathlessly. "I believe I can."

The crowd made way for him, and he was hauled up to the abbess's side. His youthful lanky figure dwarfed the abbess in the gloom, but the sight of him brought little reassurance.

"How can *he* know, a lad like that?"

"Nothing can save us now!"

"No, listen," older voices chimed in. "We've known this darkness before and lived."

"Silence," Hild cried. "You *must* listen."

Aldfrith began to speak and, though they still murmured, his voice gained in strength and at last they listened.

"It is the moon, passing across the face of the sun," he told them, "a rare occurrence, but a natural one. Wise men can predict it. Have no fear, this darkness will not last for long. The sun will return to you."

Brother Bosa came at last, and he stepped forward and spoke up quickly.

"Aldfrith is right, it *can* be predicted, but we have been so busy preparing the Synod we've had little time of late to study the heavens…" his voice trailed off apologetically.

There were murmurs of relief at his words. A flock of seagulls swooped all around them and cried piteously, just as disturbed by the darkness as the people. Just as the last sliver of light vanished, the birds fell silent and sped arrow-straight out to sea. It was as dark as sundown and only a faint grey-blue haze was left in the sky where the sun had blazed, just an hour ago. A wail of terror went up.

Hild's voice rang out again.

"The sun will return! Brother Bosa will lead us now in prayer!"

Bosa's voice boomed as he chanted a psalm in the Latin language. Those who could understand the words tried to join in while lay folk clutched their loved ones, moaned and shook with fear. A chill wind swept over the clifftops. They wrapped their garments more tightly around their shoulders, and as their cries increased, a great stamping of hooves rose from the stables; the frightened beasts bellowed.

Even some of the older folk lost their courage.

"It was not like this last time."

"No – not this bitter chill and darkness."

"Last time it was a warning – this is death!"

But Brother Bosa's voice boomed on and, by the time he had finished his prayer, a fine jewelled circlet of light crept out from behind the dark shadow. Everyone strained upward, beseeching the Christian God to save them, though many of them had fingers crossed too, in hopes that Thor and Woden heard them. The thin gleam of hope grew brighter, and there were gasps of relief, followed by joyful whispers.

"The sun is coming back! Praise God!"

"The sun returns! We are saved!"

The gleaming ring of light grew more substantial with every passing moment; it turned from silver to gold and as they watched in wonder, a touch of warmth returned. The shadowy shapes of faces emerged from the darkness, quiet and awestruck.

Fridgyth smiled as the warmth of the sun spread through her body, from head to toe. It was sheer joy to be alive, and she was reminded of the morning she'd woken in Ketel's hut and realised she'd lived through the plague.

"The young scholar was right... but will it stay?"

"It happened just as he predicted; he's a grand young sage."

"Praise the Lord for wise young men," the abbess cried, and she reached up to hug Aldfrith. He received this token of affection meekly. At last, the reeve suggested that with the abbess's permission everyone should return to their work.

Hild was smiled broadly now.

"I have a better idea," she said. "The sun is still in the sky, and we've missed our noontide meal. Let us eat now. Mildred, I hope our meal is not ruined by the fright we've had."

"I think not," Mildred replied. "We'll serve the food at once."

The kitchen workers led the crowd across the courtyard to the refectory. There were small bursts of nervous laughter and a few looks of dread still lingered, but Hild's robust good sense and Aldfrith's rational explanation had calmed most of their fears.

Elfled walked past Fridgyth.

"No more lessons today," she announced. "How could I *write* after such a morning? My hands won't stop shaking. Mathild, Wulfrun, let's eat and then we'll ride."

Fridgyth reached out with relief to kiss Della, who followed the princess.

"Were you frightened, honey? All's well now, I think."

Guy hurried after them, pushing his way frantically through.

"Gunda," he said. "I must find Gunda."

"She's gone ahead to the refectory with the other kitchen lasses," Fridgyth told him.

Just as she was about to follow in his wake, Fridgyth saw Sister Ermintrude – one of the oldest scribes – stumbling towards the preaching cross from the direction of the scriptorium.

"God help us!" she cried, her arms flailed in an effort to stay on her feet. "God help us!"

Hild and Aldfrith were still there, with Brother Bosa. They looked up at the nun with concern. Fridgyth knew that Ermintrude suffered badly from aching joints and only moved fast with great effort. Whatever it was that made her rush about like that must have caused her great distress. With a weary sigh, she went to see what the trouble was. Her meal must wait.

"Poor man! Poor man!" Ermintrude cried.

Fridgyth had never seen her like this before.

"What is it?" Hild demanded.

"Brother Dunstan – it's Brother Dunstan – I know him by his tonsure. He's fallen down the scriptorium steps, and I fear he's dead! Please come!"

Without another word Hild, Bosa, Aldfrith and Fridgyth set off towards the scriptorium.

Ermintrude hurried after them, still gabbling wildly.

"I, I went back you see – to make sure my manuscript was safely stored and then I saw him. Oh God – poor man! I thought it was one of the scholars but…"

"Not Samson?" Aldfrith asked, his brow furrowed with concern.

"No… no! It's Dunstan."

They saw, at once, that a body wrapped in a dark red cloak lay very still on the ground, at the bottom of the outer stairs. Dunstan was the only one left who'd refused to adopt the Roman tonsure; his forehead was still shaved and his dark hair long at the back. Hild moved aside to let Fridgyth come forward.

"Is there anything you can do for him?" she asked.

The herb-wife bent down and carefully examined the young man. She could see, at once, that Ermintrude was right, Dunstan had ceased to breathe, and it looked as though he'd had an awkward fall, for his legs were twisted underneath him. She suspected both limbs were broken, but knew that such injuries, terrible though they were, should not have brought instant death.

"I can do nothing. He is dead," she acknowledged. "But I'm not sure how."

She bent down and gently started to turn poor Dunstan's body. Brother Bosa stooped to help her; they carefully straightened the crooked legs. Perhaps death had been merciful, for the man would be unlikely ever to have walked again. Fridgyth examined his face closely; it was deathly white but unmarked… then as she slipped her hand from beneath his head she felt something warm and saw that a patch of fresh blood marked her palm.

"Ah… he has hit his head very hard."

"Did he fall in the darkness, do you think?" Hild asked.

Despite the shock of this discovery Dunstan, Aldfrith looked nervously about him.

"But where is Samson?" he asked, as though Dunstan's plight were not enough for them to worry about. "I lost him somehow in the darkness as we hurried to the preaching cross."

Hild picked up his concern.

"We'll make a search," she said.

Fridgyth was more worried about what had happened to Dunstan. She continued to examine the back of his head, and found a deep cut and a terrible looseness under her fingers where the skull was smashed.

Suddenly a clang rang out. It was the bar that sealed the heavy church doors from inside. Before anyone could move to investigate, Samson came round the corner of the church, followed by Argila.

"Thank God you're safe!" Aldfrith cried.

"We took refuge in the church when darkness came," the young man said.

"Where better?" Hild approved. "But did you see what happened here?"

"Ah no!" Samson cried, shocked to see Dunstan's body.

Argila strode in front of him and stooped over the body.

"No, we saw nothing," Samson said. "But wait – maybe I heard a thud and cry."

They all stared down again at the broken body.

"Could he have caught his head on the steps as he fell?" Bosa asked.

Argila slowly got up, nodding his head.

"That might explain the hurt," Fridgyth admitted. "But he must have gone with a terrible bang, for that wound has certainly brought about his death."

"I must agree with the herb-wife," Argila said.

Aldfrith bent over Dunstan's body.

"He borrowed my cloak," he said.

"You may take it back, if you wish," Hild said.

"No... no," Aldfrith shook his head and spread the cloak carefully to cover the shattered limbs. "He is most welcome to it. It's just that I cannot remember bringing it with me today."

"No, you did not," Samson said quickly. "I borrowed it and brought it to the scriptorium this morning, but then I found the day was hot – until the sudden darkness came."

Bosa and Aldfrith carefully picked up Dunstan's broken body and carried him between them to his cell.

Hild watched them go, sighing deeply. "You go and have your meal," she said to Fridgyth. "I shall join you in the refectory once I've seen the reeve. We'll have to question all those who were in the scriptorium."

Fridgyth went to her hut to wash before she went on to the refectory. Her hunger faded, and she found herself to be trembling a little, as questions raced through her mind. There certainly were questions that should be asked.

Why was Argila always there on the edge of trouble? Why had he and Samson hidden themselves away in the church, rather than gone to the preaching cross as everyone else had done? A bang on the back of the head as he fell down the steps could well be the cause of Dunstan's death, but then so could a blow! And Dunstan had been the only one left after Cenwulf's death who had refused the Roman tonsure.

Fridgyth sat down at the table and stroked her cat. Was it not a little strange that the two monks who'd refused to change to Roman usage were both now dead? A staunch supporter of Wilfrid might see these deaths as opportune. But surely there could be no doubt that it was an accident?

Then she remembered Aldfrith bending over the body, and how he'd recognised his cloak. Was it possible that, in the darkness, someone had mistaken Dunstan for Fina's son? Dunstan's dark hair was very different to Aldfrith's, but what if he'd pulled up the hood of the cloak, as he might well have done in the cold wind that came with the darkness? She saw Argila bending over the body again. Something about the way he moved had troubled her. Had his right hand swung instinctively to his left side, as though to rest on the pommel of a sword?

Stop seeing trouble where there is none, she told herself firmly. It's the abbess and the reeve's business to question this, not yours. Perhaps they were lucky that there'd been no more disasters when such sudden darkness fell. She must go to eat first, and then go to tell her bees what had happened. She set her cat aside and went to get her lunch.

CHAPTER 15

GENTLEMONTH

News of Brother Dunstan's death had spread fast, and the refectory was noisy with shock and alarm. Even the dedicated monks and nuns couldn't manage to maintain their usual silence and, on such a day, Hild was tolerant of the hubbub.

Fridgyth went out to the upper pasture as soon as she'd eaten. As she checked the hives, she quietly announced the death of Dunstan and confided to them the thoughts and fears that troubled her. The bees buzzed gently around her, undisturbed to hear such shocking news and, as usual, she soon felt somewhat comforted and soothed by them. Having set her hives in order, she went to see how Caedmon fared and found him busy mending hurdles.

"Were you not afraid when the sun went?" she asked. "You should have brought your beasts back inside the stockade."

He shook his head and smiled.

"Sister Sun would not desert us," he said calmly.

Fridgyth wished she had such simple faith.

Dunstan was buried with due solemnity and everyone who'd been in the scriptorium just before the sudden darkness was questioned by the reeve and abbess. It emerged that there had been panic amongst the scribes, for they, more than any, depended on good light to do their work.

"I can't get much sense out of any of them," Hild confided to Fridgyth. "Nobody can tell us who was the last to leave. It may have

123

been Brother Dunstan and, in the chaos, nobody ahead of him would have heard him stumble or seen him fall."

"It troubles me" Fridgyth insisted. "That Dunstan was wearing Aldfrith's cloak. If some ardent supporter of Alchfrid, or even Prince Ecfrid, had learned that he is Fina's son…" her voice trailed off, her fears flew wild.

Hild smiled and shook her head at the herb-wife. It seemed it must be assumed to have been a tragic accident.

The shock of the sudden darkness was not so soon forgotten, for despite Aldfrith's explanation, there were still those who put it down to the anger of the Christian God.

Despite these fears, the sun stayed in the sky, the days grew longer and the year kept turning. Gulls and seabirds swooped over the clifftops, fighting over their chicks and their territory, and their cries could be heard everywhere. Three-Milking month passed into Gentlemonth, when the sun rose from the eastern sea to circle overhead and set in the western sea at night, making it seem forever daylight.

"*Sister Sun goes swimming,*" Caedmon sang quietly in the meadow, as he openly strummed his harp.

> "*She swims through the short night,*
> *And rises in the morning,*
> *Refreshed from her bathe*"

Fridgyth's garden thrived, while only the usual small accidents and sicknesses needed her attention. She sent Della to study with the princesses as often as she could spare the girl. Guy accompanied her back and stayed there to talk to Ketel about winds and tides and sea-roads. Sometimes Della brought scraps of vellum from the scriptorium inscribed with mysterious words in the Latin language. Hild gathered about her a brilliant group of scholars who promised a glittering future for Northumbria.

"What does this say?" Fridgyth asked one evening, as she admired the neat pattern of shapes beneath a beautiful and accurate painting of marigolds that the girl had brought back with her.

"Cal…end…ula offi…cionalis," the girl spelled out. "That is the Latin name for marigolds. Guy did this fine work and told me I could bring it home for you to keep; for I told him how you use marigolds to make your special balm."

"That was kind of him," she said.

"Samson told me all the uses of marigold," the girl went on. "It's good for healing wounds or soothing a bruise or sprain, or a broken heart."

"You're all passing me by in knowledge," Fridgyth said wistfully.

Della shook her head to refute this.

"No – that's not true. In the scriptorium they draw plants and quote their uses, but I've never seen them pound the dried marigold petals in goose grease as you do and produce a pot of healing balm all ready for use."

"These colours glow so vivid on the page!" Fridgyth said, delicately touching the painted flower.

"Boiled onion skins make that colour," Della said. "And gorse flowers will work as well, but these hues will fade, just as they do on wool. In the scriptorium the best scribes use the most expensive dyes to paint on vellum. Eadfrith fusses so over the making of the colours – pigments he calls them. He says we mustn't touch them, and he's quite fierce about it. Some are precious; some are dangerous: red lead, green copper, yellow orpiment and at times they use real gold!"

"You are stepping into a world I know nothing of," Fridgyth said with a shrug, "even though it lies just outside my door."

One bright morning early in Gentlemonth, Fridgyth sent Della off to the scriptorium and then went to the visitors' guest hall with a stomach potion for the reeve's wife. As she crossed the courtyard, three of the dedicated nuns hurried towards her from their isolated enclosure. Such a thing hadn't happened since the sun went dark. They headed towards the main gate in silence, but were closely followed by a noisy straggling group of lay sisters coming from the family huts.

"Ship's coming into harbour," they shouted. "There's a great barge, riding in on the tide and Mother Hild's gone down to meet it!"

Over the winter, there'd been little movement on the sea, and even the better weather had brought only a few ships to Streonshalh. The sickness, which had taken root in so many of the seaports, had made traders fearful, but Gentlemonth was known for good sailing weather. Even some of the metalworkers tramped past, and it was a rare thing that they left their hearths during the hours of work.

Fridgyth rushed into the visitors' guest hall and pushed her bottle of mixture into the hands of a startled lay sister.

"Deliver this to the reeve's wife," she ordered, then hurried out to the main gate herself.

As she stumbled down the steep path, she saw a twenty-oared galley out on the sea, and she stopped for a moment and watched as it made its way fast into the safety of Streonshalh harbour. A good crowd had already gathered at the quayside, headed by the abbess and the reeve. As soon as she reached the bottom of the hill, Fridgyth pushed her way though the onlookers to stand at their side.

As the rowers struggled, stiff-legged, from the oar thwarts it became clear that these were no oar-slaves. Each man wore a plain monastic habit and bore the Roman tonsure on their heads. The abbess recognised their leader.

"Prior Sigurd," she murmured to Fridgyth.

"You know him?"

"Yes indeed – Prior Sigurd from the Kingdom of the East Saxons. He's prior of Bishop Cedd's monastery in the south. I met him once when he visited Bamburgh. He couldn't come for the Synod, so what brings him here now? Does he know we've suffered the plague, I wonder?"

Courtesy made the abbess go forward to meet the prior, as royal representative in Streonshalh, but instead of the usual kiss of welcome she held up her hand in warning.

"Prior Sigurd, you must leave – at once," she said. "Forgive this discourtesy, but for your own safety I beg you go. We have had the plague here, and though we now believe ourselves clear of it, all seaboard towns in Deira are touched by the pestilence."

The onlookers were hushed and rather shocked to hear the way she spoke, but Prior Sigurd seemed neither surprised nor offended.

He insistently came forward, took her hand and kissed it.

"Lady, we are not afraid." Prior Sigurd's voice was deliberately loud, designed to carry to all those on the quayside. "Our home too is plague-ridden, and the new king has turned his back on the Christian God. Chaos rules in his kingdom and Woden's ravens fly over our land."

The people gasped to hear his words.

"We seek asylum here in Deira, and we ask just one night's rest in your monastery, then we wish to see out our days at the burial place of our beloved Cedd."

"You'd go to Lastingham?"

"Yes, Lady."

The abbess looked pityingly along the line of monks and oblates. There were thirty of them – some frail and aged and others very young. One child no older than seven stood quietly beside the prior, watching Hild, wide-eyed, and waiting for her judgement.

"We're all in God's hands," she said at last. "I'm truly sorry to hear of your distress, but Lastingham may still suffer from the sickness that killed your leader. Can I say nothing to deter you?"

"No, lady," Prior Sigurd shook his head.

"In that case," Hild spoke with resignation. "We offer you the best we can in hospitality and we'll set you on your way across the heather moors towards Lastingham."

Prior Sigurd kissed her hand again, and a tear slid down his cheek, the relief too much for him. Hild held out her hand to the small boy and, as he took it with a charming smile, the tension eased. "Come with me, brave fellow," she said. "You must climb our steep hill and eat with us."

Everyone had to move back from the waterside to allow the visitors to come ashore. With many whispers and curious stares, the people of Streonshalh accompanied the visitors up the hill to the monastery.

Elfled and her fellow pupils had escaped from the schoolroom and had come out through the main gate, full of curiosity. The princess's eyes lighted on the young boy that Hild led, so tiny to be tonsured and dressed in monastic robes; she went to take his other hand.

"I'll tell you a riddle!" Elfled said. "I wear a tunic of white and a jacket of grey. My name is a fish, and my home is a cliff. What am I?"

The boy looked at her with amazement.

"My name is a fish, and my home is a cliff?"

Behind the princess Wulfrun smiled and mouthed the answer to the child, half covering her lips with her hand.

"Is it... a herring gull?" the boy was quick to pick up her suggestion. "His name is a fish – a herring."

"That was very clever of you," Elfled said.

The visitors were ushered into the monastic guest house, and Brother Brandon rushed about trying to accommodate them, courteous but terse at the arrival of so many unexpected guests.

Elfled begged leave to take the small boy out into the upper pasture to play. Hild hesitated, but Prior Sigurd overheard her plea.

"Billfrith is our youngest," he said. "He has endured much over the last months. Let him have this brief chance to play."

"Wulfrun will keep a good watch on them," the abbess agreed, "And perhaps we should all go out into the meadow while the sun is warm. I'll ask the kitchen workers to bring out food and drink while Brother Brandon prepares beds for you all; you must be exhausted and hungry after so long a journey."

Elfled led Billfrith out into the upper pasture, charmed by the child's fair hair, golden skin and solemn manner.

"Come and see our perfect ones," she said, determined to try him with another riddle. "They are little men and women, wearing white habits; they feast each day at a green table. They never fast, nor ever use a fingerbowl. Are you clever enough to guess what they are?"

Billfrith shook his head.

"No, but I can list the names of all the kings who've ruled the East Angles and I can chant the Latin words of twenty psalms and all the Book of Genesis."

Everyone smiled at his gravity.

"That is more than I can do," Elfled allowed. "Look – you'll see them in their white habits as soon as we get through the gate."

Billfrith saw at once.

"Calves, they are white calves!" he cried, clapping his hands.

"Little men and women in white habits… perfect ones."

Caedmon went into a stammering state of panic at the sudden arrival of so many important visitors in his pasture. He herded his calves into the far corner by the beehives and quickly marked off a small area with wattle hurdles to protect his beasts.

An air of celebration developed in the sunlit upper pasture. Lay sisters spread soft wool rugs on the grass. The abbess and Prior Sigurd came outside, and the reeve ordered chairs to be brought for them. Hild declared a day of holiday in celebration of the visitors' unexpected, but safe, arrival.

Sister Mildred set six fast-slaughtered sheep to roast on spits and, while the delicious scents of the meat began to drift across the meadow, kitchen workers handed round oatcakes and fresh baked flat bread. In the brew-house, pitchers of ale and mead were broached; in the dairy, cheeses were unwrapped and cut.

Aldfrith, Samson and Eadfrith came out from the scriptorium, to search for their fleeing students. Guy and Della followed and sat down on the grass; they quickly joined in the spirit of festivity and enjoyed the sun. Fridgyth was pleased to see her apprentice there amongst the scholars and proud that the girl appeared to talk to them with confidence. She also observed that Mathild looked uncomfortable when Guy paid attention to her. The shy princess shrank away from him and moved closer to Samson, more comfortable with his peaceful, dreamy manner. Now he'd make a kind husband, Fridgyth thought, and the quiet princess deserved such a one. She'd ask Hild about it when she got the chance, but feared she'd be sharply told to stop match-making.

Argila sat on the edge of this group of cheerful young people, saying little, but watching them all.

"Come join us, Fridgyth," Elfled ordered. "Help us keep these wild young men in order."

Fridgyth sat down with them, but kept a fair distance from Argila.

"This Billfrith speaks like a tiny bishop," Elfled cried, delighted at the young boy's maturity.

The child smiled at her words.

"I should like to be a bishop one day," he confided.

Prior Sigurd sat by the abbess and watched his young charge with indulgent tolerance; few days in Billfrith's ordered life would be like this one. Cloda and Begu came to sit beside Fridgyth.

"Good to see them all happy," the herb-wife said.

"Happy for now," Cloda said with a sigh. "But butterflies live only for a day."

"Is that dream-speak?" Fridgyth asked.

"Our Cloda dreamed of a field of golden flowers," Begu announced.

"And here we are all sitting amongst the buttercups," Fridgyth said. "Why are you so gloomy? It sounds like a pleasant dream to me."

"Flowers quickly fade and die," Cloda said quietly. "But let us enjoy this bright day!"

Ketel sat amongst the carpenters who were setting up the timber framework of the new school buildings. As the mead-cup came to him, he raised it to Fridgyth in silent greeting.

"Drink hail," she called warmly back to him.

CHAPTER 16

FLOWERS QUICKLY FADE

The afternoon wore on, and Fridgyth noted that Gunda watched the group of royal scholars jealously. The girl toiled around the meadow to offer food to residents and visitors alike, but at every opportunity her gaze was drawn back to her brother, as he charmed Elfled with endless riddles and compliments. Fridgyth had plenty of sympathy for the girl; why had Hild not moved her out of the kitchen yet? She'd speak to her about it again. The new school building should be finished by the autumn and Gunda ought to be offered a place.

Once everyone had eaten and mead and ale were passed around, the abbess called for her harp. In response to the pressing demand, Hild opened the singing herself with a brief Latin chant in which she expressed gratitude to God for the visitors' safe arrival, but she quickly handed the instrument on to Coen and invited him to sing something lively, to suit the occasion.

Fridgyth looked for Caedmon. He sat on the edge of the gathering with his harp hidden away, fearful to go anywhere near Coen and unwilling to wander far from his calves. Coen's song was met with wild applause, and he followed it with another, but suddenly frightened screams broke out in the far corner of the meadow. Elfled leapt to her feet, and Wulfrun, at once, moved protectively in front of the princess.

Some of the children in the far corner ran wildly about, they wept and wailed and flapped their arms, the calves too ran amok. Adults struggled to their feet, ready to go to the rescue.

Samson saw, at once, what the problem was.

"It's the bees!" he said quietly, and he set off fast towards them, Aldfrith close at his heels and Argila too.

Fridgyth's heart sank to her boots. One of her hives had somehow been knocked over, and the bees, frightened by the attack on their home, were swarming angrily. Children shrieked and screamed, and some of them were stung; their wild reaction inflamed the bees even more.

"Freya's breath!" Fridgyth cried. "We'll have to smoke them, and fast – I need charcoal from the cooking fire."

"I'll fetch some," Della said, and she set off, at once, to where the fire still glowed beneath the spits.

Monks and nuns backed away as fast as they could, while parents grew as frantic as their children.

Fridgyth snatched a bee-skep from a pile she always kept by the gate, but Samson was ahead of her. He took the woven basket from her hand.

"Leave them to me!" he said.

He spoke with such surprising authority, that Fridgyth somehow found herself obeying him.

The swarming bees settled on the back and shoulders of a small girl whose mother was distraught. The child, unaware of the danger, looked about her, frightened mainly by the expressions on the adult's faces.

"Mam?" she whimpered.

"Peace!" Samson said, warning those around to be still.

Somehow his voice cut through the panic, and many backed away.

"Trust me." Samson soothed the frantic mother. "Stay still, darling!" He squatted down to child's level, the woven skep there in his hands. "Now... look at me!"

"Trust him," Fridgyth said, giving her support.

The child was white with terror and trembling, for she sensed that something was terribly wrong.

"Look at me. You will be safe," Samson commanded.

The child obediently lifted her eyes to the strange young man, and it was wonderful to see how her expression changed from desperate fear to perfect trust. Samson began to hum gently, almost as though he sang the bees own song, while all the time he held the child's gaze. Then, with one swift, smooth movement, he passed the skep over her head and rose to his feet. The few who had stayed close enough to see clearly, gasped with relief, for all the bees had swarmed safely into the basket and the child remained unharmed. The mother swooped down on her little one, crying her thanks.

"Well done," Fridgyth praised him, amazed as all the others were.

"I've got the smoking charcoal," Della called, as she hurried towards them.

Suddenly everyone was laughing.

"No need… no need," they told her.

But Samson welcomed her assistance.

"The smoke will help," he said. "Come, let us take the swarm home."

So Samson and Fridgyth set off towards the hives, and Della followed closely, clutching the hot smoking bowl tightly in a fold of her apron. Fridgyth righted the hive while Della blew on the charcoal, and Samson held the skep to catch the smoke. He swung the skep gently towards the hive again, and the drowsy bees streamed obediently back inside.

"Thank goodness for that," Fridgyth cried, turning to Samson with gratitude and relief. "You are a bee-charmer, no doubt of that."

Samson bowed.

"A small skill, rarely used or appreciated," he said with a quick shy smile, as he slipped back once again to his usual reticence.

He stayed to help Fridgyth settle the bees and check all the hives, then walked slowly back at her side to rejoin the gathering.

They found that Wulfrun had produced a vial of ragwort juice from the collection of useful tools that swung at her girdle, and she and Mathild were treating those who'd been stung. Mathild's kind and gentle manner did more to soothe their hurts than Wulfrun's swift and practised dabs with the sharp-smelling herbal mixture.

"They've done well," Fridgyth said. "Princess Mathild will make a good mother one day," she said mischievously, looking up at Samson.

He nodded and smiled.

"Yes, you are quite right, herb-wife," he said. "You observe people closely."

They stood together, watching for a moment, but then Samson spoke again.

"I too like to observe people," he said. "And I've noticed that your friend the cowherd bears a harp upon his back, but never offers his services as a bard!"

Fridgyth turned to him nodding warmly.

"You have observed well. My friend Caedmon is a true wordsmith, and he plays the harp as well as any bard, but an awkwardness of speech makes him fearful to perform in company."

"But, he'd like to sing," Samson said with certainty.

Fridgyth sighed.

"Yes, he'd like to sing. Can you work your magic on him then, as you did with the bees?"

Samson stroked his chin in thought.

"I'll think on it," he said.

Fridgyth, emboldened by these small confidences, looked over to Aldfrith and Argila.

"You and your friend Aldfrith always seem to have Argila at your side," she commented.

She thought that Samson looked slightly amused at her words.

"More warrior than monk, I'd say," she insisted. "Be wary," she advised low voiced. "Be wary on your friend's behalf. There are those who'd wish Aldfrith harm, if they knew his parentage."

Samson nodded thoughtfully.

"I will indeed."

He bowed to her and went off to join his friends.

Fridgyth saw, in her mind again, the moment when the bees swarmed. Argila, had been on his feet so fast it was hard to be sure, and surely he had reached as though to grab a sword, just as Wulfrun had stepped in front of Elfled, alert to the possibility of danger.

Fridgyth frowned as a new idea came to her. Could she have mistaken Argila's intentions? Might he be assuming the role of bodyguard to Fina's son? But would Oswy's son, have a Frankish bodyguard?

The sun sank low in the sky and the bell tolled for vespers. The dedicated monks and nuns got up quietly, to return to their hermit-like existence, and Hild and the Prior led them back inside the stockade, heading for the church. The lay brothers and sisters began to clear away the remains of the meal, while Elfled and her friends wandered back to their more comfortable accommodation. It had been a day full of the most unexpected events, and Fridgyth was tired.

Next morning, Prior Sigurd insisted that he and his band of monks should set off for Lastingham. Horses and mules were provided, and Brother Bosa and a small group of guards went with them to guide them onto the heather moors.

The usual steady routine was resumed at Streonshalh but, three days later, Fridgyth was summoned to the monastic guest house, where two lay brothers who'd served the guests had taken to their beds. The scene was frighteningly familiar... for the men vomited continually and one poor fellow had a lump in his groin.

Fridgyth swore under her breath.

"Blessed Freya! Yellow plague, again? Which god do we blame for this?"

She set to work with her potions, to try to reduce the fever, and with Della's help she lanced the boil. By the next morning, one patient had died, and three more lay brothers had fallen sick.

Over the next three days, she and Della worked to contain the sickness and save the young men, but they all died and two more fell sick. On the fourth day Hild came over from the abbess's house to consult with her.

"Stay away!" Fridgyth warned.

Hild shook her head, her face grim.

"Too late for that I think; there's sorry news from Melrose. We must call a meeting."

The whole community was summoned to the preaching cross, and they gathered unwillingly, though it was a still warm afternoon with a cloudless sky and the scent of flowers in the air. Many drew their monastic hoods closely about them and avoided contact with their neighbours, for rumours of the sickness were rife. Hild brought

Fridgyth to the front and then stood solemn-faced between Brother Bosa and the reeve as she made the dreadful announcement.

"We are visited by pestilence once again, and this time it's within the monastic bounds."

Sounds of suppressed weeping came from the crowd.

"There's yet more to tell," Hild cautioned.

In a tense, low voice she announced that a messenger had arrived from Melrose. Cuthbert had been taken ill with a plague tumour in his thigh. It seemed that three of the monks who'd journeyed home with him after the Synod had died soon after they'd got back to Melrose. The plague had spared the monastery through the coldest months, and they'd hoped the sickness had gone, but now it had reappeared, striking with a vengeance, as the weather grew warm.

There were small, suppressed cries amongst the crowd as the significance of this dreadful news sunk in.

"We must flee this place!"

"But the sickness might pursue us!"

Elfled, who was standing at the front, went very pale at the mention of Cuthbert's name.

"Not Cuthbert… not my dear Cuthbert," she whispered.

Wulfrun put her arm around the princess's shoulders to comfort her.

"He's strong," she said. "Remember how Della suffered and survived, Fridgyth too. If anyone can struggle through the sickness, it will be Cuthbert."

Elfled swallowed hard as she tried to maintain her dignity.

"But I'm a…fraid," she said, with a trembly hiccup.

Mathild reached out and took the young princess's hand.

"We're all afraid," she said.

A fearful silence settled over the gathering.

"There's temptation to flee," Hild acknowledged with her usual openness. "But we've seen that those who flee often carry the sickness with them. So I say we must have courage, stay here and trust in God. I'm closing the refectory," she announced. "Food must be collected from the kitchens and eaten alone. This scourge spreads fast, and we don't know how, but there may be some hope in us keeping a distance from one another. The monastic guest house will be used as a temporary infirmary; this is where the pestilence has started, so let us try to imprison it within those bounds."

There were gasps of shock. The monastic guest house was normally forbidden to anyone who hadn't taken vows. Some of the dedicatedly religious were appalled.

Hild went on, unperturbed.

"No visitors will be accepted for the time being, unless it is a matter of starvation. Anyone who's taken with the plague must go, at once, to the infirmary. Do not stay at home with your family if you are sick – you'll risk their lives as well."

There were many frightened murmurs.

"And pray," Hild ordered, her thin face pinched but her voice still calm and strong. "Our dedicated monks and nuns keep vigil in their cells. We're in God's hands and must endure together; anyone who takes advantage of this time of hardship will be severely punished."

Suppressed whispers flew around.

"I knew the dark of the sun bode evil!"

"That darkness brought this plague!"

"It's God's judgement on the Synod!"

"Brother Cenwulf was right! There was no plague in Deira before we turned to Rome!"

"Before Wilfrid, you mean – where is he now?"

"In Compiegne. Our northern bishops aren't good enough for him, and now we have the plague!"

The memory of Wilfrid's handsome face and charm meant little now and, from her hawk-like look and determined mouth, it was clear that Hild would not tolerate panic or blame.

"Leave quietly," she ordered.

The crowd dispersed, and Ketel went with a band of carpenters to board up the refectory. Fridgyth and Della returned to their patients in the monastic guest house, and a fearful quietness crept over the monastery. That afternoon, three more lay-brothers were taken sick as well as the reeve's youngest child.

As the sun went down, Fridgyth paused in her work and spoke to Della.

"Can you watch for a while?" she asked. "I must tell the bees, what has happened or I fear they'll swarm."

"Oh yes," she agreed. "Your bees must be told."

A dreadful pattern developed As the days slipped by: one member of a family would come to the infirmary sick, then the next day more from that same family would follow. The sickness spread to the rope-makers, then the herdsmen and the carpenters. Brother Brandon found it irksome that his ordered establishment should be turned upside down and put in the charge of the herb-wife. At first he fussed and rushed about everywhere and gave orders that nobody could manage to obey, until one day he failed to appear. When Fridgyth went to his small cell to investigate, she found he too was sick; he died the following day and his death left the herb-wife indisputably in charge.

Della never asked to go to the scriptorium anymore, but worked doggedly at Fridgyth's side to alleviate suffering, along with the small band of lay brothers and sisters who were allotted the dreadful task. They designated the upper floor for men and the lower for women, but made a few exceptions when husbands and wives, or mothers and sons, wished to die together.

Despite Fridgyth's protests, Ketel came to help them; he brought fresh straw from the stables so that they could make extra pallets on the benches and the floor. Each day he took on more and more of the heavier work and transported the bodies to the cemetery for burial in a cart pulled by the grey mule, Drogo. All plans for his new quayside buildings had been set aside.

Every evening, just before the prayers of the night, the abbess came to the monastic guest house entrance, with a young oblate as torchbearer and Eadfrith as scribe. They stood there grim-faced in the shimmering torchlight, while Fridgyth solemnly recited the names of those who'd died that day and Eadfrith wrote them down.

"We'll name them in our prayers," Hild said.

Some nights Ketel sent Fridgyth and Della back to the herb-wife's hut and took charge of the makeshift infirmary himself. Fridgyth would press his arm in gratitude, too weary to argue.

Late one night Hild appeared in the doorway of the hut; she

carried a lantern.

"You'd do best to keep away," Fridgyth reminded her.

The abbess sighed.

"Maybe so," she said. "And I know you must be exhausted but, dear Fridgyth, I miss our little talks, and I find myself very much in need of sensible advice."

"You'd best come inside then," Fridgyth said.

CHAPTER 17

WEED-MONTH

The abbess sat down heavily at the table, her brow drawn with anxiety. Fridgyth sent Della to bed and then poured out two beakers of elderberry wine.

The abbess took her drink gratefully.

"I'm torn," she said, her face haggard with worry. "I've care of all these souls who follow me as their leader, and I must do my best for them, but I've Elfled's welfare to consider. I think I should send her to her parents' – maybe she'd be safer at Bamburgh. Samson and Mathild might go with her, but I cannot send Aldfrith."

Fridgyth saw the dilemma: guardianship of these young royals was a great responsibility.

"How could you bear to be parted from Elfled at a time like this?" she asked.

"I must do what is right for her, my own feelings are unimportant."

"Elfled won't want to go to Bamburgh and leave you!"

Hild's tense face softened.

"I'll miss her and fret over her, but if it's for the best I must make her go."

Fridgyth shrugged.

"It could help to keep her safe," she acknowledged. "And Samson's company would cheer her, though I think he would be sorry to be parted from Aldfrith. You might send Guy to escort the princesses to Bamburgh, Elfled loves his company. I found him outside my hut last night, hoping to see Della and I told him, for his own sake, to stay away."

Hild nodded and sighed.

"Yes you are right. Elfled would go if I sent her friends with her... but Aldfrith must stay here. He'll carry on with his studies, and I can only pray that he stays free of sickness."

Fridgyth sighed.

"Some might not care were he to fall victim to this plague," she said, her face glum.

Hild looked up sharply.

"Nobody who knew him could wish him ill."

"No, indeed," Fridgyth hastened to agree. "You know I am his greatest admirer, but..."

The church bell suddenly rang insistently, and Hild rose to her feet at once. She gave a quick nod and strode away into the darkness.

Early next morning, a loud knock on her door woke Fridgyth. As she struggled out of bed, she wondered what had happened and found the abbess there again, her cloak clutched over her night gown, her veil awry.

"What is it?" Fridgyth cried. "Not Elfled?"

"No." Hild shook her head. "It's Samson. There's little point in me sending Elfled to Bamburgh. We are too late it seems; Samson was taken ill in the night and they've all been so much together. Will you come and look at him? Argila says he thinks it must be the pestilence, but I'd like your opinion too. I fear Elfled may be next and Aldfrith too."

Fridgyth snatched up her cloak and followed Hild across the courtyard to the royal guest house. What they found in Samson's bedchamber confirmed Fridgyth's worst fears: the young man was vomiting violently, while Cloda watched him like a she-wolf her young. Aldfrith, his sleeves rolled up, appeared to be doing all the dirty work.

"There's little I can do for him," Fridgyth said quietly. "Fetch fresh water from the well and see if he can sip it. I'll send a cooling mixture for him."

"Samson cannot go to the infirmary," Hild said. "As a royal prince, he must be kept apart. I'll see that good food is sent over from the kitchens, and we must keep the princesses well away. I have confined Elfled to my house. She is furious with me. Neither Cloda nor Aldfrith will leave Samson's side. He's in good hands here."

Fridgyth nodded her agreement.

"You go back to the infirmary," Hild said sadly. "There are many more who need you there, and Argila will help here."

Fridgyth passed Argila who stood grim-faced in the shadowy hall as she left. She felt momentarily resentful but, at the sight of Ketel and Della struggling with a new crowd of patients outside the infirmary, she soon forgot all about him. She strode across the courtyard and pushed her way through to join her friends. The foul smell of sickness in the building was a vivid reminder of the horror of the boat-makers' huts.

"Come inside," she ordered, swiftly taking charge. "One at a time now, there's no point in pushing or wailing either."

Della blew out her breath, relieved to see the herb-wife back. "It's getting worse," she said.

The days wore on in such a muddle of misery, that Fridgyth could hardly think whether it was day or night. First Gentlemonth passed into Second Gentlemonth and at last the Month of Weeds arrived, and still the sickness raged. The reeve's child died, and his mother too and yet, despite all the death around them, both the herb-wife and her apprentice remained strong, as did Ketel. It occurred to Fridgyth that maybe once a sufferer had recovered they might somehow stay safe from the sickness. She insisted that all her helpers take a turn in the upper pasture each day, to drink at the well and breathe the fresh, salt laden air. Even so, many of them still succumbed to the disease.

Ketel and Drogo became a dreaded but respected team as they took the bodies from the infirmary to a new patch of land, beyond the orchard, that Hild had set aside for the purpose, when the old burial space was almost full. Fridgyth fretted that he should be left to do such work by himself, but few proffered help; she had to acknowledge that if he could manage it alone, it was probably for the best. A steady stream of corpses left the makeshift infirmary, and it was a sad day when the reeve followed his wife and youngest child into the burial ground. And yet, even through the darkest days, some recovered, and the dedicated monks and nuns stayed free of the sickness in their huts.

Towards the end of the Month of Weeds, Fridgyth and Della set up a quieter, cleaner recovery space in the hall of the monastic guest house. They kept the doors open so that the warm summer air could reach the survivors, and went in and out of the kitchens to fetch good food for the lucky few. The foodwife did her best and, as numbers were so reduced, there were no shortages.

One afternoon a flurry of excitement around the entrance to the infirmary, made Fridgyth look outside. She saw the abbess standing there.

"Come out to me," Hild begged. "Speak to me in the upper pasture. I won't touch you or come near, but there are things I need to speak about."

Fridgyth followed the abbess at a distance, glad to be outside for a while. As Caedmon saw them, he ushered his charges away towards the hives.

Hild turned to her friend as soon as they sat down together.

"Samson lives, but Cloda tells me he is still very sick," she said.

Fridgyth stared at her.

"Still sick?" she murmured.

Truth to tell, in amongst all her other concerns, the plight of the young nobleman had somewhat slipped to the back of her mind. She knew she'd have heard if he'd died and so she'd assumed he'd been making a slow recovery, like some of her own survivors. Cloda would have given him the greatest of care?

"I expected him to be recovering by now," she admitted. "I would have thought he'd either have recovered… or died."

"Cloda won't leave his side," said Hild. "And Mildred prepares special invalid food for him, same as she does for the other sufferers."

"Mildred does her very best for us," Fridgyth agreed.

The creamy porridge that she sent out from the kitchens was much appreciated by those who were recovering.

Hild sighed.

"What a year this has turned out to be! We seem beset with

troubles. The Streonshalh bulla has disappeared, the official seal that validates my most important documents."

Fridgyth frowned. She knew the small leaden seal well.

"You could have another made," she suggested.

"I could indeed – but why would anyone steal such a thing, unless they wished to write messages in my name, with dishonourable intent."

"I can see why that thought would trouble you," Fridgyth agreed.

"And now there is something else," Hild paused, as though uncertain how to put what she wished to say. "Mathild has gone to help Cloda nurse Samson. I forbade both princesses to leave my house, but she has disobeyed me."

Fridgyth stared for a moment, then pressed her lips together in understanding.

She remembered Mathild's dreamy look as she sat with Samson that day in the upper pasture.

"She loves him," she said quietly.

"So it seems." Hild shrugged, unimpressed. "Why does nobody tell *me* these things? What should I do now? I need your counsel in this matter. Mathild has thrown away her honour and reputation by this act of disobedience, and she may well have thrown her life away too. Elfled is furious that she's left them, and Wulfrun blames herself. She set herself to guard my house like a young warrior, but never thought she should watch for those inside escaping out."

"Wulfrun's not to blame," Fridgyth said at once, but then she sighed and couldn't help but smile a little. "She's a mystery, that girl Mathild. I'm amazed she'd the boldness to do it. I've underestimated her; it took courage."

Hild pulled a wry face.

"Courage? I suppose so. Her feelings towards him must be very passionate."

Fridgyth shook her head smiling a little.

"We've forgotten, old friend... you and I. We've forgotten how strong such feelings can be. The girl has chosen her fate and must live or die by it."

"It *was* extraordinarily bold of her," Hild admitted. "She has declared herself to the world. What thane will marry her now? I cannot keep it secret; already the kitchen workers know she's there."

"Well," Fridgyth said. "Maybe Samson will marry her himself if he lives. I think he may well return her feelings."

"Might he indeed?" Hild's eyebrows shot up. "You see, I knew you were the one to consult!"

"Well," Fridgyth said. "The more I think about it, the more I'm impressed by her boldness; better to blush than die of loneliness, I'd say. What does honour matter, when they die like flies around us?"

The abbess looked thoughtful for a moment and then she sighed with a nod.

"I needed your warm good sense in this. You're quite right, Fridgyth. Mathild's *survival* is all I should fret about. Samson's too."

"Better a good husband than exalted lineage," Fridgyth said. "And Samson is a cousin to Elfled, is he not? Is he promised to the church?"

Hild glanced at her uncertainly as though she'd like to say more, but she answered mysteriously.

"Only for safe keeping," she said.

"What does that mean?" Fridgyth asked.

Hild sighed and shook her head.

"It's best you don't know. Some day I'll explain. You've got enough to worry about just now, and you were wrong about one thing: I haven't quite forgotten such feelings. It's just that I'm practised at quelling them. You've made me remember the wild young woman I once was. I wouldn't have hesitated to do such a thing at Mathild's age, if only the man had been right."

"I doubt I'd have had the courage," Fridgyth said with a sigh.

She hadn't put up much of a fight when Ketel went off to marry Berta; she'd been offended and proud and refused to look his way or even speak of him. Maybe she'd have done better to ignore the shame and fight for him.

Hild got up to go.

"You've put my mind at rest."

"I'm glad," she said, waving aside the abbess's proffered hand.

When Fridgyth got back to the infirmary, she found Della hard at work. Three young orphan sisters had been brought in very sick.

"So – it has reached the weaving sheds," Fridgyth said.

"I don't like their pale looks and their hands and feet are cold," Della whispered in Fridgyth's ear. "They vomited like you've never seen, but now they've gone quiet and still."

"Fetch extra rugs," Fridgyth said. "Then take the stones from around the hearth and wrap them in cloths to warm their feet. I'll brew up some sage and honey and spoon it into them; we must try to make them sweat."

They both worked hard, but couldn't revive the girls.

Fridgyth clicked her tongue in frustration over them.

"It's not the same," she said. "No swellings, no fever – just white skin, terrible sickness and frozen cold hands and feet; it must be another disease. Not one I recognise."

All three sisters died that night. Fridgyth frowned as she bent over their pale, white bodies.

"Not a mark on them," she said, "But I thought I caught the scent of garlic on their breath. Did you feed them garlic broth?"

Della shook her head.

"They couldn't even keep water down, but I also caught the taint of garlic. Could they have eaten too much garlic do you think?"

"No!" Fridgyth shook her head. "Garlic can't do anything but good… I keep telling Mildred to chop the leaves into the pottage, as much as she can. You'd best ask Ketel to come for them."

"I think there's something else that smells of garlic," Della said, wrinkling her brow in an effort to remember. "Something Eadfrith warned about."

"You're not much help," Fridgyth told her roundly. "Was it a toadstool or a poisonous berry?"

Della shook her head.

One of the older recovering patients struggled to her feet and started to make for the door.

"I'm going home," she said.

"Just a few more days, honey," Fridgyth said. "Then we'll let you go, and willingly."

Later, when she lay down to sleep that night, Fridgyth found that there *was* something still there at the back of her mind that troubled her, and suddenly she remembered how she and Eadfrith had discovered Cenwulf dead in his hut just after the Synod. They'd come to the conclusion that he'd died of gluttony, partly because of the odour of garlic, which his starved stomach would have been too shocked to cope with, along with the red wine. But surely the same thing couldn't have happened to these three girls, they'd never been encouraged to fast. As workers in the weaving shed they'd have enjoyed a steady supply of good wholesome food and their plump, muscular bodies bore witness to that. Had Cenwulf died of some disease that she hadn't recognised after all?

Over the next few days, some of Coen's warriors were brought in vomiting and with plague-swellings; it was a shock to see such strong young men brought low and weak as babes. Fridgyth had been angry over their treatment of the cowherd, but now felt only sadness for them. She was glad that Caedmon was still outside in the meadow with his calves, away from all this foulness. Perhaps his work would help to keep him free of the disease, for it seemed that the seamstresses and shoemakers suffered the most, cramped together in their small workshops. Though Fridgyth expected it every day, no more victims came from the weaving sheds. Early each evening, after she'd drunk from the well, for a brief blessed spell, Fridgyth would visit her bees and then sit beside Caedmon to rest awhile. As the days passed, the number of his charges grew – as herdsmen had fallen sick, the cowherd had taken their animals into his care. His spotless vellum calves now mingled with a flock of young oxen, goats and geese that bellowed and cackled beside the gently lowing calves. A small gang of orphaned lads had come along with the beasts and Caedmon persevered in training them up as herdsmen, as patient with the lads as he was with the creatures.

CHAPTER 18

MARIGOLDS

One afternoon, as she walked back from the well, Fridgyth saw Cloda cross the courtyard with a tray of food. Troubled thoughts of garlic and red wine, made her call out to her; the old woman stopped, looking somewhat annoyed.

"I haven't much time," she said. "I don't like to leave my poor boy for long, but I don't approve of waste either."

"Where do you take this food?" Fridgyth asked.

Cloda shrugged, and it crossed Fridgyth's mind that the Frankish woman herself looked thinner of late, almost gaunt.

"I take it wherever it's needed," she said, "sometimes to the herdsmen's families, sometimes to the weaving huts or stables. It's good food that shouldn't go to waste. I've heard that Ranulf's youngest doesn't thrive, so I'm heading for the family huts."

Fridgyth saw that it was Mildred's creamy porridge in the bowls, all sprinkled prettily with dried marigold petals: fine food indeed to be given away.

"You should eat more yourself; you are looking thin. You need to keep your own strength up if you are to be any use to Samson. I saw you take food across the courtyard yesterday. Where did it go?"

Cloda was offended to be questioned by the herb-wife.

"To Mada's old mother – she grows very weak. Was that not charitable? And what I eat is surely my business and nobody else's."

"Did you give food to the three sisters from the weaving sheds?"

Cloda's mouth dropped open; this was too much.

"Anyone would think I'd done wrong, but this is only decent Christian charity."

She marched away holding her head up high.

Fridgyth stared after her. If she'd taken porridge to the weaving sheds, it couldn't have done the girls harm... unless it was a great deal richer than they were used to?

She stopped just outside the entrance to the monastic guest house. She was needed in there, she knew, but the deaths of the three young weavers still troubled her. She suddenly swung round and headed for the weaving sheds.

Wulfrun's mother, Cwen, was chief webster there, in charge of the many women who worked at the looms. Streonshalh needed a good supply of colourful woollen hangings to cut out draughts and brighten the wattle and daub of the walls. She came out, with her younger daughter, Gode, to greet Fridgyth; they were all old friends.

"I have a strange thing to ask," Fridgyth said quickly.

"What's that?" Cwen asked.

"Can you remember what it was that the three young sisters ate, just before they became so ill?"

Cwen was surprised. She frowned in thought for a moment and then she nodded.

"Ah... but I do remember. Those lasses thought it such a treat. They shared a fine big bowl of porridge, with thick cream mixed into it."

"And where did that food come from?" Fridgyth asked.

"Sister Cloda brought it for them. She's been so very kind that way."

Fridgyth drew in her breath sharply.

"I remember it," Gode added. "Helga threatened to steal the food, but she was only teasing them."

Fridgyth bit her lips in thought. "Porridge, you say, with cream?"

"They swore it was delicious," Gode said. "All laced with cream and honey; the top made pretty with dried marigold petals."

"It was food from the royal guest house... they ate like princesses." Cwen smiled at the memory; then her eyes flooded with tears and her mouth twisted in grief. "It was their last meal."

"I'm so sorry to raise unhappy memories," Fridgyth said, "but there's one more thing… may I speak to Mada?"

Cwen shook her head.

"She's not here," she said. Her mother died this morning. I told her not to come to work."

Fridgyth's mouth dropped open in shock.

"But I wasn't told she was sick! Why didn't Mada bring her mother to me?"

"There was no need," Cwen assured her. "There was nothing you could have done… it wasn't the plague. She was very old and frail, all skin and bones, poor thing. Nobody was surprised that she went… just old age"

"But still, I must see Mada," Fridgyth said.

She turned sharply on her heel and set off to go round to the back of the shed, where the weavers' huts stood.

Cwen and Gode stared after her.

"What's wrong?" Gode asked. "Have we done wrong?"

"I don't know," Cwen said, worried by the herb-wife's odd behaviour.

"Mada, Mada!" Fridgyth shouted as she strode towards the weavers' family huts.

Mada came out, red-eyed, her hair ruffled and unkempt. Fridgyth went carefully to take both Mada's hands in hers; the tough, leathery skin spoke of years in the weaving shed.

"I'm sorry Mada," she said gently.

Tears came again to Mada's eyes, but she swallowed hard and managed to keep her dignity.

"She was so old. I knew she had to go soon. I have asked Ketel to come and take her away for burial."

"You are sure it was not the sickness then?"

Mada shook her head.

"She was just frail and worn and thin."

Fridgyth wondered how to discover what she needed to know, without provoking more grief.

"Was she eating?" she asked at last.

Mada shook her head.

"Not for days. Not until Sister Cloda kindly brought her a fine cream pudding laced with honey and marigold petals. She ate that, and I thought it might bring her appetite back, but perhaps it was too rich. She settled back to sleep and never woke again."

"May I see her?" Fridgyth asked, "Just for my own peace of mind?"

"Yes, of course," Mada said.

She took Fridgyth's arm and led her into her hut.

The herb-wife was touched to see how lovingly Mada had laid out her mother. The old woman had been washed and dressed in her best gown, her sparse hair combed, and a small posy of marigolds laid in her thin hands.

"Did you say the food that Cloda brought was laced with marigold petals?" Fridgyth asked.

Mada looked surprised.

"Yes it was, it looked lovely, fit for a queen."

Fridgyth stooped over the frail corpse and then she caught it: a faint scent of garlic that seemed to hang over the body. Her heart began to race as she recognised the familiar odour and remembered that Cloda headed towards another needy family. She turned to Mada.

"Forgive me, honey," she cried. "I must see to something – it's terribly important!"

She hurried away out of the hut, and Mada stared after her in astonishment.

The sun was low in the sky and the light faded fast. Fridgyth broke into a run; her tools clinked on her belt and her breath came in sharp gasps. There was no sign of Cloda anywhere. Without even the common courtesy of calling out a name, she marched into Ranulf's family hut. The lay brother looked up from the hearth that he tended with surprise, as did Hilary, his wife, who was kneeling beside a straw pallet where their youngest son lay. The anxious mother held a spoon in her hand, ready to feed her child from a fine earthenware bowl.

"Stop! Don't touch that food!" Fridgyth shouted.

They stared at her, shocked. Fridgyth went, at once, to Hilary and snatched the bowl from her, relieved to see that it was still full.

"Have you given him any?" she demanded.

Hilary shook her head, her mouth agape.

Fridgyth carried the bowl straight through the hut and out to the back, where she scraped the contents onto the midden heap. Hilary and Ranulf followed her slowly, looking stunned.

At last Ranulf managed to speak.

"That was good food," he said.

"I think not," Fridgyth snapped. Then she realised how rude her behaviour must seem to them. "Forgive me," she begged. "I can't explain, not yet, but promise me that you will eat no more of the food that Sister Cloda gives away; I think there's something wrong with it."

"Something wrong?" Ranulf murmured.

"Do you promise me?"

They were puzzled and distressed at her brusque request, but Hilary managed an answer.

"You are our respected herb-wife," she said, her voice flat with disapproval. "If you say so, then we'll eat no more of Sister Cloda's food."

Fridgyth glanced down at the child, who was restless and coughing but had no plague-swellings that she could see.

"Take this bowl back to the kitchens, then go to my garden and pick fresh leeks and thyme," she said. "Make him broth and add fresh goat's milk. Please trust me in this."

With no time to explain further, she stepped out into the gathering darkness. Her head spun. What was to be done now? Something was terribly wrong, but she couldn't see clearly what it was. All she knew was that four people had died, five including Cenwulf, all of them smelling of garlic. She knew it hadn't been the plague .

The only thing that linked these last four deaths seemed to be Sister Cloda and her acts of charity. She felt that urgent action must be taken to prevent more deaths, but what should that action be? Who should she speak to about it? She could speak to Hild, but dreaded to trouble her further.

A small group of weavers clustered outside the weaving shed. Despite the fact that Cwen had called them back inside, they stood there still gossiping. As Fridgyth walked back towards the infirmary, she caught snatches of their words.

"Something's wrong with Frankish Cloda's food?"

"But we've all been eating it."

"The girls ate it, didn't they?"

"Aye they did – but then they died!"

"Go back to your work," Fridgyth told them sharply.

They moved slowly back to the weaving shed, more resentful than ever.

"And who is she to give us orders?"

"Freya's work she did… not fit for a Christian place."

Fridgyth turned on them, hands on hips.

"I shall remember that, Joan Webster, when you are sick and come to me!"

The speaker paled a little and vanished inside the weaving shed.

Fridgyth walked on and saw that Della had closed the infirmary shutters for the evening; she felt truly grateful that her assistant, young though she was, showed such good sense. She strode up the steps and went inside, relieved to find that Ketel was there with his daughter.

"I'm sorry to leave you so long," she said. "But I've have been trying to discover what made those girls so sick and… I think it might have been something wrong with their food. I'm even beginning to question what happened to Brother Cenwulf."

Della yawned.

"Father's here to help me," she said sleepily. "We've managed fine. Something to do with food, you say – you don't mean that those girls were poisoned?"

The word shook Fridgyth; her thoughts had tended that way, though she'd never used the word, even to herself.

"Not deliberately," she said, hurriedly. "People can be poisoned accidentally if the food is somehow contaminated." That must surely be the explanation, for nobody here in Streonshalh would poison food on purpose.

Ketel looked up.

"Sister Mildred would have something to say about that suggestion, I think."

Fridgyth nodded. Ketel was right – Mildred would not take kindly to the idea that her food was tainted.

"Mildred's a fine foodwife," she said. "But with so many to feed and hot weather like we've had, it's easy for milk to turn sour, or grain to moulder in the keeping…"

They both stared at her in concern as her words faded lamely, for they knew that stale milk didn't bring about death and though mouldering grain might bring disease, it was nothing like this sickness.

Della shook her head.

"Nobody would poison those orphaned lasses," she said. "But as for Brother Cenwulf…?"

She left the question unfinished. Fridgyth couldn't deny that there were those who'd have been glad to be rid of Cenwulf, but surely they wouldn't poison him.

"You're both weary," Ketel said, sensibly. "Thoughts grow wild when you're weary. Go back to your hut and rest, both of you. I'll keep watch here tonight. It may all seem clearer in the morning."

Fridgyth nodded gratefully, and she and Della set off together across the courtyard. As they came out from the infirmary, they saw the little gang of gossips shrink back inside the doorway of the weaving shed.

Fridgyth was so tired that she soon fell into an exhausted sleep, but her dreams were full of strange unconnected images: earthenware bowls, the gossips in the courtyard, a posy of marigolds in a dead woman's hands, Brother Cenwulf's cell door swinging open again and again and Brother Dunstan tumbling down the scriptorium stairs.

She was relieved when morning came.

"You sleep a bit longer," she told Della.

She set off as usual towards the infirmary to relieve Ketel but, before she got there, Ranulf's eldest son came rushing across the courtyard to her.

"Mam begs you to come to our hut," he cried.

"Someone taken sick?" she assumed.

He shook his head.

"No, but Mam says you must come, for it might be important."

Fridgyth allowed herself to be escorted to the family huts once more. Hilary looked out for them and waved the herb-wife inside. Then she grabbed her by the arm and dragged her straight through the hut, past the hearth and out to the back.

"Look! look!" she cried.

Fridgyth was flustered and, at first, couldn't see what it was she was meant to look at, for all there was out at the back was the midden heap. Then she began to understand – the heap was covered with dark furry bodies. Rats had feasted on the porridge that she'd scraped from the bowl and died at once; they lay on their backs stone dead – no time to creep away and hide.

Hilary was distraught.

"How right you were to throw the food away," she cried. "We thought you'd gone mad, but you saved our lives. What was wrong with it? Was it poisoned? It must have been poisoned."

That word again – the word that Fridgyth dreaded. She wished she'd been more discreet and carried the food away with her. She should have examined it carefully.

"Please keep this quiet for a while," she begged, "I'm trying to find out what was wrong with the food, but if wild rumours fly around it won't help at all."

Hilary hesitated for a moment, but then nodded her head.

"You saved our lives," she said. "Come back inside. We'll do as you ask, but I warn you – others already know that something is very wrong."

"At least your boy is well," Fridgyth said, as the child rolled over in his bed and pulled the blanket over his head to hide.

CHAPTER 19

HONOUR PRICE

Fridgyth arrived at the infirmary to find that Della had relieved her father from his long night's watch.

"You are still worrying about tainted food?" the girl said when she saw the herb-wife's face.

"Yes," Fridgyth admitted.

"Well, if the food came from the royal guest house and was given away," Della said sensibly. "Surely that must mean that it was intended for someone who lives there."

Fridgyth suddenly saw what stared her in the face – Fina's son! Surely he must have been the intended victim. Then again, if someone intended to poison Aldfrith, why was he not ill? Who else in the royal guest house might be a target? Not Cloda – who could want the old woman dead? And surely not Samson? But Samson *was* sick!

Fridgyth's mouth dropped open. "I've been so stupid!" she cried. "You've made me see what I was missing. Samson hasn't got the plague at all! He's being poisoned!"

Fridgyth looked out from the infirmary doorway across the courtyard towards the royal guest house. It was a smaller building than the one in which she stood, but more elaborate and detailed in the craftsmanship that adorned it. The high wooden pediment was carved with all manner of fish and fowl where were painted gold and dark red. The valuable fittings inside had been brought from far and wide – rich wall hangings and carved wooden seats – all ornamented with gold leaf. There were wooden bedsteads with fancy iron fittings, all of them heaped with soft down mattresses, and fine patterned coloured glass had been fitted into the window frames.

Fridgyth frowned; it was hard to believe that such a beautiful building could somehow be at the centre of this troubling mystery, but there was no denying it. Cloda set out each day to give away food and those she gave it to died.

As she watched, Fridgyth saw Gunda come from the kitchens. The girl carried a tray and headed for the royal hostelry. Before she'd climbed up the few steps that led to the entrance, the door opened, and Brother Argila appeared to take the tray from her.

"Can you manage again without me for a while?" Fridgyth asked.

"Yes," Della agreed at once.

"I know I leave you with far too much to do for one so young, but I feel that I must discover what could be the cause of this trouble here."

Della smiled and shrugged.

"We have only a few patients left now. I have my helpers and father to call on if I need him – you go, I can manage."

Fridgyth went.

She hurried across the courtyard and caught Gunda just as the girl was about to go back into the kitchens.

"I'm sorry to stop you, honey," she called. "But there's something I need to know. Who is it that prepared the food that you just gave to Brother Argila?"

"Sister Mildred," Gunda flushed slightly as she told her. "The foodwife takes charge of all the royal visitors' meals. Have I done wrong? You look so... worried."

"No, no, honey," Fridgyth said, and she patted the girl's cheek. "See how fine you look in those clothes... no wonder Mildred made you server to our royal guests! Did the abbess speak to you about the school?"

Gunda hesitated for a moment, but then nodded.

"Sister Mildred cannot spare me at the moment," she said.

"I can see why," Fridgyth said. "You'd best go back to her now."

As the girl went into the kitchens, the herb-wife turned and marched towards the royal guest house with determination.

"Cloda! Cloda!" she bellowed, as she banged urgently upon the heavy door. "I must speak to you."

A lay sister opened it, distain written on her face.

"We haven't sent for *you* herb-wife," she said. "Sister Cloda nurses the sick man here. She and the princess," she added with a censorious sniff. "Well... up until now."

"I must see Cloda," Fridgyth insisted.

There came other sounds of soft footfalls from inside and Aldfrith appeared behind the woman.

"Can I help?" he asked.

Fridgyth sighed with relief. Why had she not thought to ask for him in the first place? He was the one most likely to listen properly to her and answer with sense.

"May I speak with you for a moment?" she asked.

"Please allow the herb-wife to come in," Aldfrith said, with his usual quiet courtesy. "We'd value her advice, now we've two of them sick."

The woman hurried away, leaving the door open, but Fridgyth hesitated on the doorstep.

"I must not bring the plague in here," she said.

Aldfrith looked bewildered.

"But we have it already."

"I think – maybe not," she said. "I should have realised it much sooner. Your friend Samson should have died quickly or recovered by now, if it were the plague. No. I'm convinced that there's something else, but – did you say there are two of them sick?"

Aldfrith sighed and scratched his head; he looked weary.

"Princess Mathild has taken to her bed, all chilled and nauseous. She's been nursing Samson with devotion, and I fear the sickness has spread to her."

Fridgyth's eyes widened as she tried to control a sense of rising panic.

"Tell me quickly," she said. "What is this sickness like?"

"They vomit and shiver. Their hands and feet stay ice-cold, however many blankets we use to cover them. And a smell – a faint smell of..."

"Garlic?" Fridgyth suggested."

He looked up surprised.

"Yes, that is it exactly – a smell of garlic."

"What have they eaten?" Fridgyth asked.

Aldfrith looked surprised.

"Only the food that is brought over from the kitchens," he said. "I understand that the foodwife prepares it with her own hands."

"And Mathild has been eating it too?"

"Yes, indeed. She's been trying to tempt Samson to eat by sharing his meal."

"Dear girl!" Fridgyth cried. "And now she's sick too, you say? This is not the plague, I'm sure of it – it's poisoning of some kind. Cloda gave the food away, and it brought death to those who received it." She clutched the young man's arm. "And Argila has just taken a tray inside!"

Aldfrith stared at her in horror for a moment.

"Wait here!" he said and he rushed back inside, leaving her to stand alone on the steps.

He was back very soon and apologised for his discourtesy.

"Argila is warned," he said. "And Cloda too, I should have realised what was happening myself."

"No, no," Fridgyth insisted. "How could you have guessed such a thing? What food have *you* eaten?"

Fina's son looked uncomfortable. "I... I have been fasting," he admitted. "Only bread and water has passed my lips. Sister Cloda is the same. We dedicate our fast to God and pray mercy for our friends. Cloda takes much of the food away untouched to give to needy folk, but now you say you think it has been poisoned!"

"But none of this is your fault," she told him quickly. "May I ask what Brother Argila has been eating?"

Aldfrith looked reluctant to speak again, but the importance of the question was clear to him.

"Argila eats special meat dishes sent from the kitchens," he said.

Fridgyth frowned. He was indeed a strange monk if he was served meat while those around him fasted.

"So only Mathild and Samson have supped porridge?"

He nodded, pressing a tightened fist to his chest in an agony of self-blame.

"Who else has been struck down?" he asked.

"Three young girls are dead, but you cannot blame yourself. I too should have realised sooner that Samson's sickness was somehow different from the pestilence. I didn't look carefully enough when it all began."

"Argila too believed Samson to have the plague, though I believe he seems less certain lately."

"Does he indeed?" she replied.

In fairness to him, she had to admit that if Argila had ever wished to kill either young nobleman, he'd had every chance to do it. She dropped her voice.

"I fear that your enemies may have discovered that the quiet scholar is Fina's son."

"You mean my brother's supporters?"

"Yes, I do."

"You think my friend is poisoned in mistake for me?"

She nodded, and her face betrayed intense concern.

"No," he said firmly. "I think not, but you must speak to the abbess," he said. "If poison is suspected she must know about it. We have feared some such thing... though we never thought it would be poison."

Fridgyth looked hard at him.

"What did you fear?"

He shrugged and continued with some reluctance.

"An attack maybe... an ambush, or something that might appear to be an accident," he touched his shoulder. "You treated a wound, and we asked you not to upset the abbess by speaking of it."

Fridgyth's eyes narrowed.

"I knew it was no accident."

He nodded.

"Someone stretched a rope across our path, out on the way that leads to the heather moors. They'd chosen the spot carefully, for we'd left the monastery far behind us. It was where the gorse grows thick and the trees begin. Samson was flung violently over his mount's head when the poor beast bucked with shock and pain. As I leapt down to help him, a spear flew out and caught me – it came from a patch of holly bushes close by."

"Did you see who attacked you?"

He shook his head.

"Oh we saw him, but he was hooded like a Streonshalh monk, a dark cloth tied across his nose and mouth for disguise."

She could no longer hold her suspicions back.

"But Argila was out riding that day," she said. "Can you truly trust Argila? I suspect he's no monk at all. Could he have been behind this attack?"

Aldfrith shook his head.

"No, no. Argila rode to our rescue, sword at the ready. He fought off our attacker and took a spear wound in the thigh."

Fridgyth was aghast. So that is why he struggled to walk and claimed to suffer from the ague.

"I'm sorry we couldn't confide in you then."

Aldfrith looked shaken and distraught, but Fridgyth waved his apology away.

"Hooded, like a Streonshalh monk," she murmured. "Was he mounted then, to get away so fast?"

"When Argila attacked, he ran into the thicket. My friends were concerned over my hurt and, before they could rally, we heard the sound of flying hooves."

"So he escaped on horseback, though he fought on foot and with a spear?"

"A hunting spear," he said.

Anyone could help themselves to hunting spears at Streonshalh, Coen's gang kept a good supply and handed them out whenever they were required.

"We swore we'd take better care," Aldfrith said. "And we did, but then when Dunstan fell down the scriptorium stairs, we wondered if it was the accident it seemed."

Fridgyth was alert at once.

"He wore your cloak!"

"He did. And now you tell me poisoning is suspected! I regret our reticence in speaking out. You *must* tell the abbess at once."

"Yes, indeed," Fridgyth agreed. "I'll go to her straight away, and you must make quite sure that neither Samson nor Mathild takes another mouthful of that porridge. Give them a little bread and water, and please tell nobody outside this house what we suspect."

"I will see to it," he promised.

Fridgyth left him and set off towards the abbess's house. She didn't much relish telling Hild what had been going on. She crossed the courtyard deep in thought and, as she arrived, was rather taken by surprise when the Frankish goldsmith Fredemund, came quietly out through the abbess's doorway. He too looked a little startled to see the herb-wife, but hurried away towards the main gates. Fridgyth went to tap on one of the wooden shutters close to where she knew Hild was likely to be sitting. The signal was recognised at once and the shutter pushed open by the abbess.

"Come out to me!" Fridgyth ordered urgently. "It is most important that we speak."

Her voice was harsh with anxiety.

"No, you come inside to me," Hild replied. "Elfled and Wulfrun are having lessons with Eadfrith in the princess's chamber and you don't need to go anywhere near them."

Fridgyth nodded and headed for the door.

Once inside, she came straight to the point, before she'd even sat down.

"We don't *just* have the plague to deal with," she gasped. "I'm convinced that Samson and Mathild are being poisoned."

Hild turned pale and stared, aghast.

"I'm sorry to trouble you so," Fridgyth rushed on. "But I cannot keep this from you."

"No indeed," Hild replied at last. "You cannot. Come and sit down, you'd better tell me everything. Are Samson and Mathild safe for now, do you think?"

"Yes. Aldfrith will see to that, and he assures me that Argila can be trusted."

Hild smiled grimly.

"Yes, we can certainly trust Argila, and it's time you knew why.

But first you must tell me what this is all about!"

Fridgyth sat down and sighed deeply, relieved to share her suspicions. She related all that had happened and Hild cut in now and then to make certain she understood clearly. Fridgyth finally finished with the terrible conclusion that had come to her when she heard of Aldfrith and Cloda's fasting.

"And they're not the only ones who fast," Hild acknowledged.

"What! You are fasting, too? At times like this I'd say we need to eat – but it must be good, safe food," Fridgyth added humbly. "I'm left to wonder if poor Cenwulf might have been a victim of this poisoner too. The food he ate and the wine he drank may have been somehow intended for Fina's son"

Hild looked up at her, shocked.

"Do you think Elfled could have let it slip that Fina's son is here?" she asked. "Or might Ecfrid's supporters have set a poisoner to work? I shudder to think of it, but if Alchfrid of Deira wanted to get rid of his half-brother, he wouldn't be the first of his kin to do such a thing."

"No, indeed," Hild said quietly. "I was a babe in the womb, when my father was poisoned at the court of Cerdic, King of Elmet. My family took refuge there after Edwin had been driven into exile."

Fridgyth closed her eyes; she remembered with horror that the abbess had more reason than any to fear poison.

"Did you ever discover who was responsible?" she asked softly.

Hild shook her head.

"That is the treacherous nature of such evil. We never knew; the poisoner is usually paid well to do the awful work for another."

"Terrible... Terrible!" Fridgyth murmured.

They sat in tense silence for a moment, until Fridgyth felt she must press on with the matter in hand.

"I believe those two lasses from the weaving shed were poisoned by mistake. They ate the food intended for our royal guests. I know they have no kin to claim their honour price in compensation for their deaths, but..."

"Nobody to claim their honour price, you say?" Hild cut in angrily, her face quite white. "I welcomed those girls to Streonshalh! I brought them to live here under my guardianship! They had as much right to safekeeping as anyone. I… shall claim their honour price. If the guilty person is discovered, they shall be made to pay recompense to this monastery, as if it was my own children that had been murdered. I am a royal princess, my honour price is high!

CHAPTER 20

THE YOUNG BEE

The two women sat together in stunned silence for a moment. As Hild's anger and shock subsided a little she leaned forward and touched Fridgyth's arm.

"Forgive me," she said, more calmly. "You're the last one I should shout at! Please go on."

Fridgyth went on reluctantly.

"Well… I fear that Mada's old mother is another victim of this poisoner," she said. "Cloda meant nothing but good, but she gave away food intended for Fina's son. Samson had some of it, and Mathild too."

Hild looked up surprised.

"Intended for Aldfrith, you say?"

"Yes – do you not see? This poison is intended for Fina's son! That surely must be true."

Hild shook her head; she smiled bitterly now.

"Dear Fridgyth, you have seen what we've all missed and come close to uncovering a horror in our midst, but I doubt very much that Aldfrith is the intended victim of this wickedness."

Fridgyth was shocked, but not convinced.

Hild went on.

"I see I should have told you sooner, but it seemed safer that as few as possible knew. This must be for your ears only."

Fridgyth nodded, puzzled.

"In truth," said Hild. "By right we ought to bow to our friend

Samson and call him Dagobert – he should be King of Austrasia."

Fridgyth's mouth dropped open, and she stared in complete amazement.

"Austrasia…?" she gulped. "That is one of the Frankish kingdoms, is it not? But I thought the true heir to Austrasia died long ago? I recall something about a child… who died in a monastery?"

"Your memory serves you well," Hild nodded. "That *was* the story voiced abroad but, fortunately and thanks to those who supported him, the child didn't die. His existence was kept secret, and the concealment gave him some protection whilst he grew up in Ireland, far from the kingdom that should be his."

"You are saying that our Samson is Dagobert, heir to this Frankish kingdom?"

Hild nodded.

"Dagobert was five when his father died. Grimoald the palace mayor had him tonsured and sent off to a monastery for his education, then later he even told the mother that her son was dead. The Queen was pressed to adopt Grimoald's son Childebert as heir to the kingdom."

Fridgyth was almost lost for words.

"But he… that lost child… is Samson! Who turned up late for the Synod and slept in my infirmary!"

Hild nodded.

"Dagobert's nurse persuaded the Bishop of Poitiers to save her little one."

"His nurse?" And suddenly Fridgyth understood why Cloda always spoke of him as her little one. "His nurse was – is – Cloda."

Fridgyth was agog at what she heard.

"Indeed. Cloda took her nurseling over land and sea in disguise to Slane Monastery. The prince received an excellent education there and, when he grew too old for a nurse, Cloda came to join my nuns. There's more to our Cloda than anyone would guess!"

"So… Dagobert came to Streonshalh to find his old nurse. That explains a great deal that has puzzled me. The boy isn't Irish at all!"

"No indeed," Hild shook her head. "All might have been well, but Austrasia has a new palace mayor – Ebroin; he was once a supporter of Dagobert's father, so knew that the child survived. He is now as ruthless as his predecessor and ambitious for power. He sent spies and assassins abroad to discover Dagobert's whereabouts and kill him. The prince was warned by one of his father's most faithful friends and had time to flee from Slane and come to Streonshalh. That old friend of his father is Argila."

Fridgyth gasped.

"I knew the man was no monk," she said. "And it *was* him that I saw arrive in so strange a manner, in a boat down by the rocks."

Hild nodded.

"I'm so sorry that you felt threatened by his presence. Argila's only interest is to see Dagobert back in Austrasia and on his father's throne."

Fridgyth struggled to take it all in.

"And I kept asking myself why Aldfrith came to Deira, when he'd have been much better off in Ireland with his mother's kin. He risks himself, in order to seek safety for his friend. Is Elfled really Dagobert's cousin?"

"Oh yes," said Hild. "Distant cousins; both descended from the ancient line of Merovingians on her mother's side. When I took the boy to Eanfleda, she offered him Northumbria's protection. As a young girl she had been sheltered for a time by Dagobert's grandfather – when her mother and brother fled Deira after Edwin was slain – so it was the least she could do.

It was the least she could do, for as a young girl she was sheltered by Dagobert's grandfather for a time?"

Fridgyth was stunned.

"Elfled's ring… the bee?"

"Yes – a golden bee is the symbol of the Merovingian."

"The young bee… Samson is the young bee; he is Dagobert?"

Hild nodded.

"Now you will understand what a responsibility it has been to have these two young princes here."

"Oh yes," Fridgyth could see.

"I didn't mention to the Queen that Dagobert arrived at Streonshalh in the company of Fina's son. Oswy knows of course…

but now," Hild said, and she frowned in concentration. "What must we do?"

Fridgyth's worst fears were not only confirmed but heightened.

"An assassin lives amongst us," she said. "We must uncover him fast."

She waited in silence then; only Hild could decide what to do and Fridgyth didn't envy her.

"I will not tolerate a poisoner within my monastery!" the abbess said at last, and she spoke through gritted teeth. "But it will be easy for an atmosphere of suspicion to grow amongst us, for neighbour to take against neighbour, while the poisoner watches quietly and revels in the mistrust they bring to us. We must *not* panic. I'll go to the royal guest house first."

Just then a din started in the courtyard, and the two women crossed to the window. Hild looked through the open shutter to see Cloda pulled roughly about, by a gang of shrieking weavers.

"I always said she was a sorceress! Stone her!"

"She and her dreams bring evil here."

"Poisoner!" another cried. "She poisoned the food, and she poisoned the sun!"

All the time they picked up stones and clods of earth to pelt her.

"Those lasses died because of you!"

Cloda staggered and fell, as the first stone caught the back of her head.

"Your wickedness has brought the plague to our door!"

Hild threw wide the shutter and leaned out.

"Stop!" her voice rang out. "Stop at once!"

They stared at her, and the abbess hurried from her chamber and strode out into the courtyard. The women had let go of her, but Cloda couldn't get up. Her habit was torn, and blood ran down her neck.

Hild reached Cloda and helped her to her feet. She hugged her protectively, but then she turned an accusing look on Fridgyth.

"How do they know?" she asked.

Fridgyth stood white-faced, appalled at what she seemed to have started.

"I questioned Cwen and I stopped Ranulf feeding the food to his child," she admitted defensively. "I had to – and these women saw me."

Hild turned on the women.

"Yes, we fear poison!" she admitted, speaking through gritted teeth. "But it has nought to do with Sister Cloda. The source of this vile wickedness will be discovered *only* if we can keep silence on the matter. Go to your huts and remain inside until I say you may leave. If you venture out or speak of this to a soul, you'll be punished so that you'll wish you'd never been born."

The effect of her quiet fury was powerful. Stones were dropped, heads drooped in shame and they turned and hurried to their homes at once.

"Cloda, you will come to my house," Hild said.

"But my boy… he…" Cloda tried to speak, but trembled so much that her words slipped away.

"Your boy will be safe with Aldfrith and Argila," the abbess cut in. "Though *you* it seems, are not. Come back with me."

Cloda hobbled towards the abbess's house, supported by Hild. Fridgyth hovered behind them.

"Fridgyth – meddle no more," Hild ordered sharply, as she looked back over her shoulder. "I shall see to this."

"But…" Fridgyth's mouth had gone dry.

"Go back to the sick," Hild said curtly.

They disappeared inside the abbess's house and closed the door behind them. Fridgyth was left alone, feeling desolate and angry.

Why had she not been more discreet? Why had she not seen that suspicion would turn to Cloda? She heaved a great sigh and went back to the infirmary as she'd been bidden.

There were no new plague victims, and that was some relief, but her mind whirled with astonishment after what Hild had told her.

She found it impossible to sleep, and lay awake all night. Had they slipped into that dangerous state of affairs Hild had warned of? Did neighbour suspect neighbour, while the poisoner watched and gloated? She regretted that she'd allowed the women to jump to all the wrong conclusions, but she'd had to take action – what else could she have done? Hild must surely see that.

She rose and dressed the next morning in such a state of jangling disquiet that Della asked if she was sick.

"No, no," she answered quickly. "There's much on my mind, honey, but nothing for you to worry about."

Much on my mind, indeed, she thought as she plodded over to the infirmary. How to discover a poisoner who plied his trade in a well-organised monastery was just the first and most urgent problem.

'Meddle no more,' Hild had said.

Fridgyth froze when she saw Gunda carry the tray across the courtyard. Just as before, Brother Argila came down the steps to take it from her. Hild had given orders for nothing to be said and nothing to be changed, but surely somebody should go into the kitchens and ask questions. Who better than the herb-wife?

Fridgyth saw that Brother Bosa and Coen were called to the abbess's house. Hild had taken some action she supposed, but she set little store by the investigative skills of either man. Bosa was a highly educated, self-effacing holy-man, while Coen was a boorish bully. If only the reeve still lived, he'd have taken charge and supported the abbess with his sharp mind and strong sense of justice. Hild must feel his loss bitterly.

'Meddle no more' – Hild's words rang in Fridgyth's head, but her feet carried her into the kitchen. Nobody was surprised to see her there. Confusion was everywhere: vegetables were chopped; bread was kneaded, punched and slapped onto wooden boards; workers toiled to clean pots with sand that they scrunched in their raw hands; and utensils were rinsed and dried, at speed, under the foodwife's loud direction.

"Marigold petals," Fridgyth murmured to herself as she wandered over to the larder. This was where Mildred kept herbs in earthenware jars on the shelves. The herb-wife began to examine the contents of the pots, but there were so many that she was unable to find what she was looking for.

"And what might mistress herb-wife be doing in here?" a loud voice behind her made her jump.

Sister Mildred had come quietly to the larder and stood there, hands on hips. She looked severe, but there was a touch of amusement in her voice.

"Well, mistress foodwife," Fridgyth answered chirpily. "I've come for bread and porridge. I've patients still recovering, and they need plenty of good sustenance. I wonder if you've dried marigold petals to spare. I seem to have run out of them, and I want to pound a pot of balm."

"Just help yourself mistress herb-wife, don't ask first!" Mildred snapped.

"I will then," Fridgyth replied boldly. She'd always found that the best way to deal with Mildred was to reply in kind. She continued to look around, as she sniffed into pots. "But you don't seem to have any," she said.

Mildred pushed past her and, as she moved along the shelf, she lightly touched each pot.

"Rosemary, thyme, pepperwort, fennel, chervil, plantain, garlic... but no marigold petals it seems."

The big woman scratched her head and frowned for a moment; then she seemed to lose patience.

"I haven't time to waste on frippery," she said. "I thought I had marigold, but it seems I haven't. We can manage well enough without. Haven't you plenty of marigolds growing by your hut?"

Fridgyth nodded; there were indeed thick clumps of marigolds all around her hut, but she made one last attempt to discover what she wanted to know.

"I hear you make porridge for the sick young scholar who lodges in the royal guest house, all prettified with marigold petals."

"Huh!" Mildred frowned, folding her arms defensively. "I do not. As I said, there's no time for frippery, even for royal visitors, not while I have workers dropping of the plague around me."

Fridgyth was bewildered, but tried not to show it.

"So – you've never sprinkled marigold petals onto the porridge for the royal guest house?"

Mildred shook her head.

"Certainly not," she said. "Now – the bread and porridge for the infirmary is ready on the trestle as usual, and it will go cold if you don't take it."

Fridgyth looked where she was bidden and saw the food waiting for her recovering patients. Could Mildred possibly be lying about such a trivial and harmless thing as marigold petals? The delicate petals could do nobody any harm – they were simply used to add colour. Something was wrong here. Fridgyth had seen golden petals there on the porridge on Cloda's tray – seen them with her own eyes.

"I thank you," she said politely and went to pick up the tray.

"Shall I carry it for you?" Gunda came up behind her and offered.

"Thank you, honey," Fridgyth said.

As they walked across the courtyard together, Fridgyth tried a different tack.

"Was it you who put those pretty marigold petals on the porridge for the royal guests, honey?"

The girl hesitated and flushed a little.

"No time for marigold petals now," she said, "so much to do – so many sick."

"Ah… you don't have to tell *me* that," Fridgyth said, reaching out to take the tray. "Now, don't you come inside the sick-house, honey… you go back to Mildred."

She hoped her questioning of the girl would not get back to the fierce-spoken foodwife.

Fridgyth's mind was now in more of a muddle than ever. Mildred had always seemed honest, forthright even… yet who'd be better placed to slip poison into food? She recalled that Sister Redburgh had even joked about it. Could those jokes cover serious intent? The use of poison in the midst of the plague was clever, and the foodwife was no fool. But Mildred was Deiran through and through in her support for Edwin's line, so why should she wish to poison Dagobert? Perhaps Hild should not yet rule out the possibility of Fina's son being the intended victim. At least Aldfrith had been warned and would now be wary of everything he and his friends ate.

Once she'd distributed the food to her patients, Fridgyth slipped out again. She hesitated in the middle of the courtyard for a moment when she saw Hild leave her house and head off towards the church.

The abbess must have seen her standing there, but she neglected to give her usual friendly wave; Fridgyth was hurt. If she could find a way to reveal who the poisoner was, surely instant forgiveness from the abbess would follow – even though she'd been told not to meddle.

As Hild vanished behind the preaching cross, Fredemund the goldsmith stepped out from the shadows of the stable thatch and set out to cross the courtyard. He looked as though he headed for the abbess's house again, but when he saw Fridgyth he bowed politely, changed direction, and went off towards the main gate instead.

Fridgyth went quickly to knock at the abbess's door. A wooden shutter creaked open, and two tousled heads looked out. Elfled and Wulfrun called out a joyous welcome.

"Oh Fridgyth, Fridgyth come in and see us," Elfled called. "I am so miserable indoors all the time and Mother Hild allows me to do nothing but study. We have to write a whole psalm before Eadfrith comes to look at our work and now that Mathild has disgraced herself…"

"Your safety and well-being is Mother Hild's first concern," Fridgyth cut in sharply. "And I wonder if that handsome young Frankish goldsmith comes to relieve your boredom sometimes," she added, with a quick glance back towards the main gate.

The two girls exchanged a guilty glance, but said nothing.

"I seem to remember you admired him, Wulfrun," the herb-wife felt she had no time for delicacy.

"Wulfrun does nothing dishonourable – she is not like Mathild," Elfled spoke up for her companion.

Fridgyth had more pressing and urgent needs.

"I want to see Cloda," she said. "It's really important."

"I don't think Cloda will want to see *you*!" Elfled returned sulkily.

But Wulfrun gave the princess a sharp glance.

"Perhaps… if no more were to be said about the goldsmith, we might get Cloda to speak to you," she said.

"Yes… that would be fair," Elfled agreed.

"Fair is fair," Fridgyth allowed with a sigh.

CHAPTER 21

IN THE SCRIPTORIUM

At last, the door opened a short way, and Cloda looked nervously out.

"Dear Sister Cloda," Fridgyth began; for she now felt huge respect for Dagobert's old nurse. "I cannot say how deeply sorry I am that I caused trouble for you."

"And deeply sorry you should be," Cloda replied sharply. "I could call you before the abbess for judgement over this. Your careless words have brought dishonour to my name. I could demand compensation from you! I'd have every right to call the abbess herself to stand as a witness for me."

"Indeed you would," Fridgyth admitted apologetically. "Sister, please forgive me. Your boy... the prince, he owes his life to you... I know that now. Your honour and courage are above question, absolutely above question."

"You have no idea," Cloda said, mollified a little. "No idea what my poor boy suffered. He was five years old when I took the shears to his dark curls... I had to tonsure him myself, on the bishop's orders, in order to save his life. I shaved his little forehead – it was the only way I had to keep him safe. Samson, I renamed him. I promised him that, one day, his hair would grow again and that he too would grow in strength. I could have wept to do such a thing... but my tears would have made him more frightened still. Oh, you can have no idea what that feels like herb-wife."

Fridgyth stood for a moment in silence, ashamed and touched by the old woman's words, but then a sense of urgency came back to her.

"You are right dear Sister Cloda, I cannot imagine how terrible it must have been for you, but unless we discover who is behind this new threat to your prince, there may be more innocent deaths. I really need to know whether the porridge for the royal guest house had marigold petals sprinkled on it, or not? I ask because I trust your word completely and lives may depend on your answer."

Cloda's eyes brimmed with tears.

"Marigolds… marigolds… I see them in my sleep and in waking. Tainted food it was… and I have killed three girls… those screaming hags were right about that."

"No, no, it was *not* your fault in any way, Sister," Fridgyth said. "You acted purely in Christian charity, but I must know if marigold petals were sprinkled on the food and whether it came to you, from the kitchen, decorated like that."

There was a brief pause and then she answered.

"Sometimes there were marigold petals on the food, sometimes not," Cloda said at last.

"Thank you, Sister," Fridgyth said.

She was about to hurry away, but turned back.

"Did you say that you saw marigolds in your dreams?"

Cloda nodded wearily.

"I close my eyes at night and see marigolds falling all across the land and, as I watch, their glorious golden hues turn dark, and they begin to ooze with filth and maggots; it is a terrible dream."

Fridgyth pressed her lips together; Cloda's dreams had more than once proved to be prophetic.

"Dear brave Cloda," she said with a respectful bow, "I will do my best to search out this foul poisoner."

Trusting her helpers in the infirmary to take charge of the sick, she walked directly back to her hut and fished about amongst the baskets of dried herbs in search of her own store of marigold petals.

"I had them in a little bowl," she murmured. "I know I did."

She found that she couldn't lay her hands on them easily. Why should marigold petals be so significant? They added little taste to food, just a touch of bright colour. Why would someone go to the trouble of stealing hers? It was extraordinary: she'd have given them freely to anyone who'd asked. In any case, marigolds grew everywhere, free for the picking. Why not just pick them openly? Unless someone had a secret use for them and did not want to be found out.

After more frantic and fruitless searching, she stopped for a moment as her eye caught the fine detailed painting of marigolds that Della had brought back from the scriptorium. Guy had done it especially for her, and Fridgyth had been so impressed by it that she'd hung it up like a rich man's wall-hanging. Sadly the colours of the painted marigold had faded now – but what had Della said about that? Something like – *'they keep fine pigments in the scriptorium, colours that will never fade, precious dyes that we must not touch for they are dangerous!'*

"Dangerous," Fridgyth said the word out loud, and her heart suddenly thundered and set her mind to work at speed. How might pigments or dyes be dangerous? Could they be dangerous to handle, or to swallow?

She stood there for a moment, while her heart raced. What might this mean? What should she do? Then, suddenly, she knew where she should go next and quickly set off and puffed her way across the courtyard. She got past the church before the abbess emerged from her services, for she could still hear the sound of their chanting inside. Fridgyth hadn't been in that part of the monastery since the dark of the sun and the terrible discovery of Dunstan's body. Now, she climbed boldly up the outer wooden stairway that led to the scriptorium and slowed down a little to catch her breath as she neared the top. Despite her confidence as herb-wife and friend to the abbess, she'd never entered this important building before; there'd never been the need. The scriptorium was the hub of all the study and craftsmanship that produced precious religious books. It had been the haunt of Brother Cenwulf; now, at least, she wouldn't meet him there.

Those who worked inside were dedicated monks, nuns and scholars: often oblates or novices who'd been promised to the monastery at an early age. They trained over many years and toiled away in silence, excused from morning services, so as not to interrupt their delicate and important work during the hours of daylight. Beautiful manuscripts were created with illuminated lettering, the like of which she'd sometimes glimpsed in the abbess's house.

It took boldness to step through the doorway of this hallowed place, and Fridgyth found herself in a long, well-lit room full of quiet workers. Many faces looked up at her, and all of them betrayed surprise that they should see her there. Fridgyth had a strong urge to turn and hurry away, but there were questions that needed answers; more and more she began to feel that the scriptorium workshop might hold vital information. She struggled to find her courage and reminded herself that, as herb-wife, she was party to all the scribe's most intimate secrets. There was Sister Ida, with her sore legs, that itched, and on the other side of the room was Brother Bardolf, with his windy stomach, alongside Brother Peter, who suffered from painful piles. She turned to the nearest nun; it was Sister Ermintrude.

"I *must* speak with Master Eadfrith," she said. "It's a matter of the greatest importance."

Ermintrude got up from her work at once. She frowned and tapped her mouth to show that she kept silence, and then beckoned Fridgyth to follow as she hobbled down the length of the scriptorium. They arrived at a small workshop that was separated from the main room by a door. Eadfrith was there, bent over a collection of small pots. A rough hempen apron, speckled with tiny dots of colour, covered his monastic robe. He looked up as they arrived, startled to see the herb-wife there.

"I'm sorry to disturb you," Fridgyth said at once. "But I must speak to you on a matter that is both urgent and of great concern."

Eadfrith nodded and pulled forward a stool, indicating that she should sit down. Sister Ermintrude made a small huffing sound, pushed the door shut behind her and went back to her work.

"Are you keeping silence again?" Fridgyth asked.

Eadfrith smiled.

"Well, yes," he said. "I was… but if it's as urgent, as you say, then I shall break my silence. We must keep our voices low, so as not to disturb the scribes."

"Yes, we *must* keep our voices low," she agreed. "Believe me I would not intrude like this, unless it was necessary and I have no wish to be overheard."

Eadfrith pulled up another stool and gave her his full attention.

"How can I help?"

"It's something that Della once said to me," she began. "She told me that there were certain pigments kept here that the younger scholars must never touch... that they might be somehow dangerous."

"Yes," he nodded. "Some colours must be handled with the greatest of care and others are so precious, that—"

"But it is the dangerous ones that I must know about," she cut in. "Please tell me, Eadfrith, what pigment would you use to emulate the colour of marigolds?"

"Well... onion skins, soaked and boiled with a little salt..." he began.

"No, no," she interrupted him. "That will fade – even I know that. Is there a stronger yellow colour that will truly last, but perhaps may be dangerous to handle?"

In answer, Eadfrith got up and went over to a heavy wooden workbench that was built into the wall. He lifted a small dish carefully with fine tongs and set it down between them; the dish contained a yellow powdery material that glittered a little.

"What's that?" Fridgyth asked.

"We call it orpiment," Eadfrith said.

"It isn't quite the colour of marigolds," she said, disappointed.

Eadfrith took a large scallop shell from a pile beside him and carefully spooned a small amount of the powder into it. Then he added a few drops of liquid from a jug, as Fridgyth fidgeted impatiently.

"Watch," Eadfrith said.

He took up a fine brush and gently stirred the dull powder in the scallop shell. He made sure that none was spilled, and kept his face well away. As Fridgyth watched, the contents of the dish began to take on a brighter hue.

"What is that?" she asked, indicating the fluid that came from the jug.

"Egg white," Eadfrith said. "That is harmless, of course."

As he stirred and stirred and added more egg white, the colour lifted and the pigment gained in strength. A miracle took place there in the shell as the powder lightened and brightened. At last, the scallop shell swam with liquid sunlight, a perfect match for the glorious hues of marigold blooms.

"Stop," Fridgyth said quietly.

Eadfrith paused and looked at her.

"Why will you not let the girls touch orpiment?" she whispered.

He carefully set the shell and brush aside, then scrupulously examined his own hands, gently brushing them down though they seemed clean already.

"It's poisonous," he said, his voice low and earnest. "A deadly poison; sometimes we call it King's Yellow."

Fridgyth quietly drew in her breath. Here was her answer, here in front of her in a sea-worn scallop shell. Had the harmless marigold petals been used simply to disguise the strong colour of a poisonous dye?

"Why King's Yellow?"

Eadfrith shrugged.

"Orpiment has brought many a king to his throne, or so they say; it's hard to prove. If given in a large dose, it brings about instant death. However, in small doses the victim appears only to sicken. When a king wastes away and dies and his younger brother or cousin steps boldly forward to take his place, they will whisper that… perhaps King's Yellow has been at work. The strong colour must be disguised, but the substance carries little taste… in strong red wine…"

The young oblate stopped and looked up at Fridgyth with horror.

"Ah no!" he gasped. "Brother Cenwulf… he drank red wine!"

Fridgyth nodded solemnly.

"And three young girls have eaten porridge sprinkled with marigold petals and died – an old woman too."

"No," Eadfrith said, now deeply distressed. "And a symptom of orpiment poisoning is the faint smell of garlic on the breath. How could I have neglected to think of that?"

Fridgyth shrugged.

"Poison was the last thing on our minds!"

"We were quick to judge! I should have thought of orpiment!"

"It is not your fault," she said firmly. It seemed to her that every decent soul tended to blame themselves as soon as they understood what was afoot. "The abbess and the reeve both agreed that Cenwulf died after a fit of gluttony."

"But, how is it possible that orpiment is getting into food or drink?" Eadfrith asked.

"There is only one explanation,' Fridgyth said with quiet certainty. "Someone is deliberately putting it there."

The young oblate looked u –, white faced and shocked.

"Samson… this is what is happening to Samson!"

"Not anymore," she told him quickly. "I have made sure of that!"

Fridgyth and Eadfrith stared at each other, silence all around them.

"What do you know of Samson?" she asked at last, her voice very low.

Eadfrith glanced down and hesitated.

"We became good friends before his illness struck. Both he and Aldfrith confided in me… enough for me to know that each of them might have enemies."

Fridgyth nodded.

"I'm afraid Samson and Mathild have both suffered poisoning from this pigment, but they live. Aldfrith has been fasting and escaped it. Please think hard about this now," she leant forwards. "Does Sister Mildred, the foodwife, ever come in here?"

He looked shocked.

"Mildred? No – never. You cannot suspect Mildred!"

"Good," she nodded. "I don't have Mildred down as a poisoner, but she makes it clear she'd like to see Prince Ecfrid on the throne of Deira, and maybe she'd want to get a rival out of the way."

Eadfrith frowned in thought. "No, no… it would make more sense to poison his elder brother Alchfrid, 'the stranger king', but Mildred would never poison anybody. She might openly challenge, but poison – no."

"You're right," Fridgyth agreed. "Mildred is too courageous to use poison. She'd lead a rebel army rather than do that, but somehow poison is getting into the food that is served in the royal guest house."

Suddenly Eadfrith glanced back at his scallop shell of marigold coloured pigment and got to his feet, distressed.

"I *am* to blame," he said.

"No," Fridgyth got up too, exasperated. "*You* haven't poisoned anybody."

Eadfrith shook his head.

"No, but… I'm making this new mixture because I couldn't find the older colour that I had already prepared. It's gone… gone! I should have asked why! Orpiment vanished, and I was ashamed to admit that I'd lost such an expensive pigment. It's brought here from Rome at great cost, and it is a difficult and delicate task to prepare it. I said nothing about the loss, just set out to prepare more."

"That *doesn't* make it your fault," Fridgyth insisted, forgetting to keep her voice low. "But we must think fast what to do. If not Mildred, who could have taken it? Who else knows how lethal the stuff is?"

Eadfrith shrugged and swung his arms wide.

"All the monks and nuns who act as scribes. Everyone who works in the scriptorium is warned of its nature."

"Then let us look at it another way. Which of the scribes goes to the kitchen for their food?" she asked.

"None of them," Eadfrith was sure of it. "Lay brothers and sisters bring our meals to us here, since the refectory closed."

"So lay brothers come," Fridgyth frowned. "And sisters too?"

In the quietness that followed, the door of Eadfrith's workshop gently swung to, making a light clack.

Eadfrith looked up.

"Was someone concealed there, to listen to us?" he whispered.

They both got up and went quietly out into the scriptorium. All heads were down, hard at work and still in silence.

Fridgyth walked to where Sister Ermintrude worked.

"Who came through here just now?"

Ermintrude glanced up; she frowned and tapped her prim lips again.

"You must tell me!" Fridgyth demanded, her voice echoing in the quiet room.

Every monk and nun in the scriptorium looked up in shocked disapproval.

"I saw nobody," Ermintrude said at last. "Now you've made me break my silence, and I'll have to make an act of contrition."

Eadfrith took off his spattered apron and hurried towards the outer door, his brow furrowed with worry. "I should go to the abbess's house to help the princess with her lessons now. I'll speak to the abbess of our concerns at once."

He ran down the steps and across the courtyard.

CHAPTER 22

KING'S YELLOW

Fridgyth followed fast behind Eadfrith; her stomach churned with anxiety, and her breath came in heavy gasps. The courtyard was busy with monks and nuns who flooded out from the church. They said nothing as they parted, an expression of utmost dread there on the young man's face.

Fridgyth went on towards the infirmary, uncertain what to do next. Hearing the patter of feet behind her, she turned to see Gunda, once again carrying a tray across to the royal guest house.

"Stop!" she cried.

Gunda froze, and Fridgyth hurried towards her. She saw, at once, that the food the girl carried was bland and colourless. "It's all right, honey," she said, touching the girl's arm gently. "I just needed to be sure there were no marigold petals. You may go on your way."

The girl went on, and Fridgyth set off for her hut, but then something about the sound of the girl's footsteps made Fridgyth look back at her. Gunda, was still holding the tray, but she had stopped to talk to Guy, who'd come out from the abbess's house to speak to her.

Fridgyth took two more steps and then stopped to glance back at them again. Guy must go from the scriptorium to the kitchen to see his sister… might he know something that would help? Suddenly the sight of them there together troubled her. Was it the tender way that Guy touched his sister's arm, or a fleeting sense that Gunda drooped against her brother's chest, in need of support?

Guy returned to the abbess's house and Gunda hurried on to the royal guest house. Fridgyth's thoughts chased wildly here and there. Seeing the two of them standing there so close made her wonder.

"Not one person... but two?" she murmured to herself. "But... not them, not them."

Instead of going to her hut, she wandered out into the upper pasture and sat near her bees to try to clear her head. Surely she was close to madness. She'd felt for poor Gunda, ordered to work in the kitchens despite being clearly capable of more. More recently she'd watched her with respect and noted the way the girl tried to please the foodwife – so much so that she'd become chief server to the royal guests. As for the talented Guy, who'd helped so willingly with Ketel's plan for the boat-makers' hall... she'd even encouraged Della to cast a glad eye towards him!

Two people... two of them... one from the scriptorium, the other from the kitchen.

Someone like Guy could get hold of the orpiment and someone like Gunda could put it in the porridge – and carry it to the royal guest house.

She sighed and shook her head, as a wave of sickness rose in her throat. Yes, Gunda had carried food to the royal guest house, but she couldn't be the only one who had. Who else linked the scriptorium to the kitchens? There must be others – but she couldn't think of them.

It wouldn't be difficult to add a little orpiment and disguise it with marigold petals. Gunda could have used Mildred's supply of dried petals and Guy might have taken more when he visited the herb-wife's hut. Could that have been what he was doing, when she found him there, waiting for Della, just before Samson was taken sick? Once a strong young man was made sick, he'd struggle to take another large dose of orpiment, but if he was steadily given small quantities, he'd continue to be sick and slowly die. Such a thing had been happening to Samson.

Hungry young girls, like weaver lasses, would eat greedily and die quickly, just as a fasting man, tempted by strong wine, might drink deeply. Oh, poor Cenwulf... had they misjudged him so cruelly? As for Mada's mother, just a small dose of orpiment might kill one so frail.

Fridgyth was shaken to the core. She'd rather Mildred had been the guilty one than these handsome, talented young people with brilliant futures ahead of them. But now that the idea was there, she couldn't banish it and other memories came back. Gunda and Guy, outside the kitchen, that first time she'd seen them. Cenwulf had sent the girl to drudgery, and she'd been furious to be treated so; Fridgyth had sympathised deeply with the flash of fury she'd seen on the pretty face.

She hated the thought of it, but couldn't deny that it fitted well. How could they possibly have thought they'd get away with such a thing? Were they to be discovered – which they surely would be eventually – how did they think they'd make their escape? But she found an answer to that too as, with a fast-beating heart, she looked down towards the boat-makers quay. There was the strong little fishing boat that Guy had learnt to handle with Ketel's help, tied up at the quay, all ready and waiting with oars and furled sail.

"The lad knows all the sea roads round here," Ketel had said.

She got to her feet, feeling sick and trembly. Where would she find evidence of their wrongdoing? She went back inside the stockade and headed to the infirmary. There were few patients there, but she had no time to worry about them.

She made straight for Ketel and snatched hold of his strong leather tunic.

"Trust me in this – trust me," she begged.

"Trust you in what?" he asked, shocked at the desperate expression on her face.

"Go down to the quayside," she said. "Take some of Caedmon's herders with you and guard your boat. Let nobody take it, or any other boat for that matter. Cut the moorings if you must – but let nobody leave by sea."

Ketel could do nothing but gawp.

"But – should I not take Guy with me?"

"No! Guy least of all! If ever our friendship meant anything to you, do this for me now," she begged. "I cannot explain, just trust me."

He nodded.

"I will."

"Bless you!"

He headed for the door, and Fridgyth felt weak with relief.

As she followed Ketel outside, she was vaguely aware of Della watching in astonishment. She wondered what to do next. As she passed the stables another memory came to her: that day last autumn when Aldfrith and Samson were attacked, Gunda and Guy had been out together, riding. She'd seen them return herself.

There must be evidence, to prove her suspicions. Wrongful accusation was a crime in itself and could bring severe punishment. She set off again, across the courtyard, to find where Gunda slept.

The novices' dormitory was almost empty except for a nervous young girl whose fresh woollen habit announced that she was newly arrived at the monastery.

"Which is Gunda's bed?" Fridgyth asked at once.

"Gunda?" the girl stared, puzzled.

"She's the pretty one who works in the kitchens, the one with the handsome brother. Tell me quickly!"

"That one – she sleeps there," the girl whispered, hurriedly, and she pointed to a mattress in the corner which was set up against the daub-plastered wall.

Fridgyth strode to the place and dropped down on her knees beside the small wooden chest that stood by the mattress. She ruthlessly flung open the lid and plunged her hands deep inside and rummaged amongst clothing, combs and cloaks. She fished about frantically, while the girl stood watching her, pale and shocked.

"There's good reason for this intrusion," she tried to explain.

But she couldn't find any sign of the evidence that she needed. She threw back the woollen bedspread and examined the straw mattress thoroughly, flinging the hempen cover aside. Then she felt a moment of relief – there was nothing to prove Gunda guilty.

Fridgyth sat down on the messy bedding, feeling terrible. How could she even have suspected such a thing? Was she loosing control, thrashing around so wildly searching for proof? 'We must move with stealth,' Hild had said. This wasn't stealth. Did she do poor downtrodden Gunda the most terrible wrong? Was she making things worse and worse by her erratic behaviour?

Then, as she got up, her heart gave an uncomfortable thud, for she saw that the straw-stuffed mattresses in the novices' dormitory did not lie on the floor – it was set on practical low wooden truckles that kept the bedding dry and free of vermin. Fridgyth had to get down again and put her cheek against the trodden earth of the floor to look underneath, and there, just as she feared, was a scallop shell and a small bowl. She blinked hard, but there they still were, just visible in the dark shadows. Reaching in, she pulled them out, one was her own shallow earthenware bowl half full of dried marigold petals; the other was a scallop shell, just like the one she'd seen Eadfrith use in the scriptorium. It contained a small amount of golden sludge.

The girl, who still stood behind her, gasped, as Fridgyth struggled to her feet, a container in each hand.

"She was here," the girl said. "I saw her, then she slipped away."

"Who – Gunda?"

"Yes."

"She saw me?"

"Yes – and she looked as though…"

"What?" Fridgyth demanded.

"As though she'd like to… kill you!"

"Freya's teeth!" Fridgyth swore. "What a mess! She saw me bring out these things?"

"Yes," the girl was firm about it.

Fridgyth stood in the novices' dormitory flushed and sweating as black dots danced in front of her eyes again. What a hotchpotch she'd made of it all. She'd have to face the abbess and admit it. The young novice watched her anxiously; this was not at all the sort of thing she'd expected when she came to Streonshalh to join the royal abbess.

"Go at once to fetch Hild," Fridgyth ordered.

"The abbess?" she said. "I am new here! I cannot tell the abbess what to do!"

Fridgyth could see that the girl was terrified and tried to speak more calmly to her.

"Say the herb-wife has made a discovery in the novices' dormitory. Believe me, she'll come and I'm the one she'll be angry with, not you."

The girl reluctantly set off, just as the bell for noontide prayers began to toll.

Fridgyth felt as though she wanted to weep. She put the pot and the scallop shell carefully down on the floor again and sat heavily on Gunda's truckle bed, head in hands. What could have possessed them? How could these fine young people bring death to the monastery? Fridgyth felt betrayed. She'd been planning to give the girl all the support she could, just as soon as this dreadful period of sickness had passed. Had she been too slow in her efforts? Had Gunda become desperate, slaving away in the kitchens?

But now Gunda that had seen her search beneath her bed, what would she do? She could not escape with her brother by boat, Ketel would see to that. Suddenly Fridgyth saw in her mind's eye a terrible sight… Gunda and Guy hanging from a gibbet. No – she couldn't bear the thought of it – she wasn't up to this – she was too old and too foolish for such things. The abbess had been right to tell her not to meddle!

There came the sound of a light skid, followed by the sharp thud of the door shutting. She looked up as a familiar smell came creeping towards her nostrils. The novices' dormitory was filling up with smoke. Fridgyth stumbled to her feet as a sudden flame flared up close to one of the beds and quickly died down again. The source of the puttering smoke was an earthenware bowl, just like the one she used when smoking the bees. It was not only packed with glowing charcoal, but also fuelled with a pile of dry straw that burst, once again, into flames that leapt and caught the nearest linen covered mattress.

Fridgyth strode past the bowl, heading for the door and kicked it sharply away from her as she went. The door shook as though somebody tried to open it from the other side and let her out.

"Thank you! Thank you!" she called. "Let me pull from this side."

She gripped the latch and heaved, but found that it seemed to be fastened from the outside now – either fastened or somehow blocked. She tried to push hard against it again and, though it gave a little, it wouldn't open. She stared wildly about her now, stepped backwards, and tripped over the heavy wooden bar that the novices used to lock themselves in at night. She picked it up with shaking hands and rammed it at the door. It gave a little more, but all this time the smoke thickened around her and she choked. The kick she'd given the bowl had made things worse, for the nearest bedding had now caught fire and the next two beds picked up the blaze. She fumbled at her girdle for her latch-lifter and tried again to get the door open, but to no avail.

"Help! help!" she shouted. "Fire in the novices' dormitory."

Surely somebody must be close enough to hear. Was this to be the end? Was she to die like a beast caught in a trap? Would the new girl be bold enough to speak to the abbess quickly? Hild would come... but would she come in time?

Fridgyth looked around for water frantically, but there was none. Snatching up a woollen cover, she tried to use it to beat at the burning bed; she reduced the flames but sent thick black smoke billowing all around her. There was just one window, set quite high, with open wooden shutters, but the flicker of flames and puthering smoke barred her way. It became difficult to breathe. She dropped the rug and took up the wooden bar again and rammed it at the door with renewed vigour. The crack between the door and the frame widened and she could see that something fastened it on the outside.

A terrible clarity came to her – not trying to let her out – fastening her in! She had no doubt that it was Gunda who had done it – the girl she'd tried to help now wanted her dead.

"Like Cenwulf!" she muttered. "I have crossed her path and somehow got in the way of what she intends. Help! Help!" she bellowed again. Surely someone would see the smoke billowing from the high window.

Knowing that the latch-lifter couldn't help, she looked, in desperation, to her other tools, and loosed the sharp shears that swung from her belt. As she pushed the metal blades through the crack of the door, she screwed up her eyes to see where she should aim. Her hands were slippery with sweat and she couldn't see clearly enough through the smoke to find the right spot. Her lungs felt as though they'd burst with the need for air, but the crackle of flames at her back brought furious energy and at last she managed to snip her way through whatever it was that had tied the door closed. She burst out from the building, still grasping her shears, into the arms of the startled abbess.

"Dear God, Fridgyth! What now?" Hild cried.

She staggered as she caught her.

Smoke and flames followed the herb-wife from the building and the abbess saw, at once, that there was no time for explanations. She turned to Eadfrith, who followed close behind with the terrified young novice.

"Fetch gardeners and kitchen workers," she ordered. "Bring water fast and staves and rakes! Fetch Coen! We need all the help we can get! You go to ring the refectory bell," she told the novice.

Fridgyth gasped and coughed and wiped her smarting eyes, but she quickly realized that the precious evidence she'd sought was still inside the burning dormitory.

"I must go back inside," she said.

Hild grabbed her arm.

"Don't be such a fool!"

"There's evidence in there – evidence of poisoning. They locked me in and set it on fire – why else would they do that?"

"Who did this? Who was it?"

Fridgyth wanted to weep and her mouth twisted in bitterness as she spoke their names, "Guy and Gunda."

"No!"

She nodded.

"Surely not!"

Fridgyth simply pointed. Hild looked back to the smoke-filled doorway and saw that a novice's twisted hempen girdle hung there, cut in two by Fridgyth's shears.

"She fastened me inside!"

Hild moved to touch it, but now it was Fridgyth's turn to pull her back; the fire had taken hold inside and flames leapt and flared.

"Let no more life be lost," Fridgyth shouted above the roar of the flames. "You have seen this evidence at least and know that I was trapped in there."

Help came then and frantic workers quickly surrounded them, armed with buckets, brooms, rakes and spades. Hild took charge. The refectory bell rang urgently; soon monks and nuns joined the struggle to save the long, low building.

Della rushed out from the infirmary to discover what was wrong. Fridgyth berated her for leaving the patients, but Hild welcomed her and told her to take the herb-wife back to her hut and look after her.

"But Guy and Gunda, they are getting away," Fridgyth protested.

"Go," Hild insisted. "Leave them to me."

Fridgyth was unwilling to leave, but black dots swam in front of her eyes and her knees began to buckle. She struggled to stay upright and was forced to lean on the girl as they went back to her hut.

Once there, Della helped her wash and tucked her up in bed.

"Drink this," she ordered "Camomile for shock, celery seed to clear the throat, honey to soothe."

"Couldn't do better myself," Fridgyth admitted, as she sipped the drink between bouts of coughing. "But you shouldn't be here. What of our plague sufferers?" she protested.

"There are only five left, and they thrive well; the rest have gone back to their kin," Della told her. "I will go back to them once I've seen that you are resting."

"Only five of them left and no newcomers?" Fridgyth closed her eyes. "That at least is a blessing," she said.

CHAPTER 23

LOVER'S TRYST

She woke to find the abbess sitting by her hearth, her habit smoke-stained and singed a little.

"What has happened?" she asked, struggling to sit up.

"The fire is out," Hild said, "By sheer force of numbers and determination. The dormitory has gone, but the fire's not spread to other buildings. With all the deaths we've had, there's room to house the novices in the guest house, and our new school is almost built."

"And my evidence…?"

Hild shook her head.

"All is black and burned up there, though Eadfrith sifts through the mess; he knows what we need to look for. I've sent the guards to search for Guy and Gunda."

"I made Ketel go down to the quayside, to st…stop them escaping b…by b…boat," a fit of coughing took hold of Fridgyth and prevented her from saying more, while her eyes streamed. Hild picked up a beaker and helped her sip more of Della's medicine.

"I'll send warriors down to the quayside. They can take Ketel's place and let him come back to help his daughter."

Hild went to the door of the hut and issued instructions to Brother Bosa, who'd waited there; then she returned and sat down again.

"Now are you sure, Fridgyth?" she asked hesitantly. "That sweet-looking girl?"

Fridgyth nodded her throat raw.

"There was a shallow dish of marigold petals – one of my own and a scallop shell, just like the ones they mix orpiment in, both hidden beneath Gunda's bed. The new novice saw me find them; she is my witness."

"Was anything in the scallop shell?"

"Yes, a smooth golden sludge; we both know what that means."

"King's Yellow!" Hild whispered in a shocked voice "Eadfrith told me what you feared."

"Guy must have stolen it from the scriptorium," Fridgyth said, her voice grew in strength, but sounded, to her ears, as though it came from a long way away. "Ketel will never believe it of him and as for Della…"

"We all liked Guy," Hild said quickly. "Elfled adores his company… this will go hard with her." She pressed her lips together and looked stern. "And I told you—"

"Yes I know – you told me not to meddle," Fridgyth answered sharply. "But if I hadn't meddled there might well be more of us dead by now, all white and still and smelling of garlic! I even wonder if they may have tried a dose on Cenwulf," she said. "The girl hated him. He treated her unfairly in my eyes, but that is no reason to murder him?"

"No, indeed."

"They tried other ways I think and failed; when the plague came, and there were so many dying… they came back to King's Yellow."

"And we all thought Prince Dagobert had the plague."

"I thought it," Fridgyth acknowledged guiltily.

"Even Argila thought it!" Hild said. "To pick out poison amongst so much dire sickness is very hard and it's clever indeed of the poisoner."

"You *do* believe me then?"

Hild paused to look at the evidence dispassionately.

"They were certainly well placed to do it," she acknowledged. "The brother could steal the orpiment and the sister put it in the food."

Fridgyth sighed heavily.

"Gunda carried the tray to the royal guest house. It would have been easy for her to sprinkle on a mixture of ground orpiment and dried marigold petals, so that the colour from the flowers too, seeped into the food. The poison lay there looking innocent beside Argila's meat dishes. What a fool I was. I was determined to help the girl. I begged *you* to put her in your new school."

Hild frowned in thought.

"And I… I offered her lessons with Elfled in my house when the plague began. I thought to see her in a safer place, but the girl insisted she'd stay in the kitchen. There were so many other things to worry about, that I never thought to see her refusal as strange."

Fridgyth narrowed her eyes.

"Ah… she told *me* that Mildred couldn't spare her! You see, she knew she was well placed in the kitchen. But why, oh why did they do it? That is the question I cannot answer. Why wish evil on a fine young prince who showed them nothing but friendliness?"

"A poisoner will be well paid," Hild said. "But I would like to know who held the purse?"

Fridgyth remembered the feast in the upper pasture.

"Gunda was wretched to see Guy in the princesses' company – a very unhappy girl, I think!"

"They came from one of the Frankish kingdoms with Bishop Agilbert," Hild saw possibilities there.

"What now?" Fridgyth asked.

"Well… there is evidence against Guy and Gunda; they must be brought to account."

Fridgyth nodded, but her eyelids began to droop.

Hild saw her weariness and got up.

"Rest again."

She left and could be heard as she gave orders for able-bodied lay brothers to be issued with arms, in order to mount a wider search. Fridgyth was relieved that she was taken seriously, but was too weary to think clearly. Cold sweat ran down her back as she lay on her cot feeling desperately feeble. How could she have found clear evidence and then allowed it to be lost so carelessly?

Despite her weariness, it proved impossible to rest; she tossed and turned for a while, then struggled to her feet to wash her hands and face, her fine green gown was smoke-stained and blackened round the hem.

Distracted, she felt that she needed to find Ketel and Della; they, above all, deserved to know why she'd behaved in such an extraordinary way. Shakily, she managed to walk to the door of her hut, but was forced to pause a while to grip the doorframe as the sudden fresh air made it hard to breathe. She struggled to catch her breath and then battled on.

As she passed the stables, a commotion broke out inside and Wulfrun strode out, looking unusually agitated. She was followed by one of the stable lads; it was Cenric.

"I only did as I was bidden," he called. "I've done nothing wrong, I say."

"The Princess's mare has gone," Wulfrun told Fridgyth, unaware, at first, of the wild state of the herb-wife. "This lad says Guy took Seamist out and Seacoal too."

Fridgyth stared at the girl. Had Guy stolen the princess's mare… to escape?

"Fridgyth – are you well – your gown is burned – did you help to beat out the fire?" Wulfrun asked, at last taking in the terrible state of her.

"I only did as I was told," Cenric still defended himself.

"Elfled will be angry," Wulfrun went on. "She was frantic to know that Seamist was safe as soon as we heard about the fire. She trusts Guy more than most, but she's never given him permission to ride Seamist. Nobody rides Seamist but the princess, and it seems he's taken the gelding Seacoal, too."

Cenric took the opportunity to slink back inside the stables.

"The birds have flown!" Fridgyth spoke her own distracted thoughts aloud.

Wulfrun looked bewildered.

"Well… the princess will be furious," she insisted, continuing to see the problem from quite another point of view.

"She will indeed," Fridgyth agreed. "And when she hears that Guy has stolen Seamist, she'll see him as he really is."

"Stolen Seamist?" Wulfrun was deeply shocked at the idea. "Stolen her? I did not say Guy had stolen the mare!"

"But that is what has happened, honey," Fridgyth, spoke with conviction. "He's stolen the princess's mare, and there's worse to tell – but I'll leave that to the abbess, I think."

Wulfrun stared at her for a moment, appalled; then without another word she turned and ran back towards the abbess's house.

Fridgyth went into the stables and saw that there were indeed two empty stalls where Seamist and her twin, the gelding Seacoal, should have been.

Cenric was still skulking there.

"The oblate ordered Seamist to be made ready," he protested. "I just do as I'm bidden."

"I'd keep quiet about it if I were you," Fridgyth suggested.

Drogo, the mule, lifted his head from the next stall and snorted as he picked up her scent. Fridgyth went to him.

"Ah, Drogo," she whispered, stroking the rough hair along the beast's back. "What have I done? This gets worse and worse."

She fondled the mule's ears, seeking comfort in her distress.

Two strong young people with fast horses could be well away by now; it would be easy for them to vanish into the wild moors that bounded Streonshalh. They could be anywhere, and her wild actions had caused their frantic flight.

Cenric flopped down on to the pallet in the corner, his face as miserable as the herb-wife's. Fridgyth gave Drogo's ears a final tug. She must report the horse theft to Hild.

Later, in the abbess's house, Hild listened to her with a grim expression on her face.

"Go to bed Fridgyth," she ordered; her voice flat and cold. "Leave everything to me. You look like death. Go back to your hut and go to bed. I'll send Coen to search the countryside all around us, and I will arm the monks as well as the lay-brothers."

Fridgyth went back to her hut and slept at last, exhausted. When she woke the next morning, dreadful images flooded back into her mind. She got up and went, at once, to find Della and her father in the infirmary.

"No more brought in sick?" she asked.

Della smiled.

"Nobody," she said. "Well... only Sister Cloda came, complaining that she couldn't sleep for disturbing dreams. I gave her a valerian brew to drink."

Fridgyth tried to smile.

"You've done so well, honey," she said. "Perhaps we're coming to the end of the plague."

Ketel appeared in the doorway, he looked relieved to see her up and about.

"I feared you were hurt when I heard of the fire," he said.

She went to him and hugged him.

"It takes more than a bit of smoke to finish me. I thank you for your great trust in me, and now I will tell you both why I have deserted you for so long – I daresay you have heard something already."

"I heard something," Della admitted, "but I couldn't believe what I heard."

Fridgyth sighed.

"Let me tell you the truth," she said.

As they listened to all she had to say, their expressions grew more grave and shocked at every word.

"I heard it was Gunda they hunted, but didn't believe it," Della said, dashing away a tear that rolled down her cheek. "And Guy..."

Ketel put his arm around his daughter.

"It seems we have all been tricked," he said.

"I'm so sorry," Fridgyth said. "I pushed you two together. I thought so well of the lad."

Della shook her head.

"You were fooled, just as I was," she said wistfully. "He had... such a charming way with him, and he said that he..."

She turned away from them in an attempt to keep her dignity, but Fridgyth found it more painful than if she'd cried openly.

Coen returned with his warrior band having searched all night unsuccessfully. Hild ordered that they set out again as soon as they'd eaten, but it was clear to everyone that there was little chance now to catch up with the fugitives. Rumours flew wildly around the monastery.

"Too handsome for his own good, that lad, Guy, I never trusted him."

"Proud-faced, the girl was – I always said it."

"Foreigners – their speech was strange!"

"But half our monks are foreigners."

"Hard to know who's who these days, when a Rheged man sits on Deira's throne!"

"King Oswy's nobbut been here a while himself!"

"And nor have you… your father came here with Aelle!"

"No, that was my grandfather!"

One good thing was that Cloda was cleared of blame. Dagobert's identity, which had been whispered abroad, became the subject of astonished speculation. Folk were stunned to discover poisoners in their midst. Coen's warriors returned, having failed to catch their quarries. Hild sent them out again with reinforcements of armed lay brothers and monks. It was partly because there were so few men left within the monastery bounds that Fridgyth noticed Fredemund once again, as he wandered past the herb-wife's hut and out through the side gate, just as the sun began to set.

She went swiftly to follow him, alert to further trouble and curious about his furtive behaviour. He too was Frankish, like Guy and Gunda. Despite her promise not to speak to Hild about him, she was uneasy about the way he seemed to hang around the abbess's house when Hild was at her prayers.

Caedmon had taken the calves inside for the night, and the goldsmith strode unhindered through the meadow towards the sloping hillside. He stopped at the wattle fences that had been set up to prevent the calves from slipping over the edge, where there was a steep drop down to the harbour.

What was he up to? There was definitely something suspicious about his movements. Fridgyth slipped behind the beehives so that she could watch him unobserved.

Fredemund carefully unfastened one of the wattle hurdles and went further down the slope to a spot that most sensible people avoided. Since its early days, the monastery's rubbish had been tipped down onto a precipitous, stinking area of drops and ledges known as the Abbey Midden. Each shallow ledge was piled with rotting waste, and the stench was foul. The young man must be mad – he seemed to climb down amongst the stuff as though searching for something. But then Fridgyth saw that he was not alone, for Wulfrun too wandered across the pasture to join him. What was this – surely not some lovers' tryst? She didn't think much of their choice of place if this was an assignation and was astonished to see Wulfrun climb down too amongst all the rotten debris.

Fridgyth got up from the hives and went to confront them; this was simply ridiculous. She marched across the meadow and stood with her hands on her hips, looking down at them.

"And what, pray, do you mean by this?"

Her voice boomed loudly in the evening stillness.

The young people looked up, horrified.

"It is not what you think," Wulfrun cried.

"Well," Fridgyth said. "If this is what you call a moonlight tryst, then I'm sorry for you both."

The goldsmith glanced at Wulfrun.

"We must tell the herb-wife what we do, I think!"

"Those are the most sensible words I've heard all day," Fridgyth said. "You'd best come back up here, but not too close. Now tell me: what *are* you doing?"

They struggled back and stood a little way from her.

"It's Elfled," Wulfrun began, "she's desperate, and we are trying hard to help her."

"What has this got to do with Elfled?"

Wulfrun went on with reluctance.

"The princess was so very angry when the abbess forbade her to go outside the house that she raged into the abbess's chamber and took up her precious bulla, the seal of Streonshalh, and she threw it out of the window."

"Ah – so that's where it went." The missing seal had been just one more small worry on Hild's long list. "Elfled was the thief!"

"But the princess regretted her action at once," Wulfrun went on hurriedly. "But when she ran to look out of the shutter, the seal had vanished. She could only see the boy with the mule cart, heading for the midden."

Fridgyth's mouth suddenly began to twitch at the corners. The bulla was important, yes, and the abbess had been concerned that a thief should have stolen such a thing. She'd been fearful that it might be used dishonestly in her name, but Elfled's actions over the last few months did not seem so very wicked in the context of so many other terrible happenings.

. This was no matter of life or death.

"So," Fridgyth said, as she struggled to keep a straight face. "So, you two wade in the rubbish to try to get it back for her?"

"Elfled is distraught that Seamist has been stolen," Wulfrun said. "And I thought that if we could find the bulla for her... at least..."

Fridgyth looked at the dishevelled sight they made, two handsome young people covered in slops and stinking badly – she could keep the smile from her face no longer.

"This is no jest," Wulfrun protested.

"Oh, honey, you don't know the last few days I've had; this is just the best end I could hope for."

And suddenly she was laughing, laughing wildly with great relief.

The goldsmith looked at Wulfrun, and he too began to smile, as the herb-wife tried to calm herself.

"Well, do you think the abbess will forgive the princess then?" Wulfrun asked, still sounding a little offended.

"The missing bulla is the last thing on the abbess's mind just now," Fridgyth said, calmer now but smiling broadly. "Go back inside, get washed and tell Elfled to forget it."

"I'll do what I offered," Fredemund intervened. "I'll make the abbess a new bulla, and it will be more beautiful than the first, and then the princess may present it to her in place of the old one."

"You have a good man there," Fridgyth said to Wulfrun. "I didn't realise how good till now. I'll speak to the abbess on Elfled's behalf. Wait a while until all this present trouble is over, and then we'll sort this out with the abbess. Now, go back inside and wash!"

CHAPTER 24

A HERB-WIFE ON A MULE

The laughter brought relief, though it might easily have slipped into tears. Fridgyth followed the two young people back across the pasture and then went back to her hut to find Della. A fire glowed in the hearth, and the cat curled up in front of it. The girl placed bread and cheese on the table, and Fridgyth sat down, close to tears again.

"I don't deserve such a fine apprentice," she said.

That night, Ketel left one of the lay sisters in charge of the few patients that remained and came to sit by Fridgyth's hearth.

"You saw it all," he said, as he tried to cheer her. "Nobody else saw it, only you. I was completely taken in, and my lass too."

Fridgyth pressed his muscular arm, grateful for the comfort, but she couldn't stop fretting.

"The abbess told me not to meddle, but I... I couldn't leave well alone and that is why they've got away."

When Della went off to her sleeping pallet, Ketel pulled his stool close to Fridgyth's and wrapped his arms about her. She leaned back against him, grateful for his steady warmth and support. She enjoyed the rough prickle of his beard against her cheek, but as his hand strayed to her breast, she sighed and pulled forwards.

"I cannot give more," she warned.

"I understand," he said, as he loosened his grip.

They sat together for a while longer, and at last he patted her hand and struggled to his feet.

"The abbess has asked to see me tomorrow," he said. "I don't know whether she wants help with the hunt, or maybe she feels it's time to start up work on the boat-makers' huts again. If we set to work at once, we might have shelter down on the quayside before winter comes."

Fridgyth looked at his face; his skin flickered gold in the firelight. She felt suddenly regretful that this strange, sad period of working together seemed to be coming to an end.

"That's best for you," she said. "We'll see each other, and we'll still be friends."

"Yes, we'll always be friends," he agreed.

But she detected a tone of disappointment in his voice, and she knew he'd hoped for more.

"What of Della?" Fridgyth asked.

"Della will do as she wishes," he said.

He bade her goodnight as he set off back to the guest house. Fridgyth felt more regretful than ever of her gentle rejection of him. Now that he'd gone she felt cold and tired and miserable; she went to bed.

The next morning, three more of those who had recovered from the plague returned to their family - they looked gaunt but were free of disease with just a slight touch of yellow about their complexion. No more new cases came.

Fridgyth sent Della to give the abbess the good news and Hild herself came over to the infirmary.

"Do you think it's finished?" she asked, her manner still a little cool.

Fridgyth shrugged, afraid to tempt the Wyrd sisters of fate by appearing too confident.

The two patients that remained looked lost on their small pallets in the wide hall, so they were carried to the old infirmary beside the herb-wife's hut. Hild ordered the monastic guest house to be swept clean and scrubbed with ash lye, so that it could be returned to its former purpose. Brother Oftfor was appointed the new guest master and he began, at once, to supervise the cleansing of the building. Hild reopened the refectory and announced that everyone should come together for the evening meal, which would be a small feast in thanksgiving that the plague seemed to be at an end. As this news went from mouth to mouth, interest in the hunt for poisoners waned a little, and a much-needed air of celebration began to spread from building to building, hut to hut.

"Is it over, then?"

"Well the abbess seems to think so."

"Tonight we feast in thanks."

By late afternoon the last two plague sufferers were well enough to return to their family. Della went to see them safely into the care of their kin and Fridgyth was left alone in her hut, apart from Wyrdkin who wound around her feet. She sat for a while and stroked the cat's soft fur, as she struggled with a heavy sense of guilt. At last, she got up and set off for the upper pasture to find Caedmon, a moment's brief respite with him might lift her spirits.

She sat there in the sun, listening to the bees and remembering how Dagobert saved the child from their attack. The year had turned, Weedmonth had passed, and the Month of Offerings had begun. The young plague orphans stayed on as Caedmon's helpers and were becoming fine herdsmen; the wattle fences were in good repair and the calves tugged contentedly at the grass; it was a comforting sight.

Caedmon came to sit beside and, for a while, he strummed softly on his harp, but the gentle sounds he made were lost as a gang of Coen's warriors returned from another fruitless search, leading their horses past the meadow towards the main gate.

They nudged each other at the sight of the cowherd with the harp.

"Next time we feast," one shouted. "Tha'll play for us cowherd and bring thy cows to chant the chorus."

"And a mule to bray the words," another wit added.

They'd ridden all day and never caught sight of Guy or Gunda; they were thwarted in their purpose and in a foul mood.

"Useless fools," Fridgyth muttered.

They'd destroyed her moment of peace and the churning in her stomach returned. Surely something could be done to resolve this situation? She couldn't rid herself of the overwhelming desire to take action herself.

Caedmon looked up and set his harp aside, disturbed more by

her fidgeting than by the crude-calling of the warriors.

"Be still," he said. "We are nothing but ants, b-beneath the stars."

She smiled and pressed his arm, but could not be still. Finally, she struggled to her feet and left him abruptly. She strode through the side gate, past rows of cabbages, and on to the stable. The stable lads rubbed down the sweating horses, complaining at the extra work caused by the manhunt. Fridgyth went quietly past them to stroke Drogo's soft grey ears again. The notion had come to her that maybe one who travelled quietly on a mule could track fugitives more effectively. While these angry bands of warrior youths rode strong geldings and carried fearsome weapons, they could also be seen and heard a long way off. Who would share their suspicions with these frightening rough-mouths? An ageing herb-wife on a mule would be a familiar sight and much less of a threat. Many who lived and worked about the abbey trusted her and, what's more, almost everyone owed her favours.

Fridgyth stroked the beast and scratched his ears, her spirits rose at the thought of action. If she went to speak to the abbess she'd be forbidden to leave; if she asked no permission, there'd be nothing Hild could do. The abbess was already angry with her, so how could she make things worse? One thing was clear: she couldn't happily stay in Streonshalh, fretting and forever chiding herself. She gave Drogo a friendly slap on his rump and went off to the kitchens with a lighter step.

Mildred looked up sharply.

"Ah, it is you mistress herb-wife. I thought for a moment it was the other one, but she'll never show her face in here again. And to think how I trusted her…"

"You were not the only one," Fridgyth said, ashamed that she'd ever suspected Mildred.

"More bread!" the foodwife exclaimed, seeing Fridgyth help herself. "Your patients eat well."

"Oh yes, mistress foodwife, there's just a few of them left," she lied, hoping that nobody who knew better overheard them. "Those who recover have great appetites."

She helped herself generously to bread, cheese, smoked mackerel and oat cakes and carried them all back to the stables. She threw a saddle and panniers across Drogo's back and packed away her food. Then she took a leather drinking flask out to the well and filled it with fresh water. Caedmon was still there in the meadow and watched her curiously. She realised that she would have to leave a message for the abbess, but if she spoke to Ketel he'd be sure to prevent her leaving.

"Would *you* speak to the abbess for me?" she asked, "if I were to go away for a while?"

Caedmon looked astounded and shook his head. "N-not I," he said.

Fridgyth gave him a pleading look.

"It must be you – I cannot trust anyone else. Would you wait till tomorrow, and then tell the abbess that 'a herb-wife on a mule may go where warriors cannot.'"

He shook his head. "I c-can't s-speak to the abbess," he protested.

"I'm putting my trust in you," she told him sharply as she turned on her heel and strode away.

Back in her hut Fridgyth bundled together a few clothes.

"You'll have to live on rats again," she warned Wyrdkin, as the cat rubbed against her feet. "Don't you go giving me another surprise, not like last time?"

She could see that it was unfair to ask Caedmon to carry her message, and now a better idea came to her. Snatching up a willow skep, she went out to the vegetable garden where she dug up a few of the best onions, leeks, and parsnips and cut some leafy kale. She snipped small bunches of sage, thyme, fennel and rosemary and arranged them in the basket, then headed for the royal guest house. The lay sister opened the door to her. This time there was no argument, and she was shown into the small hall, where she hovered uncertainly in the doorway. Dagobert and Mathild sat together propped on cushions; both of them looked pale and thin. Aldfrith played a game of merrils with Argila. The old warrior had discarded his monk's robe for a warrior's leather jerkin; a gleaming short sword hung at his belt. His hand went, at once, to clasp the hilt, but he relaxed and smiled as soon as he saw who it was that disturbed them.

"You're welcome, herb-wife," he said warmly, bowing to her. "You see me as I am – no monk."

Fridgyth inclined her own head, and flushed slightly.

"I regret my past foolishness," she managed to say. "And I beg a moment's speech with Prince Aldfrith."

Fina's son got up at once, setting the game aside.

She offered him her basket of produce.

"Everything in this skep is fresh from my garden," she said. "A good broth made from these vegetables will do much to strengthen your invalids. You know the source of poisoning is discovered now, I think."

"Yes, thanks to you," he said.

"Now, thanks to me, they have escaped," she said, with a shake of the head. "But I mean to do my best to put that right. May I beg a favour? I need somebody that I can really trust."

"What can I do?" he offered at once.

"The abbess must receive a message from me tomorrow at noon, no sooner, but..." and she flushed again. "I cannot write it... I know only runes."

He understood at once and put the basket into the hands of a lay sister.

"Come with me," he said.

Fridgyth followed him through the hall into a wooden booth. He pulled open the shutter and light flooded the small space, illuminating the inkhorn, quill pens and a stack of parchment that sat on a carved wooden table.

Aldfrith picked up a sheet of vellum and sat down.

"What is it that you wish to say to the abbess?"

"Oh, you mustn't use calf-skin for this," she protested.

He looked uncertain for a moment, but then answered her firmly.

"This is an important message, I think," he said. "Vellum is fitting. How would you like to start?"

Fridgyth hesitated, ashamed of her ignorance.

"How *should* I address her?"

"To the Holy Abbess Hild, greetings in God? This is how bishops write to her."

Fridgyth hesitated; it sounded too fine for a humble herb-wife.

"Please put, *'To my dear, respected Abbess Hild, greetings from a loving friend'.*"

Aldfrith dipped his quill in the ink, bent over the sheet and in a beautiful regular script he began to write.

Fridgyth bit her lip and spoke again.

"I deeply regret… my carelessness and wish to put right the ills I have brought about, I go in search of the fugitives, to this end."

He paused and looked up, the quill hovered over the parchment.

"The abbess would *not* wish you to do this."

"No, but it is needful for my sense of honour," Fridgyth told him firmly.

He began to write again.

"*A herb-wife on a mule may go where warriors cannot,*" she continued. "*She may see what warriors cannot see and hear what warriors cannot hear.*"

Aldfrith looked up and nodded.

"I understand," he said. "And I think the abbess will understand too."

She watched him, wishing that she too had this magical skill.

"That is all I need to say, I think. How should it be finished?"

"May God's grace watch over you?" he suggested.

"*May your god watch over you*," she said. "I cannot sign my name, but I can draw a rune."

Aldfrith dipped the quill in the ink and handed it to her as he got up. She took his place on the stool and carefully inscribed the rune Ehwas.

"The horse," he recognised the mark.

"Ehwas signifies friendship. The abbess knows runes from her childhood, as well as the Latin."

"I believe she does," Aldfrith said. "And I shall make sure that she receives it tomorrow at noon."

Fridgyth thanked him and then hurried back to her hut; there was much to do. She very much wanted to explain her plan to Della, but couldn't risk jeopardising the venture. So when the bell rang to announce the evening meal, she simply told the girl that she'd been called away to a birthing.

"But the refectory is opened up again," Della said, excited. "You'll miss the first meal! No matter – I shall come with you."

Fridgyth shook her head and smiled.

"No, I can manage fine, alone," she said. "Go and enjoy your meal."

She felt a moment of regret as she watched the girl go and realised that she was becoming the nearest thing to a daughter she would ever have. Della would wake next morning and find Fridgyth still not back, and she'd assume only that the birthing had been difficult. It would be noon before she'd begin to worry and, by then, the abbess would have the letter. Della would go to her father and tell him of the herb-wife's duplicity. How would they feel? Might they both hate her for leaving them in this way?

She went, determinedly, to the stables where Drogo waited patiently, ready saddled. She loaded him with her bags and moved towards to the door, but as she did so a shadowy figure emerged from the end stall. Whoever it was appeared to be leading a black and white gelding – Turnstone.

She froze. Was her plan ruined before it was started?

"I c-can't speak to the abbess for you, but I c-can come with you." She sighed, relieved.

"No, Caedmon," she insisted. "You cannot leave your calves."

"My c-calves are safe with the boys," he said.

Fridgyth smiled. His quiet presence would be a blessing. Hild would probably be reassured to hear that Caedmon had gone too; she knew well that they were friends.

"Come then," she said. "You are as hare-brained as I."

CHAPTER 25

CALLING IN FAVOURS

Drogo was used to her scent and the sound of her voice so he made no fuss or noise. They went round by the herb garden and vegetable plot and out through the side gate, to avoid unwelcome questions at the main gate, though the sight of the cowherd and the herb-wife on an errand of mercy would cause little stir. Yet another search party of warriors and laybrothers rode up the hill towards them at a good pace, their voices loud and complaining. She pulled the mule off the path and bent down as though to examine one of his hooves. She needn't have worried; they didn't even glance at her.

"T'owd Abbess will be angry again."

"Shut your mouth!" another replied.

"Even Woden's ravens can't search in the dark!"

"No – any chance of catching them's long gone."

"These vision-struck Christians must see that!"

Fridgyth straightened once they'd passed.

"They pass like a herd of oxen," she muttered.

The men clattered on towards the main gate, while the herb-wife and the cowherd headed quietly downhill towards the ford, as dusk gathered about them. Fridgyth was touched to see that Caedmon had his harp strapped to his back.

They slowed up as they approached the river crossing, for they knew that everything depended on them making the right decision there. The herb-wife got down from Drogo's back, glad to see that the tide was out; the water ran shallow across the ford. One broad, level track stretched out ahead of them and ran inland on their side of the River Usk; while another turned left, to wind southwards up the hillside where it would eventually meet the coastal path that led towards Hackness. On the far side of the river, the path split again. Which direction would the fugitives have taken?

"Was the tide high at noon, two days ago?" she asked Caedmon.

"It w-would have been coming in," he said.

Fridgyth stared hopelessly at the darkening ground. The guards had repeatedly ridden over any hoofmarks the guilty ones might have left. Might the brother and sister have risked deep water to prevent pursuit? She would begin, at once, to put her own special skills to the test. She looked about her at the cluster of wattle and daub huts set close by the ford. These huts housed the ford-keeper and his family and the basket makers who made their living from the willow wands that they gathered from the marshy river's edge. One hut stood closer to the water than any of the others.

"Lindi will know," Fridgyth said, and she began leading Drogo towards the hut.

Old Lindi was blind and suffered from aching joints and fevers, but she still managed to weave skeps of every shape and size from the willow wands and reeds that her grandchildren collected. Fridgyth knew she would most likely be alone in the evening and went to tap on one of the closed wooden shutters.

"Lindi?" she called. "Lindi… can you help me?"

There was the faintest sound of rustling; then a voice called out from the dark hut.

"Herb-wife? Is that you? By Freya you startled me!"

"I'm sorry," Fridgyth replied meekly.

"I didn't call for you!"

"No, it's me that needs your help," Fridgyth replied.

They heard the shuffle of footsteps and the clack of the wooden inner bar being lifted. Out came Lindi, clutching a woollen cloak tightly against the cold air. The old woman was as much at home in the gloom as if it were daylight.

"What's this all about?" she asked, alert and slightly trembling. "Is that a mule I hear? Freya's teeth, I can smell the beast! And who else have you here?"

"It's just me and the cowherd, Lindi. We're sorry to disturb you, but we need your help; terrible things have happened up at the monastery."

"I know," Lindi agreed. "Everyone knows. As if there weren't enough trouble with the sickness rife. Poisoners, they say. I've heard Hild's warrior band go splashing through the ford as if their lives depended on it, hunting dogs baying and such a shouting and cursing that you'd think the sun had gone dark again. At first I asked our little Gilli, 'Has the sun gone dark again?' But she told me 'no Grandmother – they hunt murderers.'"

"Your Gilli's right," Fridgyth said. "But the ones we seek fled two days since on the best horses and the trail's gone cold. I wondered if you might remember two days back, after noon… I know you often hear things that others miss?"

"Ah," Lindi understood. "Best horses you say and two of them?"

"Yes," Fridgyth said.

"Was it Princess Elfled's horse they took?"

"It was!"

Caedmon smiled in admiration that the old woman could know that.

"I heard two horses thunder by," the old skepmaker went on. "And I *was* puzzled for I was sure those fast light hooves belonged to the princess's mare, but the beast screamed in protest and was most unhappy with her rider and I said to Gilli, 'That can't be the princess riding the beast'. Gilli looked out, and she told me that it was a lady she didn't know and a man with her that she thought she *had* seen before."

"That must have been them," Fridgyth said eagerly. "Can you tell us which way they went?"

"Of course I can," said Lindi. "They crossed the ford, though the tide was coming in and the water was deep. I could hear it washing across the stones, and both of the horses stumbled, but the riders urged them on with curses."

"Could you tell which direction they took when they reached the other side?"

"They took the river path, honey," she said with certainty. "They headed upriver towards Ruswarp Mill."

"Bless you," Fridgyth said with satisfaction. "Your next pot of comfrey balm shall cost you nothing – and the next, and the next."

"Huh! If I live that long," Lindi spoke with resolute humour.

Fridgyth remounted hastily, and they rode on across the ford, as the old woman hobbled back to the comfort of her hearth. The water was shallow enough to leave them dry and, as Drogo struggled out through the mud at the far riverbank, Fridgyth kicked his fat sides and turned his head along the inland path. Despite the unsettling memories that this route would bring back, her spirits lifted, for it seemed that her plan was working; her blood raced with excitement.

"I'm not too old to go adventuring," she declared, as she kicked the mule's sides again. "Can't he go any faster?"

"He does his best!" Caedmon told her sharply.

They moved steadily along the track beside the river as it grew darker. To their relief, a heavy cloud rolled away from the moon and sent silvery light across the land.

"Blessed Freya," Fridgyth whispered. "This is better than fretting at home."

They rode on faster, enjoying the gentle slip-slap of the river and the glimmer of the moon's reflection on the water. But it was with a sense of sadness that Fridgyth turned a familiar bend in the pathway. Soon they'd pass her old home. It was a long time since she'd been there. As she arrived at the spot, she pulled Drogo to a halt.

"That's it," she murmured, "the old cunning-woman's hut."

Caedmon halted too, for he knew well what this place meant to her.

Fridgyth held her breath as she peered into a dark clump of yew trees. In the moonlight, she could just make out the tumbled shape of a hut, a broken thatch and a garden robbed and gone to ruin.

"I came back here, to my mother, after the year of terror," she told him. "I was a young woman still, but barely alive and my husband and my children had gone."

Caedmon waited patiently.

"Mother helped me live again, though she was dying herself; she forced me to keep going. What would she say to see me now, all lofty-nosed and dressed so fine – the abbey herb-wife?"

"She'd be proud of you," Caedmon said, with certainty. "The abbess changed my life too when she came here and freed me from slavery."

"Better for us both," Fridgyth agreed. "The abbess brought peace and plenty to Usk Valley, but I've messed it up. I suppose I could still come back here… if I cannot catch these desperate folk and bring them back to face justice. That rotting thatch would mend, I think."

They waited in silence for a few more moments, then Caedmon said, softly, "Let's go on," and, once again, his words fell smoothly from his lips.

"Yes," Fridgyth agreed, kicking Drogo's sides more gently this time.

The sense of elation waned, and they became cold and tired, as the dark shape of Ruswarp Mill came into view. Not wanting to pass the mill without asking after those they followed, Fridgyth decided it was time to stop. Even though she'd brought all the miller's five children into the world and would be seen as a trusted friend, it wouldn't do to wake them at this hour.

"We've gone far enough for now," she said wearily. "It won't be the first time that the miller has found me asleep in his stable."

Caedmon climbed down from Turnstone's back. He too was familiar with the outbuildings and led the way confidently to the stable behind the barn where the grain was kept. The mill's two ponies were stabled there, and the cowherd knew they'd find food for their own beasts and straw for their sleeping requirements. The miller's dog barked once, but was quickly silenced by Caedmon's gentle hand on his neck. It wouldn't be as easy further afield but, for the time being, it seemed they could move quietly around the countryside, calling in favours as they went.

Wrapped in her cloak, Fridgyth lay down to sleep on clean straw, while Caedmon settled across the threshold.

They both slept soundly and were discovered soon after dawn by the miller's eldest son, who came out to feed the ponies.

"Herb-wife's here! And the monastery cowherd too!" he called to his mother. Then, returning his attention to his guest called "Come inside, Mam's poaching eggs and making flat bread. Are you on your way back from a birthing?"

"I don't think I was," Fridgyth replied, as she struggled to sit up. She rubbed her eyes, finding it hard to remember what she *was* doing, until she saw Caedmon rise to his feet from his sleeping spot in an empty stall and the last few days' events slid into focus.

"Poached eggs sound good," she said. "Would you be so kind as to feed our beasts along with yours?"

"I've done it already," the lad smiled cheerily.

As they wandered into the home-place Ethel, the miller's wife, looked up.

"Eeeh… you should have woken us and come inside," she said.

She set out bowls of bread and poached eggs for them both, garnished with sweet-scented thyme. They smelled delicious, and Fridgyth discovered that she was very hungry.

"Bless you, Ethel," she said and started to eat with relish.

"Well, what was it?" Ethel asked. "A bairn arriving or an old one leaving, it's usually one or the other that brings you out this way in the middle of the night?"

Caedmon left it to Fridgyth to explain.

"Have you heard about these poisonings?" she said. "I need to catch up with those who are responsible."

Ethel raised her eyebrows in surprised.

"Everybody's heard about it," she said. "But why are *you* bothered about them? Coen and his men have horses, dogs and arms. It's their job to track murderers down, not the herb-wife's! Leave it to them, I'd say. Wicked Frankish folk – coming here and bringing us trouble."

Fridgyth had a moment of wavering uncertainty – was she growing soft-witted as she aged? She'd seen it before – women who grew fuddled in the head, going off, never to be seen again, leaving everything and everyone they cared about behind them. Was she thick-witted to wander about the countryside like this, thinking *she* could do better than younger, agile, trained men? But the thought of returning to the monastery and admitting failure and foolishness made her heart sink to her boots.

She took another mouthful of Ethel's delicious, warm bread and her courage returned. Foolish or not, she'd have a damned good try at finding Guy and Gunda. She'd a stalwart companion in Caedmon and a just cause. She drank a mouthful of ale spiced with honey and sweet cicely and felt better. Coen and his men would never be offered such a breakfast. Her confidence in herself was fully restored.

"A herb-wife can ask questions that warriors cannot," she told Ethel. "And she can get more truthful answers, too."

The miller's wife looked thoughtful at that.

"Aye, maybe so... maybe so," she admitted.

"Did *you* see anything of a young lad and lass travelling through, two days since?"

"Young folk? You mean these murderers are young? I hadn't realised that; dear lord... and a lass as well as a lad?"

"A bonny lass and a handsome lad," Fridgyth said.

Ethel shook her head.

"I've only seen the monastery guards who came asking if we'd seen poisoners and horse-thieves. I never thought they'd be young, like you say... but I've seen nowt of them."

Fridgyth sighed and took another drink, but the miller's son caught the end of the conversation as he came in. He winked at the herb-wife.

"I've seen a pair of fleeing lovers."

She put down her ale and looked at him, her eyebrows raised.

"A pair of fleeing lovers, you say? The two we seek say that they are brother and sister, but I come to wonder... they might appear as lovers."

The lad pulled up a stool and sat down.

"They'd two good horses – dappled greys – that carried them fast along the main track as though they'd head towards Eforwic, but then instead of turning westwards, they chose to go up-river, where they'd not be followed easily. The lass wept and wailed, and I guessed they fled from her father."

"D-dappled greys!" Caedmon was alert to the significance of the words.

The miller's son scratched his head.

"Yes – greys, I think, though I never saw them close up like. They're not the first pair of lovers to hide up in the Usk valley!"

He smirked sideways at Fridgyth.

"There's nowt surprises a herb-wife," she told him roundly. "No need to be prim-mouthed with me."

"Well… they didn't behave like brother and sister, and they didn't look like murderers," he insisted.

"And what *do* murderers look like?" Fridgyth asked.

The lad looked nonplussed.

"You have a point there, herb-wife," he admitted.

Fridgyth's eyes narrowed with suspicion as her thoughts went back to the time when she'd seen Guy and Gunda together outside the abbess's house. There'd been something about them then that had disturbed her – a closeness and a tenderness that seemed perhaps more than what should be between a brother and sister. She stuffed the last morsel of bread into her mouth and rose from the table.

"Show me where they went!" she said.

The lad got up and led the way outside.

"Could they really be the ones – the murderers?"

He was excited now to think he might have seen the wicked pair.

"They might well be," Fridgyth conceded.

"There," he pointed into the distance, to where the Usk eventually flowed through a high ravine. "The track grows narrow and the sides of the river are steep and treacherous; you must be wary and have your wits about you if you want to follow those tracks. Coen's men turned back, for they reached that spot at sundown and were unwilling to follow so steep a path. You can easily slip into the river in the dark or if your beast stumbles. I'd only go up that way if I were…"

His words petered out as he realised what he was saying.

Fridgyth nodded.

"If you were desperate," she said, finishing his words for him. "And the ones we seek would indeed be desperate. They have little knowledge of the countryside round here."

She looked upriver and sighed at the very thought of attempting to struggle along that route. But she had Caedmon with her, and she knew he would never let her down.

"Well… if that is where your lovers went, then we must go there too. This seems more likely than anything else I've heard, and at least *we* may do it in daylight. Have *you* ever been that way before?" she asked Caedmon.

He shook his head.

"Nor I," she said.

CHAPTER 26

SONG OF THE BEES

They thanked their hosts and set off with grim resolve. For the best part of the morning, they followed the winding, narrow path above the river. Fridgyth tried to suppress her sense of urgency, as safety seemed suddenly more important than anything else, but Drogo proved to be sure-footed and Caedmon handled his gelding with care.

The more she thought about it, the more she became convinced that the miller's son's description fitted Guy and Gunda, and she began to wonder if they were really brother and sister after all. They didn't look much alike when she came to think of it, and she also recalled Gunda's agony of jealousy when she saw Guy flirting with the princesses that sunny day in the meadow; too passionate an emotion, for a sister towards her sibling.

She kicked Drogo's sides with renewed energy.

The wildness of the rocky ravine eventually gave way to more gentle slopes, and they arrived at noon in a remote hamlet.

"Where is this?" she asked the cowherd.

He shook his head.

It was a hidden valley, not far from Streonshalh as the crow flew, but hard to access due to the steepness of the ravine. Six monastic huts were set around a carved wooden preaching cross, all newly built. The cross was skilfully hewn and decorated with figures and plants.

"An angel," Caedmon pointed out.

Fridgyth smiled.

"Yes, but see here – they've put a mother goddess with her sheaves of corn on the back of the cross; I understand that well – a good harvest must come first."

There were more small wooden crosses, roughly worked, stuck into the ground beside small humps of recently disturbed earth.

"Graves?" Fridgyth wondered? What else could they be?

Further up the hillside, where the land shelved a little, there was an old farmstead. A few calves looked up from small enclosures, while goats and fowls roamed free. The fields were freshly turned, the clean lines of the furrows all ready to be sown; it seemed the distant hamlet thrived. Smoke rose from thatched roofs, but there was nobody in sight and an uneasy quietness hung about it all.

"Where are the monks?" Fridgyth whispered. "Are they the dedicated ones, who rarely speak and leave their huts?"

"No – look there," Caedmon said, pointing to a patch of long grass that had been flattened around the doorway of one of the monastic huts.

Fridgyth saw what he was pointing to: everywhere else the grass had grown long and undisturbed, but this one patch had been recently trodden.

"This hut's been used, but the others've been deserted for days, or even weeks. Do you think those we seek might have sheltered here?"

Caedmon nodded solemnly.

"But still, I cannot help but wonder – where are the monks? These huts are new and well made, but it seems they've deserted them."

"H-horses have been here," Caedmon was quick to see the signs of beasts that had passed recently: fresh horse droppings.

But Fridgyth was still distracted.

"Why build new cells and a fine worked cross and then abandon them?"

Caedmon pointed out hoof prints that headed further along the river path.

"They travelled this way I think, the riders that we seek."

Fridgyth tore herself away from the puzzle.

"In that case we must travel on and follow them."

As they crossed the lower slopes of the valley beneath the farmstead, they at last saw a man out in the fields sowing seed. Fridgyth steered Drogo in his direction, determined to discover more about this strange place. He saw her approach and backed away.

"Peace," she called out, and she held up her hand in the three fingered sign that she'd seen Hild use.

"I'm the herb-wife from Streonshalh."

He stopped and reluctantly came forward, but he made the familiar flat-handed sign to ward her off.

"Stay afar!" he called. "There's plague about."

She understood his concern and kept her distance.

"The plague is gone from Streonshalh," she said hoping to reassure him. "But still I'll come no closer. Have a young couple passed this way?"

"Aye," he said at once. "They sheltered down there." He pointed to the group of monastic huts. "But they'd have done best to carry on," he added.

"Why do you say that?" she asked.

The man shook his head.

"We gave warning, but they took no notice. I think they were done in and spent a night there."

"Warned them of what?" Fridgyth asked uneasily.

"The plague," the man said. "Those huts are pestilence ridden."

"But where are the monks?" Fridgyth said with a frown.

"Dead o' the sickness," the man was impatient with her slowness and indicated the smaller crosses stuck in the ground.

At last understanding dawned. Even out here in this isolated spot the disease had taken its toll.

"Where did the monks come from?" she asked.

"They came from Lasting's Ham. None of us wished them ill," he said defensively.

"But why did they come here?"

The man shook his head.

"We wanted none o' their religion for we worship the Harvest Queen here, but last Eastermonth our headman gave permission for them to build a few of their little huts. They set up their carved idol but, no sooner had they settled here, than they began to fall sick."

Fridgyth nodded sadly.

"We'd feared the Harvest Queen was angry and kept well away from them then. The old man was the last to go, so we laid him in the earth as quickly as we could, in a shallow grave behind the huts, alongside his brothers. We were sorry, for they were peaceful, hard-working fellows, but they wouldn't listen to us. Nobody's been there since, save the ones you speak of."

Fridgyth looked back at the graves as a disturbing thought came to her. "Could they have been the monks who came to Streonshalh, do you think?" she asked Caedmon, "Prior Sigurd and the young boy, Billfrith."

"I think n-not," Caedmon said. "These men must have been here b-before ever Prior Sigurd set out for Lastingham."

She was relieved to see that none of the graves looked small enough to belong to young Billfrith.

"If ever there were plague ridden huts, it's those," the man said. "We should burn them."

Fridgyth sighed.

"Aye… you'd do well to burn them," she agreed. "But can you tell us which way the two young people went?"

He nodded.

"They rode away in the direction of Lasting's Ham, whipping their horses like demons, but these tracks aren't fit for going at speed. I thought any moment they'd be thrown and break their necks. Who rides a decent horse like that?"

"Which way is Lastingham?" Fridgyth asked, breathlessly.

"You go up onto the heather moors," he said. "But you'd do best not to follow them. They say that Lasting's Ham is full o'ghosts."

"Full of ghosts?" Fridgyth stared at him. "No matter! We must follow wherever the horses went."

The man turned and walked away, shaking his head. Fridgyth and Caedmon set off once more along the river path, both of them quiet and thoughtful.

They followed the hoof prints and soon Caedmon looked back to

Fridgyth, showing her where the tracks left the river and headed up a steep hillside crowned with heather.

Fridgyth groaned; she was worn out already, and the pull up there would be difficult. The farmer's words had brought a deep sense of sadness back to her. She forced herself to dig deep into her store of common sense, and tell herself that they did well. Caedmon tracked their quarries like a hunting dog, better than any of Coen's hounds by far. Food was what she needed; food, rest and a drink of mead. She waved to Caedmon and dismounted, leading Drogo towards the sound of running water. A clean spring bubbled out from the rocks, where it ran downhill to join the river. While Drogo drank, she flopped down beside him on the grass.

Caedmon came back to join her leading Turnstone.

"I must rest," she told him. "Just for a while… I'm not as young as you, you know."

He smiled.

"You're not s-so much older."

She opened her saddlebags and found apples and bread that was still soft from Ethel's griddle, along with goats' cheese and smoked mackerel that she'd brought from Mildred's kitchen.

Fridgyth shared her meal with Caedmon and insisted that he take a good swig of mead along with her. The mead seemed to do him good, for he took the harp from his back, settled down in the warm sun and began to strum. He sang gently under his breath, surrounded by the buzzing of bees.

> *"They come as guests,*
> *Garbed in black and gold, they glide*
> *Joyous they jig in the heather."*

Fridgyth laughed, as she understood.

"You sing of the bees!"

He nodded and continued with more confidence now,

> *"They cry drink-hail from crimson cups,*
> *Honoured hearth-friends, they hum their thanks*
> *Greeting guests at every garnet-gilded stall.*

Sun fades; day turns dark, shade to shadow,
Carousing and carolling they glide homeward,
Nectar-drunk, they bawl and bellow,
Rowdy, rough-mouths,
Singing honey-soaked songs"

Fridgyth clapped in delight.

"I'll never see bees the same way again," she said. "Rowdy rough-mouths, that is so true of them. You know – if you just called the bees God's children, I swear the abbess would enjoy your songs."

"My mother c-called all beasts God's children," he said.

"Was your mother a Christian, then?" Fridgyth was surprised.

He looked uncertain.

"Not like the abbess I think, but she used to tell me the s-story of a man called Daniel who was put in a wild cat's den. He was saved from harm by a father god, who made the beast remember that the man had once taken a thorn from its paw. I loved that story. Mother often spoke of a father god and I think it was the same father the Christians worship."

Fridgyth frowned, but nodded.

"I think the story of Daniel *is* one of the stories the Christians tell. Can you remember any more?"

He nodded.

"I can remember them all."

"You should make your mother's stories into songs and sing them to Hild," she said.

Caedmon looked thoughtful and continued to strum on his harp.

"*God's children come as guests,*" he tried.

"*Garbed in black and gold, they glide…*"

"It could work," Fridgyth told him. "I'm sure it could work and the abbess would delight in it."

"W-would my song not give offence?"

"No. Certainly not; the abbess is as broad-minded as you or me. She'd laugh at the image of the drunken bees!"

The sun was past its zenith. Aldfrith would have given Hild the message by now. Fridgyth was weary with her journey, so she folded her cloak beneath her head and lay back in the heather to rest. The sun grew hot, and Caedmon set his harp aside, he left the herb-wife to sleep, while he wandered off up the hillside.

Fridgyth woke with a start, unsure how long she'd slept. She opened her eyes and struggled to sit up, as the heather around her swayed wildly. At once she sensed that she was watched, and certainty came as she heard a giggle.

"Who's there?" she demanded.

Suddenly she found that she was surrounded by dirty faced children, who reared up from amongst the heather with stones in their hands.

"Plague bringer!" A shower of small stones hailed down on her.

"Our Harvest Queen will curse you!" another cried.

Fridgyth was astonished, but quickly realised that her clothes might look monastic to them, so they'd see her as one of the Christians, whose worship they believed had angered the ancient ones. The stones stung, but didn't do any great injury.

"By Freya if you want curses, you shall have them!" she bellowed, as she scrambled to her feet.

"*By Woden's dark ravens that swoop across the sky,*" she cried, and her voice grew in strength and anger.

> "*By the thunder of Thor's hammer, fire-bright,*
> *By Freya's stalking cats, night-dark,*
> *By Hretha's death wail I shall curse you.*
> *And Freya will rot your harvest in the fields!*"

Drogo put back his ears, threw up his head and brayed as if in fear of his life. The children dropped their stones and stared, aghast. As her curses rained down on them, they screamed, turned and scattered.

Caedmon came leaping back down the hill and Fridgyth sat down again with a thump. For a moment she struggled to get her breath, but at the sight of Caedmon's horrified face she broke into smiles and laughter came instead.

"Just children," she said, as she shook her head. "Just skinny wild children – more frightened of me than I of them."

He smiled and helped her up and then they both collapsed with laughter. The food and rest had done her good, and even the vanquishing of her young attackers felt like a small victory. When they had both got their breath back, she turned once again to the matter in hand.

"We must get on," she said, as she reached for Drogo's leading rein.

They set off once more and left the river behind them, to follow the horse tracks uphill. When they arrived at the top at last, they stared open-mouthed at the sight before them. They were confronted by a wide open, sweeping landscape that seemed to stretch on forever. And a cobbled road ribboned away straight across it into the distance.

"I think I've heard of this, but I never truly believed in it," Fridgyth whispered.

"The g-giants' causeway," Caedmon's eyes were wide in disbelief. "Built by the giants W-wade and Bel."

"Hild told me it was made by the Romans when they were masters in this land, long ago, but it looks more like the work of giants to me!"

"W-where does it lead?" the cowherd asked.

"I've no idea," Fridgyth admitted. "What matters to us is whether Guy and Gunda took to it."

It didn't take Caedmon long to find hoof marks and droppings. "I think they did!" he said.

"Then so must we," said Fridgyth.

They set off along the road, and found that they could travel along it at a good pace. They rode closer together, sensing that they might be seen more easily from a distance in the open land. With some relief, they spotted that the hoofmarks left the cobbled road to turn onto a smaller track and led down into a sheltered valley.

As the sun began to set, they found a grassy glade with a stream that ran through it, and plenty of gorse scrub for kindling. Caedmon looked back at Fridgyth.

"A g-good place to camp?" he suggested.

They made a fire and ate what little food they had left. Wrapped in their cloaks, they settled to sleep back to back to share each other's warmth. At the sound of a distant wolf-howl, Fridgyth turned herself about and tried to curl her body tightly around the cowherd's. He shuffled away from her uncertainly.

"I want nothing but warmth and security," Fridgyth murmured sleepily. "You are far too young for me."

He made no reply, but moved back again and settled himself to support her head against his shoulder. Soon they both slept.

CHAPTER 27

LASTINGHAM

Fridgyth woke at daybreak and found that Caedmon had already seen to the horses, having left his cloak wrapped round her.

"A good companion," she murmured, gratefully. "I couldn't have a better one."

But, despite the cowherd's kindness, still it was a struggle to face the morning chill and get her stiff joints moving. They slaked their thirst with cool water from the clear stream and searched their saddle bags for scraps of dried bread. Ghost monastery or not, Fridgyth hoped that they would soon come to Lastingham – for there, at least, she knew there'd be food and shelter.

"They must have made good speed," Caedmon said. "This d-dung is at least two days old."

"Oh yes," Fridgyth agreed. "Lindi said 'they rode like demons,' but they'd be hungry before long. They fled in panic – no time to take food. They couldn't stop for breakfast at Ruswarp Mill and we know they got short shrift from the farmers. Where did they think they were going?" Fridgyth mused, "Why would they go towards Lastingham?"

But the tracks led on and, that evening, they rode out from the shelter of the trees to find a wide sloping valley cut by a winding stream. A well-built church rose up from the head of the valley, surrounded by monastic huts, some barns and what looked like a guest hall.

"Lastingham," Fridgyth said, with satisfaction. "It *must* be

Lastingham. Do their horse tracks still lead this way?"

Caedmon nodded.

"Why come here?" she asked. "They'd do better to head for Eforwic, where they might lose themselves amongst the throng."

"Lost? H-hungry?" Caedmon suggested.

She nodded. Perhaps neither of them really knew where they were going after all. This countryside was unknown to them – Guy rode out hunting at Streonshalh, but was unlikely to have come this far. They'd planned to escape by sea and find a harbour to the south where they would never be recognised, but she and Ketel had put a stop to that.

"I think you are right," she said. "Maybe they stumbled across Lastingham by accident, but they must have been desperate for food."

She paused for thought. It might not be sensible to go rushing into the monastery, demanding that the monks detain their visitors and hand them over to Hild for judgement. If Guy and Gunda *had* taken refuge there, they must have invented some story to explain themselves and they'd likely race away as soon as they caught sight of them. The herb-wife and the cowherd were not exactly an official Streonshalh delegation… but if Fridgyth could find Prior Sigurd, he might remember her.

Suddenly Caedmon was pointing ahead. There were two dappled horses in the distance: Seamist and Seacoal, hobbled and riderless; they wandered close to one of the monastery barns.

"That's a grand sight!" Fridgyth dismounted. "Without their horses, they can't escape at speed. We must catch them, but we'd best go warily."

Caedmon took the mule's leading rein and fastened Drogo and Turnstone to a tree. They'd be safe there and free enough to crop grass.

The herb-wife and the cowherd set out on foot towards the barn and the hobbled horses. The place was very still and quiet. Caedmon stopped to put up his hand to shade his eyes. He looked round at Fridgyth and shook his head in a troubled way. She saw what concerned him. Three fields of good barley had not been harvested? It was overripe and would soon be sprouting. As they got closer, they saw that there were flattened swathes amongst the standing stalks, where the fowls had broken into the field to feast on the grains. A small gate in the low stockade stood open. A cockerel crowed and geese and hens wandered freely, pecking at the ground. There was no sign of fowl-keepers.

Fridgyth remembered the farmer's words.

"A monastery full of ghosts," she murmured. "I can see why folk might think so."

Where was the smoke from their fires? Surely the plague hadn't killed them all?

Caedmon touched her arm and pointed to the southern hillside. Apple trees were heavy with unpicked fruit. They approached cautiously, but still there was no sign of life other than the two horses and the fowls that pecked and rooted everywhere. Seamist tossed her head and caught their scent on the breeze. Caedmon strode ahead and the mare limped to meet him, hobbled with a rope that was fastened between her front legs to stop her straying far. Suddenly he cried out in concern.

"What?" Fridgyth hissed. She frowned at the noise he made.

Seamist's mane was matted and her back whip-scarred.

"If the princess saw this…" Caedmon muttered, his face standing out white and angry in the gloom. He unhobbled the mare and stroked her soothingly. "Poor lass," he said.

Together they examined the beast bit by bit. Raw sores covered her back and withers.

"Can none of the monks here treat an injured horse?" Fridgyth asked, for her own anger rose as she saw the extent of the injuries.

They turned to Seacoal, glad to find the big gelding in a better state. The quiet that hung over Lastingham was more and more disconcerting. At the sight of Seamist's wounds they'd dropped all effort to be quiet, and nobody ran to see what the noise and fuss was about.

Unlike the monastery at Streonshalh, there were none of the familiar sounds of a vibrant community: no clamour of work, no thud of a carpenter's hammer and no clack of wood on wood as came constantly from the weaving sheds. This silence at Lastingham, interrupted only by the crowing of the cockerel, was most unsettling.

At last, they heard the light patter of feet. The sounds seemed to come from inside a wooden building that stood somewhat set apart from the other monastic buildings and a good way from the barn. A faint wisp of smoke drifted up from the thatch, so thin that they hadn't noticed it before. They strode towards it, but as they came close and the sound of footsteps continued and they both stood still and held their breath. Fridgyth rested her hand on the hilt of the sharp knife that swung from her belt.

A small figure emerged from the darkness of the building, burdened with a heavy bucket in one hand and a large basket in the other.

Fridgyth let go of her knife at once, for despite the gloom she recognised the light fair hair and sunburnt skin.

"Billfrith?" she whispered.

The child stopped in his tracks and blinked at them as though he couldn't believe what he saw. He looked a great deal thinner than when he'd set out for Lastingham with Prior Sigurd.

"I came to feed the horses," he said, as he carefully lowered the bucket, which was full of water. "But there is so much to do."

He took two more steps and stumbled. Caedmon stepped forward to relieve him of his basket and saw that it contained a mash of oats. He turned, at once, to take both food and water to the horses.

"Where *is* everyone, Billfrith?" Fridgyth asked meantime.

He looked from her to Caedmon, and she could see that he struggled to speak.

"The plague," he managed at last. "I'm… the only one left."

Fridgyth crouched down in front of the child, and reached out gently to hold him, more concerned for *his* welfare at that moment, than punishment for Gunda or Guy.

"Tell me what happened here."

"Are you angels?" he whispered, for he still stared as though he couldn't believe that they were there. "Have you come to take me too?"

"No, indeed," Fridgyth said with a touch of a smile. "We don't look much like angels, do we? Do you not remember me? I'm Fridgyth the

Streonshalh herb-wife, and that is Caedmon the cowherd. We were with you that day in the meadow – remember? You enjoyed watching the white calves with Princess Elfled."

"The little men and women in white habits," he said, and he smiled vaguely, as though he recalled a pleasant dream.

"Where is Prior Sigurd?"

"Gone," Billfrith shook his head and was solemn again. "They've all gone into the ground. We had to put them there. At first I helped Brother Ned, but then he died too and now there is only the man and woman who came here the day before yesterday."

Caedmon came back to them, leaving the horses feeding.

"Go on," Fridgyth encouraged, as her voice fell to a whisper. "The man and woman are here you say? The ones that rode these poor horses?"

"The woman has the plague," Billfrith said.

"Ha!" Fridgyth caught her breath, shocked; she didn't know whether to be glad of it or weep.

"The man wouldn't leave her," Billfrith went on. "I told him he should, but I think it's too late now. He's sickening too, and I try to look after them both *and* the horses."

"You've done well," Fridgyth said. "But where are they?"

"In the infirmary," Billfrith pointed to the building he'd come out of. "I'll have to put the woman in the ground soon. Will you help me when the time comes?"

His voice wavered as he spoke and Fridgyth wrapped her arms around him. "All will be well now," she promised, "We've come to help."

Billfrith lunged suddenly forward and clung to her. She rocked him gently while the cowherd looked back at them.

"All will be well," she soothed.

At last the child pulled back, he dashed tears away. "I'm… so glad you are here," he said, as he struggled to regain his dignity once more.

"Show me where they are," Fridgyth said, her sense of urgency returning.

Billfrith took her hand and led her to the infirmary. Caedmon followed, but she stopped him.

"This is my job," she said. "Since I survived the plague I think I'm safe from it. You may not be. Leave this to me. You tend the beasts and light a fire out here, for we'll need warmth and light. Best if we sleep outside the buildings. I have seen how huts can carry plague."

The cowherd looked as though he'd argue for a moment, but then he glanced back at the horses and pulled one of the small treatment vials that he kept from his leather bag.

"I'll put this to good use," he said and strode away.

"Now show me," Fridgyth said to Billfrith.

The foul smell inside the infirmary made her want to retch. The dregs of a fire gleamed in the central hearth, but it was hard to see in the dim light it gave.

"Have you candles?" she asked the boy.

He went to fetch some from a box on the floor – the best beeswax candles.

"I took them from the church," he said. "Brother Ned said we'd be forgiven, for there was nobody left to take the services there."

Fridgyth lit two candles at the hearth, aware of a sudden nervous movement in the corner of the room. She set it in a wooden candlestick that she found beside the hearth and took the other to have a good look around. The infirmary floor was covered with mattresses set in rough rows; they were all skewed in a mess of dirty straw and soiled bedding. Only one pallet in the corner was still occupied and a man who'd been crouched over it turned as Fridgyth held up the light. Guy's handsome features were still recognisable, but he was dirty and tearstained and his hair was matted. Fridgyth didn't think she would have known Gunda. A large swelling beneath her chin made her head loll uncomfortably to the side. Her pretty face was distorted out of all recognition. Fridgyth saw that she need not have feared they'd escape and ride away. She doubted that either of them would ever ride again.

"So you are here," she said, her voice flat and harsh.

For a brief moment, she saw the panic of a hunted beast that sought to escape in Guy's eyes, but the impression was fleeting. Acceptance and utter misery followed fast. He looked away from her, shamed.

She felt little pity. Billfrith went to lift a rug that Gunda had thrown down in her delirium. Fridgyth watched, as the child tucked it carefully about the young woman's sweating body.

"You are very good to her," she said quietly. "Much better than she deserves."

"Brother Ned said we must treat all who come to the infirmary with equal kindness and never judge," Billfrith said.

Fridgyth nodded; it was a principle that she herself struggled to apply.

"Brother Ned said that I must try to keep sufferers warm and covered, even though they sweat."

"Would you fetch me water?" she asked, as she steeled herself to be calm and think of the child.

Billfrith nodded and trotted off purposefully

When Billfrith had gone, Fridgyth allowed both grief and anger to rise up and do battle in her heart. She recalled the sweet-faced girl who'd watched Guy so jealously in Streonshalh's pasture and remembered giving her the clothes that she now wore, reduced almost to rags.

"Are you really brother and sister?" she asked.

Guy shook his head awkwardly, all pretence over. As he moved, she saw that he too had a small swelling beneath his ear and dark circles under his eyes.

Fridgyth sighed. How had it come to this? But then she brought to mind the image of the three young girls and a wave of anger washed back. She looked around, found a wooden stool and pulled it close to sit on, while she tried to calm the rage that rose in her. Justice had surely come to them, swift and merciless, but the knowledge that they were punished was not enough. Fridgyth needed to know why they had done such terrible things?

Before she could say more Billfrith returned. Fridgyth got up and kicked dirty straw away to make a clear space on the floor for the jug and beaker that he'd brought, then led him by the hand, back to the open doorway.

"Is there food left in Lastingham?" she asked, as she paused on the threshold.

Billfrith nodded.

"There are cabbages, kales and parsnips in the garden. I've not gone digging there since Brother Ned died, but I've milked the two goats and made porridge. We've a sack of oats left from last year and a bit of barley meal."

"Show Caedmon the vegetables and barley and he will help you make pottage for us all. Have you herbs?"

Billfrith nodded.

"There's sage, thyme, rosemary and garlic."

"Excellent," Fridgyth approved.

"Pottage," Billfrith smiled at the thought. "It's a long time since I had pottage."

"I'll look after these two now," Fridgyth told him. "But there's just one more thing I must ask."

Billfrith waited solemnly.

"Have you had this sickness yourself? Have you had painful boils or fever?"

Billfrith shook his head.

"I'm safe from the plague. Prior Sigurd said it was a miracle."

"It is a miracle, but how could he know?"

He shook his head at her lack of understanding.

"The miracle took place long ago."

"Tell me about it," Fridgyth said.

"Prior Sigurd found me as a babe, when he travelled in the Frankish lands. I was alone in a hut and screaming. I had the marks of the yellow plague on me – see, here and here." He pulled down the folds of hood on his small tunic to reveal two deeply pitted indentations on his neck. "I lived while all my family died around me. That was the miracle."

Billfrith related the story fluently. It was a tale told and retold many times.

"I screamed so loud," he continued. "Prior Sigurd said he thought I'd wake the dead. He took me and wrapped me in his cowl and brought me back with him to the land of the East Saxons. He said God kept me safe for a special purpose, and I need never fear plague again."

Fridgyth nodded, seeing now that the golden tint to his skin was the mark of the plague survivor.

"I'm sure Prior Sigurd was right," she agreed. "Like me, you have survived."

She lifted her chin and showed him the crackly scar that marred her neck.

The boy examined it with interest, but then his chin suddenly trembled. It was relief that moved him, not sorrow.

"I feared I was to be left alone once more, and I didn't know how that would be."

"Go and find Caedmon," she told him. "You will not be left alone, I promise you that."

CHAPTER 28

NO BLESSING

Fridgyth watched the boy go with a deep sigh, and then steeled herself to deal with Gunda and Guy. As she turned back into the stench and gloom of the infirmary, she felt that it was the last place on earth she wanted to be.

"Why?" she asked Guy at once, her voice suddenly sharp and challenging. "Why, when fate brought foulness and misery enough, did *you* bring evil to Streonshalh?"

He made no reply and anger rose so sharply in her that she wanted to walk out – to set the infirmary on fire – to make them feel the fear she'd felt. How would they like to scrabble helplessly at a locked door with torn fingers, to choke with smoke in their throats, while flames leapt ever closer? Neither would have the strength to escape. The old gods would see the justice of such an act – revenge not a crime – no more than they deserved.

She took a deep breath. It was not what Hild would do. She could never return to Streonshalh after such a deed… and it would never satisfy her need to know.

Gunda's breath rattled harshly – beyond speech; Guy must tell their story. Fridgyth pulled up a grubby straw pallet and threw a rug over it, her emotions swung from anger to sorrow.

"Lie there!" she ordered.

He crawled onto the pallet and flopped down, gasping. Guy suffered as he deserved to suffer, but if, by some chance, he lived then it would be her duty to see him face Hild's judgement.

"Gunda?" he muttered, as he tried to turn his head to see his companion.

Fridgyth picked up another mangled rug from the floor, scrunched it up, pulled him forwards by the shoulder and then propped him back against it. He looked a little more comfortable in that position, and he could see Gunda.

"Now I want to hear the truth from you," Fridgyth said.

He licked his lips.

"Water?" he begged.

Fridgyth folded her hands across her chest and sat in silence.

"Water," he whispered again. "Pity me… for I dread the fires of hell!"

"And so you should," she growled. "Answer my question first – who is Gunda if not your sister?"

Tears slipped down his cheeks, oozing from eyes that were puffed and swollen. He shook his head in misery. "Sh-she was, she is – my love."

Fridgyth poured some water into the beaker and put it into his hands. He managed a few sips, but she wasn't going to let him rest.

"Then why?" she asked. "Why not be content that you had a fine young woman who loved you? Why commit foul crimes?"

He shook his head and shuddered.

"It began long ago… when I was sent to a monastery built by Mayor Ebroin's father."

Fridgyth grimaced.

"Ebroin! We knew *he* must be behind it somehow. How did you come to deal out poison?"

"My older brother inherited our father's land, so I was promised to the church. Gunda… she was the cook's daughter in the monastery I was sent to."

Fridgyth sighed. It was not such a very unusual story: a young noble, promised to God by his family who fell in love with a girl from a family of serfs. It was frowned upon, but why should it lead to murder? Most men would quietly take the girl as a lover and if children came they'd be brought up in the monastery, dedicated to God as oblates, as so many children were.

"So – why come to Streonshalh?" she demanded. "Why poison young girls?"

Guy's brow crumpled into wrinkles of pain.

"The girls were a terrible accident," he whispered." We couldn't know that Cloda would give food away."

"Don't you dare lay blame on Cloda – she is nothing but good and brave. Who was the poison intended for? I need to know for certain; I want to hear it from your own lips."

"F-for the one who lives in hiding… Prince Dagobert."

"So Hild was right," she said. "Was it done on Ebroin's orders?"

"Yes. It was in payment."

"Payment for what?"

"Permission to set aside my promise to God… for us to be married," he choked out the words. "Bishop Bera supports Mayor Ebroin in our kingdom of Austrasia, and he can give permission for such a thing. Both of them want Dagobert dead… the end of his line."

"So… you and Gunda came to Streonshalh, determined to poison the young man who had every right to call himself your king? How did you know he'd be at Streonshalh?"

"We didn't," he admitted, shaking his head. "Ebroin's spies reported that Dagobert had left Slane in the company of Flann Fina, Oswy's son. Where would they go? It was judged they'd head for Northumbria… we didn't know we'd find him at Streonshalh, but our masters heard that Bishop Agilbert travelled north for the Synod."

"What luck for you," Fridgyth sneered. "You didn't have to search very far."

"Merovingian monarchs are sorcerers," Guy said, and he nipped his fingers quickly together in the sign against evil.

Fridgyth gasped.

"Him, evil?"

She remembered his gentleness, when he'd saved the child from the swarming bees.

"He doesn't appear evil, but…"

"Huh! No more than me," Fridgyth folded her arms across her chest. "But I could be very evil towards those who'd attempt to burn me to death."

"It was never meant," he cried hastily. "We knew you'd seen danger in the porridge and the marigold petals. You were suspicious and had found us out. Forgive us… please forgive us. Bishop Bera told us Dagobert was evil." he answered lamely.

"This Bera is the evil one," Fridgyth told him, her voice faint with suppressed fury. "And by this act of death you'd show your love for each other?"

"I was to come alone at first," he whispered. "But Gunda refused to stay behind. She said we'd do it together, and we were sent with a letter of recommendation to Bishop Agilbert. We'd travel as a brother and sister, who wished to study in Northumbria."

Fridgyth's eyes narrowed.

"Did Agilbert know your purpose?"

"No… no," Guy shook his head.

"What was it that was asked of you?"

"We were to seek out the whereabouts of Dagobert and bring about his death in whatever way we could. A scholar and his sister would seem unlikely assassins… so they said."

"Yes indeed," Fridgyth agreed. "You were not the first I suspected, and you have murdered others along the way. What of Cenwulf? What had he done to deserve such a shameful end?"

Guy shrugged.

"He sent Gunda to work in the kitchens, and though she could work well in there, it was the last place she wanted to be."

"So he deserved to die?"

He frowned and glanced across at Gunda's wrecked face, her breath came in shallow gasps.

"Cenwulf – he saw us kissing and realised she was not my sister. He forbade us to see each other or even speak. So we tested out a dose of orpiment, to discover how much was needed…"

Fridgyth gasped at such ruthlessness.

Guy looked up and glared at her.

"Once you have decided to kill… it makes little difference who… or how many."

She shuddered at the sudden malice in his expression, but she hadn't finished.

"How did you persuade him to drink the wine?"

"That wasn't difficult," he answered with a sneer. "Gunda saw that Cenwulf drank far too much at the Synod feast. She took him a goblet of wine the following night, saying the King had sent it."

"Poor Cenwulf… he must have thought it an honour. And what about poor Dunstan? Did you kill him too? There is no point in dissembling now!"

Guy admitted it.

"I took advantage of the sudden darkness, for I believed him to be Dagobert. I hit him and sent him tumbling down the stairs."

"You hit him from behind! What did you hit him with?"

A flash of anger came to him.

"I hit him with a marble paperweight. What does it matter to you? Once one is set to commit murder, honour is lost. You can know nothing of the terrible madness that comes with such a task."

"I'm glad that I do not," she retorted, more calmly. "And then you set an ambush and speared Oswy's son in Dagobert's place, while Argila fought you off?"

"Yes," he admitted. "If it hadn't been for that cursed man, we might never have needed to use poison again, and those girls…"

"So now it's all Argila's fault they died?"

He slumped back against the makeshift pillow.

Fridgyth resisted the urge to raise her hand to him, swallowed hard and began again.

"You might well have got away with your foul plan, if it hadn't been for Cloda's generosity and these *accidental* deaths. How did you know that Samson was Dagobert?"

Guy seemed unwilling to say.

"How did you *know* him?" Fridgyth shouted.

"It was the ring," he said hastily, trembling at her sudden fury. "The ring he gave to Princess Elfled, a symbol of the Merovingian line."

"The young bee! Dear Elfled," Fridgyth said softly. "Yes, she showed it to everyone. So you recognised him almost as soon as he arrived at Streonshalh?"

"Yes," he nodded weakly. "We took our leave of Bishop Agilbert at once, and Brother Cenwulf... well, you know the rest."

Fridgyth sighed.

"I begin to see why Gunda hated it so much in the kitchen! The cook's daughter, who hoped to marry a noble's son, forced back to where she'd started from. But then she found she was well placed to poison food. It was all right for you in the scriptorium, spending pleasant days in the company of princesses."

"It was only supposed to be for a while," he said sullenly.

"So then the plague came and you thought to hide your wrongdoing amongst the other deaths, knowing well the symptoms of King's Yellow? The plague must have seemed a blessing," she continued, ruthlessly.

"Yes," he admitted quietly. "No blessing now."

"You could have run away together – earned your keep as a layman-scribe in any monastery. You are more than capable of that."

"I wish... I wish we had done such a thing," Guy admitted. "But we were promised wealth and honour in our country. Who does not want such things?"

Fridgyth too had lived in desperate poverty and she was honest enough to admit that she'd dread a return to it. She sat in silence for a while, to mull over what he'd said. She had her answers now. Both Guy and Gunda were very ill, and it wouldn't be long before Hretha, the Death Woman, came for them both.

Gunda was suddenly shaken with a racking cough, and Guy raised himself to watch over her. The love between them was obvious; Fridgyth could see that.

The girl seemed to settle a little, though she scarcely breathed.

"I fear the fires of hell," Guy muttered.

"And so you should."

"But Christians speak of repentance... even for deeds like this."

Fridgyth heaved a great sigh.

"Best pray that Brother Cenwulf still holds to that belief, for you may meet him in the afterlife and Brother Dunstan too!"

But, as she sat there, an idea came that might help her too. "Perhaps, after all, you can confess your sins – not to me, but to

Abbess Hild," she said.

She got up and went out of the infirmary to find Billfrith helping Caedmon to prepare the meal.

"Is there a scriptorium here?" she asked.

"Yes," Billfrith said, at once.

"Can you take me there?"

The boy led her into the deserted scriptorium, where half-finished manuscripts lay stacked and rolled, some set in place on a table, quills at the ready, as though the scribe expected to return at any moment. They found a piece of good vellum, two sharpened quills and a horn of ink.

"We need another candle, too," she said, bearing in mind the darkness of the infirmary.

Billfrith helped her carry everything back, and Fridgyth reappeared by Guy's bed with the lighted candle and put parchment and pens into his hands.

"Now," she said, dipping the quill in the ink for him. "You may write your confession, and I will see that Mother Hild reads it. If you put everything down as you've told me, then perhaps your god will judge you a little less harshly."

He hesitated for a moment and his hands started shaking wildly at the very thought of writing, but the force of habit was strong and he managed to put pen to vellum and began to write at last.

Fridgyth held the inkhorn and watched as line after jumbled line of small marks appeared. His hands still shook, and the patterns he produced were uneven, most unlike the confident, swift strokes of the pen she knew he'd once been capable of. She could never read it herself, so must trust that death-fear drove him to write the truth.

It seemed a long while, but at last he stopped.

"I have confessed it all, and for us both," he said. "I pray for mercy... though I know we've little hope of it and I will tell you this: we were not the only ones sent to these lands to kill Dagobert."

Fridgyth nodded, for he confirmed what she had suspected all along.

"Perhaps that small thing may stand in your favour, when you go to face your god."

Gunda slumped suddenly to the side and a familiar rattle came from her throat. Fridgyth picked up the beaker to give her water, but as she tipped the girl's head back, she saw that she'd ceased to breathe. Guy moaned and struggled to reach her. Fridgyth watched them mercilessly for a while, but then she gritted her teeth and pushed his light pallet towards the girl. Guy took hold of Gunda's hand, lay back exhausted and closed his eyes.

Fridgyth picked up the roll of vellum and stood for a moment to look down on their ravaged faces; she felt that her heart might burst with bitterness. Gunda's desire must have been all-consuming and yet in different circumstances the cook's daughter, so dainty and ladylike, could have fulfilled the role of young noble's wife admirably. Why should human endeavour be so wracked with frailty and futility?

At last, the sound of Billfrith's excited voice, forced her back to practicalities. She rolled her shoulders to ease the stiffness that had come while she was sitting there.

"As Hild always says, there is much to do," she murmured.

When she went outside she found that the sun had gone.

Despite the darkness, there was warmth and activity out there amongst the ghostly monastery buildings. Caedmon had made a fire and brought Turnstone and Drogo to the barn. Seamist and Seacoal were feeding well, and they already looked better for Caedmon's care. He'd lit a torch that set light and shadows dancing together, and now he stripped sprigs of thyme into a cauldron of vegetable pottage. The mouth-watering scent of cooking drifted on the night air, while Billfrith worked hard to turn a quernstone with his sleeves rolled up to the elbows.

"I'm crushing grain," he cried excitedly. "We'll soon have flatbread and eggs to go with our pottage."

Caedmon looked up and saw how worn Fridgyth looked.

"H… have they gone?" he asked.

"The girl has," she said. "I think the man will be dead by cock-crow."

Billfrith looked up uncertainly.

"I like the man," he admitted sadly.

Fridgyth nodded.

"But he did something very wrong."

"H…have you found out why?" Caedmon asked.

"Yes," she said quietly. "But it makes little sense."

She closed the door of the infirmary, picked up one of her saddlebags and went to the well to get washed.

As she scrubbed her hands, she thought of Gunda, and remembered the days when her own clothes hung in rags, from winter to summer. Her children had died, and she'd not been able to save them, though she'd have done anything – anything. It would be a hard thing, she admitted, to choose love and poverty over the promise of wealth, but those lovers had lost everything now.

She returned to find that Caedmon cooked rounds of flat bread on a griddle; the smell of it lifted her spirits at once. They ate well and drank from the fine stock of mead that Billfrith had brought from the monastery brew house.

"Can I sleep out here, beside you?" Billfrith asked.

"Of course you can," Fridgyth said and Caedmon smiled.

At least, for Billfrith, this day had brought relief. Once their stomachs were satisfied they fell asleep, wrapped in cloaks and lying companionably close in the warmth of the fire.

CHAPTER 29

FIRE CLEANSES

The following morning was bright and sunny, but they rose and greeted each other quietly, for they knew there was grim work to be done.

Fridgyth went into the infirmary and found Guy and Gunda, just as she had expected to find them; hand in hand, both dead.

Billfrith followed her and hovered in the doorway looking worried.

"Will you help me bury them?" he asked. "It's so hard to break the ground up."

"Of course we'll help you," she said, as she stepped outside again. "But I'm thinking there may be a better way. The Christians might not want these two buried in hallowed ground – they are both murderers."

Billfrith looked at her, shocked.

"I tried to save murderers?"

"Aye," she said. "That was their crime, but you had no way of knowing it. You behaved only with wonderful courage and correctness, but I'm struggling now to do the right thing. This infirmary is full foulness, left by the sickness. After we had the first plague at Streonshalh they burnt the boat-makers' huts and fire cleansed us of the plague, for a while at least. Holy fire…" she murmured.

Caedmon nodded in agreement, seeing the way her thoughts went.

"It might seem a terrible thing," she admitted. "But I think we should burn this infirmary down, as a pyre for Guy and Gunda. They won't be buried in Christian holy ground, and it might cleanse Lastingham of the plague."

Billfrith caught his breath, shocked at her suggestion.

"You mean to burn them the wicked heathen way?"

"You can say Christian prayers over them if you think it right."

He thought for a moment, but still looked anxious.

"Holy Cedd's tomb in the church must not be harmed," he said. "I'd never be forgiven for that."

"No, indeed," Fridgyth agreed at once. "But Cedd's tomb is far from the infirmary."

Caedmon offered his support. "When my calves are s-sick unto death, I burn the carcass and the straw they slept in and sometimes I even burn the beast's shelter down," he acknowledged.

"Very well, I *will* let you burn the infirmary down," Billfrith said at last. "It's a frightening place and it stinks of death, but you must not burn anything else. Brother Ned told me that one day Holy Cedd's brother Chad will come... he'll come to Deira and ask me how I've cared for the monastery."

"Should that day come, I promise I will speak to Chad on your behalf, and I believe Abbess Hild would speak up for you too," Fridgyth said.

He nodded.

"Can it be done safely, do you think?" she asked Caedmon.

He scratched his head and began to walk around the outside of the building.

They watched him quietly. When he came back to them at last, he nodded.

"A g-good day's hard work," he said. "We must fetch water to soak the thatch of the barn and the dormitory and then watch carefully so that sparks don't set other buildings alight – but it could be done."

"Then I think we should do it," Fridgyth said. "This is the end of the Month of Offerings – let this be our offering."

The smile that came to Billfrith's face betrayed a touch of childlike excitement.

"A bonfire!" he whispered. "We're going to have a bonfire."

Fridgyth smiled, but now that the decision had been made, doubts came. Quite often when she closed her eyes at night, she saw again the pot of burning charcoal that burst into flames in the novice's dormitory. She'd be forced to face the terror of those flames again.

She closed her eyes for a moment and took a deep breath then, as she released it, she resolved to fight those fears.

"We'd better make a start," she said.

They set about fetching water in wooden buckets to soak all the nearby thatches. Fridgyth stopped now and then for a brief respite, often doubting her decision. It was heavy work and, in these moments of doubt, she suddenly saw the leap of flames in the novice's dormitory in her mind's eye.

"Come on, there's much to do," Billfrith cried, his excitement unabated.

She forced herself to action again and told herself that she could not spend the rest of her life in fear of flames.

Billfrith's cheerful sense of purpose buoyed them on. The monastery had been built by an ancient spring that bubbled up at the head of the valley amongst bilberry plants and rocks. It fed a stone basin with a continuous supply of good water and however much they dipped their buckets, the water level did not drop.

"Blessings on your Cedd," Fridgyth said. "It was he who chose this spot."

"He chose with wisdom," Caedmon agreed.

"He had to fast," Billfrith told her. "He had to fast to cleanse the place of wicked heathen spirits."

Fridgyth smiled and said nothing. So Lastingham had once been a pagan holy place – dedicated to the goddess Brig, she guessed.

At last, all the thatches that surrounded the infirmary were well soaked. They knew they must act fast now, before they dried, so they tethered the horses far away and secured all the fowls. Once that was done, Caedmon carefully picked two burning brands from their fire and set them to smoulder inside the infirmary. They threw handfuls of dry kindling on top of the brands and stood back, ready to pick up any burning timber that escaped with pitchforks, and heave it back.

The kindling smoked and crackled for a while and, as the smoke turned black, they backed away from the building. Smoke began to billow through the window holes and up through the thatched roof. Suddenly, with a rush and a flare, flames leapt. The roar and crackle made Fridgyth's heart jump with fright.

"Burn, fire burn," Billfrith cried. "Burn away the plague."

The fire took hold fast and Fridgyth had to tell herself that the fiercer the blaze, the sooner it would all be safely done. It was a frightening sight, and all three spread out to surround the place; they worked constantly to hurl straying brands back into the fire. The timber frame and dry thatch exploded and burned fiercely.

Billfrith's excited face was smeared and blackened with soot.

"Burn away the plague," he yelled, making Fridgyth smile, for he reminded her of many a wild boy at a pagan rite.

"Amen to that," she solemnly added. "You should say your prayer now, if you want to."

He stood still then, suddenly quietened and bowed his head.

"Forgive them their trespasses," he said solemnly. "Forgive them Lord."

"Amen," both Fridgyth and Caedmon added.

"Was that right?" he asked uncertainly.

"It was a kind and generous prayer," Fridgyth said. "And one thing I've learned about Christians is that they do believe in forgiveness. I think you did well."

Timbers cracked and crumbled and, by sundown, the blaze had subsided; a smouldering heap of charcoal was all that was left. Their bodies ran with sweat, their eyes were red and sore, and their clothes reeked of smoke.

But they were left with a strong sense of achievement, that no beast or other building had been harmed. They struggled to find themselves food and wash their stained skin and clothes, but their spirits stayed high.

"The fire has cleansed," Fridgyth whispered.

"The fire has cleansed," Billfrith repeated, with a satisfied smile.

They sat by the glowing remains of the fire late into the evening, while they ate and drank, quiet after their exertion, tired and a little uncertain as to what they should do next.

"I m-must return to my calves," Caedmon murmured.

"You'd go back to Streonshalh?" Billfrith looked up at them, anxious at the thought of being left again.

Fridgyth nodded.

"Yes, we must – but you will come with us of course."

"I cannot," Billfrith shook his head. "Brother Ned told me I must look after Lastingham until Holy Cedd's brother, Chad, comes."

Fridgyth smiled and ruffled his smoke-stained hair. "Lastingham was left in good hands," she said. "Let's sleep now, and we'll talk again tomorrow."

Fridgyth woke early, to find she was alone. She wasn't concerned for she assumed that Billfrith had gone to find them food or drink while Caedmon went to see to the horses. But as she struggled to her feet she saw Billfrith running towards her from the direction of the spring, his face pale and frightened.

"What is it?" she asked.

"There's a ghost up there – a spirit-wolf," he whispered, his eyes wide with fear. "I think I will come back to Streonshalh with you after all."

"Where did you see this ghost?" Fridgyth asked.

"I went to the spring, and it was there, dressed in monk's robes, but no monk that I have ever known, not one of Prior Sigurd's, or Holy Cedd's. Such hair it had that shone like the sun and it kept so still, never moving, as if it were an idol carved in wood or stone."

Fridgyth smiled at such imaginings, but Billfrith shook his head wildly, his face tense with concern.

"You do not understand! Brother Ned told me this was an evil place long, long ago before the monks came. That was why Cedd had to fast so long to purify the land before he built his monastery. Do you think our fire could have taken Cedd's spell away and brought the evil spirits back?"

"Certainly not," Fridgyth said. "Let me go and see. I understand pagan ways very well, and I'm not afraid of this spirit-wolf."

"Oh! Could it have been an angel?" Billfrith asked, wide-eyed now and suddenly hopeful. "It had such shining hair."

Fridgyth shook her head.

"It cannot be a ghost, and I don't think it likely to be an angel. Show it to me!"

Billfrith shivered at the thought.

"But a she-wolf slept at its feet."

"You stay here, then," Fridgyth said. "I shall go myself to see this strange creature."

"No – no," Billfrith, pulled her back. "It isn't safe for you. Let's find the cowherd first."

Fridgyth shook him off and put her hands on her hips.

"I was once the Usk valley cunning-woman," she said. "I fear neither spirit-wolf nor angel."

"I will come with you then," Billfrith said, and he took tight hold of her arm.

As they came in sight of the spring Fridgyth stopped for a moment, shocked in spite of her own brave words – for she too saw a still monk-like figure in the distance.

The boy looked up at her. "You see," he whispered. "I told the truth."

"You did," she admitted, as she swallowed hard.

They crept forwards quietly, but as they got closer Fridgyth relaxed and began to smile. Something in Billfrith's description had brought a strange sense of familiarity with it, and now she saw why. It was indeed a monk, who sat as still as an idol; his palms were held up to the sky in an attitude of prayer. The early morning sun glimmered on his flaxen hair and just as Billfrith had warned, a sleeping she-wolf lay at his feet.

"It's Cuthbert," Fridgyth whispered.

Billfrith stared at her.

"You know him?" he whispered.

Fridgyth nodded.

"I'm so pleased to see him for we feared he'd died of the plague, but you needn't be afraid of Cuthbert... he's no ghost."

"Are you sure? And what about the she-wolf?"

Fridgyth shook her head.

"Cuthbert has an understanding with beasts, even stronger than Caedmon's. Wild creatures trust him and Cuthbert would never let the she-wolf harm you."

Both man and beast stirred at the sound of their voices. The wolf rose to her feet, yawned and stretched. Cuthbert touched her gently on her head; she turned to lick his hand for the briefest of moments and then leapt away into the undergrowth.

Fridgyth walked forward with confidence now and it was Cuthbert's turn to be surprised.

"Streonshalh's herb-wife?" he murmured.

"I'm so glad to see you," she said. "We knew you had the plague and everyone at Streonshalh was distraught to hear it, especially Princess Elfled… but it seems you've recovered."

"It seems I have," he laughed. "Is Elfled well, and Mother Hild?"

"Yes indeed, they are both healthy, but we've had a hard time of it and there's much to tell."

Fridgyth could see that he was thinner than ever, though his skin was nut-brown and his hair blanched by the sun.

"I've had the sickness too and recovered from it," she told him. "And this is Billfrith who survived it as a babe. We're the lucky ones, I think."

"We're blessed," Cuthbert agreed.

"I thought you were an angel," Billfrith said, shyly.

Cuthbert laughed and put his hand firmly on Billfrith's head. "Just flesh and blood," he said. "But many have died at Melrose. The sickness has run its course and spared few of us to struggle on. I travel to Eforwic to greet Deira's new king."

"A new King?" Fridgyth was startled to hear this.

"Yes – the plague has taken King Alchfrid," he said. "Now Ecfrid is to be made Sub-King of Deira and his subjects will rejoice, I think. The prince travels to Eforwic with his wife and there will be great celebrations there. Ecfrid is young, but he's Edwin's grandson, and Audrey is kind and experienced as a ruler; they may do very well together. I thought I'd go on to Streonshalh to consult with Mother Hild. I meant to stay a night at Lastingham, but when I arrived I saw great billows of smoke that drifted this way and decided to sleep out here."

"The smoke will take a bit of explaining," Fridgyth said.

"I sensed a great cloud of sadness hanging over Lastingham," Cuthbert said. "But now that I find you, I'm cheered. Do you go back to Streonshalh soon? I might travel with you to see the abbess first; Eforwic can wait a while."

"Have you walked here?" Billfrith asked looking round for a horse or mule.

Cuthbert shrugged and smiled vaguely.

"I think I set out with a mule, but I find I meet a more interesting kind of person when I travel on foot, so I gave it away."

"You look as though you need food, and we have plenty of it in Lastingham. Come back to our encampment and share our breakfast," Fridgyth urged.

They walked back to find Caedmon making porridge. He greeted Cuthbert with surprise. They all sat down to eat together, and they talked, for there was much to say. Cuthbert was deeply saddened when he came at last to understand the complete devastation of the Lastingham community along with Prior Sigurd's monks.

"And Lastingham is not the only place that has suffered so," he said.

He told them how he'd passed through many towns and villages with a similar story.

Billfrith listened in silence and looked up at them uncertainly. "I'm not sure whether I should go with you to Streonshalh or wait here for Cedd's brother. I see that Cuthbert's not afraid to be alone and, perhaps, I shouldn't be either."

Fridgyth searched for the right words.

"You *must* come back to Streonshalh with us," she said firmly. "Princess Elfled would be furious if she heard we'd left you here all by yourself."

"Would she?" Billfrith's face lit up.

Cuthbert smiled and nodded in agreement.

"Abbess Hild will send a messenger to Chad, so he'll know where to find you when he comes north again."

"Then I will come," Billfrith agreed at last.

CHAPTER 30

A NOISY PROCESSION

They spent the next few days preparing for the journey back, cheered by Cuthbert's company. Fridgyth fretted a little. Now that she was going back she felt unsure of what kind of a reception she'd get from Hild. She'd arrive back with Cuthbert, and that would help, for she knew his safe return would bring joy to Streonshalh, even if hers did not.

In the evening they sat round the fire together and, feeling unthreatened by Cuthbert's quiet presence, Caedmon strummed on his harp.

"Sing of the bees," Fridgyth ordered him. "But try it the new way."

"God's children come... as guests," Caedmon began.

He managed the whole song without hesitation and Cuthbert's face lit up as the cowherd sang.

"I love your picture of the bees," he said warmly. "It says so much to me. I think, when our God made all the creatures, he made them with a sense of merriment – rowdy rough-mouths… that's just what bees are like."

"Fridgyth thinks I should try to sing about the Christian God," Caedmon said, "I'd like to sing of him, as though he were a celestial carpenter. I could tell how he made the earth like a house and the sky like a roof above us, all workmanlike. But would it offend, do you think?"

"I couldn't think of a better way of putting it," Cuthbert said.

Fridgyth listened to them, happy to see Caedmon talking to

Cuthbert with perfect confidence; the nervous stammer had vanished from his speech. She saw that Billfrith slept soundly, wrapped in his warm blanket, so she left the two men to their discussion and quietly settled to sleep herself.

The next day they prepared to leave. They decided to travel on foot so that they could load the horses and the mule with goods and food. It seemed wrong to leave so much to go to waste. They judged that Seamist and Seacoal were almost back to full strength and fit to carry baggage. They gathered apples from the orchard, wrapped cheeses from the dairy and brought kegs of mead and ale from the brewery. Streonshalh wasn't far away, and there was no urgency to get there; so whenever weariness overcame them, they could stop and camp for the night.

They set out early the following morning in sharp sunlight, sad to leave the deserted monastery to the field mice and foxes. They made a noisy procession for Fridgyth drove the two goats and Lastingham's geese ahead of her. The hens complained in wicker cages, strapped either side of the horses, and the rooster crowed all the way.

They travelled back through the woodlands and found the good camping place once again, beside the stream, close to the Roman road. They made a fire and ate together but, as they settled down to sleep, Fridgyth had the uncomfortable sense that they were being watched. She remembered that the last time she'd felt like that she'd been proved right, but she said nothing to the others. Wolves howled in the woods behind them and again she thought she heard the shuffling of wild boars, but with Cuthbert and Caedmon for company she felt no need to fear beasts of any kind. She woke just as the first light of dawn was creeping across the sky and realised that she'd been disturbed by the protest of a squawking hen and then she picked up the low murmur of childlike voices.

"Grab it quick!

"Shut up, damned thing!"

"This 'un's that cursing witch, but she's sleeping now! Get 'un quick!"

Fridgyth opened her eyes and in the dim light saw dirty hands grab one of the hens in their cages.

"Hoy!"

She struggled to her feet, but the children scattered fast behind the rocks. Caedmon was on his feet quickly too, remembering their small attackers on the journey here.

"Catch them!" Fridgyth cried.

Billfrith woke at the noise, dazed and wondering what was going on. Cuthbert seemed to have vanished. Caedmon pointed towards some rocks and crept towards them, making no sound, but then he suddenly stopped. Cuthbert rose silently from behind the spot with a small child grasped under each arm.

"Ah good, you've caught the little beggars!" Fridgyth said.

Three boys rose up from behind another rock, to berate Cuthbert and throw sticks at him.

"Let 'um go! Let 'um go!" they cried.

"Good grief!" cried Fridgyth. "Why *should* we let 'em go?"

Billfrith stared, amazed to find himself surrounded by wild children.

"Peace," Cuthbert cried, his deep, soft voice cutting through the clamour.

"Where are your mothers?" Fridgyth demanded.

There was silence for a moment. An older girl came forwards to boldly snatch back the young boy that Cuthbert had gently lowered to the ground. Then they all began to shout and cry again, while some dashed off to hide.

Fridgyth saw then that they were stick-thin, the bones of their arms and legs showed through the flesh and their little bellies were bloated. It brought terrible memories rushing back to her.

"Behave yourselves and you'll all get breakfast," she announced.

At the offer of food, all clamour ceased.

"You'd give us food?" the girl asked.

"Yes, of course we will. Just cease your noise and come and sit down here," Fridgyth ordered. "We'll build up the fire. There'll be food for you all."

Caedmon stoked the fire that they'd kept through the night. The older girl looked as though she'd cry. Fridgyth took her arm firmly and made her sit. The girl sat down, still trembling but obedient.

"Now tell me, where are your mothers?"

"Mothers are dead," the girl replied.

"Of the plague?"

She nodded and others who'd run away to hide began to creep out from behind the rocks, some, too young to speak, clung to the older ones whimpering.

"Fathers too?"

"Yes," one of the tallest boys replied, "All are dead."

Fridgyth sighed and patted the girl's shoulder.

"Food first," she said.

Caedmon and Cuthbert began to pass around flat-bread, while Billfrith found the basket of eggs they'd boiled for the journey. He handed them out to the children who grabbed the eggs wildly and stuffed them into their mouths.

"Don't snatch," he said with some authority. After a while he suddenly stopped and smiled at Fridgyth. "I'm not alone," he said.

"No you are not," she agreed, and she felt that she must take advantage of the quiet moment while they ate.

"You must listen to us well," she said firmly. "We're on our way to Streonshalh, where Abbess Hild lives, by the sea. There in her monastery she keeps beds and clothes and plenty of food."

They listened, wide-eyed.

Fridgyth crossed her fingers, praying that what she said was true. "Abbess Hild would welcome you to Streonshalh if you choose to come with us. She'd find food and clothes for you and everything you need. You could make a new life there if you wish it, but none of you are forced to come."

A frightened silence held them; then the oldest girl spoke at last.

"But we are children of the Harvest Queen... the Christian God would be angry with us."

Fridgyth shrugged uncertainly, quite out of her depth – she looked to Cuthbert for help and he smiled in his kindly way and took up her unspoken challenge.

"Our Christian God sees you all as his own children," he said.

"But will there be food every day?"

"Every day," Fridgyth said with certainty.

They looked at each other and at last they nodded.

"Then we'll come with you," the girl replied.

Billfrith smiled hugely. "Then I'm not to be alone at all," he said.

AT STREONSHALH

The abbess climbed the steep hillside path back up to the monastery, while Ketel walked respectfully at her side. They'd inspected the timber frame of the buildings that had been started down on the quayside, but now Hild hesitated at the junction that led to the upper pasture full of growing calves.

"You go on ahead of me," she said. "I need a little more fresh air before I go back inside."

Ketel bowed and went on towards the visitors' guest house.

All through the inspection, Hild had held onto her dignity with an iron will. Now she walked away from the stockade, past the meadow and headed down the hillside towards the ford. She felt desperate to get away from the monastery and the heavy responsibility that she bore, even if it were just for a few precious moments. The swallows had flown south for the winter, but the herring gulls still swooped and soared over her small windswept kingdom, squabbling all the time and crying like cats. She felt as though she wanted to screech her complaints to them, for there was now no trusted friend to listen to her without judgement or condemnation. Inside the monastic buildings, all she felt was emptiness.

"So many gone," she murmured, as she marched through brittle grass that turned strawlike at winter's approach.

At last, she stopped and sat down on a softer patch, high above the river crossing. She pulled open the leather pouch that swung from her belt and took out Fridgyth's message; she unfurled the parchment. Her eyes ran over Aldfrith's fine script, reading it carefully once again; then her finger stretched out to press the rune as though the touch might somehow bring her closer to its maker.

"Fridgyth," she sighed. "Not Fridgyth too, please God?"

She felt that her faith was being tested very hard. Was the plague truly God's judgement? Was it a sign of wrath from heaven as so many believed? Or had it been simply chance that Oswy chose to call the Synod at a time when the plague spread through the southern lands? Whatever the reason, the plague had come and Deira could never hope to be free of it again.

The disappointment she'd felt at the Synod seemed a small thing now. What did it matter that her monks shaved their crowns, or that Easter came on a different day? What really mattered was that they'd become so few in numbers that they'd struggle to survive. At least the dedicated monks and nuns in their isolated enclosure had stayed free of sickness, and she thanked Fridgyth's wisdom and experience for that.

Over the last few days, messages had arrived that announced the deaths of many of the clever young women she'd invited to join her school. What was the use of a fine timbered building with study rooms, a refectory and dormitories, all standing empty on the clifftops?

The one person she felt she could truly trust had fled, full of guilt and self-reproach. Fridgyth alone had seen the wickedness that grew around them. Truth was, Hild was angry with herself, believing that if any should have seen evil in their midst, it should have been her. The abbess had never felt so alone.

She stayed out there as the sun sank in the west, and she felt somewhat calmed at the sight of lapwings, that skimmed and dipped over the river, as the water rose with the tide.

As the sounds of the bell for evening prayers reached her, she got up to return but, before she had time to set off, a sense of commotion on the far riverbank made her shade her eyes and look across. A small but noisy gathering appeared to march along the distant bankside path, with horses and a mule in tow, and they seemed to head for the ford. Instead of hurrying dutifully back up the hill to her prayers, the abbess stepped forward, frowning as she tried to see more clearly.

"What's coming now?" she murmured apprehensively.

There'd been few visitors of late, only the lone messengers who brought bad news. This strange crowd appeared to consist mainly of children and was like no other: certainly it was no warrior gang or visiting thane. Curiosity overcame Hild's usual strict sense of duty, and she ignored the insistent bell and set off to walk down the pathway towards the ford to investigate.

Dust rose all around the small company, and a cheer rose as they reached the ford. The ford-keeper emerged from his hut to warn them that the crossing was deep, and they must be careful. The old blind basket-maker came out of her hut, disturbed by the noise, to discover what went on.

Hild saw that the travellers hesitated at the water's edge until a matronly figure strode forward, hitched up her skirts and stepped down into the water to test the depth. It was a little deep; they'd get wet, but it was passable and it seemed they couldn't wait to get across. The woman led the mule down into the water, and the others followed eagerly. At once, the sound of shrieks and laughter rose, as they all began to splash across on foot.

The figure at the front began to look more familiar to Hild with every step she took.

"Can it be Fridgyth?" Hild murmured, and a touch of joyous hope leapt in her stomach at the sight.

But what was Fridgyth doing with all these little ones? Children struggled through the water towards her. The small ones were perched high on baggage or in the arms of the older ones. There were hens that squawked and cocks that crowed and flapped, while geese honked wildly as they were carried through the water. Now she saw a tall young monk with flaxen hair, who strode towards her, one child on his shoulder and another clinging to his chest.

"Blessings!" she murmured. "That is Cuthbert there!"

Had her prayers been answered after all? And there was the cowherd too! Trust Fridgyth! Only she could return with this strange crowd.

The herb-wife waved vigorously, as she hauled the mule behind her. The abbess waved back wildly, picked up her skirts and ran to greet them. Fridgyth waded out of the water and let Drogo's bridle drop. She stumbled a little to the side, her face suddenly touched by anxiety as she considered whether she'd be welcomed back?

Hild flung her arms about her.

"Dear friend! Dear friend I thought you lost, quite lost! And you have brought me Cuthbert too!"

"I'm not easy to get rid of," Fridgyth grinned hugely, relieved at the warmth of her welcome. "And nor is Cuthbert either. I'm wetting you."

"What do I care?" Hild pulled back for a moment. "I blamed you, dear friend, when I should have blamed myself. Can you forgive me?"

"Neither you nor I are to blame for anything," Fridgyth said.

"No, indeed," Hild agreed as she hugged her tightly again.

Fridgyth's aspect turned grim.

"I found them," she said. "And discovered what was behind it all. I'm satisfied that I understand how it came about, but I've not managed to bring them back to face your judgement."

Hild shook her head.

"I only care that you are safe; God will judge them."

"He will indeed, for they are both dead of the plague."

Hild gasped and nodded.

"Then justice has prevailed," she said quietly.

Fridgyth turned to Drogo, who waited loyally, dripping wet, behind her. She reached into one of his saddlebags and brought out the rolled parchment.

"Guy wrote a confession," she said. "You must read this, then I think you will know it all."

Hild took the parchment in both hands.

"You have done very well," she said. Then she turned her delighted face to Cuthbert.

"We thought you were dead," she whispered, and a tear slid down her cheek.

He laughed and hugged her.

"But what is all this?" Hild asked, as she waved the parchment at the noisy crowd.

Fridgyth's expression became serious, and she reached out to pull Billfrith to her side.

"All the monks of Lastingham are dead. We found only young

Billfrith there. This boy has struggled to keep the place, all alone."

Hild was shocked.

"Oh, poor boy," she gasped and she bent down to kiss him on both cheeks. "How you must have suffered… and all those holy men lost to us! Dear lord have mercy on their souls," she whispered quietly. "But who are all these children?"

"I hope you won't say I've done wrong," Fridgyth said, uncertainly. "They're orphans of the plague, and we found them struggling to live out on the heather moors. They've been raised as pagans – but I know you've taken such to your heart before."

Hild looked beyond her to the ragged, frightened children as they came out of the water to meet her, dripping and shivering, faces eager with hope. She swallowed hard, for the sight of them made her want to weep.

"You bring a blessed gift to us," she said quietly. Then she raised her voice and spoke to them. "I have a home all ready and waiting for you; my new school is needed after all. Here, give that little one to me." She took a heavy toddler from the arms of its older sister. "Come on, all of you – up the hill. We've dry clothing, beds, plenty of food and tomorrow we'll hold a feast to welcome you."

CHAPTER 31

THE KING OF BEES

There was more laughter and smiles of relief as they set off up the hill towards the stockade. Fridgyth and Hild marched together at the head of the strange procession and, as they reached the main gate, they found others drawn there by the commotion. Elfled and Wulfrun appeared, with Cloda and Begu. Mildred and her helpers had come all agog from their kitchen to discover what was going on and see how many more they'd be expected to feed.

Elfled snatched up Billfrith and kissed him, then she burst into tears at the sight of Cuthbert.

"I thought you dead, my dear Cuthbert," she whispered.

"No time for tears," Hild told her sharply.

"Where are we going to put all these children?" Elfled asked, quickly becoming practical again.

"In the new school," Hild said, with a delighted smile. "And have you seen who else Fridgyth has brought back to you?"

Elfled searched anxiously through the crowd to examine all the new faces as the children came up the hill. At last she saw the twin steeds, come snorting patiently amongst the throng, loaded with baskets and babies.

"Seamist! My dear Seamist," she cried, "And Seacoal too!"

She pushed through the crowd to take the leading rein from a startled, gaunt young girl; she threw her arms around the mare's neck and buried her face in her mane.

"A good thing she didn't see Seamist when we found her," Fridgyth confided to Hild. "Caedmon has worked a wonder with the beast."

"Bless him," Hild said. "It gave me comfort to know he'd gone with you and a bit of hope that you'd come back to us."

Fridgyth hesitated outside the main gate and glanced down the bankside towards the quay, where she could see that work had started on the new boat-makers' workshops.

Hild saw her looking.

"He's not there," she said.

Fridgyth raised her eyebrows and smiled.

"You know me too well – where is he then?"

"In the visitors guest house, of course."

"Still there?" she said, smiling.

"Oh yes," Hild said. "I'm not likely to be getting rid of him!"

Then she saw Ketel come down the steps of the guest house with Della at his side. They both received the new arrivals politely although they looked a bit surprised, as everyone did. Fridgyth caught his eye for a moment and saw both relief and a welcome in his smile. He moved towards her.

"My dear herb-wife," Hild said, her tone suddenly formal, "I think you should meet Streonshalh's new reeve."

Fridgyth stared puzzled; the only person there in front of them was Ketel.

"You mean Ketel?"

Della's grin was so huge that Fridgyth knew it must be true.

"Who better for the job?" Hild asked.

Della came forward, open-armed, to hug her.

"I'm so sorry for deserting you like that, honey," Fridgyth said.

"I'm just glad that you're back," the girl replied. "I've kept your hut, fed your cat, birthed a babe, treated burns and coughs… and now I'm the reeve's daughter."

She smiled broadly with pride.

The father was not so easy to placate, and Fridgyth saw that she'd hurt the man when she vanished so abruptly without a word.

"I'm so sorry," she said. "I feared you'd have stopped me going if I'd told you what I planned."

"I would have," he admitted, "or I might have come with you."

Then he held out his arms and, when she came to him, he rested his cheek against hers for a while; it was both warm and comforting.

"I'm so glad you're back," he whispered.

Fridgyth pulled away from him, smiling and bold again.

"So... it was not the boat-makers' huts that the abbess wanted to speak to you about. I shall have to mind my manners with Streonshalh's new reeve."

"I hope you'll not be *too* courteous," he said.

"Fridgyth, come help us get these children settled," Hild called. "They will only go inside if you go with them."

The new school building was the finest dwelling that any of the children had ever seen; they walked through the fresh-smelling, lofty spaces wide-eyed and awed, their voices hushed. As darkness fell lamps were lit, fires were stoked and kitchen workers bustled in with trays of food and drink. Lay-sisters brought soft new covers to make up beds. At last the herb-wife left the children, happy enough to get used to their new home. She crept away to her hut, glad to find a fire burning in the hearth and Wyrdkin, who purred a wild welcome.

She slept, exhausted, that night, with the cat wrapped around her feet. Della left her alone, sensing that she might need quietness to settle back into her home again. In the morning, she woke and made herself breakfast. She sat in her hut contented and hugely relieved to be home and welcomed there. It was a fine morning, and she wondered if it was not too late for her to plant out baby leeks again – there'd be a new moon that night and leeks thrived well when planted out as the moon waxed.

At the sound of voices outside, the cat wandered over to the open door, curious as ever, and Fridgyth realised she'd got visitors approaching.

She stared at the four people who walked towards her hut and, for a moment, wondered if Wilfrid had returned in his purple cloak; but then she saw that Dagobert led the way, hand in hand with Princess Mathild; while Aldfrith and Argila followed on behind.

Dagobert looked very different – the young prince had discarded his monastic habit in favour of a richly trimmed tunic and cloak.

Every part of him gleamed with golden bees: a diadem set with garnets circled his brow and a hoop of gold swung from one ear, while gold bands decorated his arms: he looked magnificent.

Mathild walked at his side, as beautifully dressed as ever, her cloak now fastened with an exquisite gold and garnet brooch, her own brow circled by a dainty fillet of gold. However, the most significant change was in the proud way that she held herself; this was a strong young woman who'd expect to be obeyed. Aldfrith looked more of a monk than ever and Argila the image of a mature, battle-scarred warrior.

"Welcome," Fridgyth said, as she moved forward rather nervously to meet them. "You all look so… different."

Aldfrith bowed and smiled.

"May I present to our respected herb-wife: Dagobert Prince of Austrasia and Princess Mathild, his betrothed."

Dagobert's eyes gleamed darker than ever against his pale skin. His body was still wasted, but his smile was warm. He snatched Fridgyth's hand and kissed it.

"Herb-wife, I owe my life to you and I come to thank you and bring you a small gift."

Fridgyth dropped a curtsey, awed as she remembered that here was one who should be king in his own country.

"I don't deserve your thanks," she protested. "I've done it all so clumsily. You know the guilty ones are dead?"

Dagobert nodded.

"But I'm alive and well warned by what has happened here. Assassins come in all shapes and sizes; we must be more wary."

Fridgyth wished to warn him further as she remembered Guy's last words to her, but she hated to dampen his happiness.

"King Oswy has offered me the protection of Bamburgh," he went on. "And I shall go there to stay with my kinswoman the Queen… and I will take my new wife with me."

He dropped a kiss on Mathild's cheek. Fridgyth glanced quickly at the girl, touched to see that she was not too proud to blush.

"I offer my humble blessings on your union," she said, curtseying again. "You are truly the bee-charmer now… no… you are the king of bees. Were these precious things hidden in your saddle bags when you came to my hut?"

"Indeed they were," he said. "The abbess has given her consent to our marriage, and we'll be wed before we leave for Bamburgh. I've a noble bride on my arm, so there'll be no more skulking in monasteries now. I shall fight for my kingdom and make myself worthy of Mathild. As soon as Bishop Wilfrid returns, I'll beg his help in this matter of my rightful kingdom."

Fridgyth nodded.

"Aye... Wilfrid knows the Frankish lands well," she said. "If anyone can help, it should be him – and I think our bishop may have to work hard to please the King and Queen when he returns."

Dagobert nodded.

"Wilfrid knows my kingdom better than I do, but I mean to put that right."

Fridgyth kissed them both.

"I'm happy for you," she said. "You are worthy of all honour and this one is brave." She forgot her reticence and patted Mathild on the cheek. "I often say the quiet ones are the bravest."

Mathild held out closed, cupped hands, for she held something hidden there.

"This is for you, a token of our gratitude," Dagobert said. "It is a small thing, but it has been treasured by my family."

Fridgyth began to refuse, for she expected some precious jewel that she couldn't possibly accept but, as Mathild opened her hands, she saw that they covered a small ointment pot – the top was decorated in coloured glass in the shape of a bee and was just the size she used to store marigold balm.

"Ah," she gasped in pleasure.

"A good present for a herb-wife," Mathild said. "This smooth, cool stone is called alabaster. It's just right for you to store a precious ointment in."

Fridgyth began to shake her head regretfully, but she couldn't take her eyes from the beautiful pot.

"The prince may be offended if you refuse his gift," Aldfrith warned with a smile.

Fridgyth's fingers closed around the gift.

"Well then, I'd be foolish to offend a future king," she said. As she took the pot she noticed that sleek dark hairs now covered the front of Dagobert's head, where the Irish tonsure had been. "Your hair grows again," she murmured.

He lifted his diadem and raked his hand through the short hairs, like any lad, self-conscious of his appearance.

"It began to grow while I was sick," he said. "I couldn't tolerate them shaving me. Cloda believes the time is right – like Samson, I regain my strength."

Fridgyth glanced at Fina's son and saw a flaw in this plan.

"Will *you* stay with us in Streonshalh?" she asked, for she knew he'd wish to avoid Bamburgh.

He smiled and shook his head.

"I'm to travel to Iona and become the scholar I wish to be."

She nodded.

"I'm sorry that you must leave us," she said, quietly, "but I think you'll be happy there, and we will not forget you in Deira."

When they took their leave at last, Argila bent over Fridgyth's hand with gallant courtesy.

"Herb-wife, I regret that I couldn't tell you who I really was. In other circumstances I think we might have been friends."

"Yes, indeed," she said warmly. Then she pulled him close and whispered in his ear. "There are others that look for him, and they mean him harm."

"I will be alert," he said, with a solemn nod.

Fridgyth watched them as they left, with her hands curled tightly about the pot.

Delicious smells issued from Mildred's kitchen all day long. The children began to settle into their new home and excited whispers flew around as they anticipated the delights the feast might bring. Everyone gathered at sunset in the great hall of the guest house where the Synod had met, and Fridgyth was stunned to be given the seat of honour at Hild's right hand. Cuthbert sat on the left. Fridgyth was offered the horn of mead before anyone else – even Dagobert.

"Drink hail and welcome back to our herb-wife," Hild cried.

She was answered by loud cheers.

"Ranulf observed that all the huts which received your kittens, were spared the plague," she went on. "A small miracle we thought! You're close to being made a saint, dear Fridgyth!"

The herb-wife stared at Hild with blank amazement, while the whole gathering erupted with laughter; they clapped and stamped their feet.

As jollity subsided a little, Elfled got up from her place and came forward into the central space, flanked by Wulfrun on one side and Fredemund on the other. In her hands she bore a small but beautiful object, wonderfully wrought.

"What is this?" Hild asked, still smiling.

Wulfrun touched Elfled's arm to lend support. The princess was pale, but she spoke bravely.

"Mother Hild I have come to confess."

Hild looked puzzled and began to shake her head.

"Dear child – this feast is not the place."

But Elfled was determined and spoke quickly.

"I was so angry, Mother, when you forbade me to leave the house that I took your precious bulla and threw it out of the window!"

There was a sudden shocked silence. Everyone in Streonshalh had heard of the search for the lost seal. Hild stared at the princess, amazed.

"But... Fredemund the goldsmith has made a new bulla for you," Elfled went on. "We wanted it to be made of gold, but we had none, so Fredemund has polished one of the snakestones that you love so much and turned it into a new seal. I'm very sorry for my wickedness and sorry that I had no gold for Fredemund to use."

Hild looked severe and beckoned Elfled forward. She took the object and examined it carefully, then looked up at the goldsmith.

"It is a most beautiful gift," she said at last. "And you princess, I do forgive. It has taken courage to stand up before everyone and present this gift to me; I will be very happy to use this snakestone as my seal."

A gasp of relief ran round the hall, and everyone clapped again, while Hild reached forward to kiss her foster child. Then she looked up and waved to Mildred, who waited impatiently in the doorway.

"Let the feast begin," she cried.

Everyone ate and drank their fill and the abbess was as full of cheer as any of her guests. Though it grew late, the children stayed wide-awake with excitement. Hild called for the harp and invited some of the younger warriors to sing.

"Billfrith can sing," Elfled announced.

"Can he?"

Hild beckoned the young boy forward. This feast was for the children, and she felt it fitting that Billfrith should be the first to sing. He took the harp with a smile of confidence.

Fridgyth felt almost personal pride to see the boy so brave and happy; his high voice warbled sweetly and brought smiles to the whole company. When she saw Caedmon leave the feast, she got up to follow him, a determined look in her eyes – surely it was now or never. After he'd sung so boldly for Cuthbert she'd hoped things might be different.

The cowherd wandered out of the great hall and headed for the stables.

"Oh yes… I know where you will go," Fridgyth murmured to herself. "You'd rather sing to the beasts."

She kept herself well hidden amongst night shadows and followed him, but then saw that she was not the only one who'd seen him go. Another tall figure moved quietly ahead of her and, for a moment, the moonlight glinted on the gold chain about his neck. Dagobert too had left the feast and seemed to have had the same idea as Fridgyth. He strode after the cowherd and crossed the courtyard.

Fridgyth crept after them both, curious to watch and see what was happening but careful not to be seen. Dagobert followed Caedmon into the stables and Fridgyth crept in too. She could see nothing in the dim light at first but, as her eyes grew used to the darkness, she saw Caedmon make himself comfortable on the straw pallet which was set aside for whichever stable lad should guard the horses though the night. That evening they were all at the feast and, for once, the horses had been left to fend for themselves.

She saw a dark shadow move and caught the glint of gold in the moonlight, through the shutters. Dagobert stood there in the stables too and watched Caedmon as he settled and seemed to fall asleep, for he'd eaten well and drunk as much as anyone.

Then slowly, very slowly, Dagobert moved towards the sleeping form. Caedmon shifted and murmured a little in his sleep, as Dagobert began to speak in a low voice that followed a strange rhythmic pattern – almost a song.

"Sleep Caedmon… sleep," he said. "Sleep and forget all cares."

The cowherd made no response and it seemed that he had fallen fast asleep just as he was bidden. So – this was how Dagobert talked his wounded friend to sleep. Fridgyth was fascinated.

But gradually the words changed, though the same low voice and rhythmic pattern stayed.

"Sing, Caedmon, sing," he said.

The cowherd muttered in his sleep and turned restlessly.

"C-can't sing." he replied, as though in answer to Dagobert's command and all the pain and humiliation he'd suffered could be heard there in his voice.

"But Caedmon… you *can* sing," Dagobert said and his voice became firm and strong. "Caedmon you *must* sing for the abbess… sing for the abbess."

He repeated these instructions over and over again, his tones gradually becoming softer until he let his words drop away to silence at last. Fridgyth hardly dared to breathe for fear that she might break what seemed to her a magic spell. The power of his words had touched her too, so that she almost felt the urge to obey.

But the cowherd spoke in his sleep again and this time his voice was calm and his stammer had vanished.

"What shall I sing?" he asked.

Dagobert's voice was filled with warmth.

"Sing of what is in your heart Caedmon."

"I shall sing of the sky-maker, the world-carpenter," he murmured. "I shall sing of the earth and sky that God made for us, the sun, the moon, the grass, the trees, the plants, the flowers… the beasts and birds."

"Yes," came the warm reply.

Suddenly there was joy in Caedmon's voice.

"I will sing to the abbess," he said. "I will sing to Hild."

Then Dagobert's voice grew in strength and power.

"Caedmon, when you wake, you will go back to the feast and sing to the abbess. Caedmon, you hear me now – awake!"

There was silence for a moment and Fridgyth did not dare to move. Caedmon got straight up from the sleeping pallet and bent to pick up something in the darkness beside the pallet.

"I *will* sing to the abbess," he said.

He left the stables and headed back to the great hall, unaware of either Dagobert or Fridgyth. As he passed close by, she saw that it was his harp that he'd picked up from the ground. Dagobert came slowly from the shadows, seeming unsurprised to find her there.

"I think perhaps you *are* a sorcerer after all," Fridgyth whispered.

Dagobert held out his arm to her courteously.

"Come, herb-wife, we must hear the cowherd sing."

EPILOGUE

Caedmon picked his way through the crowded hall until he stood before Ketel. The new reeve saw determination in his eyes and the harp in his hands. He rose, at once, from his seat and steered the cowherd towards the harp-stool, where Coen sat. Everyone clapped and cheered politely, as he came to the end of his song, but it grew late and folk began to yawn. Some of the children had fallen asleep, but not Billfrith who sat at the abbess's feet. He leapt up when he saw Caedmon there.

"Caedmon must sing," he cried. "I have heard him sing before and he is a great word-weaver!"

Coen backed away with a smirk on his face, but Hild sat up straight and gave Caedmon an encouraging smile. This man had protected Fridgyth and assisted her loyally through a very difficult task; the abbess would give him her total attention and courtesy, however rough an attempt he might make at his song.

Ketel introduced him and a hush fell over the hall.

Caedmon began to strum and the sweetness of his touch on the strings made his audience wake up and take notice.

Then he began:
Now must we praise, the keeper of heaven
The mighty maker, the measurer,

Fridgyth slipped back into her place beside the abbess, but Hild didn't notice, for her eyes were on Caedmon, her face wrapt with interest and surprise.

He made first the earth for mortal men
High heaven as a roof, to cover our heads,
Then the world of wonders…

Fridgyth caught Dagobert's eye and they exchanged a conspiratorial smile. The whole hall had fallen silent to listen – and Coen's mouth dropped open in shocked surprise.

"Brave beasts of burden he shaped,
And seeds he set in the ground to grow."

Caedmon's voice carried well and he sang with a richness of tone that brought pleasure to the audience, while the meaning of his words was clear to everyone."

Hild turned to Fridgyth.

"A word-weaver indeed!" she whispered. "Your friend the cowherd is truly a word-weaver. See how the children listen to him. I have wanted something like this for a very long time!"

Fridgyth nodded wisely, hiding her glee.

Caedmon sang on and Hild leant close again.

"Fridgyth, this is the greatest gift of all! Tell Ketel to bring your cowherd to my house tomorrow morning. I have much to say to him."

As Caedmon's song drew to a close, he was greeted with cheers and the stamping of feet. He looked stunned for a moment, uncertain as to how he came to be there on the harp-stool, surrounded by such an audience and receiving wild applause. But the confusion did not last long, for he got up and bowed modestly.

The abbess rose from her seat and clapped with warm enthusiasm but, when the applause died down, she announced the feast was at an end.

"It is time for us to go to our beds," she said. "Let us go with these bright pictures in our minds."

As everyone began to leave, Fridgyth sought out Ketel and passed the abbess's message on to him. He agreed, at once, to take the cowherd to the abbess in the morning. He was delighted that such a result should come at last.

"Shall I tell Caedmon now," he asked, "so he is warned? Or will it make him fret, do you think?"

"Let him sleep soundly tonight," she said. "But I think our cowherd may have left his fretting days behind him."

They stood together for a while, both wanting to say more, but uncertain how to speak the words, until the silence between them became somehow awkward.

"I must go to my bed," Ketel said at last and he dropped a kiss onto her cheek.

Fridgyth too turned to go, just as Della came forward and caught her arm.

"I am to go with the princess and Wulfrun," she said excitedly. "We'll sleep in the school building, to make sure the children feel safe in their new home."

"A good idea," Fridgyth approved. "You go, honey, I shall be fine."

The herb-wife left the hall and set off through the darkness towards her hut, smiling to herself and pleased that Della was so well accepted by the princess as one of her friends. But gradually, as she left the crowd behind, her footsteps slowed. Was she really so fine all alone?

Throughout the feast she'd experienced a warm sense of belonging… she was Streonshalh's respected herb-wife and even though she'd made mistakes, she'd known that she was loved and needed.

Now, as she walked through the darkness, she wished there was some way for the feeling to continue. Tonight, it would feel good to have strong arms around her. It might even be pleasant to feel the slight roughness of a scratchy beard against her cheek. Well… at least Wyrdkin would be waiting for her.

But when she reached her hut she found the hearth cold and the cat out hunting. She sat there for a while, unsettled. Tonight, she really did not want to sleep alone. A flush of shame crept up her body that such a thought should come to her. Surely she was too old for such foolishness, but she remembered what she herself had said of brave Mathild: better to blush than die of loneliness!

If a shy young woman like Mathild could act so boldly, then surely an ageing herb-wife who'd seen so much of life could do the same? She got up with sudden determination, her heart beat fast and her hands trembled a little at the thought of what she planned. She washed herself and combed her hair, and then she smoothed sweet-scented lavender balm into her scarred neck. Then, not daring to stop and question the sense of what she did, she hurried out into the darkness and headed for the visitors guest house.

The courtyard was quiet now and as she crossed it her footsteps quickened and her breathing came light and fast. What a fool she'd been to push him away... they'd all be after him now that he was the new reeve. Might she even be too late?

A lay sister saw her as she entered the building, but she said nothing, only smiled and looked away. Did they all know what she was about? No matter! She was the herb-wife on a mission of mercy, though the one who needed mercy might be herself.

She crept through the great hall where the hunting dogs, and some of Coen's men, slept amongst the litter and debris of the feast. She knew from the old reeve's time where he would sleep: in a chamber well curtained at the far side of the hall. Her heart thudded so fast that it seemed as though the whole world must hear it. She reached the curtained doorway and stood there to listen. At first she could hear nothing from inside, but then she smiled as she caught the faintest sound of a snore from within. It seemed most likely that he *was* alone and, if she had anything to do with it, he would not lie there snoring for long. She slipped inside the curtain and crept into the bed.

Ketel's snoring stopped abruptly.

"What... who is this?" he muttered.

"Hush!" she ordered. "Do you want the whole of Streonshalh to know that the herb-wife creeps out of her hut at night? Now move up and let me in – tonight I need warmth."

"Oh do you?" Ketel said, giving a low chuckle. "Well, *I* would be happy if the whole of Streonshalh were to know of such a thing."

The End

CHARACTERS FROM
ANGLO-SAXON SOURCES

Hild: A royal Abbess who ruled a double monastery of monks and nuns at Streonshalh (Whitby) and Hartlepool. She was related to both King Oswy and Queen Eanfleda. Hereric, her father was poisoned, leaving his uncle, Edwin, as chief claimant to the throne of Northumbria.

Princess Elfled: The daughter of King Oswy and Queen Eanfleda. She was given to Hild to as an infant, to be raised to become a nun, in fulfilment of a vow made by her father before the battle of the Winwaed.

Caedmon: A cowherd at Hild's monastery – his story was told by Bede. He is often regarded as the father of English poetry.

Eanfleda: Queen of Northumbria, daughter to King Edwin and granddaughter to King Aethelbert of Kent and Bertha the Merovingian princess. She married Oswy, thus uniting the two warring factions of the Northumbrian Royal family and was a strong supporter of the Roman style of Christianity.

Oswy: High King of Northumbria. King Edwin (his uncle) killed his father, Aethelfrith, and claimed the throne of Northumbria. Four-year-old Oswy fled with his elder brother, Oswald, to Iona, where they were raised by Columban monks. They returned to claim the kingdom of Northumbria soon after the death of Edwin. Oswy married Eanfleda, daughter of Edwin.

Alchfrid (Alchfrith): Oswy's son – usually thought to be by his first wife Rienmelth of Rheged. His father made him Sub-king of Deira. He was a strong supporter of the Roman style of Christianity and friend of Wilfrid of York. He vanished from history after the Synod of Whitby.

Ecfrid (Egfrith): Oswy's son by Eanfleda – as a child he was a hostage of the Mercian King Penda and succeeded his father, Oswy, as King of Northumbria.

Dagobert the Second: A Merovingian prince and heir to the throne of Austrasia. He was exiled as a child of five and raised in an Irish monastery. Eventually he regained his kingdom (briefly) with the help of Wilfrid of York. His story was recorded by Eddius Stephanus in his *Life of Wilfrid*.

Flann Fina: Son of Oswy and Princess Fina. He was raised in Ireland and studied in the Irish monastic schools and later on Iona. He eventually became King Aldfrith of Northumbria, on Ecfrid's death.

AUTHOR'S NOTE

Bede's reference to Hild's monastery at Streonshalh/Whitby:

'After the example of the primitive Church, no one there was rich, no one was needy, for everything was held in common, and nothing was considered to be anyone's property.'

From Bede's *History of the English Church and People* (Penguin Classic Version)

Fridgyth the herb-wife first appeared as a secondary character in Wolf Girl (my novel for young adults published in 2006 by Corgi – Random House)

I wanted to write a historical novel for adults with an Anglo-Saxon setting, so decided to make my ageing herb-wife the main focus of a murder/mystery that became more of a 'why done it', than a 'who done it'.

Clear evidence and information for this period is sparse, so I've enjoyed creating a picture of Abbess Hild and her monastery that is more 'how I would like it to have been,' than an attempt at accuracy. Where historical sources are clear and interesting to me, I have used them, but I've also used my imagination freely.

Bede recorded the plague in the year following the Synod. 'A sudden plague, which first decimated the southern parts of Britain and later spread into the province of the Northumbrians, raged for a long time and brought wide-spread death to many people.'

Streonshalh/Whitby is not named specifically as a town that suffered from the plague, but a characteristic of the disease was that it started in seaboard towns and then spread inland. The devastation brought by the plague at Lastingham is mentioned by Bede, who tells us that Cedd died there soon after the Whitby Synod. Thirty monks from Bradwell-on-Sea travelled north to live by his shrine and all of them, barring one young boy, died of the plague.

Some historians have suggested that the yellow plague could have been jaundice, others have suggested that smallpox might have been responsible and yet others believe it to have been an early form of the bubonic plague and that it left survivors slightly liver damaged, with a yellow tinge to their skin – this is the explanation that I've used.

The main story of the attempt to poison Dagobert is invented, but Eddius Stephanus (Stephen of Ripon), chronicler of the *Life of Wilfrid*, tells how Dagobert the Second was 'banished in his youth by enemies' and raised secretly in an Irish monastery. His friends and relatives discovered that he was still alive and, with the help of Wilfrid of York, he regained his kingdom. Queen Eanfleda, a great patron of Wilfrid, seems likely to have been one of the relatives who discovered Dagobert and introduced him to Wilfrid. According to Bede, Eanfleda's younger brother, Wuscfrea, was sent to Dagobert's grandfather (Dagobert the First) for safe keeping, after his father, King Edwin of Northumbria, had been killed so it is possible that Eanfleda too could have spent time at the court of Dagobert the First, as a young woman.

There's no historical reference to Dagobert the Second ever having been to Northumbria, but I think it likely that he would have spent some time there to plan his successful return to Austrasia with Wilfrid of York – and it also seems likely that he received some financial support for this from Queen Eanfleda.

Aldfrith or Flann Fina was King Oswy's son by the Dalriad, Princess Fina, and was raised in Irish monasteries and on Iona. He eventually become King of Northumbria after Ecfrid's death and was known as 'Aldfrith the Wise.' He became a great patron of learning and the arts; his reign is often referred to as Northumbria's Golden Age. According to Bede, he was invited to accept the throne of Northumbria by Elfled Abbess of Streonshalh (his half-sister) and Cuthbert, Bishop of Lindisfarne, who met together on Coquet Island to discuss who should become king after Ecfrid.

I can't find any reference in historical sources to a friendship between Dagobert and Aldfrith, but they were both educated in Irish monasteries at about the same time and both had connections to the Northumbrian royal house.

The exact date of the Whitby Synod is still disputed by historians. The sequence of events in the story simply follows what seemed logical to me and fitted my purpose.

Orpiment or King's Yellow was used as a pigment for colouring illuminated manuscripts – now known to us as a trisulphide of arsenic, it is very poisonous.

I have used the word 'leech' to indicate a healer who has studied the healing arts in a more formal manner under the auspices of a monastery. Anglo-Saxon Leech books contain mainly herbal remedies. Lesley Smith – in her study of Anglo-Saxon leech books says –'the word "leech" in the Anglo-Saxon language translates to "doctor" and many believe that the animal was named after the practitioner rather than the other way round.'

The 'snakestones' referred to are the spiral-formed ammonite fossils, still found in the cliffs around Whitby. A heraldic image of three ammonites is often used as a symbol of both Whitby and Abbess Hild.

Theresa Tomlinson
Whitby – August 2012

www.theresatomlinson.com

ACKNOWLEDGEMENTS

The author would like to thank Sue Jaggs for her excellent editorial help, Alan Tomlinson for drawing the maps, Michelle Brown of The British Library for information on orpiment and Christiane Kroebel of Whitby Literary and Philosophical Society, for reading the manuscript and giving encouragement and help.

The following works have provided much information and inspiration:

Bede's *History of the English Church and People* (Penguin Classic)

The Age of Bede (Penguin classics) translated by J.F. Webb and D.H Farmer

Study of the Plan of the Monastery of St Gall by Horn and Borne published by University of California Press

Northumbria in the Days of Bede by Peter Hunter Blair, published by Llanerch Press

Northanhymbre Saga by John Marsden published by Llanerch Press

Stephen Pollington's *The Mead Hall*

Kathleen Herbert's *Peace-Weavers and Shield Maidens: Women in Early English Society*

Colin A. Ireland's translation of *Old Irish Wisdom Attributed to Aldfrith of Northumbria*

Bill Griffith's *Aspects of Anglo-Saxon Magic*

Gale R. Owen's *Rites and Religions of the Anglo-Saxons.*

Visits to Whitby Abbey Visitor Centre, Whitby Museum and Bede's World have provided further information and inspiration.